THE SCARS OF BATTLE

CHRIS GLATTE

SEVERN ⛵ RIVER
PUBLISHING

Severn River Publishing
www.SevernRiverBooks.com

ISBN: 978-1-64875-360-2 (Paperback)

ALSO BY CHRIS GLATTE

A Time to Serve Series

A Time to Serve

The Gathering Storm

The Scars of Battle

The Last Test of Courage

Tark's Ticks Series

Tark's Ticks

Valor's Ghost

Gauntlet

Valor Bound

Dark Valley

War Point

164th Regiment Series

The Long Patrol

Bloody Bougainville

Bleeding the Sun

Operation Cakewalk (Novella)

Standalone Novel

Across the Channel

To find out more about Chris Glatte and his books, visit

severnriverbooks.com/authors/chris-glatte

1

SEPTEMBER 14, 1943

Lae, New Guinea

The heat beat down on Clyde Cooper like a physical force, compounding his misery. Mosquitos buzzed his ears, but he hardly heard them anymore. Beneath his sweat-soaked and torn uniform, his skin itched incessantly and his body ached.

"How long we been here?" Gil asked.

Gil's Italian accent normally sounded pleasant to Clyde, but sitting in the dirt of New Guinea, being eaten alive by the elements, it grated on him. But he answered anyway. "What's it been? A month, I guess."

"That all? Seems longer."

"Your yapping doesn't help," Clyde snapped.

"Gesù Cristo, what's the matter with you?"

"You gotta ask?" Clyde gestured at their surroundings. "You see where we are? You smell the stinking jungle? Hell, it smells worse 'n you do, and that's saying something. I can hardly stand my own smell, and the last time I tried bathing in the river, I almost got eaten."

Gil slapped Private Gutiérrez on the shoulder. "You remember that, Guti? I almost shit my pants I was laughing so hard."

Gutiérrez scowled back at him, "You *did* shit yourself and it wasn't 'cause of laughing, you stupid wop bastard."

Gil's smile faded and he shook his head. "I haven't had a solid shit since touching down in this paradise."

The chitchat died down and Clyde tried to drift off to sleep, but he knew he wouldn't get much. He'd never been more tired in his life, yet he couldn't seem to sleep longer than an hour or two at a time and never deeply.

He tried to picture Abby and their soft bed back in Seattle. He imagined her tapping on the bed, asking him to join her for a nap. She glowed like a goddess and he thought he actually smelled her light perfume. He felt himself oozing into the bed beside her. Contentment swept over him like a heavy veil. She touched his shoulder gently, then more forcefully.

"Wake up! Look who showed up. Ollie's risen from the dead."

Clyde wanted to throttle Gil, but through bleary eyes, he saw a familiar soldier ambling his way.

The squad got to their feet and surrounded Ollie, slapping his back and shaking his hand.

Clyde got to him last and Private Oliver turned serious. He extended his hand. "Cooper, you saved my ass out there. I thought those sons of bitches had me for sure."

Clyde shook his hand. "I just happened to be there, Ollie. Any one of these guys woulda done the same thing. Besides, you promised to show me New York and I'm holding you to it."

"Deal."

"I didn't expect you back so soon. You all healed up?"

"Mostly. They wanted to keep me longer, but I convinced 'em to let me go."

Gutiérrez shook his head slowly. "You crazy? You were back there with the nurses and you left early?"

"They didn't send me back to Moresby—I wasn't hit bad enough. I didn't see any damned nurses where I was."

"Well, shit, what's the point of getting wounded if they don't have any nurses to look at?" They laughed.

Clyde asked, "You see Geyer? He got hit the same day you did."

"Yeah, I saw him. He was on the stretcher beside me that first night, but they put him on a plane the next day and I haven't seen him since. Doc said he needed surgery at a proper hospital."

A hush settled over them as they thought about their point man.

Oliver asked, "You guys mixed it up with the Nips any more?"

Clyde answered, "Nah. We've been chasing ghosts for weeks now. It's like they disappeared."

Sergeant Huss, their squad leader, busted into the group. "What the hell's going on here?" He smiled when he saw Oliver. "Well, lookee what the damned cat dragged in. You got here just in time, Oliver—we're about to move out."

A collective groan swept through the squad.

The rest of the platoon was already on their feet as the NCOs delivered the news. Men shuffled and stomped their feet, attempting to get the blood back into their legs. A few darted off into the underbrush and dropped their pants to their ankles.

"Where we headed, sergeant?" Clyde asked.

"Northeast. That's where the Japs are, son."

"I thought they were running with their tails between their legs."

"They are, which is why we're gonna let the navy give us a lift so we can cut off their retreat." He slapped at a bug and his hand came away bloody. "We leave in half an hour." He leveled his eyes at Clyde. "Leave your stuff, but follow me. Lieutenant Milkins wants a word with you."

Clyde exchanged a worried glance with Gil, then followed Huss through the mud toward the command tents. When they got out of earshot of the squad, Clyde asked, "You know what this is all about, sergeant?"

"Of course I do. Now shaddup."

Huss strode to the company command tent. He held up a hand for Clyde to stop, then poked his head into the tent flap. "I've got Private Cooper here for you, sir."

"Send him in."

Clyde gulped, wracking his brain for whatever infraction he must've committed. Huss stepped aside and Clyde entered. He couldn't see much as his eyes adjusted to the darkness, but he smelled food and his stomach rumbled.

He saw Lieutenant Milkins scraping the bottom of a bowl with a spoon. Clyde braced and saluted. "Private Cooper reporting as ordered, sir."

Milkins pushed the bowl aside and stood. He fixed his uniform. Compared to Clyde's, his looked fresh and clean. He returned the salute and approached him. "At ease, Cooper. It's come to my attention that Corporal Quincy's dysentery finally got the best of him. They evacuated him to the rear."

"Yes, sir. I heard he wasn't doing too well."

"That leaves a hole in Second Platoon's Third Squad. You've got some college, don't you?"

"Uh, yes, sir. A few classes at the JC back home."

"You're a few years older than most of the others. Sergeant Huss says the men look up to you. I've passed it by Lieutenant Jameson and Captain Stallsworthy, and everyone agrees."

Clyde stared straight ahead, still not sure where this was leading.

"You're being promoted to corporal, Cooper. You'll be assistant squad leader to Sergeant Huss."

Clyde stood dumbfounded. His thoughts went to his brother, Frank. He'd made corporal, but it hadn't happened this quickly. He remembered how proud his brother had been of those two stripes.

Clyde finally stammered, "Uh, uh, thank you, sir. I'll do my best."

Milkins handed him the corporal insignia and shook his hand. "I'm sure you will, corporal. Sergeant Huss will help you along to start with. Do whatever he says and you'll be fine."

"Yes, sir."

"Dismissed."

Clyde sat on the edge of the boat with his legs hanging over the gunwales, dangling over the green waters of the Bismarck Sea. The air still felt stifling, but the occasional splashes of sea spray made the trip almost tolerable. The impossibly green countryside slipped by only a half mile off the bow. It looked idyllic. The perfectly blue sky meeting the verdant greens of Papua New Guinea mesmerized him. It seemed impossible that a world war raged all around.

"Sure am glad we don't have to walk through all that country," Gil said.

"Yeah, the navy's got it good. But I wouldn't want to see this old crate in a storm. Doesn't seem too seaworthy."

"Guess that's why we're sticking close to shore." Clyde raised an eyebrow and Gil clarified. "In case we have to swim if she sinks."

"It's more of a barge than a boat," Oliver added. "Wouldn't last a day in the Atlantic."

Clyde glanced back and saw the other four barges carrying the rest of Able Company, pushing through the warm water. Two .50-caliber machine guns were mounted fore and aft on each boat in case of a Japanese air attack. He pointed to the sky. "If the Japs spot us, they'll have a field day with us. Fish in a barrel. Their base at Rabaul is just over there a bit. From what I hear, it's full of Zeros and bombers."

Gutiérrez flicked his cigarette over the side. "From what I hear, our flyboys have been hitting that base hard." He pointed out to sea at the dark shape of a ship. "I'm more worried about Jap gunboats and subs. Wish that guy would tuck in closer. What good's he doing way out there?"

"You a naval expert now, Gutiérrez?" Sergeant Huss chided. He pushed in beside them and lit a cigarette. He pointed at the peaks and valleys of New Guinea. "The Japs are out there somewhere. Those sons of bitches are the only ones you gotta worry about. Let the navy and the flyboys worry about ships and planes." He smacked Clyde's shoulder. "A word."

Huss walked away from the squad a few steps. He offered Clyde a cigarette and Clyde took it and lit up off the sergeant's zippo.

Huss said, "Now that you're an NCO, you gotta distance yourself from the men more."

Clyde looked at him with a slight scowl. "But they're my friends. How'm I supposed to just turn that off?"

"As a team leader, you're expected to order men into battle. You can't play favorites out there. The men have to know that you're impartial and that each man's treated the same. Do I need to move you to a different squad?"

"No, sergeant. It's just a lot to take. I didn't ask for this promotion."

"Cry me a river, corporal. When we reach Finschhafen, things are gonna happen fast. Second Platoon's gonna lead the way. Keep the men ready and pay attention. I can't hold your hand all the time out there."

"You can count on me, sergeant."

The barge suddenly swerved, almost knocking them over the side. The popping of distant guns filled the air. Someone yelled, "Incoming enemy Vals!"

Clyde steadied himself and looked up. Black and white pockmarks sullied the perfect blue sky. Black shapes dove between the wall of flak put up by the distant navy destroyer. Clyde couldn't take his eyes off them as the dots grew and manifested into four distinct aircraft. They looked to be coming straight at the barge.

"Get down!" Sergeant Huss screamed, clutching at Clyde.

Clyde hunched and pulled his carbine off his shoulder. The rest of the convoy of barges split off and zigzagged back and forth across their wakes, causing them to yaw and roll.

The gunners finally opened up with their .50-caliber mounted machine guns. Clyde watched the tracers arc up to meet the diving planes. Despite the racket, they looked wholly inadequate for the job.

One plane suddenly swerved out of the dive. The nose rose and fell as though the pilot had lost control. Flames erupted from a wing, then tore away, sending the plane into a violent roll. Black smoke streamed and marked its deadly path toward the calm seas. The other three kept coming, growing in size until the red meatball on the wing was clearly visible.

A small dark shape separated from the first dive-bomber's belly. The pilot pulled up and separated itself from the bomb. Clyde watched in horror as the bomb dropped straight toward the barge. The navy gunners kept hammering their triggers, sending piles of hot brass into the bottom of the barge.

Clyde ducked as the bomb exploded twenty yards off the bow, sending up a massive gout of water mixed with shrapnel. Sea water dropped onto the deck, immediately drenching them and filling the barge with two feet of standing water. The barge slowed and the shockwave rocked it, threatening to tear it apart at the seams.

The barge turned hard to port as the next bomb released from the second Val's underbelly. It sailed past the lead boat and smashed the sea between boats three and four. The screeching sound from the diving planes and the incessant pounding of the .50-calibers were drowned out as the five-hundred-pound bomb exploded.

The third dive-bomber released the next bomb, but instead of pulling out, it continued diving. Chunks of the plane tore off as the massive .50-caliber rounds found their mark. The canopy bloodied as the pilot's body shredded. The combined explosion of the bomb and the fireball from the plane sent a massive wave straight at the lead barge.

Clyde gripped a heavy tie-down stanchion as the barge smashed through the wave. The barge lifted then dropped, sending shudders through the mostly wooden frame. More seawater streamed over the sides and everything not tied down floated and sloshed.

The boat suddenly lurched as it slammed into something semi-solid. Paratroopers and naval personnel alike flung forward, some mashing into hard objects.

The barge slowed to a stop, and the machine guns had stopped firing. The gunners had been thrown from the mounts. Clyde pulled himself from the waist-deep water and searched for the remaining bombers. He saw them speeding away only yards above the sea, chased by .50-caliber rounds from the other barges. The tracers skipped on the water and arced into the sky, but none touched the fleeing enemy bombers.

The barge stopped dead in the water, and the engine sputtered. The other barges slowed and circled, the gunners searching the sky.

"Why are we stopped? Are they coming back?" Clyde asked a pale-faced seaman.

The stunned sailor didn't answer, but the ensign in charge of the barge poked his head out of the small bridge area. His voice cracked and broke with fear. He yelled. "Abandon ship! That wrecked plane we slammed into put a hole in the keel. She's going down fast. Get out! Get out!"

Clyde noticed the angle of the boat had changed. It was subtle at first, but the angle increased steadily until he had trouble standing upright without holding onto something.

Lieutenant Milkins's voice sounded calmer than the panicking ensign's. "Stay on the boat as long as possible. The other barges are coming. Offload whatever we can onto them before we sink." The paratroopers clutched their packs and weapons and sloshed their way to the edges.

Clyde stood with his squad mates in waist-deep water. Everyone watched the skies nervously. The other barges pulled alongside and ropes secured them together. The sinking barge stabilized somewhat, allowing the paratroopers and naval personnel to offload most of their gear.

Milkins supervised the entire process. The ensign had already taken his own advice and launched himself into the warm waters. When they'd salvaged what they could, Milkins ordered, "Okay, now it's our turn. Over the side."

They crammed onto the other barges. They stripped and wrung out their gear as best they could. The sun warmed them as they dried out and the barges chugged up the coast toward Finschhafen.

Gil shook his head. "Well, that sure was fun."

Clyde nodded in agreement. "I'll be happy if the rest of this mission is half as much fun."

The barge's relatively flat bottom allowed the paratroopers to debark directly onto a beach located a mile south of the town of Finschhafen on the Huon Peninsula. The Japanese had put up a tough fight here and the paratroopers didn't know what kind of opposition they'd find on the beaches. They flung themselves out of the barge and ran for cover as quickly as possible. But instead of Japanese soldiers, curious Australian troopers waved and greeted them.

"Oi, what are you Yanks up to?" one overzealous Aussie inquired as he offered his hand to Sergeant Plumly.

Sergeant Plumly, Second Platoon's platoon sergeant, slapped his hand away, stepped forward, and squared up in front of him with a dark scowl. "What's it to you, *mate*?" He said the last word as though it tasted vile.

Lieutenant Jameson, Able's ranking junior officer, stepped between them, and the Aussie stiffened his back to attention when he saw his rank.

"Kindly take me to your commanding officer, private," Jameson ordered.

The Aussie glanced at the still-glowering Plumly, then smiled back at Jameson. "Yes, sir. Right this way. He's in the mess tent last I saw."

Jameson turned to Sergeant Plumly and said, "Get things squared away here. Be ready to head into the jungle within the next two hours."

It didn't take long to offload the barges. When they finished, the men of Able Company watched the barges churn away from the beach and head back the way they'd come.

Clyde and the rest of Second Platoon separated themselves from the others, knowing they'd be the ones leading the way inland. Sergeant Huss stuck close to Lieutenant Milkins and Clyde stayed with Third Squad. He made sure each man had enough water and ammunition and their weapons were in working order.

Clyde felt foolish in his new role as assistant squad leader. He didn't like being in charge. He wished he could just go back to being a private first class. He inwardly cursed Corporal Quincy for getting the shits bad enough to be taken off the line.

They lingered on the edge of the beach while the afternoon sun beat down. The sparkling sea looked inviting. Clyde wondered if he had time to dip his head one last time. As a corporal, he could step away for a moment. Isn't that what Huss had told him to do—distance himself? But he wouldn't feel right cooling himself off while the others suffered, so he stayed put and sweat.

Finally, Lieutenant Jameson returned and issued orders. Milkins passed it along to the senior NCOs and then Huss filled the rest of the squad in. The company would move inland using local tribesmen as guides. Second Platoon, and specifically, Third Squad, would take the lead and find somewhere suitable to set up a base of operations.

"How long we gonna stay out there?" Clyde asked Huss.

"We're carrying three days' worth of food, Cooper. You can figure it out from there."

The four tribesmen wore very little. Three carried long spears and the last man carried a small bow and a bushel of arrows. It looked like a toy. The front of their hair stood straight up, making their foreheads appear elongated. All had deep grooves in their faces and broad smiles.

Huss raised his voice. "Third Squad, we're taking the lead on this one. Scouts out!"

Private Rogerson from the reconnaissance squad trotted forward with the four native guides. Clyde gave him a nod as he trotted past and said under his breath, "Better you than me, compadre."

Huss waved them forward. "Okay, move out, turds."

Clyde unslung his carbine and made sure he had a round in the chamber and had his magazine well seated. He took a deep breath and stepped into the simmering jungle.

They traveled along a trail most of the way. If not for their guides, they wouldn't have even found the trail, let alone stayed on it for long. Clinging branches and spiny vines snagged their uniforms, making each yard a misery. The tribesmen moved through without a sound, leaving hardly a trace.

Clyde tried to concentrate on the surrounding jungle. If an enemy lingered nearby, he wouldn't see them until they were right on top of one another. But even the impending possibility of combat couldn't keep his attention for long.

Fresh cuts bled and sweat stung as it dripped into them. It had been a full month since they'd hurled themselves from the C-47s over Nadzab Airfield, but he felt he'd never get used to the miserable feeling of patrolling through a steaming tropical jungle. As far as he was concerned, they should let the Japanese have the hellish place. Good riddance.

They patrolled inland for hours before they finally stopped at the edge of a large clearing. They hunkered down and the word passed to take a fifteen-minute break.

Clyde had rationed his water up till now, but he tilted his canteen back and gulped it down. The tepid, halazone-laced water tasted wonderful. He wiped his mouth with the back of his hand and took in the surroundings.

He noticed the other paratroopers didn't sidle up to him like they used to before they'd saddled him with the goddamned corporal stripes. Even Gil seemed standoffish, as though he'd wronged him somehow, even though he'd had no choice. *They'll get used to it.* He hoped.

Soon Huss appeared. He waved Clyde over. "The company's gonna set up here. This'll be base camp for the next few days. Squads will patrol from here until we find the goddamned Nips."

He pointed east. "There's a creek over there with clean fresh water, so have the guys shit somewhere else." He pointed in the opposite direction.

He looked him in the eye. "We've got the duty tonight. There's a trail the natives say gets used by the Japs to the west of our position. Jameson wants it watched."

Clyde's heart sank. All he wanted to do was get to the creek and soak his head and feet. "We got time to take a quick dip in the creek? Everyone's almost out of water."

"Hell no. Send two men to fill canteens. We're losing daylight. Milkins wants us set up before it gets dark and I agree with him." He wiped his brow, leaving a dark dirt stain across his forehead. "We move out in twenty minutes."

Clyde nodded his understanding. He wanted to complain. It didn't seem fair that the squad who'd led them in would also be first on watch duty—not to mention having a boat sunk beneath their feet that morning. But he didn't because he knew he may as well bitch to the sun about the heat.

He agonized over whom to send on the water detail. He picked Privates Wallace, Hellam, and Hicks. Gil didn't give him a second glance. Clyde felt relief, but knew he shouldn't be surprised. The paratroopers were volunteers and professional soldiers through and through. His chest swelled with pride. If he had to endure this hell, at least he'd be doing it with the greatest group of warriors in the U.S. Army.

The paratroopers of Third Squad finished digging foxholes just as the sun set. The trail they straddled wasn't much more than an animal track, but it showed signs of being used by more than just animals, so they set up for a fight.

Clyde settled into his foxhole alone with his thoughts. Huss had assigned the night watch duty rotation. They had given him the last watch slot, which meant he may get a few solid hours of sleep before then. As the assistant squad leader, he'd already checked the men's positions and made sure they had plenty of ammo, knew the callsigns, and the watch rotation. Now he could finally relax.

He opened a small carton of crackers and munched them without really tasting them. The wafers had little taste in the first place, so he chased them with a long slurp of water. The cool creek water was a vast improvement. He looked forward to the morning when he'd hopefully be able to strip and wash his body in the creek.

As darkness fell, he watched the surrounding jungle. He watched trees, bushes, and rocks turn into nondescript lumps in the darkness. He tried to memorize their locations so he wouldn't mistake them for enemy soldiers when he looked again—hopefully after a few solid hours of sleep.

He also marked the nearly invisible locations of the foxholes scattered around. Huss had them set up in an L shape around the trail to maximize the firepower they could bring if the Japanese came that night. But as the darkness deepened, it seemed impossible to see, let alone engage an enemy force. An entire regiment could pass by and they might not notice.

He sighed and lowered himself into the bottom of his hole. It still smelled of fresh dirt. During the excavation, he'd dug up countless worms and bugs. In the darkness, he couldn't see them, but he could hear their small sounds all around him. He hoped they'd leave him alone long enough to fall asleep. He touched his wedding ring and spun it on his finger, trying to bring images of Abby to mind. He finally fell into a dark, dreamless sleep.

What seemed like only moments later, he woke to someone knocking their fist against his helmet. He pried his eyes open, unsure of his surroundings.

"Wake up, Cooper. It's your turn for the watch."

He tried to focus on the dark outline lying down next to his foxhole, but he couldn't decide who it was. "Wh—what? It's already time?"

"Yes, goddammit."

He recognized Gutiérrez's acid-laced voice. "That you, Guti? See anything?"

"Yeah, it's me, and no, I didn't see nothin' out of the ordinary."

"Okay, you're relieved. I've got it from here."

Gutiérrez grunted and crawled back to his foxhole. Clyde wiped his eyes and readjusted himself so he could see over the edge of his foxhole. He touched his carbine propped beside him, then touched his ammo pouch. He placed a grenade on the lip and tried to focus. Sleep still threatened to pull him back into its sultry grasp. He smacked his cheeks to wake himself.

A quarter moon had risen while he slept, and the soft gray light filtered through the treetops. He could see fifteen yards down the trail.

He didn't check his watch, but knew dawn was still two hours away. His body ached all over. His legs felt tight and he stomped his feet to bring circulation back to them. He felt grimy and itchy, but he did his best to ignore it and concentrate on his job.

The intensity of the night sounds always impressed him when he actually stopped to listen. He'd heard it enough to tune it out mostly, but he concentrated on it now, knowing a change might signal something approaching, either the four-legged or two-legged kind.

His mind drifted. He wondered what Abby was doing at that moment. What time was it in Seattle—or Texas? *I don't even know where she is*, he thought bitterly.

He froze. He'd heard something, something unnatural. The insects' incessant roar dimmed slightly. He stared down the trail, focusing on all his senses. He saw nothing out of the ordinary, but felt something approached. He gripped his carbine and slowly brought it up, never taking his eyes off the trail. An icy shiver ran through his body, despite the warm air.

The sound again. It sounded like the soft click of metal scraping on wood. He brought the carbine's stock into his shoulder, then thought better of it and clutched the grenade. His muzzle flash would give away his position. The grenade would be enough to wake the rest of the squad and also shock the enemy.

His ears thrummed as his heart threatened to burst out of his chest. His mouth went as dry as dust. Movement at the far edge of where he could see the trail spiked his adrenaline and convinced him he wasn't imagining things.

He brought the grenade to his chest and slowly wound his finger through the pin. Then he saw them. One moment, nothing, then a line of six Japanese soldiers carrying rifles slung over their shoulders. They moved as though they feared nothing.

Clyde pulled the pin quickly and hurled the grenade as though delivering a fastball to a talented hitter. He yelled, "Japs front!"

The enemy force stopped in their tracks for a frozen second, then the grenade exploded a few feet from them, sending deadly fragments of metal into them.

Clyde quickly clutched his carbine, aimed and pulled the trigger, but nothing happened. He cursed himself, pressed the safety and tried again. He fired into the lead man. The soldier had taken the brunt of the grenade blast and staggered as the .30-caliber carbine rounds slammed into his torso.

By now, a few of the other paratroopers were up and firing. Clyde shot through his entire magazine in seconds. He fumbled to reload, but by the time he managed it, the last enemy soldier had disappeared into the night, running like an Olympic-level sprinter into the murky darkness.

Clyde fired off a few more rounds, aiming where he thought he might be. The roar of gunfire increased for a few seconds as the rest of the squad woke up, but soon Sergeant Huss's husky voice broke through. "Cease fire! Cease fire!"

Clyde couldn't catch his breath. He felt as though he'd run a fast mile, but he hadn't moved even a foot. Gunpowder wafted over him, obscuring the trail, but he could see enemy soldiers down—some wounded and moving—trying to crawl aimlessly out of the killing ground.

Huss yelled, "Was that you, Cooper?"

Clyde struggled to wet his mouth and finally managed to croak, "Yeah. It was me."

"Are there more of 'em?"

"I—I dunno. I don't think so."

Huss said, "Cover me." After hopping out of his hole, he moved forward in a crouch, his Thompson submachine gun at the ready. He stopped at the first downed soldier. He swept his weapon side to side, then stood and stepped over the first man. His machine gun barked three times as he ended the second man's attempt to crawl away.

Keeping his eyes down the trail, he said, "Team One, move up with me. Rest of you, cover us."

Clyde wanted to leap out of the hole and join them, but he was in charge of Team Two, so he stayed put and tried to calm himself. He watched the paratroopers rifle through the enemy's belongings. They finally returned, some grinning, some looking sick.

Huss stood over Clyde's hole and asked. "How many were there? You get a count?"

"I saw six of 'em."

Huss nodded and looked back at the carnage. Smoke still wafted from where the grenade had exploded. "Well, then two got away."

"We going after 'em?"

"Hell no. The others will wonder what the hell all the racket was about. We need to get the hell outta here." He raised his voice. "We're moving out."

Clyde hopped out of the hole and stared toward the men he'd helped kill. He wanted to check out his handiwork and made a move to do so, but Huss stopped him with a meaty hand on his chest.

"Leave it be. You did good, corporal. Now move out."

2

SEPTEMBER 1943

Myitkyina District, Burma

Shawn Cooper watched the railroad tracks from a high cliff ledge. Operational Group Bellevue expected a train at any moment now. They'd arrived three days before and had been watching the tracks ever since.

Lieutenant Danny Umberland tapped Shawn's foot and asked, "Anything moving out there?"

"Nothing we're interested in. Coupla deer. Think we could get away with dropping one and getting some fresh meat?"

"You not happy with the Iguana Didi brought us?"

Shawn gave him a look, but Umberland shook his head. "No, too risky. That train should be here soon. Captain Burbank would have our balls on a spit if we messed this mission up just to vary up our culinary palettes."

Shawn already knew the answer, but he'd been lying on this hunk of rock for three hours and wanted the distraction.

He lovingly patted the scope mounted on the Springfield rifle. He had it covered with a soft cloth for protection. "Too bad. Those deer wouldn't have a chance. With this beauty, it'd be like shooting fish in a barrel."

"You just keep your head in the game, Cooper. You happy with the positioning?"

"Oh yeah. Like I said, from this range—fish in a barrel."

"More like Nips in a barrel."

Shawn looked back and gave Umberland a thin smile. Umberland often tried for levity but more often than not, failed.

Shawn hadn't used the sniper rifle in anger yet, and he didn't particularly relish his role in the mission. He'd killed plenty of enemy soldiers by now, but those engagements had mostly been at night. He knew for certain his bullets had ended men's lives, but they'd just been shapes and silhouettes. Through the scope and in the light of day, this would be different—much more personal.

He wished he could turn off his conscience like so many of the others could. Lieutenant Henry Calligan came to mind foremost. He'd been one of the first OSS men into Burma, arriving with the famed—at least in the secretive OSS establishment's eyes—original Detachment 101 group. He killed Japanese soldiers and Burmese sympathizers as easily as buttering bread.

Calligan hadn't opted to join them on this mission. The brass deemed OG Bellevue ready to operate on their own. It had been a full month since they hit the labor camp workers and soldiers who'd been repairing Detachment 101's handiwork on the train tracks section. Since then, Bellevue had been on countless patrols. They'd covered vast distances of jungle and plains and had a good idea how to get around now.

Calligan had watched them leave Camp Knothead the week before. He'd nodded and grinned, but he didn't look convinced of their readiness. He'd spoken in hushed tones to their guide, the Kachin tribesman Didi, as they streamed past. Shawn would've given up a month's wages to know what they'd discussed.

Umberland checked his wristwatch, then slapped Shawn's leg. "I'm heading back to the radio. If the team gives me any advance notice, I'll let you know, but be ready. The Japs will be heavily armed and probably moving fast."

Shawn understood the mission, but stated anyway. "I still think we should just blow up the track like we did last time."

"Command thinks it's more valuable to take out the engines than the tracks. If they run out of locomotives, the tracks don't matter anymore. And we get the added bonus of destroying a bunch of Jap equipment and supplies—not to mention killing more Japs."

Shawn tried to flash a grin, but couldn't force himself. Instead, he just nodded, lifted the scope's cover, and peered through.

Just before leaving, Umberland's tone changed. "I know it's dirty work, but we didn't start this thing. You okay, Shawn?"

"Yes, sir. I know my duty."

"Remember, officers and engineers if you get a shot."

"Got it."

Umberland sauntered back into the thin jungle. Shawn pivoted his sights, searching for the rest of OG Bellevue hidden in holes around the railroad tracks. He saw nothing out of the ordinary.

He gulped against a dry throat. Despite what Umberland said about targeting the civilian engineers, he didn't plan on doing that. He understood the rationale, kill the engineers until they ran out of them, but he decided he wouldn't be the one to pull the trigger if he could help it. They'd most likely die in the attack anyway, but it would be one less thing he'd have to live with.

He found the strip of ribbon he'd placed about three quarters of the way to the tracks. It hung limply from a bent piece of kunai grass, showing no wind. The air felt hot and heavy, but at this range, not much would affect his shot. He said a quiet prayer, willing the Japanese train not to show up. *If Captain Burbank knew, he'd drum me out of the unit. Am I the only one who doesn't relish all the killing?*

His mind went to Ilsa, the beautiful spy he'd met and fallen in love with in Panama. *Love?* He wondered. Those days seemed ages ago. Would she even recognize him? He'd lost weight, leaving only sinewy muscle over bone. The last time he shaved, over three weeks ago, he'd barely recognized himself in the mirror. The sharp, angular cheekbones and bloodshot eyes he'd seen in the reflection couldn't belong to him. What would he look like in a year? *Unrecognizable.* Would he ever see her again? Would his soul be too far gone to even be capable of love?

He startled when Umberland hissed at him. "You awake up there? Hutch and Mackie hear the train approaching. Get ready."

. . .

The minutes ticked by at a glacial pace. Sweat dripped from Shawn's forehead and threatened to sully his sight picture. He wiped his brow with a filthy handkerchief and cursed himself. He shouldn't be this worked up.

He panned the scope slowly, following the tracks to where it emerged from the jungle. He wouldn't shoot until the boys down in the holes set off the plastic explosives set beside the track. They'd built the bomb intent on maximum destruction. They placed the bomb into the bottom of a large steel pot and laced rocks and bits of steel left over from the train track builders over the top. The shape of the pot would direct the blast force out the top, which angled toward the tracks where the locomotive engine would be. Then they camouflaged the whole thing with brambles and brush. When the bomb exploded, the rock and metal would scythe through anything unfortunate enough to be in its path.

Shawn took his eyes from the scope when he noticed a stream of black smoke rising from the jungle canopy. It moved steadily forward. He strained to hear it, but it was still too far away. He bet the rest of the squad could feel it pulse through the dirt as it clicked along the steel tracks.

Umberland whispered beside him, "See the smoke?"

"Yeah."

He settled his eye back into the scope and waited. The stream of smoke didn't seem to advance any longer and it took on a grayish color. What did it mean?

Umberland said, "It shoulda been there by now."

Shawn glanced at him without taking his right eye off the scope. Umberland used his binoculars, fiddling with the focus knob.

"Must've stopped," Shawn said.

"Why? Do they see our guys?"

Shawn saw movement along both sides of the track where the jungle gave way to the grassy plain. He adjusted his elbows and concentrated. "Soldiers coming out. I see—there's two squads, at least."

"I see 'em, too."

The soldiers walked cautiously, swinging their rifles from side to side as they searched the area.

"They're gonna walk right past the bomb, dammit," Umberland hissed.

"If they see it, this entire mission's a write-off. Can you knock those guys down from here?"

"Of course. You know I can, but that won't accomplish much, and I'd probably only get one or two before they took cover."

Umberland cursed under his breath.

"Don't worry, the bomb's well hidden. They won't find it."

The Japanese patrol came abreast of the bomb, but they didn't falter or call out in alarm. The further they moved down the tracks, the more relaxed they seemed to become. They just kept marching as though on a Sunday stroll. A few even slung their rifles. Shawn tracked them, keeping his sights centered on an officer with a pistol belt and a swagger in his gait.

"They're gonna go right over the top of the boys."

"Yep."

"If they make a move, drop 'em."

"Yep." Shawn slowed his breathing and placed his finger gently on the trigger. It felt cool to the touch. He'd zeroed the rifle, firing three full stripper clips through it. The trigger had a heavier pull than he liked, but from this range, and steadied by the rock ledge, he wouldn't miss.

"What rank's that guy? Might be a captain or a major even," Umberland commented as he gazed through his binoculars. "You might get yourself a prize, Cooper."

The betting pool for the highest ranking officer didn't sit right with him. It felt too much like Didi slicing ears and fingers off his victims. It made him feel dirty. He'd added his own money to the pool, but only to play along. If he won, he wouldn't know what to do with the money, either. How could he send the money back to his mother? Blood money. It wasn't right. *I'll spend it on booze for the group back in Nasira*, he decided as he applied a tiny fraction more pressure to the trigger.

The Japanese officer stopped, pulled out a white handkerchief, and wiped his brow. He put his hand to his mouth and, although his voice didn't reach their position, it had an instant effect on the other soldiers. They hesitated, then moved off the tracks. The officer clutched the nearest soldier and sent him scampering back along the tracks toward the waiting train. As the soldier ran clumsily along the uneven beams, the soldiers he passed slapped him and kicked him in the butt, taunting him.

Umberland's voice had an edge of excitement. "He's giving the train the all clear."

Shawn took his eyes from the scope and chanced a glance. The running soldier tripped and fell headlong right in front of the bomb. Umberland took in a sharp breath and held it. Shawn did, too. He wanted to shift his scope to see better, but kept it squarely on the officer's chest.

The clumsy soldier picked himself up and brushed dirt off his uniform. Other soldiers leaned over laughing. He walked to his helmet, which had fallen off and rolled even closer to the bomb. It stuck and he pulled. The brush they'd cut and stacked for camouflage fell away, exposing the pot filled with rocks and metal.

At first the soldier only stared, as though uncomprehending. He leaned closer, dug his hand in, then reared back and yelled. A bright blast erupted a few feet from him. His body simply vanished as fire and the force of the bomb turned his body to particles.

The force of the blast reached Shawn's perch and rocked the rifle in his hands. Dirt and bits of rock danced as though in an earthquake. Before putting his eye back to the scope, he saw at least six other enemy soldiers torn apart and scattered across the field like confetti.

The boom thundered up and down the valley, reverberating off cliff faces and bending tall grass and stiff trees. The surviving Japanese were all on the ground, either blown over or having instinctively dove for cover.

Shawn searched for the officer and finally found him, scrambling unsteadily back to his feet. In that instant, the pops of machine guns and small arms erupted. Shawn didn't need to look to know OG Bellevue had risen from their well-concealed holes and raked the survivors with accurate fire.

The officer staggered in his sights. His mouth moved as he screamed orders that no one would hear. Shawn blew out his breath, steadied, and fired. The rifle bucked, but he kept it tight to his shoulder and watched the officer stumble. The officer's tunic turned crimson and he looked at the mortal wound as though annoyed at a stain. His knees buckled and he dropped, then flopped onto his face.

Shawn had already worked the bolt action and was searching for more targets, but every soldier lay inert or dying. The quick and violent crescendo of gunfire ceased.

Gunther, the radioman, came scampering up to them, holding out the radio. "Sergeant Boyd for you."

Umberland took it and had a quick back and forth while Gunther and Shawn exchanged wide-eyed looks of astonishment. The once-peaceful field below now had a massive, burning scar, and was dotted with bodies, some scorched beyond recognition, others full of bullet holes.

Umberland signed off. He pointed toward where the train must still be idling. "I'm sending the others to finish off the train."

Shawn saw his comrades leaping from their holes on the plain below. The wood and thatch covers they'd used to conceal them from above lay haphazardly around the entrances, leaving small black holes. It added to the feel of chaos and destruction.

"I can't cover them from here. Once they're in the trees, I won't be able to help them."

"I'm betting that was the main force. They just have to deal with stragglers and engineers."

Shawn bit his lower lip. "What if you're wrong?"

"The damned locomotive's the mission. We have to destroy it," he said gruffly. "They can take care of themselves," he finished without as much conviction.

Shawn moved to the right as far as the ledge would allow. He scrunched into a tight slot and lay on his stomach. Rock and twigs dug into him, but he ignored them as he put his eye to the scope.

He steadied the crosshairs on the farthest edge of the railroad track and, out of the corner of his eye, watched his teammates leapfrogging one another toward the waiting train. It had been less than two minutes since the explosion. The Japanese would still be reeling and wondering what had happened. Hopefully, the men of OG Bellevue would fall on them violently before they could organize and react.

Shawn raised his voice. "They're going beneath the canopy. I won't be able to see them."

Umberland scuttled over to him and scanned with his binoculars. He mumbled, "Come on, come on." He seemed as nervous about the situation as Shawn. Shawn didn't envy having to make that decision. Some of his anger melted away. Umberland was doing the best he could. He trusted him.

The popping sound of gunfire came to them. Shawn strained but couldn't see anything. His mind eased as he heard only Thompsons and carbines. But he tensed when he heard something much louder and deeper coming from deep inside the canopy. Immense geysers of dirt erupted along the railroad tracks as bullets bypassed Bellevue and thunked into the dirt.

"What the hell's that?" Shawn guffawed.

Umberland cursed, then answered, "Sounds like an antiaircraft gun. Twenty millimeter if I'm not mistaken."

"Jesus, that'll tear those guys up. Let's get down there and help 'em."

"Negative. You can do more good from here." He pointed. "If they retreat, the Nips'll be right behind 'em. They'll need your long gun skills." He turned to Gunther. "Try to raise Boyd."

Gunther turned the radio volume all the way up and tried to raise Sergeant Boyd, but got no response. The sound of gunfire mixed with louder booms from grenades. If he even heard the call, Boyd would be too busy to answer.

The firefight continued for nearly a full minute. It was the longest minute of Shawn's life. Finally, the antiaircraft fire stopped after a series of crashing explosions. Thompson submachine gun fire dominated, then tapered off quickly.

"They must've gotten the upper hand."

Gunther finally got a response. "I've got Boyd, sir," he said excitedly.

Umberland snatched the radio. "Situation?"

Shawn could hear Boyd's voice. It sounded tinny and distant. "We took the train. We're setting charges on the locomotive and everything else, too. You probably heard their big gun."

"Casualties?"

"Yeah, Fenton and Mackie are dead. Hutch is wounded, but he can walk."

Umberland shut his eyes and rubbed his forehead. "Understood. We'll come down and assist with the bodies."

"Uh, there's not much left of them. We'll get whatever personal items we can find."

Umberland looked like he might be sick. He signed off and stood. He paced as though uncertain what he should do next. He finally pointed at Shawn and ordered, "You stay up here and watch over things. Gunther and I will go down there."

Shawn nodded and put his eye back to the scope. He could see more smoke rising through the jungle canopy, and he saw the faint flicker of flames.

Fenton and Mackie gone, just like that. He knew them as well as he knew his own cousins—better, really. How badly injured was Hutch? He shut his eyes, staving off the tears that threatened. He'd have time to grieve later. Right now, he had a job to do.

He watched as the survivors streamed back into sight. They trotted, keeping their weapons ready. The last two men to emerge trailed coils of wires. They hunched and fidgeted with the detonation box. They yelled and the rest of the men went to their bellies. A series of sharp cracks and bright flashes from beneath the canopy made Shawn flinch. A secondary explosion blistered the air. The fireball pushed through the swaying tree-tops, scorching them and lighting some on fire. The shockwave hit him square in the face, followed immediately by a hot, oily wind.

Shawn licked his lips nervously. Surely the Japanese would notice. A relief force had to be on the way by now. He silently urged his teammates to hurry.

Lieutenant Umberland and Corporal Gunther finally made it to the valley floor. They sprinted toward the others. Where would the relief force come from? Myitkyina Airfield or one of the many nearby Burmese villages?

Minutes later, he got his answer. The drone of aircraft started dimly, but grew steadily. Team Bellevue had nearly made it to the cover of the jungle. Hutch held his arm and limped, but moved under his own power.

Shawn stood and searched the sky. He finally saw black dots against the blue sky near the horizon to the south. The others hadn't noticed them yet. They still moved at a normal pace. Shawn cupped his hand around his mouth and yelled as loud as he could. "Jap planes incoming! Incoming!"

His words had no effect. With the slight breeze, the distance, and their own heaving breaths, they couldn't hear him.

Shawn put his Springfield to his shoulder and fired. The others immediately went to their knees. All eyes focused on Shawn. He jumped around, waving and pointing at the incoming threat. He finally got his point across. The OSS men sprinted the rest of the way toward the jungle. Two others helped Hutch along on either side.

Shawn dropped to his belly and tucked himself into the cover of a thorny bush. He ignored the painful barbs as he watched the growing dots turn into aircraft. He couldn't see the rest of the team, but they'd be in cover by now. *I'm the most exposed.*

The roar of low-flying aircraft filled the valley. The greasy black smoke coming off the burning train drew them in like flies to shit. Two Zeros swept back and forth over the burning train. They flew low over the entire area, hoping to draw fire. Shawn didn't dare move. He fought the urge to take a potshot. It was tempting, but he knew he had little chance of causing damage unless Lady Luck smiled on him. Even if he managed to hit one, it would only invite a strafing run. Better they found nothing. Part of their mission was striking fear into the enemy, and nothing did so better than deadly hit-and-runs that left little evidence behind.

The Zeros arced into the sky, then lanced back down toward the valley. The lead pilot strafed the field where the exposed holes were still visible. Dirt and debris shot up in a long swath of destruction. The second plane loitered overhead, turning in a slow arc, no doubt searching for return fire. They finally climbed and turned back toward Myitkyina. The drone of their engines finally faded into nothingness.

Didi stepped out of the jungle and grinned. Shawn dusted himself off and smiled back. Even though he'd lost two close friends, Didi's bottomless joy was contagious. Operational Group Bellevue sifted back into the jungle. If all went well, they'd take a circuitous route back to Camp Knothead and arrive in two days. Shawn hoped he'd finally be able to get some sleep, but doubted it.

3

SEPTEMBER 1943

Austin, Texas

Abby Cooper languished on the bed she'd sleep in for the foreseeable future. Beatrice Malinsky's place didn't look any bigger than her old apartment in Seattle, but for some reason it felt bigger. Perhaps it was the bright sunshine beaming through the window, or perhaps it was the huge open expanses surrounding her in every direction, or maybe all the possibilities that had just opened up for her made everything seem bigger.

Beatrice poked her head into the room. "Well? What do you think? Will it work for you?"

"Oh yes. It's far more than I expected. Thank you, Bea. Thank you so much."

"Don't mention it. You're paying rent after all."

"Yes, but you went through a lot of trouble making this room up for me. You even put a picture frame on the mantle."

"I figured you could use it for that picture of Clyde you're always staring at."

"I'm sorry about that. I just miss him so much. It's torture not knowing if he's okay or not. It drives me crazy."

"Well, once you start flying, you won't have time to dwell on it anymore. The training's tough and they don't give you a lot of free time."

"I owe you for that, too. I know you had to pull some strings to get me accepted."

"A few. You don't have many hours, but Conklin wants you on board and you're a natural flyer. You'll pick it up fast. Besides, when they realized how few women actually had enough flight hours, they dropped the hour requirements for the WFTD program. You've got more than enough now." She smiled and crossed her arms. "But those hours came a long time ago, so you're behind a little."

"I suppose I need to get used to all these acronyms. I guess it's easier than having to say, Women's Flight Training Detachment, though."

"You're in the army now. They use loads of them."

"Am I though?"

"Well, you'll take the same oath the men do, but no, not officially. But once we prove ourselves, General Arnold said it'll happen automatically."

"Gives me butterflies just thinking about it. Thanks for putting in a good word for me *and* getting me up to speed."

"It's okay. I don't mind burning the candle from both ends. You're lucky. The WFTD doesn't expect you to be up to standards right at the start. The WAFs did. But you have to be proficient enough to make it through the first week of flying, or they'll just cut you from the program. Conklin wants you, but he has to defer to whatever the instructors recommend. If they see him giving you special treatment . . . well, it wouldn't be right."

"I don't want special treatment. I want to earn my right to be here. Just like everyone else."

"You've had a long train trip. Unpack and settle in. I've got loads of books and flight manuals you can go over at your leisure."

Abby went to her and hugged her fiercely. At first, Beatrice stiffened, but then she hugged her back.

Abby said, "I owe you a lot, Bea. I won't ever forget it."

Beatrice broke the embrace and gave her a beaming smile. "I'm happy to have a roommate. It can get lonely sometimes."

"Lonely? You? I don't believe it for a second. You must have a line of men seeking you out. "

Beatrice tilted her head and batted her eyelashes. "Oh, you're too kind." She gave her a coquettish bow, then a simmering look. "You're not too far off the mark. In fact, we should probably come up with some ground rules." Abby looked confused, so Beatrice explained. "A signal in case I have a man inside."

Abby blushed deeply. She finally uttered, "Um, okay."

Beatrice laughed and gave her a dismissive wave. "You're married. You forget what it's like being single."

"I guess you're right. Do you have men over often?" she asked carefully.

"Goodness no, I'm not a tart, but sometimes. It's harder now with the war, not as much time—although there are more uniformed men around. I must say, I do enjoy a man in uniform." Abby blushed again and Beatrice flung her thick brown hair. "I'll let you unpack. We can figure out food and everything later."

Beatrice shut the door and gave her one final wink. Abby couldn't help laughing. She and Beatrice hadn't lost a thing since high school. Their friendship felt solid and delightful. This chapter of her life would certainly be entertaining. It helped ease her mind. So far, she'd made the correct decision.

She hefted her suitcase onto the bed and unsnapped the latches. It exploded as though she'd packed live animals inside. Her clothes seeped out the sides and spilled onto the bed. She glanced at the closet, wondering where it would all fit. Some of it might have to be packed away. She shouldn't have brought it all, but couldn't decide what to leave and what to bring, so she'd brought most everything. Looking at the heap made her feel silly. Once in the program, they'd give her some kind of uniform. The train porter had nearly thrown out his back when he'd hauled her bag from the baggage compartment.

She hung clothes in the closet and placed a line of shoes underneath. She wondered what kind of footwear she'd need for flying. Beatrice wore a light pair of boots when she flew, but Abby had nothing like it. Would they give them uniforms? Beatrice wore men's coveralls most of the time. The WASP program wasn't a part of the military, although they adhered to many of the same standards, particularly where it concerned discipline.

She'd have to get used to being told what to do and how to do it, not to mention what to wear.

Once she filled the closet and the small dresser, she gazed into the bottom of the suitcase and saw the stack of letters from Clyde. She smiled and pulled them to her lips and kissed them. She inhaled, trying to find a hint of his smell, but she only smelled her clothes and a hint of mustiness. She tucked the letters into the nightstand, then arranged the pictures of him. She inserted the one of him at the picnic into the frame Beatrice had bought for her and sighed as she gazed wistfully.

She suddenly remembered the letter that Clyde's best friend Gil Hicks had written to her. She'd stowed it in her handbag and forgotten all about it. She'd written to him months before, asking him about her father helping Clyde become a paratrooper. Her father had implied it, but she suspected that he'd been lying to her. It seemed like ancient history now. Her life in Seattle seemed like a universe away and she wanted to keep it that way, but she also wanted to know what Gil had to say.

She dug into her handbag and found the letter. She held the flimsy paper and noted all the colorful stamps. The little piece of paper must have traveled a long way. She'd sent the letter to him a month ago, and his letter had taken almost as long to get back to her.

She sat on the edge of the bed and carefully opened the letter. She read it carefully. Gil's handwriting wasn't awful, but she had to guess at a few words. As she read, she gripped it tighter and tighter. Gil told her that contrary to being helped, Clyde had actually nearly died . . . twice! Clyde had said nothing about either incident during his furlough. He hadn't lied to her, but he hadn't volunteered the information, either.

She read it again. Gil had obviously left out a lot of details, but imagining Clyde hitting the tower and being knocked unconscious nearly made her ill. Why hadn't the army told her about that? Didn't they notify the family when a loved one was injured? Even more terrifying, on his last jump, he'd had to throw his reserve parachute when his primary hadn't opened. That must've been a close thing, yet he hadn't even hinted at it.

She understood his reticence, but it angered her at the same time. What else didn't he tell her? She wanted to crumple the letter and throw it into the wastebasket, but instead she swiped at a tear and placed the letter gingerly on the bed. Her father hadn't helped her husband. Quite the opposite, it seemed. Despite feeling sick to her stomach, she also felt a welling of pride. He'd overcome incredible odds and qualified for the most elite unit in the entire military.

She didn't know why her father had lied. In fact, she couldn't recall much of that conversation. It had been heated and she'd just wanted to get it over with. But her loathing for her father only grew. What had happened to him? When did he become such a monster?

She thought about Trish and Miles. A sadness swept over her. Trish had been her best friend, but she'd betrayed her. But Trish had also lost Miles, a man she obviously had been in love with. How was dealing with that loss? At the funeral, she'd seemed detached and stoic, but Abby saw pain in her eyes as she had gazed at the casket. Then the anger as Abby's father had read the eulogy, using the platform for his own gain, like some deranged politician. Perhaps Trish had turned her sadness at losing Miles into sheer hatred for Victor Brooks.

I should write Trish a letter. But then she remembered how they'd parted. Trish had demanded she return Miles's journal and she lied and told her she'd burned it. She'd actually boxed it up and put it in the mail. It would arrive in her new mailbox here in a few days. She didn't have a notion of what she planned to do with it, probably nothing, but she couldn't bring herself to give something so personal to Trish, who would use it to bring her father down.

She felt conflicted. She loathed her father at the moment, but he was still her father. She still loved him, or at least loved the man he used to be. Would she ever see the day her father turned his back on all this backstabbing evil and became a good man again? She hoped so, but didn't know how it would happen. Perhaps he needed to be taken down. Perhaps that would be the one thing that could bring him back to his old self.

He'd never been completely lovable, his affection never came in hugs or words, but he used to look at Abby with eyes of adoration and love. She remembered those looks and cherished them deeply in her soul.

But all that was behind her now. The troubles she left in Seattle wouldn't follow her here. Her parents didn't even know her address, let alone Trish. A pang of regret made her wince. *I fled. I left them in the lurch.*

The thought made her rub her temples as a headache threatened. *I've made my decision. I'm not going back—at least, not yet.*

Beatrice burst through the front door. Abby sat on the couch reading the manual for the trainer she'd be flying, the BT-9. She'd read it six times already and had marked up the margins to prove it.

"Drop everything. We're going to the club."

"A club? I don't know, Bea. I have a lot of studying to do."

"This is the last night you have before training starts. We're going out on the town and you can't say anything to change my mind."

"Well, in that case—let me get changed."

A half hour later, Beatrice pulled her old truck into the parking lot of an old tavern. Abby took in the club with some trepidation. "This is the club? It looks ready to fall down."

"It's safe enough. Come on, the whole gang's inside."

"Whose whole gang?"

"Your whole gang. The WAFs I fly with and a few of the other trainees you'll be joining."

Abby stepped from the truck and straightened her dress. Music pumped from the closed front door and she heard many mixed voices.

"Sounds like things are already in full swing." She checked her watch. "It's barely five o'clock."

"Start early end early. You check in at six a.m. tomorrow."

Abby followed Beatrice to the front door. Beatrice smiled and just before opening the door, said, "By the way, there'll be some male pilots here, too."

"Oh? From the base?"

"Some are, others flew in from other areas. This bash has gotten famous."

"I haven't heard of it before now."

"Of course you haven't. Come on, let's get inside."

She opened the door and the noise level made Abby wince. She stepped in behind Beatrice. The lights were low and the curtains over the windows only pulled halfway down, making the scene dingy and dark.

Clinking glasses, laughter, and cigarette smoke permeated the air. Abby didn't recognize anyone, but that didn't surprise her. She'd only just arrived in town.

Beatrice waved as a group of women noticed her and called out her name. She clutched Abby's hand and pulled her through the throngs of gyrating bodies. The smell of alcohol and cigarette smoke hung heavily.

A woman almost as tall as Beatrice slung her arm around her shoulders. "Beatrice! As I live and breathe. I didn't think you'd make the scene. What took you so long?"

"I had to swing by the house and pick up my new friend." She stepped aside and Abby smiled at them. "This is Abby Cooper. She starts training tomorrow. We've been friends since middle school."

The tall woman extended her hand. "Well, welcome. I'm Fonda. It's nice to meet you. Anyone who's a friend of Beatrice's is a friend of mine."

Abby shook her hand. "Thank you. It's good to meet you." She had to yell to be heard. The introductions went around the gaggle and Abby did her best to put names to faces, but she doubted she'd remember them all. Each of them exuded confidence and poise. She'd never been in such a group of women like this in her entire life. She felt lucky and intimidated at the same time.

A man approached, weaving his way through the crowd, holding up a tray full of precariously poised beer mugs. A few sloshed their contents, but he maneuvered marvelously, keeping the tray mostly flat.

"Coming through! Make way." Abby recognized a heavy British accent. She did a double take and remembered him from when she'd visited Beatrice the month before. What was his name? She remembered it was odd. Heathcliff or something like that.

Beatrice flung her arms out as he approached. "Hercules, you're a lifesaver." She took a mug from the tray as he brought it down. In a flash, the rest of the beers vanished and they left him holding the empty tray.

He shook his head and laughed. He noticed Abby and stopped. "I know you, don't I?"

Abby smiled and extended her hand. "Yes, you helped me with my bag a few weeks ago. I'm Abby Cooper, Beatrice's friend from Seattle."

"Oh rightio, I remember now. You're back for more?"

"I start training tomorrow."

He stroked his thin mustache. "Yes, of course. Major Standish Hercules at your service."

"Thank you, sir."

"Looks like you lost out on a refreshment. Stay here. I'll be back with another round."

"If it's not too much trouble."

"No trouble at all."

Before he left, Beatrice wiped her mouth with the back of her hand, then placed it on the major's shoulder. "Thanks Stan. You remember Abby?"

"Yes, I just reintroduced myself."

Beatrice strung her arm through his and pulled him close, whispering something into his ear. She gave his earlobe a quick nibble, then pushed him back toward the bar.

He blushed, but moved off. Beatrice watched him appreciatively. "He's got a nice behind, doesn't he?"

Abby covered her mouth and felt her ears heat. She didn't know what to say.

"Don't you think so?"

"I hadn't really noticed."

"Nonsense! You're married, not dead."

"Are you two . . . ? You know—together?"

Beatrice shook her head and slugged down more beer. "No. He's a bit of a prude, to be honest." She lowered her voice and leaned in close to her ear. "But I'd love to see his naked butt one day."

Someone handed her a beer. Abby took it and sipped. She wasn't used to drinking beer. She much preferred wine, or even champagne. Beer hadn't been something she'd ever been exposed to—too proletariat, she supposed, for the country club scene.

Beatrice pointed to a gaggle of women at the far end of the bar. "Those are the other students you'll be training with."

Abby took a keen interest. They weren't nearly as loud and boisterous as the WAF pilots, but they all held mugs of beer. They seemed more nervous than the rest of the crowd.

"I should probably go introduce myself."

"I'll take you over there. Be awkward otherwise."

Beatrice strung her arm through Abby's, and they cut their way through the crowd. There were more women than men, but the men were all young and quite good looking. Some had British accents and others were obviously American. They gave Beatrice and Abby appreciative looks as they brushed past them, making Abby uncomfortable. Beatrice seemed to glow with the attention. She batted her eyelashes and playfully swatted at them.

As they approached the women, Beatrice leaned close. "This group are all qualified pilots, but will be in the WFTD, just like you. They don't have enough hours to qualify for WAF training. Some have been flying for years. Don't let on that you're a cherry."

"A cherry?"

"Yeah, you know—a novice."

Abby thought she should be honest with them, but before she could say anything, Beatrice raised her voice to them. "Ladies, hello."

The women knew her. They smiled and gave her the respect she'd obviously earned. Abby hoped one day she'd be looked at similarly. They barely glanced at her.

Beatrice put her arm around Abby's shoulder. "This is my friend, Abigail Cooper. She'll be joining you in the morning."

They stared at her. Abby felt as though she were being evaluated like a cow for the slaughter.

She fidgeted but manage to say, "Hello, you can call me Abby."

The women warmed to her a little, but one of them kept her stare icy. Abby went around the group, introducing herself. When she got to the glaring woman, Abby extended her hand. "It's nice to meet you."

The woman didn't offer her hand. "Cooper, eh?"

"Yes, Abby Cooper."

"You're the low-hour pilot from Seattle."

Abby gave a quick glance to Beatrice. How could she know that information?

"Um, yes. I suppose compared to everyone else, I don't have as many hours, but I'm a quick learner and I'm eager to get started."

The woman crossed her arms and looked down her nose at her. "My name's Mandy. Mandy Flannigan. But I don't suppose you need to remember that."

The iciness in her voice made Abby cringe, but she found the courage to ask, "Why not?"

Mandy leaned forward as though speaking to a child. "Cause you won't be here long enough for it to matter."

Abby felt as though someone had slapped her. What had she done to deserve this person's ire? They'd only just met. "I beg your pardon?"

"Beg all you want—it won't help you."

Beatrice stepped forward, but Abby put a hand on her shoulder. "It's okay." She smiled at the others, who looked embarrassed at Mandy's outburst. "I'm sure we'll all become fast friends when this is all over." She smiled sweetly. "I look forward to getting to know all of you." She looked at Mandy last and lingered there. She could feel the hatred coming off her like a furnace.

She spun away, pulling Beatrice with her. Beatrice glared at Mandy, who simply sipped her beer.

"She's cocky. You want me to set her straight?"

"Of course not. She's just someone I'll need to steer clear of, I guess. How does she know about my flight hours?"

"I dunno. I guess it's probably not a state secret or anything."

Abby took a long draft from her mug, leaving a mustache of foam on her upper lip. She lifted the mug appreciatively. "I've never really had beer. It's good. I could get used to it."

Beatrice slapped her back, nearly making Abby choke. "Thatta girl. Beer's the pilot's choice out here in Texas."

Standish Hercules saw them and smiled broadly. He swooped in with two fresh mugs of beer. When he saw Abby already holding a half-filled one, he shook his head in dismay. "It appears I'm late for the show."

Abby took it from him. "That's okay. This one's almost gone, anyway."

Beatrice raised an eyebrow and exchanged a look with Standish. "Our Abby's got a taste for beer, Stan."

"Well, in that case—as you Americans say—cheers!" He raised his mug and the entire room erupted in raucous cheers.

4

Abby sat more upright in her seat as she listened to the flight instructor, Wanda Uster, explain aerodynamics and lift to the attentive students of the Women's Flying Training Detachment. Just like everyone else, she knew the material already—she'd studied the manuals exhaustively, putting in extra work just to keep up with the others, who clearly knew a load more than she did.

Wanda's voice held a south Texas twang. It sounded as though she may doze off if she talked much slower. The information would be on the test, so Abby paid close attention.

She thought back two weeks to that first day of class. She'd drank too much beer the night before and her head had throbbed. She'd only had five mugs of beer, but it had a terrible effect on her. She'd nearly thrown up, but kept it down. It would've been better to just let it all out. Beatrice had come to her rescue with strong coffee and toast, but nothing seemed to help. Since then, she hadn't had a drop of alcohol and had no desire to until she made it through training. She may not even then.

She looked around the room and took in the other students. Each of them had achieved more than the average woman so far in their young lives. Most had at least a few years of college and had maintained high marks. Abby felt a little lost at first. Although she'd been to university, she got very little out of it other than etiquette lessons from her sorority sisters, and how to pick the right man, of course.

What was Clyde doing at that moment? At least a hundred times a day, she thought about him. She'd written and received many letters, but the last one she received told her not to expect any more for a while. She dreaded what that could mean, but she understood what he implied. He'd be heading into harm's way.

She hated not knowing what he was up to. It didn't seem fair. Since her training started, she didn't have time to seek out war news, and not knowing current events seemed to make it worse somehow. Was he involved in a major operation or just more intensive training?

Wanda droned on and Abby forced herself to concentrate. She'd missed something important because the others were frantically writing notes. She tried to lean over and sneak a peek, but the desks were too far apart. After class, she would have to compare notes. Who could she ask? Mandy Flannigan wasn't an option, but the others didn't seem to mind her low-hour status.

After the first week, they'd all been required to move onto the base. They had erected barracks a few hundred yards off the airfield. The spartan accommodations and strict curfew rules assured they had few distractions. They could still go out on weekends, but during the week, they were confined to the airbase.

Beatrice hated the new rules. They hadn't made the WAFs stay on base when they'd trained. Despite missing Beatrice's antics, Abby didn't mind. It left her plenty of time to study and get to know the other girls better.

Excluding Mandy, she liked the other women immensely. They came from all different walks of life. Some came from wealth, others from near poverty, but they all had one thing in common. They all loved to fly.

The tight confines of their living quarters made it impossible not to get to know the other trainees, but it also made it difficult to avoid Mandy. She'd managed to, mostly. Mandy hadn't gone out of her way to harass Abby, but she still scowled at her and had a generally bad attitude. The other women respected Mandy's qualifications and her prowess in the air, but Abby wondered how long that would last.

During official introductions way back on the first day, Abby had felt embarrassed at her own obvious lack of experience. Everyone else had real-world flying experience and at least a hundred and fifty flight hours. The WAFs required their applicants to have a minimum of five hundred flight hours, have received a commercial license, and have a 250hp engine rating. Since very few women had those qualifications, they formed the WFTD in order to bring the unqualified women up to speed.

Even with the lower standards, Abby still found herself the least qualified of the bunch. She had wondered if she'd made a huge mistake, but decided she'd do her best, no matter the obstacles. After two weeks of ground school, she was still there.

Today would be their first time climbing into the trainers with their instructors. Abby recognized the old Stearman trainers from her first flight training so many years before. They dotted the airfield and their navy blue paint and yellow lettering shone in the Texas sun. She felt grateful to be learning in a familiar aircraft, but the others felt somewhat let down. They wanted to fly the BT-9s and the T-6 Texans tucked away in the hangars.

As the hour wound down toward the time they'd head to the flight line, Abby's nerves spiked. She fought the urge to chew her fingernails. No one else seemed the least bit concerned, but they were already accomplished pilots and the Stearman was like a bike with training wheels still attached.

Beatrice had flown with Abby every chance she got before classes started, and that had boosted her confidence. Abby had done well, remembering the old thrill of flight from that long ago summer in Seattle. But she still had trouble with crosswinds and she still bounced her landings occasionally. She'd improved markedly since those first days. Even though it was against the rules, Beatrice even trusted her to perform acrobatics, although they mostly worked on stall recovery and landings.

The biplane Stearman wasn't nearly as powerful as the P51, but it would be far more forgiving. It had a much better glide slope than the Mustang, which made Abby feel better in case she lost the engine for real.

Miss Uster checked the clock. "Okay, that's it for classroom lessons. Remember, there's a test tomorrow on the material, so study hard. But now, it's time to fly," she said with a broad smile. "Check the board for your assignments and be on the flight line in an hour." As the trainees stood and collected their things, she raised her voice and reminded them, "Remember, there aren't any toilets up there."

The group tittered and laughed. Abby slung her books in the crook of her arm and made her way out the door along with the others. A palatable excitement permeated the air. She only felt nervous. What if she forgot everything? The Stearman wasn't half as complicated as the P51, and she'd studied the airplane's flight manual cover to cover at least twenty times, but at that moment, she couldn't remember the checklist. She would have a written checklist in front of her, but what if they wanted her to do it from memory? At that instant, she couldn't remember any of it. She broke out in a cold sweat.

Mandy nudged her shoulder. "You ready for this? You look terrified."

Abby shook her head, not wanting to rise to the bait, but it made her angry. "I'm ready. I know that flight manual by heart. Go ahead. Test me."

Mandy smiled, and her beautiful straight white teeth sparkled in the lights from the hallway. "Okay." she placed a finger on her chin. "What's the stalling speed at sea level for the Stearman?"

Abby cursed herself. She knew the answer, but it escaped her at that instant. She stammered, "Er—um," Mandy sneered, but it came to her finally. "Fifty-three miles per hour."

"And the optimal climb out rate?"

Abby's eyes narrowed, but the answer came to her in a flash. "Optimal climb out is eight hundred twenty-five feet a minute."

Mandy's snide face changed to a thin smile. "Well, at least you know the bookwork. But how will you do in the air, I wonder? How many hours do you have—a hundred?"

"Not quite. Sixty-five."

Mandy guffawed, "Barely enough to be considered more than a complete novice. I have over four hundred hours. Some on multi-engine aircraft. I'm glad I'm not going up with you. You're a liability."

Abby shut her mouth tightly and increased her pace. Mandy matched her stride and kept talking. "I doubt you'll make it through the first month of actual flying. Bookwork's one thing, flying's quite another."

Abby stopped abruptly and turned to face her. "Why are you so awful?" Mandy blanched and looked around as though wanting witnesses. "It's not a popularity contest after all. I'm here to help with the war effort. Why are you here, Mandy? Besides making everyone feel bad, I mean."

Mandy lifted her chin, tucked her books close to her chest, and huffed. "I'm here to make sure people like you don't ruin it for the rest of us."

Abby looked around in confusion. "What? What in the world are you talking about?"

Mandy lowered her voice and pushed Abby into the wall. Not hard enough to hurt, but enough to let her know she was in control.

"This war is going to change everything for us women. Don't you realize that? A few months ago, this job didn't exist. Without the war, I'd still be flying for carnivals and getting paid a quarter of the male pilots, all while smiling sweetly and shaking my ass just to keep my job. Look around you. All these women worked their tails off to be here. But you? You just stroll in here off the streets and assume you're gonna make it. You don't have enough experience. What happens when you auger into the ground at two hundred miles per hour? I'll tell you what'll happen. They'll shut us down quicker than you can say Pan Am Airlines."

Abby gulped and tore her eyes away from Mandy's seething gaze. "I— I'll do my best."

"Your best? Your best is barely good enough to get off the ground. One crashed airframe and they'll ground all of us and send us back to the holes they grudgingly allowed us to squirm out of."

Abby clenched her fists at her side. Anger welled, and she stared daggers at Mandy. "Look here—I may not be as experienced as you, or anyone else here, but I love to fly. I get better and better every time I go up. I'm careful, too. Probably more careful than you, since I don't have the experience. I may never be as good as you, but you have no right to judge me before you even give me a chance."

Mandy shook her head as though dealing with a dense child. "Don't you see? This isn't about you and your dreams to fly—it's about us." She indicated the trainees streaming past their heated argument, as they tried to pretend not to hear. "These women deserve the chance, not you. You're an upstart. You're only here because you know Malinsky, the WAF's darling. You don't belong here. You haven't earned the right to be here. You just know the right people."

Abby felt like crying, but kept her tears to herself. Mandy turned from her and strode away. A few trainees waited for her and put their arms around her as she approached. Abby stood in the hall alone, dumbstruck. She just wanted to fly—to earn her wings and fly as a WAF, but she hadn't thought about what that meant for anyone else. Was Mandy right? Would they shut the program down if she bent an aircraft? No, they wouldn't have started the whole thing if they didn't *really* need it, but Mandy had opened her eyes to what it could mean for women even after the war finally ended —if it ended. Why did everything have to be so complicated?

An hour later, Abby stood with everyone else on the flight line facing the Stearmans lined up like majestic horses. Compared to the P51, the Stearman looked like a toy. She held her notebook full of notes and check-lists, maps, and tools of the trade tight to her chest. She hoped she'd remembered everything. If she'd forgotten something important, it was too late now.

All the women wore men's one-piece jumpers. Since they were made for men, they didn't fit well. Abby's hung off her thin frame, making her feel like a hanger in a closet. The instructors' suits didn't fit much better, but were adorned with brightly colored patches. The trainees' suits had no flare at all. Despite the ill fit, the instructors stood proud, with their chests out and their medium-length hair fluttering in the wind. Abby wanted to be one of them. She vowed she wouldn't let anyone down, especially herself.

Mandy had a point, but she would not quit without at least trying. If she really couldn't get it and thought herself a liability, she'd simply take herself off the trainee list. She didn't know what she'd do then and didn't want to think about it. First things first.

The thought of having to go back to Seattle with her tail between her legs almost made her physically ill. She briefly wondered what her mother and father were doing at that instant. What would they think of her if she scampered back home at the first hint of difficulty? No, she wouldn't do that, no matter what. Her mother would accept her, but her father would give her his "I told you so" look.

She'd do everything she could to get through the training, even if it meant putting in more hours of work . . . not to mention acing every written test.

Miss Foster stepped forward and raised her voice. "You checked the lists. So let's get this over with. Ladies, approach your aircraft."

Abby felt a thrill race up her spine. She didn't expect such pomp. It reminded her of some sort of jousting match from King Arthur's time. She made her way to the aircraft with the proper tail number. Her instructor stood with her meaty arms crossed and a deep scowl. Abby had seen her around and knew she had a reputation for being tough.

She braced in front of her like a soldier reporting for duty. They did not consider the WFTD a military program, but they adhered to much the same standards. She felt ridiculous standing at attention, but it was what they expected.

"Trainee Abigail Cooper, reporting, ma'am."

Abby was a half a foot taller than the stout instructor, but she felt small beside her.

"Cooper. I hope you're ready for today's flight."

"Yes, ma'am, I'm ready."

"Is that so? My name's Wanescoat. You'll call me instructor or ma'am. Understand?"

"Yes, ma'am."

"Walk me through the preflight, Cooper."

"Yes, ma'am."

Abby strode past her. She went to the engine cowling and unhinged it, exposing the engine. After checking the spark plugs and oil level, she snapped the cowling back into place. She went to the propeller and ran her hands over the edges, feeling for any nicks or imperfections. Then she went to each wing and gazed into inspection ports, making sure the leading wing edges were in perfect condition, and no wires were cut or frayed, and the ailerons moved freely. She made her way to the rear and checked the rudder and elevator, then the tail wheel assembly. Finally, she dipped her finger into the fuel to check the gasoline level.

She wracked her brain for anything she might've missed. She carried a sheet, but no one used it for preflight. It should be automatic and obvious. She forced herself not to use it this time.

"She's airworthy, ma'am."

"We'll see about that. Proceed."

Abby climbed onto the wing and gingerly stepped into the front cockpit. She eased the straps over her shoulders, keeping them out of the way yet accessible. Wanescoat lowered herself into the rear cockpit. The airframe shimmied as she shifted and squeezed her wide hips into place. Abby wondered about her weight. The airframe and power plant could handle it no problem, but she wondered if she should bring it up. Perhaps it was a test.

"Um, I suppose I need to ask you about weight and balance?"

The shimmying from the back stopped abruptly. Abby glanced behind her and saw Wanescoat glaring at her.

"It's fine," she finally said. "But if you're so interested, why don't you walk me through it?"

Abby closed her eyes, trying to bring back the information from memory, but she couldn't. She reached down and pulled out the aircraft's handbook. Every airplane had different specifications and the flight handbook had all the information spelled out so even an elementary school student could understand.

Wanescoat harrumphed. "You need the handbook? It was supposed to be studied thoroughly. You don't know this aircraft's weight and balance specifications?"

Abby felt sweat bead on her forehead. She bit her lower lip and concentrated, trying to picture the page with the information printed on it. It came to her after a tense moment. "Yes, I remember now. The crew load is four hundred pounds, assuming a full tank of gas and oil."

"That's right. Very good. So, are we within the boundaries?"

"Um, well, I'm one hundred twenty pounds." She considered asking outright, but decided it wouldn't be a good idea. "Which means, unless you're over 280 pounds—we're fine."

"And do you think I weigh over 280 pounds?" she asked with a hint of iron in her voice.

"No, ma'am."

"Good, then proceed to your checklist. Time's a wasting."

Abby went through the checklist easily.

She checked the surrounding area for any hazards then called out to the mechanic standing nearby, "Give her a few spins, please."

The mechanic pulled the propeller through a few turns to clear the combustion chambers from any leftover oil.

Once the mechanic cleared away, she went through the starting sequence by the book. The Stearman's engine sputtered, then roared to life with gusto. She adjusted the throttle, and watched the oil pressure gauges register. With everything running smoothly, she signaled for the ground crew to remove the chocks holding the wheels in place. That done, she glanced at the tower, looking for the yellow light telling her to taxi to the runway.

She taxied her way along the taxiway and lined up behind the other Stearmans waiting their turns. She went through the engine run up, making sure the magnetos held adequate charges and the rudder, ailerons, and elevator worked as advertised.

Soon it was her turn to take off. She watched the tower light turn green, clearing her for takeoff. For a moment, she forgot an instructor sat behind her, watching her every move. She felt invigorated and alive. The power of the engine rumbling through the soles of her boots, the roar through her headphones, and the wind blowing her hair in the open cockpit added to the thrill.

She pushed the throttle steadily forward and counteracted the slight engine torque, trying to swing the entire aircraft left by applying pressure on the right rudder pedal. She overcorrected slightly and the airframe slewed right, but she caught it smoothly until they darted straight down the runway.

The thrill of her back being pressed into the seat wasn't nearly as intense as in the P51, but she still wanted to whoop. She stifled the urge, deciding her instructor wouldn't appreciate the enthusiasm as much. For the instructor, this was all just so much routine.

She glanced at her engine dials. The tail wheel came off the ground and the stick felt light in her hands. She pulled back slightly, keeping a few pounds of pressure. The aircraft lifted off the tarmac smoothly. Abby couldn't help herself. She whooped, "Yeehaw!"

Over the intercom tube, she heard instructor Wanescoat say, "Yeehaw? Are you a cowgirl, Cooper?"

"Sorry, ma'am. Uh—no ma'am." She had to raise her voice to be heard through the intercom tube system.

Despite the awful acoustics, she could hear the laughter in Wanescoat's voice. "Well, you coulda fooled me. Take us to five thousand feet at our best possible rate of climb."

"Yes, ma'am."

Abby did her best to keep the aircraft climbing at eight hundred feet per minute at a steady speed of sixty-five. The stick felt heavy in her hands, even though she needed very little pressure. When she flew with Beatrice, it never felt this difficult. She blew out a breath and forced herself to relax, but it didn't help.

"That's five thousand feet, ma'am. Leveling off."

"Good. Now take a heading of zero-nine-zero for five minutes."

"Yes, ma'am." She turned due east and checked her watch. She struggled to maintain course. The plane seemed to skid through the air as she crabbed into the wind. She figured the wind blew at least twenty-five knots up here and came at her from the southeast.

"That's five minutes, ma'am."

"Okay, now make a clearing turn."

Abby obliged, turning steeply one way, then the other while checking for other aircraft. She spotted a silver glint of a fuselage in the distance. "I have an aircraft to the north about three miles out."

"Noted. Now I want you to S turn across that straight road below us. Do you see it?"

"Yes, ma'am."

Abby flew perpendicular across the road. When the back edge of her wing crossed over the road, she turned sharply left, maintaining a forty-five degree banking turn. She struggled to keep the nose from dipping and her speed from rising. Once she'd reversed course, she leveled the wings and put her heading back onto zero-nine-zero, but she'd already crossed the road by then. She turned right, making the turn steeper to compensate for her lateness. The nose dipped and she picked up speed. When she crossed the road again, she'd drifted and was still in a turn. She leveled off well past when she should have.

She heard Wanescoat say, "That's a fail."

"Yes, ma'am, I know."

"What went wrong?"

Abby wracked her brain. She'd practiced this enough with Beatrice. She'd failed a few times then, too, but nailed it mostly. "Um, I picked up too much speed on the last turn and crossed too quickly. I was behind the whole time."

"Why?"

"I—I guess I just lost it."

"The wind. You didn't compensate for the wind. It pushed you around the turn faster, then slower—it also sped you up and you didn't compensate."

"Yes, ma'am. I see that now."

"Flying is all about precision. I know you can see for miles and miles all around right now, but what happens when you can't? What happens when you have to rely on just your instruments? One little miscalculation leads to you missing your airfield by miles. You'll be delivering these aircraft to airfields all across the country. They are vital to winning the war. If you can't find your airfield, you're no good to us at all." She paused to let that sink in, then continued. "Take everything into consideration . . . especially the damned wind."

Abby nodded vigorously so Wanescoat could see her doing it. "Yes, ma'am. I understand."

"That was a basic maneuver. Should've been easy for an experienced pilot. How many hours do you have?"

"Officially, sixty-four, ma'am."

"How long ago?"

Abby gulped against a suddenly dry throat. No one had really asked her that before. She decided to be honest. "Mostly earned six years ago, ma'am."

A long silence put Abby into a mini-panic. Would Wanescoat simply kick her out of the program before she even had a chance to improve? She wanted to say something more—to let her know how committed she was, but thought better of it.

Wanescoat finally said, "Are you a quick learner?"

"Yes, ma'am. I mean, I think so. I'll put in extra hours if you'll let me. I'll do whatever it takes to make the cut."

Wanescoat said, "You're going to need all the extra help you can get."

"I've been getting lessons from my friend Beatrice Malinsky."

"A fine pilot—one of our best, but she's too busy to take on a student. Tell you what, meet me after classes. There's about two hours before dark we can use. It'll mean you'll have to stay up later studying and you'll most likely miss dinner."

"I'm fine with that. Like I said, I'll do whatever it takes."

"I'll test you in one week. I'll expect you to pass your basic flight test all over again. If you fail, that'll be it for you. We don't have time to waste on you after that."

"I understand—and thank you, ma'am. If it makes a difference, I'm usually better than that. I think I'm just nervous."

Wanescoat pushed the end of the intercom tube outside the cockpit, flooding Abby's ears with a harsh roar. Abby finally heard Wanescoat's voice again. "We'll put that on your headstone. 'I was nervous,'" she mocked. "Excuses won't keep you from dying out here, young lady. You don't have the luxury of being *nervous*. You just have to do the job."

5

SEPTEMBER 1943

POW Camp Bilibib, Philippines

Frank Cooper opened his crusted-over eyes and wished he were anywhere else but there inside Bilibib POW camp. Surely, he must have been there for years by now. April 1942 seemed ages ago. The other prisoners kept track of the time, but he paid little attention to it now. Every day was just another day of sweltering heat, insects, rats, worm-filled rice, and the incessant gnawing hunger that never really went away.

He dragged himself into a sitting position and looked around the barracks. Barracks—they could hardly be called that—were more like shacks. The thatch walls drooped with condensation, mildew, and mold. If you got too close, it rained down and covered the floor in a thin layer of bluish-gray death. Nothing inside the barracks stayed clean, despite their best efforts. Diseased rats filled the area beneath the floorboards and they ventured topside at night. Rat bites were common and painful. Some men had succumbed to infection from them. Things got worse during the rainy season. The added mud and constant wetness made even breathing difficult. The rainy season always brought more death to the POWs. Thankfully, that season had passed, but the dying never stopped, just slowed.

Larry Grinning Bear saw him finally coming out of his stupor. "You alive, Frank?"

"Yeah. I'm still here. Not sure how much longer, though."

"Well, today's moving day, so hop to it."

"Hop to it? Hop to what?"

"Getting fed. You almost missed chow. You'll need all your energy for the move."

"You really think they're moving us? They've been saying the same thing for weeks."

"Yeah, but this time they mean it. The road's done, so they don't need to keep us around as laborers anymore."

"Where you think they'll send us?"

Grinning Bear stared into the distance. "I dunno. Anywhere's better than this dump, though."

"I doubt that. What if they ship us all the way to Japan? What then?"

"I dunno, Frank. All I know is I'm glad to be doing something other than sitting around here slowly dying."

"You marines are always itching for action."

"Semper Fi."

"Yeah? You still got faith?"

Grinning Bear stopped rolling his thatch sleep mat and looked at Frank with bloodshot eyes. "I've got faith in my brother marines. You've heard the same news I have. We're slowly pushing these slant-eyed mother fuckers back." He whispered the last part. They'd shot or bayoneted men for saying far less.

"You think they'll liberate us soon? How long can this damned war last?"

"I wouldn't hold your breath, but I know it'll happen at some point. We just have to stay alive long enough."

"I'm losing my faith, Larry. I've been here too damned long. It feels hopeless."

Grinning Bear leaned in closer. "What about escape? You haven't given up on that, have you? And what about Bernice? You think she's given up?"

Frank's mind went to Bernice Callahan, the nurse he'd taken a liking to. She seemed to reciprocate his feelings, but he hadn't seen her in weeks. For a while, they delivered care and whatever medicine they could scrounge and keep from the prying Japanese, but that lifeline seemed to have dried up. The camp had run out of medicine and everything else they needed to survive and with it, his hope.

"I dunno. I pray she's okay, but I feel so helpless. She was the only thing keeping me upright."

"She's still out there. Have faith, man. Maybe we'll get news once we're on our way to the new camp. Hell, maybe they'll put us in the same camp she's in. Santo Tomas—right? And you never answered me about escape."

He lowered his voice. "I think we'd just end up with bayonets in our backsides. It seems impossible. Besides, our own officers forbade it."

"I know, I know. But what do they know? Captain Valencia acts like a scared rabbit. He does whatever Hideki tells him to do. I think he'd sell his own mother if Hideki told him to," Grinning Bear said with dripping disgust.

"Now'd be the time to try, I guess. During the move, I mean."

"Nah. They'll be even more uptight and alert than normal."

"It's impossible anyway. I don't know why we're talking about it."

A whistle blew and Frank got to his feet shakily. Instinct and negative reinforcement had trained him to come to attention when he heard that damnable whistle.

"Guess chow will have to wait. It's time to go," he uttered. He took one last look at the ramshackle hellhole and followed Grinning Bear out of the thatch door. "At least it's stopped raining, finally."

"That's probably why they're moving us. The roads are finally passable. Remember what Manila looked like during the monsoon season? The city was bad enough, but out here in the boonies, it must be far worse."

They formed up in ragged lines as the cadre of Japanese soldiers strode among them with their bayoneted rifles and lousy attitudes. Frank stood as still as possible, but he felt himself swaying like a dying blade of grass in a strong wind.

He'd done all he could to stay strong. The weekly raids into the kitchen livery continued, but even the Japanese seemed to be on cut rations, so they couldn't steal as much without raising suspicions. It meant the prisoners didn't get as much and their energy dwindled.

Their one meal a day had been slowly reduced—the water content increased in the gruel, while the rice diminished. The only protein they received came from the mealworms in the rice and whatever bugs and animals they could catch in the festering camp.

Rats were plentiful, but diseased. More than a few men had sickened and been carted off to the infamous infirmary after eating one of them— they'd never returned. Frank hoped their new camp didn't have an infirmary, at least not like the one here. Not one full of fear and death.

He'd missed his daily ration but he had a stash he could access if he could break away for a moment. Surely there'd be time to visit the latrines before they traveled.

An hour later, Frank sat in the back of a Japanese troop truck, watching the thick green jungle pass by slowly. Hunger gnawed at his belly more than usual. He hadn't been able to break away to visit his meager food stash one more time. He hated leaving it. He'd worked hard and risked his life stocking it and now it would be consumed by bugs, animals, or the sweltering jungle itself.

The truck had been a welcome sight. The thought of walking long distances, as they had forced them to do when they'd traveled to Camp Bilibib, didn't sit well. He doubted he had the strength to make it more than a few miles, and he was better off than most. Captain Hideki's insistence on daily excruciating exercises had taken a heavy toll.

They passed through a small town. The Filipino townspeople emerged and stared as they passed. Some looked fearful, and others shot daggers at the Japanese soldiers when they weren't looking. One smiled and flashed a quick V for victory sign when he caught Frank's eye. Frank couldn't help but grin back at him. *Hope?*

"You see that?" Frank asked Grinning Bear quietly.

Grinning Bear opened his half-shut eyes and shook his head.

"One of 'em flashed me the victory sign."

Grinning Bear noticed the town and the people for the first time. "They don't seem too happy."

Frank eyed the Japanese soldier sharing the back of the truck with them. He sat near the front of the truck bed and faced backward, but his gaze never wavered from the next truck back. Being put in such close proximity to the filthy prisoners obviously annoyed him. Frank wondered what he'd done to deserve such low duty.

Frank said, "You see the way they're looking at them? Pure hatred."

"Can't blame them. I don't think they're known for their charity," he said carefully.

Frank lowered his voice and covered his mouth. "I wonder what would happen if we could get outta here? I bet the Filipinos would help us."

"Now you wanna escape again?"

"Now that I see their anger—it seems possible. I don't think they'd turn us in."

"One guy flashes you a victory sign and that's all it takes for you?" He shook his head. "It's too risky. Don't try anything."

"Course not. It's just good to see we're not alone out here."

Grinning Bear nodded. "Yeah, you're right." He straightened his back and stared at the Filipinos. "Can you imagine if this sort of thing happened back home? We forget, we were stationed here, but this is their *home*."

"You're right. I'd be mad as hell."

They passed out of town and the jungle closed in again. Frank sat near the back. The truck directly behind stayed close. Frank fantasized about rolling out the back and darting into the jungle. The Japanese would have a hell of a time finding him. Then he could make his way back to the town and join the resistance, and lead the Filipinos to one glorious victory after another.

It was just a fantasy, however. He pictured what would actually happen. He'd lurch out the back, be unable to get to his feet in the mud and the following truck would run him over. Each subsequent truck would drive over him until his body became one with the road. The last truck might stop to allow a guard to leap out and drive his bayonet into his back just to make sure, or simply shoot him as they passed. The image almost made him laugh.

Someone up ahead yelled and the truck lurched to a stop. Frank smashed into Grinning Bear and the other prisoners couldn't keep themselves from piling forward. The Japanese guard pushed them off, then brought his rifle up, as the prisoners pulled themselves from the bottom of the truck bed.

More yelling, then the driver pushed the truck into gear with a harsh grinding sound. The truck leaped forward, sending the guard sprawling onto the prisoners. He slashed and punched until he could get to his knees.

The truck went off the road and pulled into the cover of the overhanging trees, then halted again. More yelling and the Japanese pointed at the sky. The guard in Frank's truck braced his rifle and aimed at the heavens. Then Frank heard it. Engines—many airplane engines.

He exchanged hopeful glances with Grinning Bear and the other prisoners, then searched the only sliver of sky he could see. The guard yelled in Japanese, pulled his rifle into his shoulder, and aimed skyward.

Frank saw tiny dots against the clear blue sky. The occasional flash and dark smudge of antiaircraft fire erupted. He couldn't tell what they were, but by the way the Japanese acted, they had to be Allied aircraft. Moments later he heard a far-off whistle, followed by distant heavy thuds and crumps.

He couldn't keep from smiling. Every prisoner's face looked skyward, and their eyes sparkled with joyous tears. Frank thought it was the most beautiful thing he'd ever seen. He wanted to leap up with a raised fist, but he knew they'd beat and probably kill him, so he satisfied himself by watching the distant bombers lumber through the pockmarks of flak.

An hour after seeing the bombers, Frank saw the results of the raid. As they passed the waters of Manila Bay, thick black smoke rose from the large port. A few ships lingered nearby. None of them seemed to have sustained damage, but a few buildings smoked and flames licked up the sides. The damage didn't look catastrophic, but to the prisoners, it didn't matter. For the first time since surrendering from Corregidor, they saw evidence with their own eyes that the war still raged on.

Frank felt a surge of renewed hope. "By God, they haven't forgotten us," he muttered excitedly.

The guard had stopped trying to keep the prisoners from talking. His obvious fear made his rage seem impotent and unimportant.

Grinning Bear asked, "Where'd they come from you think?"

Lieutenant Blunt answered. "Those were long-range bombers. Probably B-17s. They've got a lot of range. Must've come off some island or possibly China."

Frank added, "Who cares? The point is, they're close enough to strike Luzon. Which means they're on their way."

"I've never been so happy to see flyboys in my life."

The guard had finally had enough. He leveled his rifle at them and barked his ire at them in rapid-fire Japanese. The message was obvious: shut up or die. They did so, but they couldn't keep the smiles from dimpling their sallow cheeks.

Soon, however, their smiles disappeared when their destination became obvious. Just before entering the suburbs of Manila, the trucks pulled off and trundled toward the bay. They finally stopped at a small port. Anchored a half mile off the docks sat a medium-sized ship, and along the dock a veritable fleet of barges awaited their arrival.

The officers issued orders and the Japanese guards sprang into action, yelling and pushing them to dismount. In their weakened states, it took longer than they wanted and a few men paid with brutal thumps.

They herded the prisoners toward the docks. They lined them up six rows deep with their backs to the water. Fear swept through the ranks as they imagined themselves being gunned down and their bodies pushed into the bay to be consumed by crabs. But why cart them all the way here, when they could've done the same thing back at Camp Bilibib? Easier cleanup, perhaps?

Captain Hideki approached and they stood in nervous silence. He held his infamous bamboo stick. The same stick he'd used for his exercise regimen with Grinning Bear's backside. Frank noticed his friend stiffen as Hideki paced back and forth, thunking the stick into his palm over and over. He'd always had a flare for the dramatic. Whatever new hellhole they were headed toward, at least Hideki wouldn't be joining them there.

Hideki finally stopped pacing and spoke through his interpreter. "You are being given the highest honor imaginable. You are being shipped to the glorious shores of Japan itself. There, it will be your privilege and honor to serve the emperor for the rest of your days."

They stood in stunned silence. Frank felt the joy and hope the Allied bombers had brought suddenly evaporate. His shoulders slumped and his legs nearly gave out. Japan was surely a death sentence.

His body trembled. His eyes darted like a wild animal. Could he make a break for it? He cursed himself for not having the courage to leap from the truck when he might've had a chance at escape. But there was nothing he could do now. If he tried to escape, he'd only hasten his death. *Would that be so bad?*

Maybe it was time to make one final stand. If they all rushed them at once, they might get to Hideki before they gunned them down. He imagined strangling the life out of him. But no. He barely had the energy to stand upright and the others were in just as bad, if not worse, shape. Hideki could likely whip them all by himself using only his cursed bamboo stick.

Even the smoke still curling up from Manila Bay couldn't lift his spirits as he trudged to the waiting barges that would take them out to the ship, then into the very heart of the enemy.

6

OCTOBER 5, 1943

North of Finschhafen, New Guinea

Corporal Clyde Cooper crouched in the clearing where Able Company had set up their base camp. Since the night of the ambush, there hadn't been any more action. Despite patrols pushing out in every direction, they couldn't find the retreating Japanese.

Lieutenant Milkins spoke to the men of Third Squad. "Captain Stallsworthy thinks we've been here long enough. So our patrol today will be the last unless we find something." He pointed to the rudimentary map spread out on the packed dirt. "I won't be coming with you this time. Sergeant Huss is in charge. You'll head northwest again but this time you'll go out farther."

Clyde didn't like the sound of that. The last time they'd been out there, he'd had a feeling they were being watched. Nothing came of it, but he couldn't shake the feeling.

Milkins continued. "We made it to this ridgeline last time. This time, you'll push into the valley beyond. Air reconnaissance shows some kind of trail. Could be the Japs are using it. Pack enough food to stay out overnight, but try to do this quick. Questions?"

The other NCOs shook their heads. Clyde asked, "We bringing the guides with us, sir?"

"Not this time. They left last night. They've got regular lives to lead, I guess," he grinned.

Huss said, "I'll bet their old ladies got after 'em about being gone too long."

"Yeah, maybe. We've been over this terrain before. We know our way around." When there were no more questions, he finished. "You move out at 0500. Make sure your men have plenty of water and ammunition."

Huss broke the news to the rest of Third Squad as Clyde packed his bag and filled his ammo pouch with magazines and extra grenades. He kept his distance from the others but hated doing so. He'd settled into his new role as assistant squad leader, but he didn't have to like it.

Gil approached him. "You think we'll find 'em this time?"

"Hell if I know. You wanna find 'em?"

Gil shrugged. "Yes, and no. I mean, I wanna kill the little bastards but . . ." he let his words die.

"Yeah, I know what you mean. I wish we could just line 'em up in a field and mow 'em down as they crossed. Not this close quarters jungle crap."

"Exactly," Gil said as he lit a cigarette.

He offered one to Clyde. "No, thanks."

"You heard from Abby?"

Clyde shook his head. "Not out here. Who knows when our mail will catch up with us. Maybe if we get sent back to Moresby."

"We getting sent back? You heard anything?"

Clyde scowled. "I'm a corporal, not a general. They don't give me the scoop. Why you asking about Abby?"

"Why not?" Gil asked. Clyde shrugged and kept packing. Gil pressed, "You didn't tell her about Melinda, did you?"

Clyde stopped packing and stared daggers at him. He hadn't thought about his indiscretion for weeks and didn't like being reminded. "What business is that of yours?"

"It's not, but you need to trust me on that one. Never tell her."

"I heard you the first time. I didn't tell her. It's not something I could say in a letter, anyway. It'd have to be face-to-face, and who knows if I'll even get outta here."

Gil pointed his half-smoked cigarette at him, nodding emphatically. "Exactly. If you tell her and you die out here. That'll be how she remembers you."

"Jesus Gil! Are you trying to make me feel better?"

Gil stepped on his cigarette and blew out a string of smoke.

Clyde added. "We move out soon, get packed up, private."

"Pulling rank on me. I like that."

"Fuck off, Gil."

Gil smiled and said half mockingly, "Yes, sir."

Clyde knew he should give him what for, but he couldn't bring himself to do it. Despite what Sergeant Huss said, Gil was still his best friend. He couldn't just throw that away because they sewed a few stripes on his shoulder.

He hefted his carbine and joined Sergeant Huss. Huss held his Thompson submachine gun on his hip as though duck hunting. "Team Two ready to go, corporal?"

"Yep. We're ready."

"Good. Need you to pick who you want out on point."

"Uh, okay. Rogerson."

Huss shook his head. "Rogerson needs a break. Pick someone else."

"Hicks." He immediately felt bad. Did he choose him 'cause he pissed him off? That would be just as bad as favoritism, just in reverse. He couldn't win.

"Hicks it is. Let him know."

"Will do, sergeant."

Clyde felt exposed as Third Squad pushed through the jungle, heading toward the distant ridgeline. Lieutenant Milkins had wished them good luck as they left the clearing, but Clyde thought he was just happy not to be joining them. Milkins had proven himself in combat, but Clyde couldn't help holding a grudge against him. He always seemed to volunteer Second Platoon and, particularly, Third Squad for these missions. Seemed the more combat they saw, the more missions they picked them for. Why not give someone else a chance and leave them the hell alone?

He strained to see or hear Gil out in front of them on point. When he'd told him about it, Gil had spit, then nodded. The tight grin he gave him felt like an indictment. "Glad to do it," he'd said, but his tone suggested otherwise.

Clyde felt justified, though. They knew this part of the jungle. They'd been there before. By the time they reached the ridgeline and descended into the valley, Gil would be spent and it would be someone else's turn— Rogerson, most likely. By making Gil go first, he was actually doing him a favor. While covering known territory, he would get his point man rotation in. He'd be safer. He'd only thought of that later, but still.

Private Wallace, directly in front of him, suddenly stopped and crouched. Clyde hunched and felt his heart leap into his throat. Had Gil found something? They'd been patrolling for two hours and he hadn't stopped once.

He glanced behind and saw the others crouching and fanning to either side with their weapons ready. Sergeant Huss caught his eye and motioned him forward. Clyde nodded and moved in a crouch past Wallace. He whispered as he passed, "Stay put, I'll see what the holdup is." Wallace didn't respond, but kept scanning the jungle.

Clyde stopped when he got to Oliver, the last man before Gil. "You see anything?" Oliver shook his head slowly and pointed. Clyde followed his gesture and saw Gil's backside twenty yards up the small game trail they'd been following for the past hour. He looked frozen in place and Clyde wondered how he should approach him. He crawled.

It took a while, but he finally got to Gil's side. Gil didn't acknowledge him at first—just stared straight ahead as though transfixed.

Clyde didn't hear or see anything out of the ordinary. He finally whispered, "What is it? You see something?"

Gil didn't answer right away and Clyde wondered if he was playing with him. But finally Gil hissed, "No, I *feel* something."

"What?"

"Like I'm being watched."

A chill ran up Clyde's spine. He'd learned to listen to his own instincts and he trusted Gil's just as much. He concentrated on the surrounding jungle. Nothing felt or sounded out of place, but in the thick jungle, there could be an entire regiment yards ahead and he wouldn't know it unless they were moving.

He whispered. "We can't just sit here with our thumbs up our asses, Gil. We've gotta keep moving."

Gil nodded slowly, but never took his eyes off the jungle. Clyde heard someone approaching from behind. He turned to see a red-faced Sergeant Huss crawling toward them. He didn't look too happy.

When he got to them, he hissed, "What in Sam's hell is going on up here?"

"Gil senses something ain't quite right."

Huss's head looked ready to explode. "He *senses* something? What kind of horseshit is that? Is there something ahead of us or not, Hicks?"

Gil shook his head once. "I dunno. Just got a bad feeling."

Huss looked at Clyde for some kind of affirmation. Clyde shrugged, not wanting to commit one way or the other.

Huss's scowl deepened. He angrily chewed his lower lip, but finally nodded. "Okay, we'll move forward in a combat spread. Tell the men." Clyde backed away a foot and Huss grabbed Gil by the shirt and pulled him so their noses touched. "You better be right about this, Hicks."

"I hope I'm not," he answered.

The squad spread out in a wedge formation. Gil stayed out front. The thick jungle didn't allow them to spread out too far, but at least if an ambush awaited them, they wouldn't all be in the kill zone and might roll up the enemy flank if it came down to it.

They'd advanced approximately seventy yards when the crack of a rifle split the air. Clyde dropped to his belly instantly. For a moment, nothing happened, and he wondered if someone had an accidental discharge.

But then he heard Rogerson yell, "Sniper! Hellam's hit!"

Clyde raised his head, searching for the telltale smoke from the sniper's rifle, but he could only see jungle. The rifle crack came from the front, but beyond that, he couldn't pinpoint the sound. Where the hell was Hicks?

Huss yelled, "Where is he? Where's the sniper?"

Another rifle crack answered him. Clyde heard the thud of the bullet smacking into a palm tree to his left where Huss had called out from.

A flurry of answering fire from the squad shredded the jungle to the front, most of it directed toward the treetops. Clyde hoped they didn't hit Gil. He aimed but didn't see what they were firing at, so he held his fire.

The firing tapered quickly. He called to his squad leader. "Huss, you okay?"

A shaky voice answered, "Yeah. The fucker missed me by a cunt hair."

"You see him?"

"Negative."

Another shot and this time the bullet smacked the ground in front of Clyde, only inches from his head. He shimmied backward and rolled behind an outcropping of rock. Another bullet zinged off the rock, sending shards into his helmet. *Son of a bitch!*

Concentrated fire from the squad clipped a suspicious treetop nearly in half. Massive leaves and thick branches fell. Gutiérrez called out triumphantly, "I got the son of a bitch."

Clyde stayed down. He felt wetness spreading across his hip, and he wondered if it was blood or urine. He didn't feel any pain, so he must've pissed himself. He cursed and felt suddenly embarrassed. He got to his knees and glanced at his crotch, but the wetness wasn't from piss. He pulled his canteen and saw the jagged hole in the bottom. He stood on shaky legs as the rest of his water drained down the side of his leg.

Huss trotted through the jungle to him, his eyes wide. "You alright? That son of a bitch had you dead to rights." He saw the wetness and the dripping canteen. "Holy shit, Cooper. You almost got your balls shot off."

"Must've—must've been a ricochet or something. I—I thought I pissed myself."

Huss slapped his shoulder. "You're alright, corporal. Come on."

Clyde stepped over the rock outcropping that had saved his life. He saw Rogerson and Private Plontovich hovering over Hellam's unmoving body. His face was unnaturally white. He had a neat hole in the bridge of his upper nose. His bloodshot eyes looked in opposite directions, as though the sniper's bullet had cut the cords holding them in place.

Plontovich was in Team Two. He'd been his responsibility and now he was dead.

Gutiérrez said, "Should we cut him down?"

Clyde tore his gaze away from Plontovich and saw what Gutiérrez meant. Far overhead, a Japanese soldier swayed on the end of a tether wrapped around his ankle. His arms hung down and blood dripped from his fingertips.

Huss answered. "Leave him for the birds. Let him rot."

Clyde took off his helmet and wiped the sweat from his brow. His hands shook and he felt like vomiting. Gil came sauntering out of the jungle beyond where the sniper swung and bled. The sniper had let him pass to get to the rest of the squad. Gil must've passed directly beneath him.

"You alright?" Clyde asked.

Gil glanced up at the dead sniper. He put his hand out and caught a bloody drip in his palm. "Starting to rain," he said with a grin. No one laughed and he said, "Yeah, I'm alright. Spent most of my time trying not to get shot by you guys."

Clyde asked Huss. "What now, sergeant?"

"We keep pushing past the ridge."

Clyde went to his side and said, "But they know we're coming. They couldn't have left that sniper there by chance."

Huss pursed his lips, then said, "Now you've got an opinion? We'll approach the valley from due west instead of going straight up the hill."

"Shouldn't we get orders from Milkins? He'll wanna know what's going on, and what about Plontovich's body? We can't just leave him out here."

"We'll bury him so the animals don't get him. We'll mark it and pick him up on the way back out. As far as reporting in, we're too far out for the radio."

Clyde wanted to argue. He wanted to get Plontovich back to base and get the hell outta the jungle, but he knew Huss was right. Their mission came first.

"That alright with you, corporal?" Huss asked with iron in his voice.

"Yeah. I've just never lost a man like that."

"Well, get used to it. This war's just getting started."

. . .

After the brief firefight, they veered away from their initial route and headed south, parallel to the ridgeline. The jungle thinned. They kept their eyes up, looking for more snipers in the treetops.

Sergeant Huss stopped them after a quarter mile and pulled Clyde aside. "I think we're far enough around now. We'll move up toward the valley and sweep to the east. See what we can see. We'll take a ten-minute break. Swap out Hicks for Rogerson on point."

"Will do."

Soon the squad members not watching the perimeter sat and slugged water from canteens and gnawed on D-rat bars of chocolate.

Gil sat beside Clyde. He plunked his helmet onto the spongy ground and wiped the sweat from his forehead. "I'm glad that's over."

"You did good work."

He shook his head. "I walked us right into that sniper. I never even saw him."

"You felt him, though. If you'd ignored your instincts we woulda been in a neat line for that son of a bitch. We woulda lost more men."

"Maybe. But it didn't help Hellam none."

Clyde couldn't argue with that. He kept quiet. Gil had probably been in the sniper's sights at one point.

"He let me pass right beneath him. He coulda just as easily of shot me between the eyes."

"Yeah, but he didn't."

Gil looked off into the distance. His happy-go-lucky attitude had vanished. He finally muttered, "Guess it's only a matter of time out here."

"Matter of time?"

"Before the sniper chooses me or you."

"That's morbid as hell."

"Maybe, but it's true. Chance is the only reason I'm alive right now. If he'd chosen me, I'd be dead."

"You knew something was off. Maybe next time Huss'll listen and divert instead of pushing straight through."

"Just sobering to think I walked right beneath him. He coulda spit on me as easily as shot me."

"Don't let it get into your head. Like Huss said, it's gonna be a long fucking war."

A few minutes later, they rose and walked up the slope in a combat wedge formation. Rogerson led them. When they reached the top of the ridge, he stopped and the rest of the squad moved up and hunkered. The valley below was broad here. A small stream meandered through and sparkled in the sunlight. It would be idyllic if not for the war.

Nothing moved down there, at least nothing on two legs. An obvious trail paralleled the creek. It could be an animal trail, but the enemy might use it, too.

They watched the valley for half an hour before Huss finally motioned them closer. "I haven't seen anything, but we still gotta go down there and check it out. Remember, we're just out here to scout. Avoid contact if possible." Nods all around and he signaled them to move forward.

They moved slowly, staying well spread out from one another. Clyde watched their interval as much as he watched his surroundings. The paratroopers moved well, and Clyde quickly stopped worrying about them. They'd practiced patrolling for countless hours. So much so that now it just came naturally.

Rogerson led them to the valley floor. He stopped and crouched where the trees gave way to blowing grasses. The creek burbled, but they couldn't see it any longer. The trail was out there in the grass somewhere.

They listened and waited, but nothing sounded out of place. The smell of wildflowers wafted on a slight breeze. Impossibly green grass swayed and shimmered in the sun. It seemed to glow. How could there be a war going on?

Huss motioned Clyde and Team Two to stay put while he took Team One forward. Clyde passed the signal to the rest of his team and they settled in and watched for the enemy.

Huss disappeared into the swaying grasses as though it swallowed him. The idyllic nature of the place turned in Clyde's mind to a place where men could die horribly and suddenly. He scooted himself until he hunkered beside Rogerson. "I don't like not being able to see them. Go back up the hill a ways until you can see them and me. You'll be my link to them."

Rogerson nodded his understanding and moved back the way he'd come. Clyde watched him the entire way. A few minutes later, Rogerson stopped and turned. He looked out over the valley, then turned his gaze back toward the team. Clyde waved until Rogerson signaled he could see him.

Clyde kept his eyes on him. If anything went wrong, he'd be the first one to notice. Rogerson wasn't a normal member of the squad, but Clyde trusted his skills even though he didn't know him all that well. Knowing he was a scout in the paratroopers was good enough for him. The scouts were the best of the best.

Minutes passed slowly. Rogerson stood, keeping himself behind a small tree. Clyde watched intently. Rogerson ducked down slowly, then signaled frantically.

Clyde passed the information onto the others. "Someone's coming down the trail."

"Japs?" Gutiérrez asked.

"We've gotta assume so." He moved toward Rogerson's position. "Come on. We need to get into a better firing position. We can't cover the team from here."

He stopped suddenly when he noticed Rogerson signaling him to stop. Clyde held up a hand and cursed. "Shit. Hold up. They must be close."

He kept his eyes on Rogerson, who watched the trail. He expected to hear rifle fire at any moment. Private Raley had the powerful BAR up there with Huss somewhere. If they couldn't avoid contact, it was the first thing he expected to hear.

Rogerson pulled his carbine into his shoulder and settled into his sights. *Not a good sign.*

Agonizing minutes ticked by. Rogerson didn't take his eyes from the sights. Clyde didn't know what was going on, but it couldn't be good. *I'm helpless down here, dammit.* He cursed himself for not taking the whole team up with Rogerson from the start. He couldn't shoot what he couldn't see. Team One had no support from him.

A loud yell, followed with more yells and more voices, made Clyde grip his carbine even harder. Any moment, the fireworks would start. He decided he'd dart up to Rogerson's position and help suppress the enemy once it did. But instead of gunfire, more voices. Rogerson relaxed, taking his eyes off the sights. Clyde wanted to yell at him for a report, but didn't want to give his position away until he knew more.

Finally Rogerson turned, and the smile on his face told Clyde everything he needed to know. Whoever was out there, it wasn't the enemy.

Rogerson cupped his hand and called down to him. "Natives. They're *not* Japs!"

Clyde felt the tension melt from his body. He murmured, "Thank God," to himself. The other paratroopers seemed to deflate as the prospect of imminent combat faded.

Clyde's mouth felt tinny and he spit, then ordered his team, "Join up with Rogerson. Watch for any enemy sneaking around. I'm gonna see what the hell's going on over there."

Clyde pushed through the tall grass, heading toward the sounds of animated conversation. He found the trail and stepped out cautiously. Most of Team One stood with their weapons at port arms, facing away from him. Private Terry Raley aimed his BAR squarely at Clyde's chest, then quickly tilted the muzzle skyward when he recognized him.

"It's me, Raley. Don't shoot."

Clyde stepped past him, and Raley gave him a sly grin. "I nearly did, Coop."

Clyde stepped up to the gaggle of soldiers. Beyond them, he saw a mixture of male and female natives. The men held spears or bows, and the women held baskets filled with colorful items he couldn't identify. They used dramatic hand motions combined with fast talk.

Sergeant Huss looked bemused. He held up his hands, "Whoa there, hoss. I don't speak your language. Slow down."

A distinct Australian accent joined the interaction. "What are the bloody Americans doing way out here? Ay?"

A deeply tanned Caucasian man stepped out from the group. He wore the same skimpy garments as the natives, but he carried an old Lee Enfield on an improvised sling, which looked woven out of twine.

The natives stepped aside as the Australian stepped forward. Huss hefted his Thompson to his hip. He looked the Aussie up and down. "Who the hell are you?" he challenged.

"Braddock. Doctor Lester Braddock." He extended a hand but Huss ignored it.

"Doctor? Way out here?"

"That's right." He pulled his hand back. "I've been living out here since before the war started. These people need me more than ever, so I stayed."

"Are you a real doctor, or some kind of voodoo doctor?"

"Voodoo? I'm not sure what you mean. I graduated from the University of Sydney in '33 with a medical degree." Huss still looked skeptical, so the doctor continued. "I grew up in Port Moresby. I returned when I graduated and bounced around between villages before the war started. The Japs put a crimp in my travels, so I stayed at my final posting with the Naroobi Tribe ever since."

"You carry a rifle? Thought all you doctor types didn't believe in harming your fellow man and all that. Took an oath or something, right?"

"I use it for hunting mostly, but you're mistaken about that. I've seen the Jap's butchery firsthand."

"Speaking of Japs . . . have you seen any around here?"

The doctor smiled. "As a matter of fact, yes. There's a large group of them just a few miles from this very spot. Would you like me to take you to them?"

7

Clyde barely breathed as he lay beneath the thick cover overlooking the enemy camp. At least a full company of Japanese soldiers milled about in the tight valley. He wanted to get the hell outta there, but Sergeant Huss insisted on getting an accurate count, so there he lay, counting.

Beside him, Rogerson and Hicks lay as still as stones, trying to become one with the earth. He knew the rest of his team—sans Private Plontovich, who they'd buried in a shallow grave a few miles back—were behind him, making sure no one snuck up on them.

On the other side of the small creek sixty yards back, Sergeant Huss, with Team One and the Australian, Dr. Braddock, waited for their return.

Clyde had already been gone too long, but he had to get close before he could get an accurate count, which meant he had to creep.

Satisfied, he tapped Gil and motioned him to move back. He did the same for Rogerson on the other side. He watched the camp until they were both well back from his position. They barely made any noise, and none of the Japanese soldiers took notice. If they had, he figured his best chance for survival would've been to run for his life.

He pushed back a foot, keeping his eyes on the nearest soldier, only thirty yards away. The soldier turned toward the jungle. Clyde stopped and let his body sink into the rotting jungle floor. Had he heard him?

The soldier seemed to look right at him, but he didn't raise his rifle or make any other aggressive moves. He stepped forward, closing the distance to fifteen yards. He stopped, unbuttoned his pants, and took a leak. Clyde barely breathed. The piss seemed to last forever. He could smell it, and he distantly thought the man must be dehydrated.

His back suddenly itched, then burned like fire. Ants crawled up his back. He remained still, even though the fire ant stings made him want to scream and thrash. He must've brushed up against one of their hated colonies. The stings on his back were like licking flames climbing up a piece of dry paper.

Finally, the soldier snapped his britches and turned back toward his camp. Clyde stayed motionless for another few seconds as the burning grew. A chill of cold sweat swept over him. He couldn't take it another second. He spun so his head faced the direction he needed to go, then rolled onto his back and scooted himself uphill while shimmying side to side. The burning continued, but at least he was killing some of the little bastards. He finally made it to where the rest of his squad lay waiting for him.

Gil hissed, "You okay?"

"Fucking ant hill. They're eating me alive. Need to get back to the creek." He thrashed and tried to reach his back.

Gil spun him around and lifted his shirt. He roughly brushed the ants off, having to pull some that clung tenaciously, their jaws clamped tight.

"Got most of 'em, but there'll be more."

"Move out," Clyde said through gritted teeth.

They moved fast, and when they reached the others, Clyde didn't waste any time stripping and dunking himself in the creek.

Huss looked confused. Gil said, "He's got ants in his pants."

Huss crouched and grinned down at him. "Your back looks like you've been lying on a bed of nails, Coop."

"Fucking fire ants."

"You get a count?"

He glared at his squad leader as he picked more of the little devils off his legs. "Yeah, I got a count. It's an undersized company."

"You sure? Not more of 'em tucked in behind?"

"Course I'm sure. I got close enough to almost get pissed on," he said, having trouble keeping his voice level and in check.

"Okay, okay, calm down. When you're done with your little bath, we'll move out and give the coordinates to the brass. They'll wanna pulverize this place." He stood and signaled the men to get ready to move. "Japs are too close to hang around. Let's go, corporal."

Clyde stepped out and gave his body one more look. He squished a few more ants between his fingers. He didn't relish putting his pants back on, so he draped them over his pack—his shirt, too. He wrung out his underwear and put them back on gingerly, then put his pack on.

Huss shook his head when he saw his half-naked assistant squad leader. "Feel sorry for the man behind you," he said, then laughed. "You're a real piece of work, Cooper."

Clyde winced as the pack rubbed against the fresh fire ant bites. He wasn't in the mood for jokes. "Let's get moving."

Once they'd put a fair distance between themselves and the enemy, they moved quicker. Doctor Braddock and a native who'd stayed with him led them along jungle trails they never would have found on their own.

After an hour, they passed where they'd buried Plontovich. Clyde's back still burned. The bites, combined with his own sweat and the rub from his pack, made him want to tear his own skin off. But he didn't complain. Plontovich would've given anything to feel his pain.

Sergeant Huss waved the patrol past the gravesite. "We don't have time to bring him. The Japs could move and we'll miss our chance. We'll mark it on the map and send out graves registration."

Clyde wanted to protest, but he knew it was the right call. He wondered if they would ever find the body. Huss had collected his dog tags and reports would be written, so at least his next of kin would know what happened, but would his body ever return to the states, or would it rot and fester out here in the jungle forever? Perhaps he'd be the home base for a new fire ant colony. "This goddamned war," he muttered to himself.

Despite feeling generally miserable, Clyde still had duties to perform once they'd made it back to the rest of Able Company. He got the men squared away, making sure they ate, drank, and resupplied. With his duties done, he sat on a log as Doctor Braddock spread some kind of salve on his back.

"What is that stuff, Doc? It tingles."

"In a good way?" he asked.

"Well, yeah, I guess it feels better. Kinda weird, though."

"It's from combining two plant leaves and making a paste by boiling and mashing them together. The natives have many home remedies for such ailments. The jungle is teeming with natural medicines. It's fascinating, really. I've only just scraped the surface. It would be a fascinating field of study, though. The jungle might hold cures for all our ailments."

"And the natives know where to find it, I guess." His back felt better with each layer of ointment. His skin seemed to prickle, as though Braddock poured champagne or carbonated water over the bites. "You think they might know where to find the fountain of youth?"

Braddock answered seriously. "Perhaps they do. I'll have to ask them about it."

"I was kidding."

"I've seen things out here that don't seem possible. I wouldn't doubt it." He finished applying the ointment. "That'll do it. Don't bathe for a while. Let it work first."

"Feels great, Doc. I'll leave it on as long as possible. Thanks."

"Well, not too long. It'll start eating away at your skin, eventually."

Clyde spun around, alarmed. "What? You serious? How long then?"

"A couple of hours." Braddock stood, wiped his hands vigorously, and strode away.

"Leave it on a couple hours or it'll start eating me alive after a couple hours?"

Braddock just waved and kept on walking.

Gil, Oliver, and Gutiérrez lounged nearby. Oliver said, "I wouldn't trust any of that witch doctor bullshit, Coop."

Clyde rolled his shoulders up and down, still feeling the buzz from the ointment. "It works. The bites don't hurt at all—pain's gone. Besides, he's not a witch doctor, he's a medical doctor."

Gutiérrez picked dirt from his fingernails. "Same thing."

"You don't believe in doctors, Guti?"

"Belief? I didn't know they were a religion."

"You know what I mean. You don't trust 'em?"

"Hell no, and you shouldn't either."

Gil chimed in. "We'll see how you feel when you take a Jap bullet in the guts."

Gutiérrez pointed the stick at him. "Don't put that kind of curse on me, Hicks. You know better."

The screech of outgoing shells interrupted them. The distant booms followed long seconds later. "That sounds heavier than howitzers," Oliver stated.

"Naval guns. Guess our little Nip friends are getting what for."

"Probably blow the hell outta your anthill, too," Oliver added.

"I sure the hell hope you're right. Now they've got a taste for human flesh, they might be more dangerous than the damned Japs."

Wave after wave of naval fire arced overhead and slammed into the distant jungle.

"Next, I guess they'll send in some bombers and really work the place over."

"Then us just to make sure," Gil said heavily.

The thought hadn't occurred to Clyde, and he shook his head emphatically, but then realized his old friend was right. After expending so much ordnance, they'd want to know if they'd hit anything.

"At least they'll probably send the whole company this time. Maybe they'll let Second Platoon sit this one out." All three paratroopers looked at him as though he'd lost his mind. "You're right. Better get some sleep while we still can."

One day later, the bulk of Able Company, minus Fourth Platoon, moved north, then turned west, following a large river valley. The brass thought they might trap whatever remained of the Japanese company they'd bombed the day before. They sent Fourth Platoon the old route in case the Japanese pulled a 180 degree turn south to flank them.

Clyde doubted the Japanese would still be there at all. If they hadn't been pulverized by the naval guns or the multiple bombing runs that followed, he doubted they'd waste much time getting the hell outta there.

Thankfully, Second Platoon didn't lead the way this time. Despite Lieutenant Milkins's protestations, Captain Stallsworthy wanted fresh blood leading the way. Second Platoon took its place in the middle, between First and Third Platoon.

The wide river valley had a decent-sized road running through the center. They had used it for commerce between Finschhafen on the coast and the mountain tribes inland. A few trucks and jeeps trundled along the track, carrying extra supplies. Compared to the initial patrol, this was heaven. The occasional airplane swept overhead, making them flinch before seeing the friendly markings.

"I wonder what we look like from up there?" Private Wallace, a nineteen-year-old rifleman from Utah, asked. No one answered him, so he added, "Probably just specks."

Sergeant Huss looked at Wallace, then glared at Clyde. Since Wallace was on Team Two, it was Clyde's responsibility to shut him up. His heart wasn't in it, though. Wallace was just bored and impossibly young.

"Shaddup, Wallace," he finally said.

He'd gotten a good night's sleep that night, but awakened much sooner than he'd wanted. As the assistant squad leader, he needed to be up early helping Huss organize the move. So far, he didn't understand why anyone would want to be in a leadership role. He had seen no upside. Sure, his paycheck was bigger, but he didn't see that, and what good would it do him if he were worm food? At least as a private he'd be well-rested worm food.

Plontovich's face with the bullet hole in the center flashed in his mind. He'd been his responsibility. Would he still be alive today if that son of a bitch Quincy hadn't gotten dysentery and was still the assistant squad leader?

He'd gone over the sniper encounter in his head countless times. Plontovich just happened to be the sniper's target. Pure chance. If Clyde had been walking in the same spot, he'd be dead instead of Plontovich. *This shit'll drive you crazy if you think about it too much. Best not to think about it.*

He turned his thoughts to Abby. He tried to picture her flying an airplane like the ones buzzing overhead. Had she gotten into the program?

He knew very little about it, just that it was competitive. If anyone could do it, it would be his Abby. He hoped she was safe. He supposed the army would send a telegram if she wasn't okay. Would they expect him to keep fighting if his wife died in a fiery plane crash back in the states? Undoubtedly, yes.

He tried to erase that train of thought but couldn't stop thinking about her burning alive. For a moment, he wished he hadn't given her his permission. He could've said no, and she would've respected his wishes—but no. He was being a damned fool. She had a passion for flying—she'd be fine. He smiled, thinking about all the times she'd burnt their dinner. *Well, she's not passionate about cooking.* He couldn't wait to get home and hug and kiss her. He yearned just to hold her and take in her smell.

A muffled bang broke his train of thought. He hesitated a moment, then dropped when he heard another, and another.

"Take cover! Mortars!" Sergeant Huss yelled.

Clyde hugged the ground, then shimmied off the road and into a natural defilade. More popping explosions filled the valley. The trainers at Fort Benning told them that mortar shells were soundless as they arced overhead. "The first thing you hear's the damned explosion," he remembered one of them barking gruffly.

One truck had two near misses, causing the driver to steer off the road and into the soft ground of the jungle. It buried up to the axle and lurched to a halt. The next mortar round landed on the cab, sending the hood flying end over end.

Clyde ducked lower, wondering if the occupants got out in time. Doubtful. The mortar shells continued landing on the road, but mostly near Third Platoon's position.

NCOs barked orders, arraying the paratroopers to repel a possible assault. The heavy weapons crews set up their machine guns behind rocks and fallen logs. He figured the trailing mortar teams would also set up, but he couldn't see them.

He searched the jungle-strewn hillsides rising from the valley in the distance. A spotter must be out there somewhere. The mortars were far too accurate. The valley floor flooded every year, keeping the foliage and trees relatively sparse, but thick lengths of waist-high grass could hide an entire regiment of enemy soldiers. Clyde wondered if the enemy had drawn them into an extensive ambush.

Huss yelled from thirty yards in front. "Dig in! Find cover and dig in!"

Clyde repeated the order. "You heard him. Dig! Dig!"

He pulled out his entrenching tool and started digging into the soft ground. It was a mixture of sand and loamy soil. He threw great clumps as more mortar rounds rained down. Sweat poured off him, but he didn't stop until his hole could fit his body lengthwise.

He glanced back at Team Two. Most continued digging, but a few were already down and watching their surroundings with wide eyes. The enemy mortars kept concentrating on Third Platoon. Clyde figured if the enemy was going to attack, it would come immediately after the barrage.

He cupped his mouth and yelled. "Dig 'em deeper while we've got the chance!" He took his own advice and flung more soil.

He heard the cracks of rifles and stopped digging and took cover. The mortars had stopped. He could still see smoke drifting to the north on a slight breeze. He hopped into his hole. It felt wholly inadequate. He could hardly bend his knees inside, but at least it would protect him from mortar shell fragments. He glanced up at the sky, wondering if he would see a direct hit coming.

He yelled, "Make sure your weapon's clear and your ammo's close." He poked his head up, saw Wallace, and gave him a withering look. The kid could be forgetful. Wallace gave him a thumbs-up sign, although his eyes were wide as empty pie plates.

Huss hustled toward Clyde, running in a crouch. He slid in next to his hole. "Milkins got orders to be ready to move in case they attack."

"Move? Where?"

Huss smacked the back of his helmet. "If you let me finish, I'll tell ya. We'll move to the left flank and Third will move to the right flank. Stallsworthy doesn't like the way we're stacked."

More gunshots from up front made them both look that way.

"You think they're coming?" Clyde asked.

"Yeah, I do. I think that undersized company we found was just the tip of the iceberg."

"They've gotta have spotters up there. Those mortars are far too accurate."

Huss nodded and scanned the hillsides. "I agree, but don't worry about it, just be ready to move your team on my say-so."

He heard the dull thump of mortar tubes behind him. He instinctively ducked. "Our mortar boys are getting in on the action," Huss noted.

The fire from the front increased suddenly, and the distinctive sound of a Nambu machine gun joined the fray. There was no doubt now. They were coming.

"Shit, they've got one of them damned woodpeckers," Huss seethed. He slapped Clyde's shoulder and hustled back to his own hole.

Clyde yelled to the nearest squad members. "Be ready to move left when Huss gives us the word." They passed the word back from man to man.

Long minutes passed. The heavy weapons squad continued pouring mortar shells forward and the cacophony of gunfire never abated from First Platoon, but so far nothing came at Second Platoon.

Another Nambu joined and fresh explosions rocked First Platoon's position. More mortars exploded in their ranks. Clyde decided the increase came from the smaller, but just as lethal, knee mortars.

He heard orders coming down the line. Huss jumped out of his hole and yelled, "Now! Shift left. Stay with me."

Clyde yelled to the men behind him, but they were already moving. "Move! Move!" He leaped out of the hole after making sure he had everything he needed. He saw Huss sprinting, leading Team One into the grass. Clyde waved his arm and ran to catch up, carrying his carbine at port arms.

He crashed into the grasses and high-kneed his way through. It was much less resilient than what they'd had to hack their way through on the Nadzab airfield. It parted like wheat, but still cut exposed skin.

Second Platoon ran all the way to the edge of the valley, then moved up so they'd be on First Platoon's left flank. But before they arrived, a brief and violent firefight broke out. Carbines, Thompsons, and BARs answered the rifle shots from the Japanese bolt action Arisakas.

Clyde and the rest of Third Squad found cover and watched and waited. He couldn't see much, but the shots had been close and directly in front of

First Squad's position. He wondered if anyone had been hit. The fusillade cut off suddenly and his ears rang. The main event still raged in front of First Platoon, but the intensity had died down.

Men yelled, but he couldn't understand what they said. He didn't hear anyone moaning or screaming. He didn't need to remind his men to be ready. Everyone gripped their weapons and watched in every direction with wide eyes.

Huss looked back and told him to hold his position with an outstretched hand. Then he hustled forward and disappeared into the brush.

Clyde watched the jungle slope above him. He didn't like that the Japanese could use it to gain a height advantage on them, even get behind them. One squad could wreak havoc on them. It was thick jungle, steep, and probably slick as snot, but he still didn't like it.

Huss reappeared and signaled him to move up. Clyde stopped beside Huss as his men spread out around them.

Huss said, "Alright, look. That was a Jap patrol probing First Platoon's flank. The Nips are all dead or scattered. We're gonna move up and link up with First. Once we do, anything in front is fair game. Anything up the slope, too," he added. Clyde nodded his understanding and Huss moved forward.

The firefight to First Platoon's front had dropped off to a few desultory shots from both sides. He hadn't heard the Nambus for a long time and wondered if they were moving. Hopefully, they'd knocked them out of the fight.

He waited for the proper separation, then advanced slowly. He couldn't see beyond the front few paratroopers, so he concentrated on the hillside to his left.

When they finally linked up with First Platoon, they spread out and found cover. Clyde thought they'd be digging in again soon. The sun dipped low on the horizon and he didn't relish spending the night out here, but apparently they were going to do just that.

Huss waved him forward. "Come here, look at this."

Clyde walked the ten yards and stopped. Just beyond the cover, the jungle was torn up with mortars and gunfire. Shredded trees dripped pulp like wounded animals. The floor was littered with dead Japanese soldiers. Steam and smoke rose off them, like some comic book cemetery scene.

"Jesus. There's so many."

"Yeah. Plumly told me they ran straight into the machine guns. Didn't hesitate—just charged."

"Thought this was just supposed to be a blocking force. Something to slow us down so the main force could escape."

"Plumly thinks they'll come again tonight. Night time's their specialty."

"We sticking around?"

He gave Clyde a side-glance. "Hell yes. They've never faced airborne troopers, just those Aussie pussies."

"I'll let the men know."

Huss kept staring over the sea of dead. "You done good these past few days, Cooper."

Clyde didn't much like Huss, but he respected him as a soldier. He lifted his chin and pushed out his chest. "Geronimo."

"Geronimo," Huss answered.

Clyde hated watching the sun set behind the ridgeline. They'd spent the remaining hours of daylight digging in and even fortifying their positions as much as possible to guard against the inevitable mortars that would precede another attack. He hoped that day's engagement had convinced the Japanese to bug out. They'd lost a lot of men—twenty they could see sprawled in front of the line—but how many more had they hauled off or died by mortar fire further back?

The darkness settled over them like a heavy black cloak. He tried to eat something, but had to force it down. The C-rations were less than appetizing, but he ate what he could stomach. He doubted he'd sleep, so he may as well not be hungry.

They'd dug their foxholes in a zigzagging line, which connected to the other squads in Second Platoon. Each man knew his field of fire assignments. To fire outside it would mean endangering the paratrooper slightly forward. They could've dug in side by side, but the space didn't allow it.

They'd be too close together, allowing one mortar round to knock out two fighting positions.

Clyde wished they'd had more time and could've built linked trenches. But despite that, he felt good about their defensive positions. They interspersed the machine gun crews along the lines. The mortar crews were forty yards back, ready to launch flares and high explosives.

Despite Huss's cavalier attitude, Clyde didn't want the Japanese to come. He'd much rather pass a sleepless night of high anticipation than have to face waves of screaming enemy soldiers. The thought terrified him and kept him vigilant.

Captain Stallsworthy had ordered outposts to the hillsides on either side of the valley. It eased Clyde's mind somewhat. At least if the Japanese tried anything from that direction, they'd have ample warning. Now all they had to do was wait.

Three long hours passed. Since dropping into New Guinea, he'd spent a few nights in the jungle, but that didn't make it any easier. Would he ever get used to all the strange sounds?

Shadows seemed to move. More than once, he nearly fired—convinced he saw an enemy soldier. But he held his fire, remembering that first chaotic night near Nadzab. Everyone had been jumpy, expecting an attack at any moment—an attack that never materialized. The only thing that had attacked had been a few coconuts falling into foxholes and scaring the hell out of the occupants. But this felt different. He *knew* the enemy lurked nearby, but he'd be damned if he'd be the first man to fire.

A voice called out from the jungle, making him clutch his carbine tightly. The voice sounded close, maybe thirty yards out. "Help me. I'm wounded!"

No one responded. He felt reasonably sure it wasn't an American soldier, although he didn't notice an obvious Japanese accent. No one had gone missing, and he'd heard stories of Japanese impersonating wounded soldiers, trying to draw them out so they could slit their throats. Many Japanese spoke fluent English, having traveled abroad before hostilities broke out.

"I'm hit. Medic, help me. Medic."

He sounded convincing. Clyde recognized Sergeant Huss's voice yelling back. "Here's something for the pain." Clyde noticed a quick motion from Huss's foxhole. A few seconds later, a bright flash and a muffled explosion from a grenade erupted in the jungle. Clyde doubted it had gone far enough to affect the impersonator, but the explosion seemed to open a door of yelling from the front lines.

Clyde heard thrashing as if a large group was running straight at him. He strained to see shapes, but couldn't see more than a few yards in the gloom. The hated chattering of a Nambu machine gun opening fire made him duck, but he kept his eyes above the lip of his hole. Lances of red and yellow tracer rounds sliced through the jungle far to the right. He pulled his carbine tight to his shoulder.

Huss yelled, "Steady! Here they come!"

Two flares ignited overhead. The jungle was suddenly bathed in an eerie glow as the flares slowly descended beneath their small parachutes. A moment later, all hell broke loose.

The .30-caliber machine guns opened fire at the same instant. Clyde saw the enemy now. The muzzle flashes, tracers, and flares ruined his night vision, but he didn't need it to see enemy soldiers darting through the trees straight at his position.

"Pour it on!" Huss yelled, but Clyde hardly heard him. He found a target and pulled the trigger. After waiting in silence for so long, the sudden onslaught of sound and violence threatened to overwhelm his senses. He felt fear building, but his training took over. He calmly found targets and fired into them until they dropped or he lost sight of them, then he found another and repeated the process until his thirty-round magazine emptied.

He dropped into the hole and fumbled with his ammo pouch. His fresh magazine slipped from his hand and landed somewhere at his feet. He cursed himself but didn't waste time digging for it. He found another one and slipped it into place. He chambered a round and stood again.

The flares were nearly on the ground. The low-angled light cast long, swaying shadows, but he could still clearly see enemy soldiers running erratically. Bullets snapped close by his ears before he could fire, and he ducked into cover. Bullets impacted the log he'd pulled in front of his hole. He stayed down for a few seconds, but knew he had to get back in the fight or risk being overrun.

He rose and glimpsed movement to his left, out of his zone of responsibility. He swung his carbine in that direction anyway, just in time to see an enemy soldier leap into a foxhole, screaming like a madman. It was Oliver's hole. He aimed, but couldn't get an angle. He might hit Oliver.

Before his conscious mind could tell him not to, he leaped from his hole and ran toward the struggling men. A new set of flares sparked overhead and he clearly saw the Japanese soldier grappling with Oliver inside the foxhole. Neither man could get an advantage in the tight confines. They grunted and cursed at one another.

Darting shapes ran and weaved toward him from the jungle. He turned, but machine gun fire cut down three enemy soldiers twenty yards from him.

Clyde stepped forward until he stood over the hole with his carbine aimed, but unable to fire. The deadly struggle played out as though he were watching it at a movie theater back home. He kept his finger on the trigger, but he couldn't risk a shot. Oliver finally got some space and pounded his fist into the enemy soldier's face. His head snapped back and his eyes crossed—stunned.

Clyde saw his chance. He leaned forward, placed his red-hot barrel against the Japanese soldier's ear, and pulled the trigger twice. Blood sprayed Clyde's face and the soldier slumped like a rag doll.

Oliver gasped as blood splashed him. He struggled to free himself from the hole, as though the corpse might infect him somehow.

Clyde dropped to a knee and aimed back into the jungle. Fewer targets remained, but he fired at darting shadows until he'd spent the remainder of his magazine. He quickly found a new magazine and slammed it home.

When he saw no more targets, he took his eyes from the sights but kept the carbine at his shoulder. He looked at Oliver, who stared at the dead soldier curled in the bottom of his hole.

"You okay, Ollie? Did he cut you?" When he didn't answer right away, he raised his voice. "Ollie?"

Oliver snapped out of it and tore his eyes away from the dead man's face. "I—I'm okay." He felt his body as though checking for leaks. "I'm not hit."

"Find cover. They might try again."

Oliver stared at him in shock and horror. "You—You're hit. You're bleeding."

Clyde felt his face and his hand came away bloody. He felt revulsion. He quickly wiped it on his pants. "It's not mine. It's his. You good?"

"Yeah, I'm good, Coop. Thanks."

Clyde felt awkward, crouched there like an idiot. He glanced at the other men hunched in their foxholes. In the light from the flares, he saw every one of them staring at him. He hustled back to his hole and dropped inside. The firing dropped off to a few scattered shots. A new batch of flares lit up the area, followed immediately by outgoing, high explosive rounds that thumped into the jungle.

Huss bellowed, "Check ammo. I need a headcount."

Clyde scanned for more targets, but didn't find any. He still felt eyes on him. He turned. The men continued to stare at him as though he'd sprouted wings out of his back.

He pulled out a handkerchief and wiped the blood off his face. He had to wipe many times before he felt clean. His hands shook and he couldn't keep from shivering. He hoped the others didn't notice. He suddenly wanted to curl into a ball and cry like a baby. He was grateful when the flares finally sputtered out and he couldn't see the stares anymore.

8

OCTOBER 1943

Camp Knothead, Burma

Shawn Cooper slithered out of his hammock and plopped onto the hard-packed ground of Camp Knothead. Operational Group Bellevue had returned from their train ambush mission a few days before. Shawn slept for ten straight hours, more consecutive hours of sleep than he'd had in months. But instead of feeling refreshed, he felt as though a truck had hit him. Every muscle screamed and ached.

He planted his feet, twisted, and rocked side to side, trying to loosen himself. His muscles slowly lengthened as he stretched and the tightness dissipated somewhat. How much more jungle living could he take?

The operational groups prided themselves on physical fitness and they'd impressed the other OSS men with their ability to cover large swaths of difficult terrain relatively quickly. No matter the distances they had to travel, they completed them with time to spare.

Shawn secretly wished Bellevue would slow down a little, but the men were too competitive for that to happen. They strove to push harder and farther than the man next to them, which made that man push harder. The overall effect was a constant need to push and strive for more.

Bellevue had been operating out of Knothead for four months now. The constant strain had made his body strong, but he felt tired all the time. He'd lost weight he didn't know he could lose—his body carved down to only the essentials.

Thankfully, the men back at Nasira kept the camp well supplied with plenty of airdrops. They didn't lack for food. They'd even parachuted in a chef for their own personal use. Since then, the fare had improved dramatically. They ate with abandon, giving their bodies the fuel they needed to keep pushing.

They guarded Chef Watson with their lives—always escorting him around camp. Once, Watson had ventured out of the camp's immediate perimeter and a full-scale rescue operation ensued. They found him sitting next to the creek, soaking his feet. They berated him and hustled him back as though he were the president.

Shawn stumbled toward the chow hall hut. The closer he got, the more delicious smells wafted to him, and the more his stomach grumbled. He found half the Bellevue men inside enjoying one of Chef Watson's newest creations. Shawn filled a tray with thin slices of marinated meat, potatoes slathered in butter and spices, steamed vegetables, and thick slices of bread.

He sat down with the group and rubbed his hands together. "Oh man, I'm hungry."

The others barely acknowledged him. They slurped, gulped, and inhaled the succulent food as though it might be their last meal. Shawn ate as slowly as he could force himself to, although his hunger paired with the amazing flavors made it nearly impossible.

He sopped up the last meat juices with the last piece of bread and popped it into his mouth. He leaned back and rubbed his belly with satisfaction. "I don't know how he does it. He's a damned magician."

JoJo agreed. "He's one a million. Wish we could take him on missions."

"Nah, having him here makes coming back that much sweeter. It's like Christmas. If it was every day, you'd get bored with it."

"Christmas is one thing, but I don't think I'd ever get bored with Chef Watson's cooking."

Henry Calligan, the Detachment 101 veteran, plopped down across from Shawn. The table went quiet. The 101 men didn't normally mix with the

Operational Group guys unless they needed something, and it wasn't usually something good.

He placed his napkin in his lap and cut his meat meticulously, as though he dined at a fine restaurant and not in the middle of a steamy jungle in Burma some two hundred miles behind enemy lines. He chewed just as slowly. His facial expression never changed. He may as well have been eating a C-ration rather than tender, succulent meat.

Shawn leaned on his elbows. "So, what's the scoop, Calligan?" He knew he held the rank of lieutenant, but the OSS men threw convention out the window—especially out in the field.

"The scoop? Whatever do you mean?"

The others exchanged worried glances. Shawn persisted. "You don't normally join us in the mess hall unless you need a favor . . . or a mission."

Calligan placed his knife and fork beside his plate and dabbed the sides of his mouth with his napkin. "Yes, well, I suppose you're right. That's not too keen of us, is it?"

"What's on your mind, sir?"

"I want to hit Myitkyina airbase."

The room went silent. Finally Shawn asked, "Major Gunnison approved a mission to Myitkyina? I didn't think we had enough operational units here for that, and the Kachin aren't quite ready. Are they?"

"Technically, that's correct. More and more Kachin are taking up arms against the Japs, and soon they'll be a formidable force—that is as long as we keep dropping supplies and training them to fight. But I want to observe the airfield for myself. See if it's even possible. If we could hit them, destroy their aircraft on the ground, it would give us quite a lift. Take a lot of pressure off the men flying the hump into China, too."

Paul O'Keefe asked, "What you need us for? You fellers are as good at reconnaissance as anyone out here."

"Of course, but we'd want to stay out there for at least two weeks."

The OG men exchanged confused glances. JoJo said, "So what? You afraid of getting lonely or something?"

Calligan gave him a tight, humorless grin. "We'd need a considerable contingent of porters."

The men's confusion turned to anger. O'Keefe leaned forward and said, "We ain't porters, Mr. Calligan."

"Course not. We'd use Burmese and mules for that job."

"Burmese? You can't trust them as far as you can throw 'em, unless you're talking about Kachin."

"Not Kachin, regular Burmese villagers. That's what we'd need you for mainly. To keep the Burmese in line. Of course, you'd come in handy for any encounters we have with the Japanese, too. But we hope to avoid that altogether."

Shawn asked, "Have you run it by Burbank or Umberland yet?"

"Not yet. I wanted to get a feel from you guys first. I mean, you're not babysitters either."

Shawn looked around at the men as they considered the question. It was beneath them, but an operation was still an operation. He didn't see anyone showing they wouldn't be willing to go on the mission if it became official. None of them relished sitting around for long, but they'd only just gotten back and could use a few more days off.

"Any objections?" Calligan asked. When there weren't any, he picked his utensils back up and cut into the meat. He raised the perfectly cooked cutlet and smiled. "Watson certainly knows what he's doing. Reminds me of our cook back home. Millie ran a tight ship. She'd approve, no doubt."

Shawn figured Calligan came from money and he just confirmed it. Shawn's mother cooked all their meals, and he would put her up against any professional cook any day of the week.

"When would we leave?" he asked with some trepidation.

Calligan chewed and swallowed before answering. "I'll present the plan to Major Gunnison back in Nasira. If approved, I'd like to leave as soon as possible. A day or two in Nasira, then fly back here and leave a day after that."

"What's the hurry?" JoJo asked.

Calligan gave him a tepid smile. He finally said, "One step at a time, Mr. Palance. One step at a time."

. . .

A week later, Shawn walked alongside the Burmese porters as they guided their mules through the jungle. The men all came from the same village some fifteen miles north of Camp Knothead. These particular villagers didn't claim fealty to either the Japanese or the Allies. They worked for money and goods, not the war effort. Currently, the highest bidder was the Allies.

To keep the Burmese from finding the location of Camp Knothead, an airdrop of supplies landed on the village soon after the OSS men arrived. When there weren't Japanese Zeros waiting for the transport planes, the Burmese proved they hadn't been in contact with the Japanese . . . at least not recently.

Didi and the three other Kachin guiding and assisting the OSS men despised the very thought of having the Burmese along, but the Kachin were too proud to be simple porters. Calligan explained the need, and the Kachin understood, but it didn't mean they accepted their hated neighbor's presence.

The U.S. Army had supplied the Kachin in the region with army uniforms and U.S. weapons and ammo. Besides being diminutive, they looked like any other U.S. Army soldier. They were obviously proud of their new uniforms. They strutted around the porters like peacocks showing off their plumage. It took a while for Shawn to get used to seeing Didi in a uniform. He wondered if he still wore his grisly war trophies beneath his collar.

Shawn decided that the men of OG Bellevue weren't there to monitor the Burmese as Calligan suggested, but to act as a buffer between them and the Kachin. The Burmese didn't like the Kachin any more than the Kachin liked them. However, the Kachin looked ready to kill them and the Burmese looked ready to run away at the first hint of violence. Calligan had explained that their differences went back much farther than the current war. They were ancient enemies.

The supply burden on the Burmese men's shoulders and the mules made the going slow. To Shawn, the slow pace was a relief from their normal rush, but he worried about ambush. Bumping into an enemy patrol in the jungle's vastness would be exceedingly unlucky and unlikely, but the Burmese porters added an unknown element.

They hadn't told the Japanese about the airdrop, but perhaps they'd sent runners ahead to warn about the patrol. If so, the enemy might wait around any corner. To make sure there wasn't, half of Bellevue stayed back while the rest patrolled ahead, sweeping the jungle.

The procession stopped. The porters immediately unburdened themselves and sat down to rest while the mules found clumps of grass and ate contentedly. With every break, the porters wanted to smoke but were warned against it, as the smell of a cigarette traveled great distances and might attract or alert nearby enemy soldiers. They grumbled about the inconvenience, but complied.

"They seem like men on the way to work who can't smoke at the bus stop," Shawn mentioned to O'Keefe.

"Yeah. Gotta figure none of 'em even knew what a smoke was before the war landed on their doorstep. Now they can't do without 'em."

A ragged line of Bellevue men came out of the jungle. A thin layer of sweat clung to them. The lead man, Sergeant Boyd, reported directly to Calligan, who nodded and slapped him on the back.

Boyd and the others slunk back to the rest of them and took a seat. Boyd blew snot from his nose then said, "We stayed about a mile in front—didn't see any sign of the Nips, though." He focused on Umberland. "Reckon we'll keep moving or find a place for the night?"

"We'll keep moving. Calligan wants to make the outskirts of the airbase by tomorrow evening, which means we either need to step things up a bit or keep moving longer." He glanced around at the line of porters. "If we push these guys too hard, they'll bolt, and if they bolt, they'll report us to the Japs, and it'll be a fight all the way."

"They wouldn't get their payment then," Shawn stated.

"Nah, but the Japs would pay. Maybe even more."

"This smells rotten."

Boyd chimed in. "Don't fret about it too much. I think they're more afraid of the Kachin than us or the Japs. Have you seen the way they look at them? The Kachin, I mean."

JoJo said, "Yeah, like they wanna carve 'em up and eat 'em for a snack."

"Exactly. They'll do whatever we demand as long as we keep the Kachin away from 'em."

Umberland stood and stretched his back. "We need to get moving. Everyone that didn't just get back, follow me forward."

Shawn got to his feet and checked his carbine. He looked forward to getting out in front. He didn't mind the slow pace, but he was ready to get back to work. Walking alongside the porters and mules felt too much like a job.

Shawn moved away from the porters, catching their scathing glances. He couldn't decide if they glared more than normal or if they always looked like that.

Shawn's group moved in single file along a dirt track, which could barely be called a trail. Didi led them at a fast pace. Since the first group had already covered this ground, Shawn didn't mind.

When he figured they'd gone a mile, Didi slowed and the Bellevue men spread out to either side.

Umberland veered toward Shawn. "Get up there with Didi. Take the new man Veatch with you."

Shawn didn't like it, but he understood. Veatch and Plano had dropped into Knothead, along with Chef Watson. They were new and needed real-world experience.

Even though the journey from the U.S. East Coast took months of arduous travel, Shawn and the others teased them they looked as fresh as spring grass.

Shawn figured they'd likely all looked exactly the same when they first arrived. Calligan walked nearby, dressed skimpily, his skin nearly as dark as Didi's. Shawn tried but couldn't imagine Calligan ever looking different from the way he did now—as though he'd been born out there. He wondered, not for the first time, about his life before the war. Perhaps someday he'd feel comfortable enough to ask, but he doubted that.

Shawn tapped Veatch as he passed him. Veatch didn't hesitate to follow. "You're going on point with me. Didi's up here, too."

"No problem."

"You adjusting okay?"

"Sure thing. It's not California, but . . ."

Shawn glanced back at him. "Not as many cute surfer girls."

"You can say that again."

When they caught up to Didi, he looked back and smiled broadly. He'd lost half his teeth, and the ones still there were a yellowish red. He'd sharpened a few, adding to the overall terrifying effect.

Didi increased his speed, weaving through the jungle, barely disturbing the foliage. Shawn pressed forward, trying to match his stride and stealth. He heard Veatch struggling to keep up behind him.

Now that they were beyond where the first group had patrolled, Shawn didn't feel comfortable with Didi's speed, but he understood what he was doing with the new guy. Indeed, he'd done it to all of them.

As the heavy breathing and Veatch's headlong push faded into the distance, Didi suddenly stopped, then darted to the right. Shawn caught his eye and went left. They hunkered and waited.

Shawn listened to the surrounding jungle. Besides Veatch, he heard nothing out of the ordinary. He trusted Didi and knew he wouldn't be performing this rite of passage if the enemy was nearby. But he couldn't simply turn his senses off.

Veatch's struggle to keep up sounded like a freight train approaching. When the new man sounded only yards away, the thrashing through the jungle sounds stopped. The labored breathing continued, however. Veatch was doing what they'd trained him to do in similar circumstances: wait for someone to find you.

Shawn stayed as still as stone. He'd leave the rest for Didi, who had a far better chance of soundlessly approaching Veatch. Despite having a lot to learn, the new guys were still excellent soldiers and many had combat experience before joining the OSS. Shawn didn't relish taking a bullet on a lark, so he stayed put.

He heard Veatch edging forward. His senses would be on overdrive and his finger would be near the trigger, despite orders to maintain silence. When Veatch was only a few yards away, Shawn saw a sudden flash of brown and green, followed immediately by a muffled yelp from Veatch.

After a brief scuffle, Shawn moved quickly back the way he'd come. He pushed aside foliage and saw Didi crouched on Veatch's chest with an evil-looking blade at his throat. Veatch didn't dare move.

Out of the side of his mouth, Veatch stammered, "Could—could you get this madman off me, please?"

Shawn hunkered and grinned. "Not just yet." Soon, the other men filtered in and surrounded them. They all laughed at Veatch's predicament. Shawn stood and said, "Okay, you can get off him now, Didi."

Didi glanced at Calligan, who gave him a slight nod, then Didi sprang off Veatch's chest like an invisible rope had pulled him. He sheathed his knife and couldn't wipe the smile off his face. He chattered excitedly to Calligan, who smiled and nodded.

Veatch gawked at Didi as though he'd lost his mind. Then he stood and brushed himself off. "Is he crazy?"

Shawn answered. "Nope. He greets all the new guys that way."

"I might've shot him."

Calligan guffawed. "Ha! Now that would be a neat trick, since he could've slit your throat before you even knew he was there."

Veatch finally laughed. "Am I in the club now?"

Umberland said, "Club? We're a combat unit, soldier. Now get up there and take point."

Veatch looked at the grinning men of Bellevue. "Plano gonna get the same treatment?"

Umberland smiled and pushed him toward the jungle. "You just worry about not leading us into an ambush."

Shawn shook his head at Umberland's antics, then stepped in behind Veatch.

"Is this as close as we can get?" Calligan asked Umberland.

"No, but it's as close as we can get without being seen outright."

Calligan grunted and put the binoculars back to his eyes. He was careful to keep the glass lenses shrouded beneath a dark-colored cloth. He slowly scanned back and forth across the airfield and the nearby town.

Shawn lay nearby, also gazing out over the expansive airfield. The Japanese, or more likely their Burmese or Chinese "volunteers," had cut the jungle grasses and trees far back from the edges, leaving a two-hundred-yard killing ground in every direction. Parts of the ground smoldered where they continually burned the underbrush back. Beyond it stood the fair-sized town of Myitkyina itself. The airfield pointed directly at the massive Irrawaddy river, like an arrow.

Shawn asked, "Why haven't they bombed this place? It must be pretty damned obvious from miles away."

Calligan answered without pulling his eyes from the glass. "The Aussies tried a low-level attack with a mix of fighters and bombers once. The Nips have ack-ack everywhere and they know when an attack's coming, so they have fighters waiting. They lost a lot of men and planes and barely made a dent. There's also quite a few civilian structures nearby they need to worry about."

Umberland added. "We don't have enough bombers in the area for any high-level stuff, and the ones we do have are being tasked with helping the Chinese and General Stillwell."

"So here we are," Shawn said under his breath.

The officers ignored him. Shawn held the scoped Springfield. Umberland had asked him to put it together in case any wandering enemy patrols happened upon them. Even though they sat on a precipice overlooking the field and had excellent cover, he felt exposed as aircraft lumbered overhead, either coming or going.

He'd never seen a more active airfield. He counted twenty parked Zeros, a few transports, and a handful of bombers. He couldn't see what lurked inside the many camouflaged hangars dotting the circumference, but guessed they also held aircraft. No wonder the Japanese owned the skies around here. The Allies had nothing even close within hundreds of miles. Not yet, anyway.

Umberland said to Calligan. "Doesn't seem like our little raids have had much effect on them."

Calligan harrumphed and kept scanning. He stopped and pointed. "What about that culvert there?"

Umberland raised his own binoculars, and Shawn put the scope to his eye. Umberland focused on the spot. "Well, it doesn't extend very far into the field, but it would get us close to the airfield if we made it across the open ground in front."

"At night, taking our time . . . we'd make it fine," Calligan insisted.

"Yeah, except we saw the glow of this place as we approached last night.

The whole place is lit up like a birthday cake. They have nothing to fear from the skies just yet, especially at night."

"I think we need to try."

Shawn jolted from the scope, and Umberland did the same from his binoculars. They both stared at Calligan, who continued glassing the field.

Umberland said, "What's the point? We're not here to strike the place, but to see if it's possible. Sending men to that culvert might get them killed. And you want to do it just to see if you can?"

Calligan slowly dropped the binoculars from his eyes, then met Umberland's accusatory stare. "That approach needs to be tested."

Umberland's jaw rippled as he ground his teeth. He reigned in his emotions and finally said, "I'm not ready to send my men down there just yet. We'll see how things look at night."

Calligan stared at the airfield for a long minute before he finally answered. "Agreed. We'll settle into our new digs and see how they operate . . . for now."

Shawn noticed Umberland's red face. He looked ready to burst with anger. Without another word, Calligan pushed back from the knoll and disappeared into the jungle.

Shawn's belly did a flip-flop, but he felt compelled to ask. "Don't mind my asking, but is Calligan in charge, sir?"

Umberland's face mellowed and he shook his head. "I'm in charge of Bellevue, but he's in overall charge of the operation."

Shawn pursed his lips, not sure what that answer meant. Could Calligan order Umberland around or not? He thought they were the same rank. "I see," he finally said.

Umberland tapped his shoulder. "Come on. Let's get settled in. We need to get the lay of the land. We might be here awhile. Just seeing how this place operates is an intelligence boon. Nasira will be very interested in all these aircraft."

"As long as Calligan doesn't get us killed first."

"I'll make sure he doesn't," Umberland stated flatly.

. . .

They returned to the precipice that night. Shawn watched the lit-up airfield from his perch through his scope and Umberland and Calligan scanned it through their binoculars.

Umberland gave a low whistle, then said, "They really don't have much light discipline—do they?"

Calligan grunted. "They have nothing to fear from the Tenth Air Force just yet. That's why I'd love to hit them. They're not suspecting a thing." He licked his lips as though about to eat something savory. "They have a few watchtowers and a single patrol walking the perimeter. It would be easy to get in there, set some charges, and burn the place down."

"That's not our mission," Umberland stated flatly.

Calligan's tone turned angry. "What's the matter with you?"

Umberland took his eyes from the binoculars and could see Calligan's seething face lit up by the lights from the airfield. Shawn watched them both from the corner of his eye.

Calligan continued. "You act like some kind of straight-legged line officer. You're an OSS man for chrissakes—chosen for your ability to improvise and change things on the fly. How the hell'd you get put into fieldwork? You should be back in Nasira."

Umberland's jaw rippled and even in the low light, Shawn saw the vein on his forehead popping out. "It's not why we're here," he seethed, obviously trying to maintain control of his voice. "Besides, we didn't bring more plastic explosives than we normally bring. We don't have enough to make a dent."

"I brought plenty."

The silence hung heavily between them. It took almost a full minute before Umberland spoke again. "You always intended to hit it, didn't you? It wasn't just to see if it could be done. You came to do it. That's why we're here, isn't it?"

"I came prepared for anything. It's how they train field officers. I didn't know until right now."

"You lied to us, then?"

"Like I said, I just decided. I see an opportunity to kill Japanese and strike fear into them. Look at that place. It's ripe for the picking—lit up like a damned Christmas tree. They're practically begging to be hit."

Umberland obviously fought against his growing anger. Shawn could see him struggling to maintain his composure.

Shawn refocused his attention on the airbase. He had to admit it looked easier than he'd expected, but it didn't make him any less fearful. Watching the airfield from afar was one thing, but the thought of being down there planting explosives on aircraft or buildings with an entire enemy division stationed only a mile away made his sphincter tighten. But alongside the fear, adrenaline also surged through his veins and he had trouble sitting still.

If they could pull it off, it would be a glorious mission that might do serious harm to the Japanese. They could put a crimp in their air power in the entire region. Could they actually pull it off, though? It would be dangerous as hell, but he thought they could. The idea grew on him.

They spent another thirty minutes watching the airfield. A siren sounded and soon after, a bomber with one smoking engine arrived. It landed and taxied to a parking spot beside the Zeros. A truck pulled nearby and men held hoses, ready to put out an engine fire, but the engine soon stopped smoking.

Once the hustle and bustle died down, the runway lights shut off. Lights from the buildings remained on, however. Beams of light from the two guard towers sliced into the darkness, scanning the open fields surrounding the airfield. Large gaps of darkness remained, and Shawn didn't think it would be too difficult to approach the airfield undetected.

"Well, I guess they're not completely oblivious," Calligan stated.

Umberland added. "Without the runway lights, it actually looks more feasible."

Calligan slapped him on the back. "That's the spirit. I knew you'd come around."

Shawn heard someone coming from behind them. He turned and saw Sergeant Boyd's outline slithering their way.

"That you, Boyd?" he asked, alerting the others to his presence.

"Yeah, it's me." He pointed at the two officers, who stared back at him. "You're needed back at the CP."

Umberland asked, "What is it?"

"We've got visitors."

The officers exchanged a glance, then pushed back and off the precipice, following Boyd. Shawn took one last look at the airfield, then followed.

Boyd spoke low to the officers, but Shawn could hear him easily enough. "Visitors from town. Didi and the other Kachin led them in just a few minutes ago."

They walked the hundred yards to the temporary base camp. No fires lit the area and the darkness felt stifling, but Shawn's eyesight soon adjusted and he could see outlines and shapes easy enough.

He veered away from the officers and Boyd. He wanted to discuss things with the others. They'd be in the dark about the whole thing. He found the other Bellevue men huddled nearby in a tight knot. He sat down with them and they acknowledged him with nods.

Keeping his voice low, Shawn said, "You're not gonna believe this."

Sensing the inside scoop, the others pressed closer to him and listened intently.

"Calligan wants us to hit the airfield."

O'Keefe let out a long breath, as though slowly deflating a balloon. He said, "I knew it. That crazy bastard's gonna get us killed."

"I thought Umberland was going to toss him over the cliff. He was so mad."

"Maybe we should do that ourselves," JoJo suggested without a hint of humor.

Gunther leaned in. "How'd it look, Shawn? I mean, is it even possible?"

Shawn thought about the question for a few seconds, then answered. "Yeah, actually, I think it is. It's guarded, but they're not expecting any trouble. It'd be dangerous, but I think we could pull it off. Lots of targets, too."

"We didn't bring enough . . ."

Shawn interrupted JoJo. "Calligan brought extra C-4."

"That sneaky son of a bitch," JoJo said with a grin.

"Who're the guests?" Shawn wondered.

"Villagers from Myitkyina."

Shawn couldn't hide his surprise. "Really? How'd they find us way out here?"

"They're Kachin. Apparently, they infiltrated the town years ago and have been living there, keeping tabs on the Nips. Didi, or one of his buddies, knows them and they went into town to talk, and they led them back here."

Shawn looked from one to the other. "How? I mean, did Calligan know all along?"

JoJo shrugged. "Dunno, but probably. It would make sense."

"That son of a gun has secrets layered upon secrets," Shawn said. "Maybe they'll have good intelligence on how to best hit the airfield. It would help to have some local knowledge working with us."

"Guess we'll find out in the morning," O'Keefe said, then yawned and put his head down.

Shawn felt anything but tired, but he thought he should at least try to sleep. Tomorrow might be busier than he'd expected.

9

They spent the rest of that night and the next day watching the airfield. They noted an enemy patrol started at midnight, circumnavigated the airfield, and ended an hour later.

During the day, they observed two separate patrols. One in the morning and one in the evening. Both followed the same route they'd seen them take the night before. The six Japanese patrolled with their rifles slung. They trudged along, taking little interest in their surroundings.

With all the information they could put together on such short notice, the OSS men discussed their options and decided they'd make their approach right after the night patrol packed it in for the night the following evening.

They inventoried their explosives and determined they had enough to blow up ten parked aircraft and one or two hangars. It would be enough to cripple the air power in the region for a few days, at least.

The two Kachin infiltrators from Myitkyina were visibly excited at the prospect of an attack. They promised to help in any way possible, but Calligan urged them to keep a low profile and continue their daily routines. He told them they'd need them later when the big push from the north came. They begrudgingly agreed and returned to Myitkyina.

Bellevue would lead the way into the airfield, setting most of the charges. The Kachin were excellent warriors, but they weren't as highly trained with explosives, so they would cover them while they worked.

Umberland broke them into two-man teams. One would set charges while the other watched their backs. They wouldn't use cords or wires to set the plastic explosives off, but acid detonators set for approximately ninety minutes.

The detonators worked well, but they could be finicky, especially in the hot, wet environs where they operated. The detonators rarely failed, but rarely burned as consistently as they should, sometimes varying anywhere from a few minutes to fifteen or twenty. To make sure they weren't in the middle of the job when one went off, they decided on the ninety-minute mark.

With the plan in place, now all they had to do was to prepare and wait. Shawn unscrewed the scope from the Springfield rifle, carefully wrapped it in the oily soft cloth, and stuffed it into his pack. He'd leave the pack and the Springfield behind and cover JoJo with his carbine as he set charges on their assigned aircraft.

The night crept by at a snail's pace. Shawn shut his eyes and tried to relax. He used the breathing technique they'd taught them back in Maryland: in for four seconds and out for four seconds.

Finally, the word passed. The enemy night patrol had done their cursory patrol and arrived back at camp. Shawn's eyes snapped open. He hadn't slept and he didn't feel relaxed.

No one said another word as they quietly wound their way to the edge of the jungle and crouched. Hand signals directed them to the shallow trench, which would lead them toward the airstrip. From the precipice, the trench looked shallow, and from ground level, it looked even less inviting.

They moved two by two. Each two man unit a team. Shawn and JoJo led the way. Sweat dripped off Shawn's face as he struggled to keep his body in the trench. Occasionally, a spotlight's beam swept over the top of him and he'd stop.

When he'd made it halfway across, the ditch spread out and shallowed. He peeked over the lip and saw the beam of light scanning the trench in front of him a few yards. From the tower's elevated angle, the light shone into the bottom of the ditch. From here on out, they'd have to low-crawl.

He lay on his stomach and crawled as close to the left lip as possible. He made it another third of the way before he noticed the ground lighting up around him. He froze. The spotlight's beam swept over his body slowly. *I'm invisible. I'm invisible.* When he didn't feel a bullet dig into his back, he slowly turned until he could see JoJo. JoJo flashed a smile.

Shawn crawled faster, knowing the light wouldn't sweep past him again for a few minutes. He'd made it another thirty yards when something in his subconscious made him stop. JoJo nudged into his boot and stopped, too.

Shawn scanned the area directly in front. He didn't have a good reason he'd stopped—something didn't feel right. A blackness to his right caught his attention. He inched along, using his toes to push his body forward. He came face-to-face with the black blob and his head swooned.

He reached out and felt what he thought he'd find—a thin tripwire stretching across the bottom of the ditch, only an inch off the ground, attached to a precariously perched grenade on one end and a spike on the other end. The day before, they'd scanned every inch of the ditch with binoculars from the precipice, but they'd missed the booby trap. How many more would he find?

He reached for his knife and unsheathed it with barely a sound. He prided himself on keeping the blade razor sharp and when it touched the taut wire, it cut instantly. He made sure the Japanese grenade stayed in place, then sheathed the knife and pointed out the grenade to JoJo, who nodded his understanding.

Shawn slithered onward while JoJo stayed behind to inform the next two men of the hazard. Shawn made it the rest of the way without incident.

He stopped at the end of the ditch and raised his head just enough to see through the grass. The metal and concrete tarmac of the airstrip shone dully in the starlight. A Zero sat parked only twenty yards away. He didn't see any guards or mechanics.

He looked beyond the first four Zeros and spotted their assigned aircraft. The twin-engine bomber looked immense, even from this distance. As part of their extensive training, he knew every Japanese aircraft by sight. The military had codenames for all of them, and his target's codename was Betty. He also knew it by its official name: Mitsubishi-G4M.

It was the bomber with a smoking engine. Even now, he could see the nearest engine's cowling off. During the planning, they'd worried there might be mechanics working all night on it, but for whatever reason, it sat as silent as a ghost. Perhaps they were waiting for spare parts.

He watched the closest guard tower. For the moment, the guards had shut off the spotlight. He saw the soft red glow of a cigarette. The guards would be bored and sleepy. That would change.

JoJo tapped his boot, signaling that he'd arrived. Without a glance, Shawn pulled his knees beneath himself, steadied his carbine, and rose into a crouch. The guard tower on the other side of the airfield wouldn't pose a threat, so he kept his muzzle aimed at the nearest guard tower as he moved to the first Zero.

He hid beneath the wing. The smell of aviation fuel and oil hung heavily. He glanced at the open cockpit. He fought the urge to hop onto the wing and peer inside. Aircraft fascinated him and he'd had little opportunity to explore one. But now wasn't the time.

JoJo tapped his leg, letting him know he could proceed. Shawn moved beneath the fuselage to the other wing. He peered around it until he could see the guard tower. A guard flicked his spent cigarette over the side and Shawn watched it spark when it hit the ground. *Careless son of a bitch.*

JoJo hustled from cover and Shawn kept his carbine trained on the tower until he slid beneath the second Zero's wing. JoJo took up a firing position. He signaled, and Shawn ran in a crouch. He tried to see every nook and cranny that might hide a Japanese soldier as he ran. Would he see or hear the shot that would end his young life, or would he suddenly find himself in utter blackness?

The tower spotlight flicked on again. They both froze. Shawn thought they must've tipped them off, but the beam settled on the fields in the distance and slowly swept back and forth. Now they'd be able to move easier since the light would hamper and limit the guard's eyesight.

They made it to the Betty bomber's left wing and settled beneath it. Shawn scrunched his nose. The smell of burnt plastic and oil assaulted his senses. A ladder stood beneath the damaged engine. They listened and watched for any sound or movement. The methodical drip, drip, drip of oil into a pool sounded louder than it should.

Shawn noticed the bulbous window sticking from the side. It reminded him of the pimples he'd had to endure during puberty. Just behind it, a round doorway hung open, and he could see the blackness beyond. They'd planned to plant the plastic explosive in the engine if they could reach it, but seeing the open door changed the plan.

JoJo pointed at the opening, and Shawn nodded his understanding. JoJo placed his carbine on the ground and pulled off the pack holding the explosives and detonators.

Shawn checked for movement one last time. Satisfied, he hustled to the door and stopped to listen. The smell of leather seeped from the doorway. It reminded him of his father's study. Hearing nothing, he poked his head into the opening. He couldn't see anything in the darkness, but figured if anyone waited for him inside, he'd already be dead. He hefted himself into the aircraft awkwardly. He couldn't help making some noise, so once inside, he stopped and listened. Nothing.

His eyes slowly adjusted to the darkness and he saw the outline of equipment strewn across the floor, including a large machine gun. He remembered the Betty bombers having at least two mounted machine guns.

He eased toward the cockpit. Despite how large the aircraft looked from outside, the interior felt cramped. He stepped over unidentifiable equipment before he finally made it to the cockpit.

He marveled at all the windows. A few had obvious bullet holes. The damage that forced them to land here must've come from Allied fire, not just a general maintenance problem. He wondered if it had been ground fire or if one of the P-40s he occasionally saw had taken a bite.

He moved back toward the door to give JoJo the all clear. His feet tangled and he fell forward. He cringed hearing the metallic bang the stock of his carbine made hitting the metal floor.

He heard a startled Japanese voice somewhere in front of him and close. He squinted and saw movement coming from the tail-gunner's station. His mind went into overdrive. If he fired his carbine, the entire operation would be a bust and they'd have to fight their way out of there. His hand went to the knife.

The voice came again and this time without the sleepy grogginess. He grunted as he pulled the knife, hoping he sounded apologetic and harmless. Just a comrade who'd accidentally tripped.

Shawn kept the knife behind his back as he approached. The metal shine on the knife had been dulled, so it wouldn't give him away, but he thought it better to keep it completely out of sight. He ducked lower and lower as the ceiling tapered.

The voice again, but this time it had more urgency and alarm. A blackness moved only feet in front of him. Shawn lunged forward, leading with the knife. He couldn't see well enough to aim his blow, so he stabbed and found flesh. He stabbed over and over as quickly as possible with his left hand while he groped for the tail gunner's mouth with his right.

Hot blood spilled onto his hand and the smell of a ruptured bowel made him reel, but Shawn's body worked automatically as he sliced and plunged the blade higher and higher up the body, searching for vital organs and arteries. His mind detached itself from the act momentarily.

The Japanese mewed in pain just before Shawn found his mouth and clamped his hand tightly across. He stuck the blade into his neck and pushed. He felt the blade cut into the spinal cord. The Japanese seized and twitched unnaturally beneath him, then finally deflated as though he'd drained every ounce of blood.

Shawn's face was inches from the Japanese airman's. Even in the low light, he saw the life drain out of his eyes. The vomit came as a complete surprise. He didn't feel it coming and he couldn't stop it.

He pushed off the body but he felt the slickness of the blood layered thickly upon him. It dripped off his hands and he could barely hold the knife.

JoJo hissed from the doorway. "Cooper! Cooper, you okay?"

Shawn staggered his way forward until he saw JoJo aiming his carbine at him from the doorway.

He lowered the muzzle. "Holy shit, Cooper. Are you hit?"

Shawn could hardly form words, but he croaked, "No—not hit. I—I'm okay."

JoJo looked beyond him. "Can't see shit in here. Is it clear?" Shawn nodded and stood at the doorway. Blood dripped off the knife and his hand. JoJo looked from Shawn's eyes to the knife. "Sheath that and pick up your rifle. Pull yourself together and cover me from outside." When Shawn didn't react, JoJo's voice took on a steely edge. "Now."

His words pierced Shawn's psyche. He felt himself suddenly back inside his own body, not simply a detached bystander. He did as JoJo ordered. He sheathed the knife and wiped his hands on his pant legs before picking his carbine off the floor. He hopped from the bomber and onto the tarmac and JoJo went to work placing the plastic explosives.

He glanced at the guard tower. They continued scanning with the spotlight as though nothing out of the ordinary had happened. To him, the scuffle sounded loud and impossible not to hear. He turned and watched briefly as Ned and O'Keefe worked on the nearest Zero.

It didn't take long before JoJo hopped out and landed lightly beside him. "You okay?"

Shawn still didn't trust his own voice, so he nodded.

"I set the charges. Let's get the hell outta here."

They made it back to the tree line without incident. JoJo led Shawn all the way back. It wasn't how they'd drawn it up, but Shawn was grateful that JoJo recognized how the knife killing had affected him and taken matters into his own hands. He could've done the job, but simply following without having to make any more life-and-death decisions helped ease his mind.

Calligan met them at the rendezvous spot and quickly received the report from Umberland. They'd placed charges on all the aircraft they'd intended to, but couldn't get close enough to the hangars and other buildings dotting the airfield.

Calligan slammed his fist into his open palm. "I was hoping to kill all their pilots."

Umberland answered. "I know, but the barracks are too close to that second guard tower. We couldn't get close enough without tipping our hand. I made the call to abort."

"It's a lot harder to replace pilots than aircraft ..."

"I'm aware of that. Like I said, I made the call. No Jap pilot's worth one of my men."

Calligan gazed at Shawn. He crinkled his nose and looked him up and down. "Jesus, what the hell happened to you? You smell like shit, man."

Umberland said, "He had to kill a man with his knife in the tail of that wounded bomber. Must've been sleeping in there."

Calligan lifted his chin and looked long and hard at Shawn before finally saying, "Good job, son. A gunshot obviously would've ended badly for everyone."

Shawn nodded, still not trusting himself to talk without completely breaking down.

"Must've knicked his bowel," Calligan added.

The words sparked the memory as though he were back in that tail gunner's position, covered in blood and shit. He vomited uncontrollably. Calligan stepped back but not in time to keep his feet from being splashed.

"For chrissakes, man. Pull yourself together."

Shawn wiped his mouth but didn't otherwise respond. His guts and his head hurt. He needed a drink of water.

Calligan stepped away and said over his shoulder. "Come on. The show should start any minute now. It'll make you feel better."

Shawn doubted anything but time would make him feel better, but he wanted to watch the fireworks just as much as the next man. They spread out on the ledge, not bothering to conceal themselves. Every man had already packed and they were ready to march out of the area as soon as they saw their handy-work. The enemy would likely scour the area in the morning.

Shawn sat on a rock beside JoJo and O'Keefe. He kept wringing and rubbing his hands. He'd dumped water over them as well as his head, but blood still covered his clothing and clung to his fingers and lingered beneath his fingernails. He wanted to bathe in a scalding tub of soapy water for an entire day, but he'd be happy if he found ten minutes in a mountain stream.

They didn't talk, even though everyone still felt the effects of adrenaline coursing through their bodies. It had been a successful mission, at least so long as the detonators worked, but for some reason, it felt subdued.

The first explosion went off five minutes early. One of the middle Zeros suddenly erupted in fire and flames, which lit up the sky dramatically. The thunderclap of sound reverberated up and down the valley.

The OSS men discussed it in low murmurs. If they yelled and cheered as though at a college football game, they'd alert the Japanese. The guard tower shone its spotlight on the burning wreckage as though the light might extinguish the flames. The entire airfield was alive with men darting here and there.

A volley of explosions erupted, lifting the aircraft and hurling parts in all directions. The timing couldn't have been worse for the Japanese. Men awakened in panic from the first explosion now became victims as shrapnel sliced through them and flames engulfed them.

Shawn watched the Betty bomber. It remained still and unmoving beside the surrounding infernos. Flames flickered and sparkled off the front windows. What would the tail gunner's friends think if their plastic explosive didn't work and they found him gutted in his tail gunner's position?

He had to shut his eyes when the bomber finally flashed in the middle, lurched upward, and split neatly in half. The tail section dropped forward and the flames from the front section licked up the sides and soon blazed. All they'd find of the tail gunner would be a charred husk. He felt better about that, as though it might hide the heinous act. He wished he could hide it from himself—expunge it from his memory somehow.

Calligan raised his voice. "Good work, men. All explosives accounted for. Now let's make ourselves scarce."

10

Shawn Cooper and the rest of Operational Group Bellevue hunkered around the small fire. They were tucked into the bottom of a miserable valley a few miles from the Myitkyina airfield they'd attacked a few days before.

The Marshy ground and constant wetness seeped into their boots. They could've chosen a more hospitable place to bivouac, but doubted the Japanese would bother to look for them here. Being able to build a fire was a bonus, although they had to keep it burning low and only during daylight hours.

Since the attack, they'd had to cover and conceal countless times as enemy aircraft searched for them in the endless valleys surrounding the area. They had seen no enemy foot patrols but assumed they'd be searching, too.

JoJo held his socks to the heat. They steamed as the afternoon progressed. The sun would set soon and they'd have to put the fire out. He looked around and didn't see either Umberland or Calligan. "This whole mission is fubar."

Shawn rocked back and forth on the rock he sat on. "Come on, JoJo. You're not having fun sleeping in a marsh? I love it here. I wanna move here when this whole shindig ends. I'll bet land's cheap."

O'Keefe added, "They could give it away and I wouldn't take it. What the hell are we doing out here? We hit the airfield and now we're just sitting here wasting our time."

JoJo leaned in and lowered his voice. "We've been out here a full two weeks now. It took three days to get here and might take longer to get back. How much longer you figure we're gonna stay? Might have to eat the mules soon."

Veatch rubbed his hands together and held them out to the fire. "I didn't think I could be cold in Burma."

"When you live in a marsh, you're gonna be cold," Shawn said.

JoJo said, "We've done our job. It's time to leave. The porters are ready to revolt. I'm surprised they haven't left already. I would've."

O'Keefe said, "Only thing keeping 'em here's the Kachin. Without them watching them all the time, they woulda left days ago."

Shawn said, "Even that won't keep 'em here much longer."

"If they leave, they'll take the mules with 'em and we'll be stuck carrying all the gear," O'Keefe added.

"Should we bring it up to Umberland? He's gotta be feeling the same way we are," JoJo said.

Silence lingered until Shawn finally said, "I know he's as upset as we are. He had to talk Calligan out of hitting the pilot barracks. Can you imagine going in there again?"

"Calligan's crazy. He and Didi scare the hell out of me. They'd sooner skin us alive than say good morning," O'Keefe said.

Umberland elbowed his way into the circle. The group went quiet. He held his hands out to the heat. "Bout time to put the fire out."

JoJo stood and kicked mud and water onto it. It hissed and smoked. "Yes, sir," he mumbled, then sat back down heavily.

Umberland looked them over. "I heard a little of your conversation." He let that hang there. The men stared straight ahead, gleaning the last vestiges of warmth from the setting sun. Umberland said, "Lieutenant Calligan's an odd sort, but he wants the same thing we all do."

JoJo, clearly frustrated, said, "Oh yeah? And what's that? Dying of hypothermia and bug bites?"

"Winning the war." No one said a word, so Umberland continued. "As soon as the rest of the Kachin are armed and trained, they'll lead the assault here in Burma. General Donovan himself met with the Kachin chief. Some crazy name like Zhang Htaw Naw. He met with him in his home village in the Hukawng Valley. I'm sure you all heard about that, but what you didn't hear was how impressed he was with the Kachin.

"General Stillwell needs a powerful fighting force and up-to-date intelligence on Jap movements and concentrations. He's heard about the Kachin, but didn't think he could rely on them. General Donovan convinced him otherwise. This Zhang fellow has already put together nearly five hundred eager fighters." He looked around, saw Didi, and pointed at him. "Men like Didi over there. Can you imagine five hundred men like Didi? Donovan authorized arming and training them, so the Tenth Air Force is making supply drops all over the place. Once they're ready, they'll coordinate with Stillwell and the fight for northern Burma will be on. You men will be on the leading edge."

Shawn had heard some of this through scuttlebutt, but not the straight scoop. "So what are we doing way down here? We've already hit the airfield. We should be up there helping train the Kachin."

"And you will be, but first Calligan's going to set up a permanent watch station here." He pointed toward Myitkyina. "The Jap Eighteenth Division is headquartered down there. They're dropping a radio set along with a couple more 101 guys. They'll have a direct line to the air corps guys."

JoJo still wasn't convinced. "So what's Calligan need us for anymore? We should get the hell outta this cesspool."

"The drops coming tomorrow. Along with the radio and the 101 guys, they're also dropping more supplies. We'll run security for the drop."

"Awful close to Myitkyina, aren't they?" Shawn asked.

"They know what they're doing. They'll be low, well below the ridgelines." No one said anything, so Umberland added. "Look, I know conditions here are terrible, but it's almost over. As soon as Calligan has his radio base set up and secure, we'll head back to Knothead. Day after tomorrow, most likely."

The news lifted their spirits. Training the Kachin in a nice, comfortable village would be a pleasant change. From what Shawn had seen, they'd be a highly effective guerrilla force. The Japanese made a huge mistake when they brutally attacked them in their mountain villages and turned them into bitter enemies. He hated the Japanese, but the Kachin's hatred was on a whole different level. They *loathed* them.

Shawn shuddered at the memory of Didi butchering the dead Japanese soldiers—taking body parts as trophies. Perhaps they could train such brutality out of them—then again, part of guerrilla tactics was instilling a large dose of fear into the enemy. If the Japanese were afraid to leave their bases, it would make life much easier for the allies. He had a lot to think about.

Shawn woke an hour or two before sunrise to the sounds of panic and mayhem. He unsnapped the flap of his hammock, which kept the bugs from entering, clutched his carbine, and rolled onto the spongy ground. He took a moment to orient himself to the sounds. When he didn't hear gunfire, he relaxed.

He saw a dark shadow pass and recognized JoJo's features. "Hey, what's going on?"

JoJo didn't break stride. "Dunno, but I'm gonna find out."

Shawn looked furtively at his hammock. He'd been sleeping soundly and wanted to continue, but his conscience and curiosity got the better of him and he followed JoJo.

They trotted toward the rising commotion. They saw Umberland and Calligan listening to the Kachin while they gestured wildly. Shawn had been picking up bits and pieces of the Kachin language, but still had a long way to go. Calligan, on the other hand, could speak the language fluently.

"The Burmese." Calligan stated flatly. "They're gone. They want to find them and kill them," he said, as though giving a weather report.

"In this ink? How long ago?" Umberland asked.

"Doesn't matter. They could track in complete blackness, I've no doubt about that."

Umberland said, "We don't have time to chase them down. The plane arrives in a few hours. We need to be here, or they won't find us at all. Besides, I'm not gonna be a part of murdering unarmed Burmese porters, and neither will my men."

Shawn felt an immense fondness for Umberland at that moment. Say what you will about him. He cared about Bellevue's welfare. *At least someone does.*

"They might bring the Nips back," Calligan suggested.

Umberland shook his head. "They coulda done that a long time ago. I bet they are heading home. They've been miserable for days now. They don't care about this war, they just want to go home. Besides, they left us the mules. They're almost more important."

Calligan considered it for a long while. The Kachin were eager to hunt their hated brethren. They hadn't killed or maimed any Japanese yet. Shawn figured they'd love to break in their new carbines and Thompsons.

Calligan spoke to them in their stilted, singsong language. They gesticulated wildly and pointed into the jungle. Calligan switched to English and said, "I told them to forget them. They're not happy, but they'll do what I say. I tend to agree with you. I don't think they have the backbone to report us to the Japanese, unless they're unlucky enough to run into a patrol. They'd give us up to save their own skins, no doubt. But that's unlikely."

Shawn exchanged a glance with JoJo. "Should we move up the valley just to be sure?"

Calligan looked his way, as though noticing him for the first time. "Probably a prudent move. The transport will fly up this valley until they see our smoke, so it doesn't really matter where we are, as long as we're in this valley." He conferred quietly with Umberland.

Umberland turned back to them and ordered, "Wake the rest of the men. They'll be happy to get out of this damnable swamp."

It didn't take long to break camp. As the dawn broke, they moved up the valley. The spongy ground finally gave way to firm soil. The Kachin led the way, taking them through a boulder-strewn section where the hills pushed in from both sides. Beyond the narrows, the valley widened into a lush landscape with varying shades of green grass. The grass swayed in the light wind and smelled of flowers.

Shawn stopped to look. "Now this is more like it," he uttered to no one in particular. "This has been here the whole time? What the hell were we doing in that damned swamp?"

"Course it's been here the whole time, dummy," O'Keefe answered.

"Sure can be beautiful out here—if you can look past the bugs, tigers, and Japs."

They wound their way into the valley. They set up camp beneath a massive grove of towering trees on the north side of the valley. Vines hung from the tops of trees all the way to the ground in thick strands. The trees looked as old as the mountains and made Shawn feel as insignificant as an ant.

The creek, which had spread out and created the marsh at their first camp, kept to the confines of its rocky banks here, so the ground stayed firm and mostly dry. The crystal clear water burbled over the rocks, filling the valley with a pleasant sound.

"It's like we've traveled from hell and into heaven. Maybe this creek's actually the River Styx," Shawn said as he scooped water and drank deeply.

Calligan, standing nearby, said, "Don't get too comfortable, son. You boys'll be leaving once the plane finds us."

"You're staying here then?"

"Until I'm ordered somewhere else, yes."

"This won't be a bad place to be."

"I agree, but we'll have to set up an observation post overlooking Myitkyina. We're much too far away to do much good from here."

Shawn pointed at the mountains to the south. "Maybe find a path cutting through the mountains. Myitkyina's just on the other side."

"Didi says there isn't. We'll have to use the valley to access the Irrawaddy river valley, then cut back up north. But this is a good spot to get resupplied."

Shawn looked around and didn't find what he was looking for. "Where *are* the Kachin?"

"As soon as we decided where to set up, they went back down the valley."

"Why? Going after the porters?"

"I hope not. I told them to watch the marsh to make sure they didn't give up our position." He shrugged, "but they'll do what they want."

"Think they'll go after 'em?"

"I'd say it's fifty-fifty."

"Jesus, I wouldn't want those sons of bitches mad at me."

"Me either. They hate them just about as much as they hate the Nips."

"Why?"

"They've been at odds for generations. One side'll raid the other, kill men, capture women and children, use 'em as slave labor or wives. Then they retaliate, and so on, and so on, forever."

"Sounds archaic."

He stared into the distance. "Not much different from the way we go about things. We just do it on a much grander, more violent scale. It's human nature to kill one another."

A chill went up Shawn's spine. He didn't know Calligan's age for sure, but he seemed ageless, as though he'd been fighting in these jungles for thousands of years . . . only the enemies changed. He wanted to know more about him, but feared the truth might be worse than the fantasy.

"You're a cold son of a bitch, Calligan."

The comment snapped Calligan out of his stare. He turned his icy gaze on him. He smiled, laughed uproariously, and left Shawn watching his back as he walked away, still laughing.

JoJo came up beside Shawn. His head dripped creek water. He wiped his face, scratching at the stubble from many long days without a shave. "Someday you're gonna go too far with that crazy asshole."

"Nah. I'm not worried, although sometimes I wonder if he's a few bricks short of a wall."

"He's been out here as long as any of the other 101 guys. I wonder if we'll end up that way."

"What's a guy like that do after the war? Can you see that guy in a normal house, in a normal neighborhood, with a normal wife and family, going to a normal job?"

JoJo wrung out his shirt and shook his head. "Nope. Most likely end up in jail."

"Yeah, or work for the government."

"Probably both."

. . .

Three hours after making camp in the new locale, they heard the droning of an airplane. They'd seen a few high-flying aircraft, undoubtedly Japanese, but this sounded different. It sounded low, close, and familiar.

They darted out from the cover of the trees and made ready to throw a smoke canister. A few men had their weapons ready in case things didn't turn out the way they expected. If it turned out to be a Jap aircraft, it would be a waste of ammo trying to shoot it down. Better to get under cover and leave 'em alone.

The sound grew. It seemed to bounce off the valley walls, making him think it was behind him sometimes. But no, it came from down the valley. He kept his eyes on the tight cut they'd walked through only a mile west. The transport would have to gain elevation to get over it, and it would be visible at that point.

Sure enough, he heard the engine noise increase. A moment later, the lumbering transport rose, leveled off as it lifted over the cut. It didn't dip back down, but continued straight about one hundred feet off the ground. He wondered if the valley looked as beautiful to them as it did to him, or did all the endless valleys all look identical from their elevated perch.

"Pop smoke!" Umberland yelled.

Soon, a rush of white smoke rose into the languid air in a thick plume. The transport nosed down slightly, getting even lower. The engines roared as it passed overhead and the wings waggled a hello.

Shawn couldn't help waving back. He felt like a child watching an airshow instead of a deadly OSS operative deep behind enemy lines, but he felt an undeniable rush of joy. He thought he must look quite the idiot, but everyone else, excluding Umberland and Calligan, waved and jumped around, too. He wondered if the Kachin had seen the plane and were eagerly waving as well.

"Stow the smoke!" Umberland yelled again.

Ned shoved the smoke canister into a bag and sealed it tight. No use advertising their whereabouts to any passing Japanese flights. Ned came away white-faced and shook his hand as though he'd burned himself. If a Japanese Zero got wind of them, it would make quick work of the slow, defenseless transport.

The transport continued up the valley, but they'd definitely seen them.

The engines faded, then grew again as the pilots turned back toward their position.

A few seconds later, the C-47 returned, only this time it flew at three hundred feet and lumbered even slower. Four large bundles flew out the side and gray and white parachutes blossomed and slowed their headlong journey to earth. Two men jumped next. They tumbled, then snapped as the static line inside the plane pulled their chutes for them. They only swung twice before they crashed into the soft valley grass.

The transport's engines roared and it shot down the valley, picking up speed. Shawn wondered at the audacity of the pilots. The mission seemed impossible. Find and fly up an obscure valley deep behind enemy lines less than ten miles from the largest enemy airfield in the region, then find a group of thirty men and drop them a radio, supplies, and two more OSS operatives. They must be completely bonkers, or incredibly skilled, and stupidly brave . . . probably all three.

Shawn trotted across the valley toward where the two operatives had landed. When he got to them, they were finishing rolling their parachutes into tight, neat balls. They didn't look any worse for wear, despite hurling themselves from an airplane three hundred feet up at ninety miles per hour.

The nearest man smiled, waved, and said in a southern drawl, "Hey, y'all seen anyone calling themselves Operational Group Bellevue around these parts?"

Shawn couldn't keep from laughing. "You're in the right place, hoss, unless you were looking for a different Bellevue, that is. Might be another one down a ways," he pointed west.

"Well, I guess you'll just have to do." He stepped forward and they shook hands as though old friends.

"Welcome!" Shawn said. "I'm sure you'll find our little slice of Burma everything you've ever hoped for."

He looked around admiringly. "Well, it ain't south Texas, but it'll have to do."

Shawn laughed again and directed him back toward the camp. "Your 101 man, Calligan's over this way." He noticed men from Bellevue hauling the other bundles off the field. "Hope those radios survived."

"Me too. Those are more important than us by a long way," he indicated the other OSS operative. "That's Conner O'Donnelly and I'm Flynn Guthrie, by the way."

Conner bowed, as though addressing royalty. "At your service."

Shawn extended his hand to him, too. "I'm Shawn Cooper. Glad you didn't twist or break anything. Landings can be rough out here, but you landed in a nice soft patch of grass."

"You airborne?"

"Formerly of the 501st, yep. How was the flight in?"

"Bumpy and downright petrifying," Conner said. "Those pilots didn't fly much above the treetops. We even saw a Zero off in the distance. Thank God they didn't see us."

"They woulda ruined your day."

"I hope those sons of guns make it back okay," Flynn said, looking toward the now long gone transport. As they walked, he hefted the parachute silk. "What should we do with these? Bury them?"

"Normally, yes, but the Kachin women love the stuff. We'll hand it off to the men when we get a chance. It's better than cigarettes. The Kachin men'll carry it hundreds of miles 'cause they know they'll be heroes in the women's eyes and be rewarded for their efforts," he finished with a wink.

Flynn laughed. "Things are the same across the world. The men are trying to get laid, and the women are trying to dress nice."

Operational Group Bellevue stayed with Calligan and the newcomers while they set up and tested the radio. They had enough power to transmit all the way into India, with no relay stations. The hand-cranked generator made a lot of noise and required a lot of effort, but it worked beautifully.

They'd dropped two sets just in case one had taken damage on impact. Both had survived, but Burma's climate would degrade them quickly, so they could use the second set for spare parts if needed. Calligan looked positively ebullient. Shawn had never seen him so happy. He skipped around and clicked his feet like a crazy person or a Broadway dancer.

Operational Group Bellevue spent the night in the lush valley, woke early, and trekked their way westward. The sun was just rising when they passed through the narrow point of the valley and the marshlands spread out before them. They looked beautiful, but he knew the misery they held.

Shawn wondered where the Kachin had gone. Perhaps they watched them as they passed. Would they try to get the jump on them? The small tribesmen enjoyed their games, especially when patrolling. They liked to get as close as possible without being seen, then leap out from cover. It was a wonderful way to get shot. With the proximity of Myitkyina, Shawn hoped they'd behave better, but he kept a sharp eye out, just in case.

The unit moved with ease over the familiar ground. They eventually turned north and with each step, they put more distance between themselves and Myitkyina. They still saw no signs of the Kachin, or the enemy.

They increased their pace. With little fear from enemy patrols and easy terrain over rolling hills, they settled into a slow trot. Without pushing themselves too hard, they devoured the miles quickly. It felt good to be moving and helped clear Shawn's mind.

They stopped when they heard the distant pops of gunshots in the distance. They spread out and crouched in the low grass, and waited a few minutes but heard nothing else. Umberland waved them forward.

They moved in a loose combat spread. It was difficult to pinpoint exactly, but it sounded like the shots came from the low valley ahead.

They stopped when they could look down into the valley, which was nothing more than a cut in the hills where a tiny creek meandered through. Shawn remembered it from their trek into Myitkyina three weeks before. The shots could've come from anywhere, but he thought he could smell a hint of burnt gunpowder on the wind. He got Umberland's attention and pointed to his own nose.

Umberland lifted his nose, then nodded back. They hunkered lower and watched silently. Getting into a firefight was the last thing they wanted to happen. Running into even a small enemy patrol could be disastrous. If even one man escaped, which was highly likely, they'd bring more troops and hunt them like animals. Best to avoid contact, but in order to avoid it, they needed to know where it originated.

Sergeant Boyd waved to get their attention, then pointed up the valley. He signaled he could see something. Umberland moved up to him and Shawn hunkered nearby. He immediately saw what Boyd had seen. It looked like discarded clothing, but upon further inspection, it was a body. Two more sprawled nearby.

They weren't Japanese, but looked like native Burmese. They watched the valley for another ten minutes. No movement and no more shots.

Umberland called Boyd closer. They talked about their options while the others watched the valley and the relatively thin surrounding jungle.

Boyd came forward. He pointed to five men, including Shawn, to move forward. They would check out the bodies while the others watched their backs.

Shawn gulped against a suddenly dry throat. The shots hadn't been long ago. Whoever had fired could easily lie in wait to see who came to investigate. He suspected it must be the Kachin, but it could also be Japanese.

He moved from cover to cover, keeping his eyes on the treetops and the surrounding jungle. Thankfully, it wasn't too thick here. If it had been, they most likely would've never even seen the bodies. He wished they hadn't.

He didn't see or feel anything out of the ordinary. He relied heavily on his sixth sense, but he didn't feel as though he was being watched or targeted.

When they'd come within twenty yards of the closest body, they stopped. Boyd touched Shawn's shoulder and pointed. Shawn didn't hesitate. Staying in a crouch, with his weapon ready, he approached the body. It was on its stomach, face down—definitely a Burmese native.

He crouched only a yard from it and inspected it for booby traps. The Japanese could be sneaky that way. He saw nothing obvious, so he scooted until he was right beside it. He noticed the bullet hole in the man's bare back. Blood still seeped from it. He didn't see any other wounds. He went to the second and third man with the same result. All dead and recently killed with bullets in their backs.

He looked around at the treetops, wondering if a sniper had done this dirty work. But setting up way out here in the jungle's vastness made little sense. They could sit for months and not see another human being. Before their group traipsed through, Shawn doubted anyone had wandered through here in years, possibly even decades. No, these men had been killed by someone close and on the ground behind them. Had they been running? He thought so.

He moved back to Boyd and the others. "They're all dead. All three shot in the back. Looks like they were running away."

"How d'you know that?"

"I don't. Just a hunch. I don't think the shooter, or shooters, are still hanging around."

Boyd nodded and moved to the bodies to check them out himself. He and Shawn hunkered while the others spread out around them, looking for trouble.

Boyd said, "I recognize this guy. He was one of our porters."

"Really? How do you know?"

"I remember the burn mark on his shoulder." He pointed at the puckered skin. "I remember thinking he must be a tough hombre."

"You think the Kachin did this? Our Kachin?"

"Bullet hole's small. Could be from a carbine, and those boys can shoot. I'd say it's a damned good bet."

"They murdered them."

Boyd gave him a steady look before saying, "Murder? Hell, I think these fellers have been fighting one another for hundreds of years. Murder to us is just a way of life for them."

"Shot in cold blood? As they ran away? I call it murder."

"Well, I see your point, but there's not a hell of a lot we can do about it way the hell out here. For all we know, it coulda been the damned Nips."

"Didi and others did this. We never saw 'em and they never came back to the camp. They hunted these poor devils down like dogs."

Boyd looked around the valley. "Might be watching us as we speak. They're like ghosts out here. We'd never know."

Shawn stood and slowly turned 360 degrees, searching for the Kachin. He fumed. These men meant nothing to the Kachin, but they were still human. He supposed they had hopes, fears, and families, just like anybody else. To be cut down in cold blood as they ran for their lives didn't sit right with him.

Boyd slapped his arm. "Get up there and tell Umberland what we found. Have him meet us down here. We're wasting daylight." When he didn't go right away, he pushed him, "Go on—git."

"This ain't right, sergeant. They shouldn't get away with this."

"Umberland will tell Burbank about it and he'll either run it up to Nasira or just sweep it under the rug. It's outta our hands. Now follow orders, soldier."

11

OCTOBER 1943

Seattle, Washington

Victor Brooks read the newspaper with a satisfied smirk, then folded it and beamed. He held it up and shook it at his wife Meredith sitting across the table, doing her level best to ignore him.

Victor said, "That's the best damned reporting I've ever read. I may send a letter to Perkins's boss. He really nailed it."

"Something about the war, darling?" she simpered.

His silver mustache twitched in annoyance. "No. The war's too easy. Any fool can regurgitate current events. I'm talking about the editorial section. Perkins has written a real gem about the need for corporations to take more control over production. Get it out of government hands altogether. We've proven ourselves over the past two years. The government will just slow us down."

Meredith sipped her coffee, then gave him a slight smile. "Did he mention you again, dear?"

"Well, yes. As a matter of fact, he did, but that's beside the point. He has wonderful insight into the business world . . . particularly the production side of things."

"Is that the reporter that covered poor Miles's funeral?"

"Yes. He did brilliantly there, too. It's where I first discovered him."

She gave him a tight smile, then said, "Well, you invited him, after all."

He could hear the accusation in her voice. He leveled an icy gaze at her, waiting for her to turn away like normal, but she stared back. When had that change happened? It irked him.

"You don't think I should have honored Miles Burr's death? His sacrifice?"

Her eyes narrowed and he heard the biting hate in her voice when she replied. "Honor? His memory certainly deserves to be honored, but not the way you did it. That was all about you, Victor. Miles's death just gave you a way to elevate yourself to the world, and make yourself seem less . . ."

She hesitated and he leaned forward, smacking the newspaper onto the gleaming wood table. "Seem less what, Meredith?"

She jumped at the loud smack, but finished what she wanted to say. "Guilty," she hissed.

He leaned back in his chair and they stared at one another. The staff in the corners took the opportunity and left through the adjoining doors.

"Guilty of what?" he asked incredulously.

She leaned forward, defiant. "His death, Victor."

His eyes went to slits and he pointed a long bony finger at her. "Careful what you say, Meredith. You've pushed me as far as I'll allow."

She crossed her arms and leaned back in the opulent chair. She shook her head sadly. "Listen to yourself, Victor. As far as you'll allow? What will you do, assault me in my own house?"

"Your house? Ha! This is *my* house, woman."

She stood and the coffee cup tinkled from side to side on the fine china saucer. "So I'm a guest in this house? Is that it? I'm just someone you *allow* to live here? I'm one of the staff?" She shook her head. "No, that's wrong. At least they're able to return to loving homes at the end of their day. I'm stuck with you." She said it with such venom, he couldn't respond for a moment.

But he soon recovered. "What has gotten into you? You used to be so pleasant, but now you're a damned shrew."

She roared with laughter, the sound not quite happy. Victor stared at her as if she'd lost her mind.

"Don't you mean compliant, Victor? Not pleasant, but compliant—that's what you really want. Isn't it? Compliance?"

Victor stared at her, his anger rendering him speechless.

She sighed deeply, tilted her head, and gave him a sad smile. "It wasn't always this way. Remember when we first met? Remember when we courted? You hung on my every word. It was what attracted me to you in the first place. You were the one man in all those stuffed shirts who actually cared about my opinion. You gave me a voice. My God, Victor, I'd never felt so alive. You treated me with—with dignity."

Victor felt momentarily stunned. He didn't have time for this melodramatic garbage. He had a company to run—money to make. "You're living in a fairytale, Meredith. The past is just that—the past. Courting? It's so many years ago, I don't even remember. I certainly don't *want* to remember. What's gotten into you?"

She stepped from the table and pushed her chair back with a soft scraping of wood. "I feel sorry for you, Victor. The man I married was a romantic, *virulent* man. I don't know the man standing in front of me anymore."

"Virulent? Don't be disgusting. We're not simpering little children anymore. You expect people to stay the same forever? Like I said, you live in a damned fairytale."

"No, I don't, but I once did and I'll always cherish the memory, even if you won't."

Victor watched her leave. He thought about yelling at her, forbidding her to leave until he'd excused her, but he knew she'd simply leave, and make him feel even more impotent. Couldn't she see what he'd given her? Couldn't she appreciate her life? She could have anything her heart desired, yet she insisted on sitting there, making *him* feel horrible about his decisions. Decisions he'd made to make their lives better—her life better.

He grasped the china coffee cup and hurled it against the wall. It shattered, but even that sound seemed pathetic and inconsequential.

An evil thought crossed his mind. Had Meredith betrayed him? An affair would explain her recent behavior—her defiance. A flash of hurt followed immediately with boiling anger, made him grip the edges of the table. He wondered who it could be.

He doubted any of his colleagues would be stupid enough to betray him in such an obvious and dangerous way. He couldn't think of anyone Meredith would even be attracted to. His associates were mostly well past their prime. Perhaps it had been Miles. He'd fit the bill—she'd always fancied younger men. At least he saw her looking sometimes. But no, Miles had died and Meredith would hurt over such a loss. *Surely I would've noticed that . . . or would I?*

No, it wouldn't be someone he knew. It could be anyone, really. She spent most of her days flitting from event to event, one after another, with almost no oversight. She could've met someone at any of those events.

The more he thought about it, the more convinced of her guilt he became. He thought briefly of the handful of women he'd been with since marrying Meredith. Since the war broke out, he'd been far too busy, and besides, it was different for men. *It's expected.*

He hurried out of the dining room, intent on putting Sal on the case. Sal would find the scoundrel easy enough. The thought sent a shiver of delight up his spine as he thought of all the different ways he'd make him pay. Victor would not be made a fool.

An hour had passed since her argument with Victor, but Meredith couldn't help replaying it over and over in her head. She sat in front of her vanity and silently cursed herself. She hadn't wanted to antagonize Victor, but she couldn't help herself, especially when he gloated so disgustingly. She didn't have all the details about Miles's death yet, but she didn't think it happened the way he had described at the funeral. She checked her makeup. She hoped he'd simply forget the whole thing, but knew him better than that. No, he'd dwell on it.

Her heart skipped a beat when she checked the time. She had a rendezvous with Calvin during the lunch hour. A bird on the lawn caught her eye as she walked past her bedroom window. She stopped and watched as another bird descended and they bounced and frolicked around one another. What she assumed to be the female darted and dashed, making it more difficult for the male, but in the end, the deed was done.

It reminded her of when she'd first met Victor. He'd been so handsome and interesting. She'd taken an immediate shine to him, but she only let on enough to attract his attentions. Once he noticed her, he pursued her with abandon, much the same way the male bird had pursued the female. She pretended not to notice Victor at all, and it drove him mad. He practically tripped over himself to be with her. She continued flirting with other men, driving him even crazier. But she always knew she'd end up with him. He was everything she'd ever dreamed a man could be. How had it all crumbled?

She sighed. It hadn't been any one thing, but a combination of hundreds of little things, all adding up to the current loveless sum. When had Victor last looked at her the way Calvin looked at her? Poor Calvin. She'd have to put an end to things soon, or he'd be too head over heels in love with her. It might already be too late. She could see it in his eyes. He was young. He'd recover and find someone his own age and forget all about her eventually.

Perhaps she'd break it off that very day. The sooner the better, really, for everyone involved. She thought of Abigail walking in on her in the library those months ago. She'd never seen such disgust in her daughter's eyes. It hurt deeply, but it also brought them a tiny bit closer together—as though the shared secret bonded them.

She hadn't heard from Abigail since she'd left for Texas. She hadn't left a forwarding address, so she couldn't even write her a letter. Had her affair forced her to flee her home? No. Once she'd recovered from the initial shock, Abigail hadn't seemed perturbed enough for that to be the reason. Something else made her leave—or perhaps it was a combination of many things and the affair was just one more. She only knew she missed her only daughter. A sadness swept over her. What had her life become?

Perhaps she wouldn't break it off with Calvin just yet. She needed him to hold her one more time—to put her troubles on hold and simply live for the moment one last time.

She gave one final look in the mirror—her imperfections were more difficult to cover up these days. She descended the long, snaking staircase and met Sal in the foyer. "Will you take me to the club, Sal?"

"Yes, of course, Mrs. Brooks."

She touched his powerful arm and looked past his ugly scar and into his eyes. He could be hard, but she also knew he had a gentle side. She'd seen it many times when Abigail was young and would follow him around the property all day like a lost puppy. He'd pretended he didn't like it, but she knew otherwise.

"Please Sal. I think after all these years you should call me Meredith."

Sal looked surprised, but he nodded. "Okay, *Meredith*. It might take some getting used to, but I'll give it a try."

He held the door to the Rolls Royce open, and she stepped inside. It smelled like fresh leather and soap. Sal always took great care of their property. A memory of him flashed in her mind, but she quickly shoved it back into the dark recesses. He used to call her Meredith behind closed doors. Did he remember?

He slid into the driver's seat and started the engine. It growled to life instantly and he let it warm.

Meredith said, "Thank you, Sal."

He looked at her through the rear-view mirror, obviously perplexed. "Thank you for what?"

"For taking such good care of us." He raised an eyebrow and she continued. "This car, for example. It's not yours, yet it's in immaculate condition, thanks to you. It's how you've treated our family from the very beginning and I, for one, appreciate it."

He turned in the seat and smiled. "That's good of you to say, Mrs. . . . . I mean, Meredith."

She gave him a sad smile, then stared out the window.

He said, "Is everything alright?"

"Why? Because I'm not my usual horrible self today?"

He didn't respond, and she placed her hand on his shoulder. "You don't need to answer that. I'm sorry to put you on the spot, I just woke up feeling —sad. But also grateful."

He turned back to face front and watched her in the mirror. The engine ticked into a steady idle.

"I'm worried about Victor," she said quietly.

"Why?"

"I'm worried about his soul."

"His soul? What do you mean?"

"I mean, I don't know him anymore. Not really. I'm worried that he's doing—or has done—terrible things. He's not the man I married. I yearn for that man, but I fear he's gone forever."

Meredith looked at his eyes in the mirror. She saw tenderness but also sadness. She asked, "Has he?"

His eyes hardened again, and his scar darkened to an ugly purplish color. He looked away and his hands gripped the steering wheel tighter.

She lowered her voice. "Has he made *you* do those things?"

He pulled the Rolls away from the house and when they were at the end of the long driveway, all the tenderness had disappeared. He spoke and she heard the iciness. "I've done things in my life I'm not proud of. Most of it before I worked for your family. I'm my own man, Mrs. Brooks. I make my own decisions . . . and I'm still here."

"I'm having an affair."

"I know."

"Of course you would. Does he know?"

"No. But he suspects. He wants me to watch you. He wants to punish whoever it is. Just this morning, he approached me while you were upstairs."

"Poor man," she said, barely above a whisper.

"Your suitor?"

"No. Victor. I feel sorry for him. So much hatred in his heart. I feel it too, but I've come to terms with it recently. It's not worth carrying around. It ages us and only makes us bitter."

"Your suitor must be quite the man," he said it with biting bitterness. She also heard something else—something she hadn't heard in decades.

She placed her hand on his shoulder and she felt him shiver beneath her touch. His eyes softened, and she smiled at him.

"I'm ending it with him."

"Probably for the best."

"Don't hurt him."

He hesitated for an instant. "I won't."

"What will you tell Victor?"

"What do you want me to tell him?"

"If I thought it would help him break through his hatred, I'd say tell him the truth, despite the pain it would cause him, but I think it would have the opposite effect. I'm afraid of what he might do."

"I wouldn't let him hurt you." He said it with a hint of anger and a large dose of something else—care.

For the first time in a long time, she thought of Sal as something other than the hired help. She'd always held a deep affection for him, mostly because of the way he treated Abigail, and there'd been that one time of weakness ages ago, but this was something different. She'd never looked at him as a man before. That wasn't quite right—she'd never looked at him the way she'd once looked at Victor, except that once.

She removed her hand from his shoulder and went back to staring out the window. He concentrated on the road as though he'd never driven before. *This is getting far too complicated*, she thought.

Trish Watson noticed the shiny Rolls Royce pulling into the front of the country club. She'd been loitering nearby for two hours. So far, they'd asked her twice why she was there. Both times she'd told the inquirer to buzz off, but she figured they'd call the cops the next time and that's the last thing she needed.

She stepped from the shadows and approached the car. She stopped when she saw a big man step from the driver's side, adjust his hat, then walk briskly to the back passenger side. She recognized Sal immediately and turned away abruptly, as though studying the flowers. Meredith Brooks emerged from the Rolls as Trish watched from the corner of her eye.

Sal took a quick look around, said a few words, then went back to the driver's side. Meredith stood there and watched him pull away. She waved and Sal waved back. Strange behavior for a driver and his charge, but maybe they were closer than she knew. Abby had told her Sal had been working for the family since before she'd been born—still, it seemed odd.

Trish stepped toward her. Meredith stepped toward the front door of the club. Just before Trish reached her, the doorman planted his hand against her chest and stopped her.

"Where do you think you're going, missy?"

Trish didn't like being touched and reacted without thinking. She gripped the hand and twisted. The man yelped in pain. Trish stepped close, then drove her knee into his crotch. He doubled over, gasping for breath. She released his hand, allowing him to drop to the ground, where he grasped his balls and rocked side to side, moaning.

Trish's eyes darted for a place to run, but heard Meredith call out. "Miss Watkins? Is that you?"

Trish stood over the injured doorman. She raised the brim of her dock worker's hat and said, "Yeah, it's me."

Meredith strode to her and put her hand to her chest as she observed the young man on the ground. "Oh dear. It appears you've tripped and hurt yourself, Gregory."

Gregory's eyes widened and he shook his head and, through gasping breaths, said, "No—no, she—she hit me in the . . ."

Meredith leaned closer so only he and Trish could hear her. "That's what happened, Gregory. You tripped and fell. Unless you never want to work in this city again."

He stopped rocking and stared at Meredith for a long moment. She raised an eyebrow and he decided. "O—okay. I—I tripped."

Meredith smiled and said. "This is my guest, Miss Watkins."

Gregory staggered to his feet, still clutching his crotch and giving Trish a wary look. "Whatever you say, Mrs. Brooks."

"Fine. We'll stay on the patio. Please have champagne for two delivered."

Gregory stumbled into the foyer to put in her order. Trish said, "Thanks. I didn't mean to put him down like that."

"Quite impressive really."

"I don't like to be touched."

Meredith laughed. "I'll keep that in mind. I assume you're here to see me?" Trish nodded and Meredith led them around the main building to a covered patio. A few yards away, a group of golfers stood around manicured grass getting ready to tee off. No other patrons sat outside.

"Why are we outside?" Trish asked.

"Two reasons. One: I'd like some privacy and two: you're not dressed appropriately for the inside. They'd ask you to change or leave within minutes." She gave her a wry smile. "And I don't want a repeat of the performance at the front door."

"Aha. I don't own a lot of dresses."

Meredith waved it away. "Now, what did you want to talk about?"

Trish looked around suspiciously. She finally said, "You act as though you've been expecting me. Why is that?"

"Not expecting anything really, but not surprised, either."

"Why is that? We've barely met. Just at the funeral." Her voice caught slightly as Miles's image flashed in her mind. It happened less and less now, but enough to annoy her.

Trish saw the concern in Meredith's eyes and was reminded of Abby.

Meredith answered. "You're Abigail's friend. Miles's too, if I'm not mistaken. Perhaps more than friends."

Trish didn't like being read so easily. "Still doesn't answer my question."

"I watched you at the funeral. I watched you and Abigail interacting. Something seemed off. You looked both grieved and—well, angry. Then Abigail left in a huff and you tried to stop her. I figured you might try to get in touch with her."

"Do you have her address?"

Meredith shook her head sadly. "No. She didn't give it to me, and didn't leave it at the post office either. Can you imagine that? I don't know what it means."

The waiter came out with two flutes of sparkling champagne. He set them down in front of each of them. He gave Trish a withering glare. She took the flute and drank half of it in one gulp while staring into the waiter's eyes. He huffed, then left them alone.

Trish set the glass down and said, "I didn't think so, but that's not why I'm here."

"Really? Then why?"

Trish looked around then leaned forward. Her tone hardened and she tried her best to look dangerous. "I work for some people that paid me for a job. I'd nearly completed the job, but Abby got in the way." She watched the color drain from Meredith's face. "I can't find Abby, so that avenue's closed, but I have another option." She let that hang there.

Finally Meredith asked, "What kind of job?"

She sneered. "Not the nice kind you country club people are used to. A dirty job . . . involving your husband."

Meredith lost whatever color she had remaining in her face. "I don't understand. My husband hired you? Didn't you work for him on the factory floor? What's this all about?" She looked around nervously, as though seeking help.

"I had everything I needed, but Abby destroyed it all. But you can help me get it all back."

"Get what back?"

"My payday, my reputation, and my revenge."

"I'm afraid I still don't understand."

"Your husband's not a good man, Meredith. I was on the verge of having all the proof I needed to put him in prison. Although, I don't know if my employers are interested in putting him in prison, if you catch my meaning."

"His life's in danger?"

Trish shrugged as though it didn't matter. "He's responsible for Miles's death . . ." her voice caught and she silently cursed herself for the slip. "He didn't take that responsibility." She shook her head bitterly. "But that's just his latest crime."

Meredith's voice hardened, reminding Trish once again of Abby. "Careful what you say, Miss Watkins. What do you want from me?"

"Access. I want you to bring me evidence. You're his wife. You can access everything I need."

Meredith's face broke into a mirthless smile. Her eyes turned cold and Trish saw danger there. "You're asking me to help you put my own husband behind bars? You're out of your mind. Honestly, what was Abigail thinking when she befriended you? No wonder she left so soon after the funeral."

Trish smiled grimly. "You'll do it because if you don't, I'll tell your loving husband all about your affair." Trish relished the momentary flash of fear in Meredith's expression, but expected more.

"What?" Meredith finally managed.

"Calvin Larkins."

Meredith looked around frantically. "Have you done something with him? He was supposed to meet me here."

Trish was momentarily taken aback. Meredith Brooks didn't seem distraught about her knowledge of the affair as much as she did about her beau's safety, and she'd admitted her guilt through association. Trish figured she'd deny the whole thing, leaving it to her word against Meredith's. A pillar of society versus a street rat. She'd played this as her last chance at retribution and it wasn't going as she'd planned.

"So you admit it?"

Meredith leveled her icy blue eyes at her. "It's not a great secret. Everyone on the staff here knows. I hear them snickering behind my back all the time. Once Victor takes a step away from the damnable company, he'll know, too. He already suspects. Where's Calvin?"

Trish didn't know what to say. Meredith didn't seem at all bothered with her threats. "I'll go to the papers. I'm sure they'd love a juicy tidbit about a rich wife of a leading war production company having an affair with a man half her age."

Meredith sighed, then leaned closer to Trish. "There's a war on. Do you really think anyone would care? Assuming the paper would even risk printing something based only on your input. I don't mean to be cruel, but your word against mine? You'd just embarrass yourself. Now, for the last time, what have you done with Calvin?"

"Nothing," Trish finally answered. "I told him to get lost. Told him I planned to expose your affair. He left in his jalopy."

"Oh dear, well, I guess you saved me the trouble." She downed her flute of champagne in one gulp. "Now, tell me what my husband's done, and why on earth I should help you."

12

After Sal's conversation with Meredith on their way to the country club, he had no intention of following Victor's orders to watch her and find her lover. But now, here he stood watching Meredith and Trish drinking flutes of champagne together. He couldn't imagine an odder pairing.

He couldn't get close enough to hear what they talked about, but he could tell it wasn't a comfortable meeting for either of them. Had Meredith set it up or had Trish?

When he pulled up to the front of the club, he noticed Trish right away. He hadn't let on, but felt intrigued enough to watch them, mostly because Meredith might be in danger. He'd seen Trish's takedown of the hapless doorman. She'd attacked brutally and efficiently, which gained her a modicum of his respect. Although it also cemented his intention to keep a close eye on her while she interacted with Meredith.

The pair leaned close to one another as though conspiring. He wished once again that he could hear the conversation. Victor wanted to know if she had a boyfriend. Sal already knew she did. He wouldn't pass that information onto Victor. He doubted this meeting had anything to do with that, but it piqued his interest.

The meetup finally broke up. Trish stood abruptly and looked around as though sensing someone watching. He'd tucked into the shadows and had a large bush in front of him, so he didn't fear her spotting him. He watched her strut from the patio as though she owned the place. She waved at one of the staff, who watched her with obvious ire. She winked and blew him a kiss. *Cheeky gal.*

She strode past Sal's hideout without a glance and disappeared around the corner. Sal watched Meredith. She didn't look well. She stared at her empty flute of champagne, spinning it in her supple hands. He had an urge to go to her, but suppressed it and cursed himself for even considering.

He felt compelled to follow Trish. He wanted to know what she was up to. He considered simply asking Meredith. After all, the cat was already out of the bag as far as her affair and him following her. He wondered at her frank openness with him. Lately, she seemed much more like she used to be in the old days . . . *passionate*, he realized. The result of her boyfriend, or something else?

He gave one last furtive glance at Meredith, then slunk from the shadows and rounded the corner where Trish had gone. He saw her walking briskly up the long club driveway toward the street. He doubted she had a car and wondered how she'd gotten there. Had she walked?

He considered getting in the Rolls, but didn't want to tail her in such a conspicuous vehicle. He trotted to the Rolls, flung his hat into the front seat, and scooped out an umbrella. It wasn't raining, but it threatened and he could use it as cover if needed.

Trish made it to the street. She hesitated, then waved and trotted toward an old car parked nearby. Sal reconsidered his options, then hustled back to the Rolls and into the driver's side. Ostentatious or not, if he wanted to tail her, he had to use the Rolls.

From his parking space, he watched Trish enter the passenger side door. He couldn't see the driver well, but thought it was a man. The old Ford pulled onto the road. Sal memorized the color and make, then pulled from the parking lot and drove up the driveway, then onto the street. He saw the Ford trundling along, heading back into the city. He followed at a reasonable distance.

Because of restrictive gasoline rationing, the streets were almost bare of vehicles. It made this sort of work much harder. He needed to stay close enough to see any route changes, but far enough away not to be noticed. If they suspected a tail, he'd be easy to spot.

Perhaps it would be better to guess where she might go. He knew where she lived. Getting noticed might inflame whatever was going on between Trish and Meredith. He decided tailing her would be much easier on foot, so he turned off and took an alternate route into the city.

He parked a few blocks from Trish's small apartment and walked the rest of the way. The Rolls stood out even in the affluent section of Seattle, but out here it might as well have a glowing sign above it, saying, "I don't belong, I don't belong."

He lit a cigarette and leaned on a building, watching the workaday folks passing by with their faces buried in newspapers.

The war news had improved somewhat on all Allied fronts. He paid more attention to the happenings in the Pacific theater. MacArthur's Sixth Army and Kinney's Fifth Air Force were pounding the Japanese on New Guinea. The island-hopping campaign happening further east under Admiral Nimitz also made significant gains. He didn't know if Clyde had made it to the front yet, since the family hadn't heard from Abigail in months. He'd read about successful airborne operations in the region, but didn't know if it had been Clyde's outfit. Sal didn't particularly like Clyde, but he hoped he'd survive the war.

Thinking of Abigail made him sad. The last time he'd seen her, at Miles's funeral, she'd glared at him with outright hostility. He didn't know why, and it broke his heart to think he'd earned her anger. When he'd pressed her, she'd stubbornly gone silent . . . the same way her mother occasionally shut him down when she was angry. Thoughts of Meredith swirled with thoughts of Abigail. *What a mess I've made.*

The old Ford finally showed up outside Trish's apartment building. It had taken longer than if they'd driven straight there from the country club, so they must've stopped somewhere along the way.

He noted the male driver. His head nearly touched the ceiling and his thick neck told him he was a big man. He didn't get out, but simply pulled up and Trish hopped out. She didn't look happy. She slammed the door and the tires squealed for a fraction of a second as he drove off quickly.

Neither of them seemed happy with the other. He wondered who the driver was and what they'd disagreed upon.

She stopped to light a cigarette at the top of the stairs leading down to her basement-level apartment. She studied her surroundings as she smoked, while constantly checking over her shoulder.

Sal noticed two men in long trench coats approaching from down the street. Something about the way they walked with purpose made the hairs on the back of his neck stand up. He remembered the incident at the poker club and wondered if these two had Tommy guns tucked beneath their coats.

Sal's shoulder holster carrying the .45-caliber pistol suddenly felt heavy. He'd started wearing it more since the poker incident. It would raise eyebrows if the cops saw it, but he kept it well hidden and as inconspicuous as possible. His credentials as security for Brooks Industries would dispel any further doubts.

He moved up the street until he came to the corner on the opposite side of Trish's apartment. Trish noticed the men and focused on them. She didn't run, but she didn't look happy about the imminent meet either. She flicked her cigarette butt and it hissed into the gutter, still running with rainwater.

The two men stopped in front of her. One of them talked while the other moved behind her, hemming her in. Trish shifted from foot-to-foot as though she needed to pee. She didn't look comfortable, despite the grin she'd painted on her face. The talker pulled out a cigarette of his own. He didn't offer one to Trish. As if in answer to whatever he'd said, she flung out her arms and he could hear her raised voice even from across the street, but he couldn't decipher what she said.

The man lit his cigarette and listened to her tirade dispassionately. He blew out a long stream of smoke, then pushed his index finger into Trish's chest. He leaned close to her and spoke, all the while tapping his finger into her upper chest.

Instead of the lion he'd seen attack the doorman at the club under similar circumstances, Trish now looked like a cowed sheep. She nodded and kept her gaze on her feet. These men, or more likely, who they represented, obviously scared her.

They finally left her standing there alone. She watched them saunter back the way they'd come. She lit another cigarette, then took the stairs to her apartment two at a time. He heard her door slam.

Sal considered his next move. He couldn't wait outside Trish's door all day. He blew out a long breath. The best play was to follow the men and find out who they worked for. He had a bad feeling about them.

Trish sat on her dingy couch and smoked one cigarette after another. She stuffed the last one of the pack into the overflowing ashtray. She'd need to buy more, but she didn't want to leave her apartment. She wasn't afraid of Trambolini's men jumping her. If they'd wanted to do that, they would've, but she didn't feel up to talking with anyone she might run into.

She leaned her head back and closed her eyes. If only Abby hadn't burned that damned journal. She'd been so close to finishing the job. She would've been paid, she'd have those thugs off her back, and she'd get at least some semblance of justice for Miles. But without Miles's journal, she had nothing.

When she'd stumbled across Meredith's affair, she thought she might have some kind of leverage, but Meredith didn't bat an eye. And Meredith was right. No one would take her word over Meredith's, even if she were worried about the consequences, which she didn't seem to be.

She'd actually enjoyed her visit with Abby's mother. Abby told her all sorts of terrible things about her, but she seemed more like Abby than anything, and she liked Abby. She'd also been impressed with Meredith's taste in men. Calvin, although a bit of a pussy, was handsome.

She wondered about Victor. Perhaps he wasn't as awful as Abby made him out to be, either. But no, she'd seen his evil firsthand, or at least the results. His cutting corners to save money had killed poor Miles and given her a burned head.

She knew all about such men. Greed and power made him tick. Just because he owned and operated a legitimate business, didn't give him the right to do whatever the hell he wanted. Being a pillar of society and owning a war-related business just made it harder to bring him down, but no one was above the law. Well, almost no one. She doubted Julius Trambolini worried much about the law. Hell, he probably owned half the force.

Although Meredith hadn't felt intimidated by the threat to expose her affair, she'd seemed appalled to learn about the way her husband chose greed over the safety of his employees. Trish had detailed the actions leading up to Miles's death. *Appalled, but not surprised.* She realized, now.

She almost didn't tell her about the arson. But she was good at reading people and she thought Meredith might turn on her husband if given enough reasons to do so. After all, Meredith talked about him as though he were a colleague rather than her longtime husband.

She'd seen outright disgust when she detailed the fire. She'd asked a curious question, though. "Was Sal involved?" When Trish told her he'd helped plan the whole thing, it surprised her to see that Meredith looked more disappointed with him than her husband. Almost as though she expected such things from Victor, but not from Sal. Curious, indeed. But, despite all that, Meredith didn't give her what she wanted.

Back at square one. How could she finish the job and get paid?

She'd already spent most of the initial payment they'd given her. If she couldn't deliver the final product, the thugs she'd just encountered made it clear they would expect her to pay it back.

She didn't have any side projects in the works—the damned factory job had taken too much of her time for that sort of thing. She had to figure out a way to finish the job, or . . . or what? Trambolini didn't want her dead. They might rough her up—put her in the hospital—make her do odd jobs until they felt she'd done enough to pay them back. That might never end. She'd be some kind of indentured servant to the Trambolini clan for the rest of her life.

She removed her hat and rubbed the splotches of hair. The scars from the burns would always remind her of Miles Burr, Victor Brooks, and pain. She still had nightmares about being on fire. She hated the weakness of that, but the nightmares didn't care how she felt. Maybe they'd disappear if she could end the job to her satisfaction. She didn't want to end up in the hospital again.

Talking with Johnnie hadn't helped things either. He'd agreed to take her to the country club and pick her up. He was the only person she knew who still owned a car—piece of shit, but more than she had.

She'd grilled him about the secretive job he still worked. They obviously paid well. At their first meet up a few months ago, he'd asked her about Sal Sarducci. His employer wanted to know more about him. She'd turned the conversation and eked some information out of Johnnie about his employer. He worked for someone who'd had their business physically burned down and thought Victor Brooks had given the order. It took little digging to find the business that fit that bill. Beyond finding the name Trask Industries, she hadn't pursued the lead. Perhaps she should.

She hadn't been able to get Johnnie to give her any more information. He wouldn't go into detail and wouldn't let her in on the job, either. Johnnie grilled her in turn, wanting to know what she had on Victor Brooks. He even said his employer would offer her more money than whoever had hired her. She doubted that, but still wouldn't tell him who she worked for. He might not be so cavalier if he knew.

She was no closer to finding an answer. She stood, paced the small room a few times, and decided she needed more smokes. *I'll think of something. I always do.*

Sal followed the two trench coat–wearing thugs for a few blocks. They entered four different businesses. They spent ten minutes in each and came back outside without bags, telling him they'd bought nothing.

They walked the streets as though they owned them. Again, he was reminded of the men he'd killed at the poker club—Trambolini men. These men matched the description. He wasn't positive, but who else? That meant that Trish had some sort of connection with them. Had she borrowed money? The factory job she left fairly recently paid well. She wouldn't need to borrow money unless she needed a large sum.

He'd used a few police connections he still had downtown and dug into her past when he'd noticed her and Abigail hanging around together. She didn't have any family, at least none he could find in the Seattle area. She'd been arrested once for petty theft, but the charge hadn't stuck. As far as he could tell, she lived simply, each little hustle adding to her coffers. She bounced around from shady gig to shady gig like a pinball. He couldn't imagine why she'd need to borrow a large amount of money.

Then it hit him like a ton of bricks. She was doing a job *for* the Trambolinis.

It made sense. It had surprised him when he saw her on the Brooks Industries employee roster. She'd worked for months on the factory line and become a reliable worker. Had that all been a front? He remembered thinking about this before, but he'd let it slip. But now it hit him square in the face. Trambolini must have hired her to get inside Brooks Industries. But for what purpose? *Dirt. I killed Julius Trambolini's nephew and he wants revenge.*

Despite Victor and Julius having a friendly talk over dinner about the unfortunate incident and supposedly putting it behind them, perhaps Julius had put up a false front. He was gunning for Victor, possibly him, too.

He watched the thugs round the corner. He thought about confronting them. They were undoubtedly armed, but so was he. But even if he got the drop on them, they wouldn't tell him anything, even if they knew—especially if they knew. Say what you want about organized crime, but trust and deep bonds held them together. Besides, he wanted to keep this under wraps. If Julius knew he was onto them, it would become much harder to watch them.

He needed to let Victor know right away.

Sal drove to the factory and parked in one of the few provided parking spaces. Brooks Industries had expanded and they'd built on every little piece of land, including parts of the parking lot.

The sounds of heavy machinery and the smell of oil and gas met him as he strode through the door. Victor usually spent Tuesdays at the factory office, meeting with shift leads and foremen personally. He claimed he liked to see the factory working, but Sal knew he liked his subordinates to know he was always watching.

He took the stairs two at a time. He entered the small space where underlings would sit and wait to be called in to confer with the headman. A pretty secretary sat behind a large desk. It seemed much too large for her. A man dressed in a suit sat in one of the comfortable chairs, reading a new copy of Life magazine. He looked over the edge of the magazine and nodded at Sal. Sal recognized him as one of the foremen in charge of blasting caps—Miles Burr's replacement. He hoped he didn't suffer the same fate as his predecessor.

"Mr. Sarducci. What a surprise," the pretty secretary beamed.

He ignored her fluttering eyelids and stepped past the desk and stood at the locked door.

She pushed a button and spoke into an intercom. "Mr. Sarducci is here, sir."

"Sal? Send him in."

She pressed a different button, and the electronic lock disengaged with a loud buzz and click. Sal remembered discussing the fancy lock system with Victor. He thought it a silly expense. "Why not just get off your ass and turn the lock manually," he'd asked, but Victor enjoyed such things. As a bonus, it might impress—even intimidate the men sitting in the lobby.

He closed the heavy door behind him, and he heard it automatically lock. Victor gave him a wan smile. He didn't like surprises. "Here for a late lunch?" Victor asked. "Or you've already found Meredith's lover, perhaps?" His eyes hardened dangerously.

"It's not about that. We might have a different, bigger problem."

Victor scowled. "What kind of problem?"

"The Julius Trambolini kind."

"Trambolini? Tell me."

Sal explained the who, what, and where, and how he'd learned them. He didn't mention his conversation with Meredith in the Rolls, however. He respected her more than Victor lately. They'd been friends a long time, but Victor wasn't the same kid he'd known growing up, or even the man who'd struggled to build a now thriving business. He'd become—*ruthless*.

When he'd finished, Victor stroked his silver mustache. He stood abruptly and looked out the double-paned windows overlooking the factory floor. Despite the proximity of hundreds of machines and workers, barely any sound could penetrate.

"You're speculating."

"Yes, but it makes sense. I always felt there was something off about Miss Watson working here. It's not like her kind to suddenly take on gainful employment. Street rats like it easy."

"Hmm, well, you'd know more about that sort of thing than I would."

Sal bristled, but realized he didn't mean it the way it sounded.

"But what was she after? I mean, even as a worker, she wouldn't have access to anything incriminating."

"The better question is, what's Julius after? What's his endgame?"

"If it is Julius . . . perhaps I should invite him to dinner. I could figure out if he has some kind of vendetta against me. I'm good at reading people."

"Like you read him the first time?" Victor bristled, and Sal continued. "He's a master of subterfuge. He lies for a living and he's good at making you think what he wants you to think."

"This could all be just you being paranoid, Sal. It's all circumstantial."

It was Sal's turn to bristle. "It's my job to protect this family. I think it's a genuine threat. At least one we need to consider and be ready to defend against."

"What do you think he's after? If he wants revenge for his nephew, why not just have you killed? You're the one that shot him."

"I don't know for sure. But I *do* know he can't let his nephew's death go unanswered. He may go after your business. Getting dirt on you to put you out of business."

Victor grunted a sharp laugh. "Dirt? He's a mafioso boss for chrissakes."

"It's why he'd know what to look for."

"There's nothing . . ." he stopped and stroked his mustache. "I suppose the arson could be a problem."

"I was thinking the same thing. If he could prove you were behind that, no judge in the world would take your side. Hell, the judge might give Trask your business as compensation, not to mention that you'd be behind bars faster than you can say Peter Rabbit."

"Don't look so pleased. You'd be right beside me."

Sal crossed his arms and stared at his old friend. "You'd turn me in?"

"I'd be testifying under oath—I'd have to tell them everything. They'd find out anyway and if they found I lied, it would be worse for me." He shook his head emphatically. "But—but this is ridiculous. If he had something on me, he'd already have done something. The fact that you saw his men harassing our friend Miss Watson proves it. They have nothing. She failed, and they're clearly unhappy with her." He sat on the edge of his large desk. He said, "Miles certainly isn't going to talk, but what about the other two? What are their names?"

"Matthew Clevenger and Bartholomew Hanready."

Victor looked him in the eye. "Hmm. Yes, I wonder if something needs to be done about them."

Sal's eyes narrowed. "I'm not killing anyone for you, Victor."

Victor stared at him for a long moment before finally saying, "No, I don't suppose you would. I wonder if something less dramatic could be done. Do you know where they are?"

Sal raised an eyebrow. "Last I checked, they were working at 'crucial to the war effort,' jobs downtown. Why?" he asked suspiciously.

"Well, there is a rather large war going on. Surely the service would welcome the addition of two bright young men to the ranks."

"How the hell could we make that happen? Their parents run in the same circles you do."

"We'll set them up for a fall. Illicit drugs, maybe prostitutes, too. Use your imagination. I'll be sure the honorable Franklin Hornsby hears their cases. He'll give them a choice of a long prison term or the army infantry." He smiled. "Happens all the time."

"Jesus, Victor. When did you become such a cruel son of a bitch?"

Victor erupted from behind the desk and stood facing Sal, eyeball-to-eyeball. "You need to remember who you work for, Sal. I won't tolerate your weakness much longer."

Sal wanted to throttle him. He'd never heard such venom in Victor's voice, but instead of fear, it made him angry. "I can't work for you anymore, Mr. Brooks."

"This is what I'm talking about. You're like a simpering woman! Be careful what you say, Sal. You aren't exactly innocent."

Sal could feel the scar running up from his chin pulse. He looked into Victor's seething eyes. "You threatening me?" his voice was low and dangerous.

Victor didn't budge. "I'm laying down the facts. If you don't have the stomach for it, I'll get someone who does."

Sal took a step back. "I won't do your dirty work anymore, Victor. You're on your own." He turned and strode to the door. He gripped the doorknob, but it remained locked. "Open the door or I'll tear it off the hinges," he said calmly.

"Sal . . ." Victor's voice had taken on a more reasonable tone.

"Unlock the door!" Sal yelled. The door buzzed and Sal flung it open. Without turning around, he said, "Goodbye, Victor."

Victor didn't stop him. Sal marched through the waiting room, ignoring the stunned looks from the secretary and the foreman. He took the stairs two at a time. He considered walking or paying for a cabbie, but he used the Rolls one last time. He needed to pack and say goodbye to the staff at the estate. He'd known many of them for years. He didn't want to leave, but he didn't see any other choice.

He sat in the Rolls and rubbed his hand along the leather steering wheel he so lovingly oiled once a week. He'd miss the plush vehicle, but he'd miss the Brooks family more. But that wasn't quite true. Things hadn't been good for years now. Perhaps it would never be the same. He missed what it used to be like.

What would Abigail think of his sudden departure? Perhaps he'd track her down in Texas. Not knowing why she seemed to despise him tore him up inside. He needed to find out. Suddenly, he wanted nothing more than to find her and talk. He missed her more than he cared to admit, but first he needed to see Meredith. He couldn't move on with his life until he set things right with her.

13

Sal stood in the doorway of the now empty small garden house he'd lived in for the past twenty-plus years. The little kitchen and the pots and pans he rarely used hung over the equally unused stove. He'd taken most of his meals in the main house with the staff. He'd miss Chef Peterson's cooking. Would he ever eat another of her decadently delicious desserts?

He'd already said his goodbyes to the staff. They'd listened in stunned shock as he told them he was retiring. He didn't go into detail, but everyone realized something drastic had happened between himself and Victor. Tears had been shed, not by him, but by those who loved him. It almost made him reconsider, but he had no intention of groveling in front of Victor and no intention of performing any more unsavory tasks for the man.

He hefted his suitcase and closed the door of the little building. He locked the door and left the key in the keyhole. Would anyone move into the space? The staff, with the exception of Mr. Hanniger, lived in their own houses or apartments and commuted.

He walked to the driveway and heard the crunching of rocks as a vehicle approached. He'd called for a cab, but it was only a few minutes ago. This couldn't be it already. A yellow cab pulled to the front and stopped. Meredith stepped out. She was early. He stopped, hoping she didn't see him, but also hoping she would. On his way back from his meeting with Victor, he'd decided to leave without speaking to Meredith, yet. He'd do it later once he had his own place.

She leaned in and said something to the cabbie. Sal thought he may as well use the cab so he stepped forward.

Meredith saw him and smiled. "Sal, hello." Her expression turned to concern as she noticed his suitcase. "Are you finally heading off on vacation?"

"No, Meredith. I'm leaving—permanently. I'm retiring. It's time for me to move on."

Meredith recoiled, as though someone had physically struck her. "What? What are you talking about? You can't—what's happened?" She looked panicked. The cab pulled away and Sal let it go.

"It's just time. I've been thinking of leaving for a while now. I've got money saved up, so don't worry, I'll be fine."

"But—but this is so sudden. Were you even going to tell me? What if I hadn't come home early?"

"I—I don't know. I just have to leave. I can't work for him any longer, Meredith. I'm sorry."

Her eyes turned hard. "What's he done? What has Victor done?"

Sal considered telling her, but thought it wasn't his place to disparage her husband when he wasn't there to defend himself.

Meredith surprised him. "Is it about the arson? Did he ask you to do something like that again?"

He looked around nervously, then stepped forward and clutched her elbow. Her scent intoxicated him momentarily and he remembered, as he always did, her beautiful naked body spread out in front of him. He suppressed the feeling, as always, and said, "Keep your voice down. How do you know about that?"

She placed her hand on his. "Trish Watkins. I just met with her this morning at the club. She—well, she threatened to expose my affair if I didn't give her information. She wants revenge for Miles. When I didn't bite, she mentioned the arson and also what he did to Miles."

Sal scowled. "How does she know about the fire?" he wondered out loud.

"She and Miles were an item. Lovers, apparently."

"I can't believe he'd tell her something like that, lovers or not." He had a hard time picturing them together in the first place—an odd couple, no doubt.

"He didn't. She told me she read it in his journal."

"Journal? Chrissakes, there's a journal?"

"Yes, but Abigail destroyed it according to Trish. That's why she tried to blackmail me. She has no more options."

"Tried?"

"I told her I wouldn't help her bring my own husband down. She's obviously desperate. She has nothing or she wouldn't have come to me."

"What if she's not bluffing about the affair?"

She waved her hand as though shooing a fly away. "I'm not worried about that. Even if she did, no one would have a reason to believe her. And I really doubt anyone except Victor would care. It's over, by the way."

"What's over?"

"My affair. I won't see him again."

He could see the hurt in her eyes and he felt a surge of jealousy, but he suppressed it quickly. He wanted to hug her, but didn't.

Instead, he thought about the two thugs who'd met Trish outside her apartment. Trish trying to blackmail Meredith only confirmed his suspicions that she was desperately trying to get out from beneath whatever they had on her. What *did* they have on her?

Was she still a threat? Was there any more evidence she could dig up to hurt the family? He thought about the two men who'd helped Miles burn down the factory. Would Trish know about them? And if she did, would they tell her anything? No, but they might tell those thugs, particularly if they used enhanced methods of persuasion. Perhaps Victor's idea of having the spoiled brats sent to fight the Nazis wasn't such a terrible idea after all.

He scowled as he realized he was acting as though he still worked for Victor. None of this was his business any longer.

"What's going through your head, Sal?"

He broke from his thoughts. He liked when she used his first name. The intimacy rang in his ears. A memory of her husky, passionate voice while she bit his ear in shared ecstasy flooded through him.

"I've done this job too long. I was thinking about potential threats and how to counter them, but I don't work here anymore."

"You can't leave, Sal. Not now." She touched his arm and he felt her heat through his sleeve.

"I have to. I—well, it's just time for me to go."

"But where will you go? Where will you live? You don't even have a car."

"I'll manage. Won't take long to find an apartment. Couple of days in a hotel downtown is all. I've saved plenty of money over the years."

A second cab pulled into the driveway and trundled along the gravel. She put her other hand on his shoulder and looked up at him. He stared down into her eyes. He wanted to kiss her, but knew it was far too late for such things.

She said, "I can't imagine never seeing you again, Sal. I don't want that. You're a part of this family."

The rest of the staff came out of the estate and stood on the ornate stone entryway. Meredith leaned into his powerful frame and hugged him fiercely. He wrapped his arms around her and hugged her back. He could feel her shake as she cried against his chest. It sparked a vivid memory. Only she'd been naked and they'd just finished making love in her marital bed. Her tears back then weren't tears of sorrow, but of sheer ecstasy and lust.

The cab pulled up and the cabbie leaned over and rolled down the window. "This the place? You, Mr. Sarducci?"

Sal broke away from Meredith and nodded at the cabbie. "Gimme a minute." He stared into Meredith's eyes. "It's not forever, okay. I'm not leaving the city, at least not yet." He looked at the rest of the staff he'd spent so much of his life with. He felt a heaviness in his heart. He'd miss these fine people. He hefted his bag and waved. The staff, some with tears glistening on their cheeks, waved back. He stepped into the back of the cab and sat down heavily. He forced himself not to look back as they drove down the long driveway.

"Where to, pal?"

Sal read off an address and asked, "You know it?"

He gave an exasperated whistle, then nodded. "Yeah, I know it. It's in the city. Who's the dame?" When he saw Sal's glare, he shrugged and kept driving.

Meredith felt awful. After Sal left, she went to her room, plunked down on the bed, and cried. Sal had been a part of her life since she'd first met Victor. He'd always been on the sidelines, Victor's odd friend that didn't quite fit in. She knew they'd grown up together. Victor told her the story of their diverging paths with a gleam in his eye. Sal had gone off to war and Victor had gone into business. Even though they had taken massively different paths, they respected each other, and had come back together after the war. Neither man would say so, but she'd seen the love they held for one another. They'd been best friends. But not now—now she'd seen only the bitterness in Sal's eyes when he spoke about her husband.

What had happened to their relationship? *Probably the same thing that's happened to ours*, she thought bitterly. Little by little, Victor was tearing the family apart. First Abigail, now Sal.

She blushed, remembering the one night she'd made love with Sal. *No, not love. We screwed!* She blushed deeper and her ears turned hot.

She'd ended things with Calvin that very day. Now she wished she'd waited. She yearned for a man to hold her, but she couldn't very well call on him. She didn't want to confuse the poor boy.

The tears flowed heavier. *I'm a married woman, yet there's no love in my life. How did it come to this?*

What would happen if she went to Victor's bed tonight? Would he shun her or welcome her with open arms? Surely, he could be capable of love still—if even just out of a physical need. But after their argument, he'd be cold as ice.

Sitting through dinner would be awful enough. She wouldn't even know how to broach the subject of sex. Did he have a mistress? Did he even think of her in that way anymore? Once, long ago, it was all he thought about. He couldn't keep his hands off of her. They'd screwed like rabbits. Those were the happiest days of her life.

She pictured herself lying there crying. It angered her. What had she told Abigail? Be a lioness!

She wiped her tears and sat up in bed. She wished she could call on Abigail, talk with her only daughter the way they used to when she was just a little girl, so full of wonderful questions. Such a glorious imagination she had. What wonderful adventures she must be having in Texas. She'd been gone for months now. Would she be done with her training? And what about Clyde?

She suddenly felt sick to her stomach. She hadn't thought about Clyde in weeks. Guilt ate at her guts. What if something happened to him? Would Abigail abandon her flying and return home?

She decided then and there that she'd visit Clyde's parents. If she hadn't thought about Clyde in weeks, she hadn't thought about his parents in months. *What kind of person am I?*

She'd been endlessly selfish. She remembered meeting them at the wedding, of course. They were working-class people. She liked them, but they had little in common besides their children being married to one another. What would it be like when Abigail had children? Would she be an estranged grandmother? She didn't want that. She suddenly felt an over-whelming need to reconnect with her daughter. Perhaps the Coopers had Abigail's address.

Sal would know where they lived—then she remembered. She supposed Mr. Hanniger would know. He could drive her there in the Rolls. She suddenly missed Sal very much. Would she ever sit behind him as he drove her around to her various meetings? She always felt safe in his presence. She adored Mr. Hanniger, too, but it wouldn't be the same.

She checked the time. The dinner hour approached. Did she have time to go to the Coopers' house? No, she'd do it tomorrow. She didn't want to put them out. Perhaps she should call first, but she remembered they didn't have a phone. She'd just have to hope Mrs. Cooper, Cecilia, she recalled with a snap of her fingers, would be there tomorrow morning. She wiped her eyes, went to the vanity and touched up her makeup. Perhaps she'd try to make peace with Victor—then who knows?

Meredith wore a dress to dinner, which she hadn't worn in years. She remembered Victor liked it. In fact, she might have been wearing it the last time they'd made love. Would he remember? She had no illusions. Even the most romantically inclined man wouldn't remember such a thing years after the fact. Perhaps he would've when they were first married, but not now.

Victor came into the dining room and barely looked at her. He sat down, tucked his napkin onto his lap and took a long gulp of red wine. The serving staff served fresh bread and a salad. He pecked at the salad, spread butter on the bread and tore large chunks that flaked onto his plate.

She watched him closely. Sal, his oldest and most dear friend, had walked out of their lives, but he appeared unfazed. She thought about the arson, but tried not to let it cloud her mind. She wanted to focus on the positive in him. It must still exist somewhere in the depths of his soul.

"How was your day, dear?" she asked.

He glanced up and gave her a wan smile. "Fine, dear. You?"

"Awful, really."

He looked genuinely surprised. "Awful? What happened? Did you get kicked out of the Bridge Club?"

She felt his biting words like physical sword cuts, but bore up and did her best to ignore the gibes. "Well, you must know that Sal left. Surely you know that?"

His eyes hardened. "Oh yes. You heard then. I think he'll cool off and realize he's made a huge mistake. He'll be back."

"I don't think so. He packed his things and drove off in a cab. I saw him off. The entire staff did. He's not coming back, dear."

He stroked his mustache, then took another sip of wine. "Hmm. It's unfortunate, but perhaps it was time for him to move on."

"That's it? That's all you have to say about your childhood friend leaving? He's like family."

He shook his head slowly. "No. He's not family. Family wouldn't leave."

"Abigail left."

"She'll be back. He will, too. And when he does, I'll make him beg for his job back."

Meredith closed her eyes. This would be harder than she imagined. How could she seduce a man with such a vile character?

"Do you remember this dress, Victor?"

He glanced up from his bread and squinted at her. "Um, no. should I? It looks a bit dated to tell you the truth."

She stood and walked to his side. He watched her as though wondering how the animals had gotten past the bars at the zoo. She swayed her hips and leaned over so he'd get a good look at her cleavage. It used to drive him crazy with lust.

"What are you doing?"

"Let's sleep in the same bed tonight, Victor. Like we used to. You don't show it, but I know you're upset about Sal leaving. I've known you too long. We're both sad, let's console one another. It's been far too long." She leaned on the table, seductively twirling a ringlet of hair.

"What's gotten into you? Have you been drinking all day? You sound like a harlot."

"No, I'm not drunk. I—I want to be with my *husband*."

"What about your boyfriend? What about him?"

She knew he didn't know about Calvin, just had suspicions. She didn't want to lie or play games, but she also knew if she admitted it, it would be the final nail in the coffin of their marriage. There would be no kind of reconciliation. He loved lording things over her far too much to simply let it go, and she wasn't willing to beg him for anything.

"I don't have a boyfriend." She wasn't lying. She'd dumped Calvin that morning. "But that doesn't mean I don't have urges and needs."

He sat back and dropped his salad fork onto the plate with a loud clatter. "Don't be disgusting. What's gotten into you? You must be drunk."

"I'm not drunk! My God, Victor, have you no passion left? I want to make love to you. Don't you understand that? Am I not being clear?"

He stared at her for a long moment. He wiped his mouth and pushed his chair away from the table. "I've lost my appetite." He stood and looked her up and down. "Good night." He strode out of the dining room and slammed the door behind him.

His words hurt, but not as much as she thought they would. She didn't expect seducing him would be easy. Indeed, she figured it would end the way it just did. She just hoped it might lead to something more. She sighed and wished once again that she hadn't broken things off with Calvin.

She retreated to her salad and bread. The main course came out and she enjoyed the perfectly cooked filet mignon all by herself. She sipped her wine and toasted Victor's empty chair. "To my lost love." She drained it in one long gulp.

Where was Sal spending the night? She hoped he'd be alright. Men always said they were fine no matter if it was the truth or not. They were all afraid of showing weakness. A weakness all unto itself.

Amanda came in with the wine and filled her glass. "Everything okay, ma'am?"

"Fine, fine. Would you like to join me for dinner? Seems I've been stood up."

Claire looked toward the door, no doubt wondering how it would look to the others if she took Meredith up on the offer.

"I could use the company," Meredith pressed.

Claire sat beside her but kept on the side of the chair, ready to bolt at a moment's notice. "Yes, ma'am. I've already eaten but I can keep you company if you like."

Meredith cut a piece of meat and stabbed it with her fork. She held it up and studied it. "Such wonderful meat. Perfectly cooked. I hope you enjoyed yours?"

"Oh, no. The filets are for you and Mr. Brooks, ma'am."

Meredith was genuinely surprised. "I thought the staff ate the same meals we do."

"We did before the rationing. But now it's just too scarce."

"How many steaks do we have?"

"Um, I don't know, off the top of my head, but at least eight pounds' worth. Different cuts, of course."

Meredith smiled. "I'm going to take some of it as a gift for someone I've neglected for far too long."

"Very good, ma'am. If you don't mind my asking, who?"

"Clyde's parents, the Coopers. I plan on visiting them tomorrow."

"I'm sure they'll be overjoyed, ma'am."

"And buy no more meat unless it's easily available. The entire country's on rations. We should be, too."

Claire looked at her hands. "Um, I'm not in charge of buying, but Mr. Brooks has told Claude not to skimp."

Meredith realized she'd lost her hold on the household. She used to be in charge of such things, but now it had fallen to Victor through her own negligence. She'd rectify that, too. In the meantime, she'd enjoy the rest of her steak dinner.

The next day, Meredith dug through her address book and found The Cooper residence address. She didn't want to split Mr. Hanniger's duties at the house, so she hailed a cab.

After a long ride into the city, the cabbie pulled up outside a row of neatly kept, small houses packed tightly together. She'd never been there and felt bad about that. She'd never even considered visiting before. *How selfish of me.*

She paid the cabbie and stepped out of the vehicle, but poked her head back in. "I'll just see if they're home. Would you mind waiting? In case they aren't home."

He grunted his assent and she went to the low gate and opened it onto the small front yard. She imagined Clyde and his brother—*what was his name? Oh yes, Frank*—playing in the yard as children. As she approached the front door, she noticed the stars on the windows, letting everyone know they had two family members serving overseas.

She remembered that Frank, the older boy, was a prisoner of war. She shuddered, wondering what that must be like. Not knowing if he was alive or dead must be gut-wrenchingly difficult. She felt even more guilty for not checking in with them before now.

She knocked tentatively on the door and waited. Footsteps approached. She straightened herself, not knowing if she'd even be allowed inside. Since the wedding, she had basically ignored them. She certainly wouldn't blame them if they turned her away.

The door opened and Cecelia Cooper stood there. She wiped her hands on an apron. A strand of hair hung down over her eyebrow and she blew it away from the corner of her mouth, but didn't otherwise react.

Meredith wondered if she might not recognize her. "Hello, Cecilia. It's Meredith Brooks—Abigail's mother."

Cecilia nodded and gave her a tight smile. "Yes, I know who you are. What are you doing here?"

Meredith felt immediately defensive. She squelched the urge to lash out at her. Her old self would've certainly done so.

"You have every right not to want me here. I've—well, I've been selfish and awful." She turned to leave but the cab had already left.

Cecilia opened the door wider and stepped aside. "You may as well come in. I've just heated some water. I don't have straight coffee, but the chicory I added isn't too bad."

Meredith smelled baked goods wafting over her. "Thank you. I'd love a cup, if you can spare it."

Cecilia closed the door behind her. Meredith looked around at the small, immaculately kept space. She noticed pictures of Clyde in his paratrooper uniform, looking happy, and also beside him a picture, which she assumed to be Frank in his army uniform. He had a stern, no-nonsense look about him.

"Have a seat. I'll bring out a tray."

Meredith watched her disappear behind a swinging kitchen door. Beyond it, she saw cooking utensils and a messy countertop. She went to the couch and sat down on the edge. On the low coffee table sat an old tattered copy of Life magazine. It looked as though they had read it a thousand times over.

In the corner, beside a radiator, was an old, well-used leather chair. She supposed it must be Mr. Cooper's spot to read the paper. An ashtray had a few half-smoked cigars sticking out the sides. She also noticed a pipe. She could picture the two sitting here every evening, gleaning the newspapers and magazines for any hint of information regarding their two sons. It made her heart ache.

Cecilia backed through the swinging door and placed a tray with two coffee cups and a small steaming carafe. There was even a small tin of sugar cubes and cream.

Meredith said, "Oh thank you. You didn't need to go to all that trouble."

Cecilia waved it off. "Nonsense. It's not every day Meredith Brooks comes for a visit."

She might have meant it sweetly, but Meredith felt the biting bitterness.

She found herself having to override the urge to put Cecelia in her place. Two warring factions struggled inside her. One had been in power for most of her adult life, and the usurper once reigned supreme in her youth. How had she ever let the spite, hate, and pride take center stage?

"I know it seems sudden and completely unlike me. I would've called ahead, but I don't have your number."

"We don't have a phone—so there is no number to call," she stated without a hint of anger or pity.

"I wanted to visit. I—I've been—well, it's just inexcusable that I don't have you and your family in my life."

Cecilia poured the coffee. "Would you like cream and sugar?"

"Yes, thank you."

Cecilia added a sugar cube and splashed cream in carefully, as though spilling even a drop would be a crime.

Meredith realized it must be her coveted supply of cream and sugar. "Just a whisker will do, thank you. I know how hard these things are to come by."

"Do you? I wouldn't think it would affect you much."

Meredith felt her face color. She sipped the coffee and couldn't keep her nose from crinkling. It didn't taste like the rich, dark roasted coffee she normally drank every morning. She set the cup down and forced a smile. "It's lovely. Thank you."

Cecilia genuinely smiled for the first time since she'd arrived. "You've obviously never had chicory coffee, have you?"

"Chicory? No. It's—it's different."

Cecilia laughed heartily. "Yes, it's certainly different from what you're used to. I haven't tasted straight coffee for months now." She sipped her brew and smacked her lips. "You get used to it after a while." Meredith noticed she hadn't used the cream or sugar. She felt even more the fool.

She remembered the bag she'd brought. "Speaking of which—I brought you a gift."

Cecilia looked puzzled and a little suspicious. "A gift?"

Meredith hefted the bag onto her lap. She opened it and pulled out the stack of fresh meat. "It's steak. Ten pounds worth."

Cecilia's eyes nearly bugged out of her ruddy face. "Goodness sakes. How—where?"

Meredith's smile spread. "I asked the staff to gather it up for you. It's just Victor and I. We don't need even half of it. Please take it and enjoy."

Cecilia placed the meat on her lap atop her apron. She held it as though she held the Crown Jewels. "It's a wonderful gift, Mrs. Brooks. Thank you."

"Please, call me Meredith."

"Only if you call me Ceecee."

"Ceecee. Okay, wonderful."

Cecilia stood abruptly. "I'll need to get this into the icebox. Excuse me a moment."

"Of course." Cecelia went to a door in the back of the living room. Stairs led down to a basement. She descended slowly and Meredith heard the stairs creaking and groaning with each step.

She sipped the coffee and forced herself not to spit it back out. It tasted bitter, even with the sugar cube. She wanted to flood it with cream and at least three more sugar cubes, but fought the urge.

She saw a picture of what must either be Cecelia's husband or a grandfather wearing an old-style U.S. Army uniform. She realized she knew very little about the Cooper family. Were they from a military family? That would explain why Frank had been in the service before the war started.

Cecilia came up from the basement with a broad grin. "That's the first meat that's been in there since we ran out. I think I might have the neighbors over to help us enjoy it. It's too much for just me and Sid. It's been a rough year for everyone."

Meredith pondered that. Besides her daughter leaving the area, she'd barely noticed any difference since the war began—certainly not rationing. A fresh wave of guilt swept over her. She felt incredibly out of touch with normal, everyday folks. The first time Cecelia, Ceecee, gets a gift of food, she's already planning on sharing the wealth with her friends. Her old self vied to put her down, but no—she was obviously a good woman with an enormous heart.

"Have you heard any news from your oldest son?" she asked carefully.

Cecilia sat down and took a sip of coffee before answering. "Not since the Red Cross letter. He's a POW somewhere in the Philippines." She wrung her thick hands. "I know he's okay, though. Call it a mother's intuition, but I *know* he's still alive."

Meredith wondered if she'd know if something had happened to Abigail? She doubted it very much. She didn't share such a deep connection with anyone in her life. It saddened her.

"It must be so hard for you."

"It is—it is." She shrugged. "But I pray for him every day. I trust he'll come through it all okay."

"How about Clyde? Have you heard from him?"

Her eyes brightened and she clapped her hands together. "Yes. He finds the time to write us at least twice a month." She went to the bureau with the pictures on top and pulled a stack of letters from the top drawer. She waved them as though showing off her most prized possession. "The mail service is slow, but his last letter came all the way from New Guinea. I didn't even know such a place existed. He doesn't let on, but I can tell he's been through some tough times."

"Oh, it's so good to hear he's alright. I've been worried about him."

"Doesn't Abby tell you about him? I know she gets far more letters from him than we do. It's only right, of course."

Meredith felt an iciness dig into her stomach. "Does—does Abby write you, too?"

"Well, yes, of course. Not often, about once a month. She writes beautifully. You must be so proud of all she's doing. It's so exciting."

"I'm afraid I wouldn't know."

"What do you mean? She doesn't write to you?" She put her hand to her chest as though she couldn't imagine a more heartbreaking scenario.

Meredith shook her head sadly and picked at her cuticles. "She didn't even leave us a forwarding address, so I can't write her." She looked up and gave Cecelia a tight smile. "She didn't leave on the best terms, I'm afraid. But I miss her terribly." She didn't allow the tears forming in the corners of her eyes to fall. She blinked them away quickly.

"My goodness, how terrible." She set her coffee down. "Would you like to stay for lunch? Sidney comes home for lunch on Wednesdays since he has a longer break."

Meredith didn't want to overstay her welcome. She desperately wanted to ask if she could have Abigail's address in Texas, but knew it would ask her to betray Abigail's trust.

She stood and straightened her dress. "No, no. I won't impose. I just wanted to deliver the meat and see how you were doing—and to apologize for being so wretched. I'm truly sorry. I'll pray for both Clyde and Frank's safe returns."

Cecilia touched her shoulder tenderly. "Thank you. That means a lot. Please don't be a stranger. Our door's always open to you, your husband, too."

Meredith couldn't imagine Victor dropping by here, but smiled. "Thank you, Ceecee, and the same goes for you. If there's anything we can do for you, don't hesitate to ask." She almost laughed at the thought of Victor coming home to see Ceecee and Sidney sitting at their dinner table.

"We get along okay, but thank you." She held up a finger as though remembering something. "There is one thing you could do for me."

"Yes, anything."

"I wrote a letter to your daughter and haven't had time to post it. Would you mind putting it in the mailbox for me on your way out?" She went to the bureau and handed her an envelope with Abby's name across the top—and her address.

Meredith couldn't keep the tears from escaping this time. She wiped them quickly, but her cheeks remained wetted. "Yes—yes, of course. I'd be happy to." She stared at the address, memorizing it through blurry eyes.

Cecilia walked her to the door. As Meredith strode down the path to the mailbox, she stopped and turned back to Cecilia. "Thank you," she said, her voice heavy with emotion. "Thank you."

Cecilia smiled and said, "Mothers and daughters should know each other's hearts. Be well, Meredith."

14

NOVEMBER 1943

Austin, Texas

Abby felt the breeze blowing against her face. She glanced over the side of the Stearman at the endless landscape of Texas. It looked mostly brown with splotches of color here and there. Cultivated fields formed perfect squares separated by long, lonely dirt roads. The airfield cut through the desolate countryside like a finger swipe across a dirty window.

She'd been at it an entire month now. The training had been tough and constant, but she'd risen to the challenge. Her primary instructor, Pam Wanescoat wasn't sitting behind her at the moment. Abby had been checked off for solo flight two weeks before. She felt comfortable flying the Stearman. It felt like an old friend. She patted the side as though it were a living thing and said, "You're a good girl, but I'll be moving on soon."

Word had come down from General Arnold's command. In order to speed up the training and streamline the entire process, the Women's Airforce Ferry Service and the Women's Flight Training Detachment would combine to form a new unit called Women Airforce Service Pilots, or WASPs. Deborah Cochran, the head of the WFTDs, would be in charge of the new unit with Nancy Love, in charge of the WAFS, her second in command.

She turned sharply over the top of the airfield and descended. She'd been flying for two hours, practicing power stalls, spin recovery, and basic navigation.

She flew toward the tower, looking for the green light signal. She could see old Charlie Tucker standing behind the light, giving her a steady green: cleared to land. He never seemed to smile. When she'd first met him, she'd been intimidated by his grim manner, but she'd gotten to know him better and they'd become friends. She'd miss him. She waved and he waved back, giving her a rare smile.

Normally the landing pattern was full of aircraft, but not today. Today, the rest of the women were packing their bags for Sweetwater, Texas. They'd ride busses to Avenger Field and move into new living quarters as members of WASP class 43-6.

She leveled off and entered the downwind segment of her landing sequence. She saw the other Stearman aircraft lined up neatly, wing tip to wing tip. The wind was right down the runway and only 10mph. Textbook conditions.

Once her tail passed the end of the runway, she pulled back the throttle almost to an idle. The plane dropped steadily as she turned onto her base turn. She continued a smooth turn onto final and leveled the wings. She wanted this last landing to be perfect.

She evaluated her speed, drop rate, and distance to her touchdown point. Dropping on the airfield always reminded her of a bird of prey stooping on an unsuspecting rodent on the ground.

She adjusted the elevator trim slightly and rode the aircraft down smoothly, allowing a few miles per hour above a stall. The Stearman floated like a heavy leaf, dropping steadily toward the tarmac.

When the aircraft was only twenty feet above the ground, Abby balanced the plane just above a stall with micro-adjustments to the stick and rudder pedals. She added slight back pressure on the stick, keeping the wheels off for as long as possible. The plane seemed to hang in the air forever. She loved the feeling. She felt the aircraft stall for just an instant before the wheels touched down gently.

She rolled forward only fifty feet before she goosed the throttle. She expertly parked beside the last Stearman in line, swinging the plane around as she pressed on the left brake pedal and pivoted in place. Her wingtip only had two feet to spare from the other wingtip.

Before shutting down the engine she glanced up at the tower and saw Charlie looking down on her. She gave him a final wave goodbye. He lifted his chin and gave her an exaggerated salute, then looked away and scanned the horizon with a large pair of binoculars. The simple gesture made Abby tear up. She'd miss this airfield and the people she'd met there.

"Thank you, Mr. Tucker," she said to herself.

She went through the shutdown sequence in meticulous order, unstrapped, and hopped out of the cockpit and onto the wing.

Beatrice Malinsky stood nearby with her arms crossed over her bosom. Abby hadn't seen her in over a week.

Abby took off her leather flight helmet and trotted to her friend. "Bea, you're back," she said excitedly. "I was hoping I'd see you before we left for Sweetwater." She pulled up short when she saw tears in Beatrice's eyes. "What's wrong? What's happened?" She felt hollow for an instant. "Is—is it Clyde?" she asked with dread.

Beatrice shook her head and reached for Abby. "No, no, it's not Clyde." Beatrice flicked a tear away in irritation. "It's—it's Stan . . ."

Abby put her hand to her chest in shock. She knew Bea and Major Standish Hercules had been more than just colleagues, but she didn't know just how far their relationship went.

She pulled Beatrice into a tight hug. "What happened?"

"He—he was shot down over the channel. Those nasty kraut bastards killed him."

Abby was repelled by the coarse language, but continued holding her friend, who shook. "Oh, my God. I'm so sorry. He—he was a good man."

Beatrice broke the hug and wiped her face, looking around sheepishly. "I don't know why it's affecting me so much. We only spent a few nights together. He was such an excellent pilot. How could they get to him?"

Abby thought of him straining to carry her bag to Bea's ancient truck those many months before, and how he balanced the beers at the bar only a few weeks before. The memory made her happy and sad at the same time. He was gone forever. "Oh, Bea. He was such a dear man. I liked him so much. I can't believe he's really gone."

"I only found out because he trained here. It came through secondhand from one of the mechanics, but I checked the casualty lists and his name is on it." She kicked the asphalt and her tone changed markedly. "What I wouldn't give to go up against those Nazi bastards. I'd give 'em what for."

Abby nodded, feeling the same way about the Japanese undoubtedly trying to kill her husband in some faraway jungle.

She swept her arm around Beatrice's shoulders and leaned into her. "Come home with me. I need to pack, but I'll stay with you as long as I can."

Beatrice walked with her toward the small concourse building. She said, "I've already packed. I can help you."

"What? You're leaving too?"

"We're being folded into the WASPs, too."

Abby couldn't help smiling. "You mean we'll be flying together?"

"Not exactly." She wiped her eyes and blew her nose into a handkerchief. "I'm part of the training cadre."

"Oh. I guess that'll change things a little."

Beatrice took a step away from Abby and nodded. "Yes. But everyone already knows we're friends. I doubt you'll be a part of my group. They wouldn't want to think I'm giving you special treatment."

"And I wouldn't want any. These past few weeks, I think the girls are finally respecting me for my flying skills."

"You put the Stearman down like a leaf on a pond . . . without making a ripple just now."

Abby appreciated the accolades, but it had been perfect landing conditions. If she didn't land perfectly, she'd be worried. "Too bad we don't have time to toast Stan properly. I'll always remember him."

Beatrice's eyes lost focus as she stared toward the horizon. Her hand went to her belly and she muttered, "So will I."

Abby arrived in Sweetwater, Texas, on a bus with the ninety-five other women in class 43-6. Four busloads of trainees pulled up to the Blue Bonnet hotel and offloaded. They wore mostly dresses. They had ordered them to leave their coveralls at the old base, leaving them with only civilian clothes to wear. After so many weeks of wearing the coveralls, she felt over-dressed.

Abby wondered if Beatrice had already arrived. As an instructor, they had separated them from the trainees. She worried about her friend, and wanted to talk more with her about Stan, but doubted she'd ever get the chance.

A woman stood in front of the little hotel with her hands on her hips. She wore a form-fitting coverall. Abby and the others recognized her for what she was, the woman in charge.

They lined up in front of her and stiffened as they had taught them to do in the WFTD. Abby felt slightly ridiculous as her dress flitted back and forth in the light winds. She felt anything but military.

"Welcome to Sweetwater, Texas, ladies. My name is Lieutenant Trudy Bowers." She started pacing, her hands clasped behind her back. "Those of you who came over from the WFTD are already familiar with the area. Some of you aren't. This hotel will be your temporary quarters. You are now a part of something new and different. You are striving to become Women's Airforce Service Pilots, or WASPs for short.

"Your time here won't be easy. You'll train hard and we will give no quarter for failure. We don't have time to hold your hands. Three demerits and you're gone.

"Most of you have already been involved with other flight programs, but WASP training is different. You'll spend most of your time learning the rigors of flying military aircraft. Both in the air and on the ground. You're expected to learn basic military drills as well. You're expected to march, to exercise, and to learn how to function in the army. If you don't excel at each, we will drop you.

"The airplanes you are learning to fly aren't like anything you've ever flown before."

Abby thought about her time in the P-51 and understood exactly what she meant.

"The training is tough. Many will fail. We don't apologize for that. If you have what it takes, you will fly pursuits, as well as dual engine bombers." A murmur of excitement rippled through the women, but quickly quieted when Lieutenant Bowers continued. "Don't get too comfortable here at the Blue Bonnet. We'll be moving out to Avenger Field tomorrow at 0600 hours. Once there, you'll receive your room assignments, uniforms, and everything you need to function in this *man's* army." She stared at them, then stopped pacing and added, "One last thing. Do not write to your families to tell them what you're doing here. They probably already know, but we don't want our enemies getting wind of it and using it against us. Understand?"

A resounding "Yes, ma'am!"

"Good. There's a café in town. Find a room and relax. This is the last evening you'll have to do so for the next sixteen weeks."

The busses picked them up promptly at six the next morning. The late November sun hadn't even risen yet. Abby wore a coat, but her legs were bare beneath her dress and she shivered as she entered the bus.

The banter and excitement from the night before had vanished. All the trainees had shrunk into themselves and tried to stay warm sitting on the ice-cold bus seats. Thankfully, Avenger Field was a short two miles from the Blue Bonnet.

As the headlights flashed across the area, they lit up several medium-sized complexes. Each looked identical and were undoubtedly where they'd be staying. The lights also lit up a line of what could only be instructors. They stood at attention, perfectly spaced, wearing baggy coveralls. They squinted as the lights passed them. Abby saw Beatrice and her heart raced. Despite the awkwardness that might come of it, she wanted to have her as her instructor.

Mandy Flannigan sat behind Abby. She leaned forward and said, "Well, well, if it isn't your old friend. What a coincidence."

Abby turned and scowled. She normally didn't bother responding to her remarks. It never went well and just made her feel worse. But she felt ornery this morning. "Piss off, Flanny." She knew the nickname irked her more than anything else, particularly when it came from someone she didn't respect, which was most everyone.

Mandy's face flared red and she stood aggressively. "Why you little . . ."

The bus lurched to a stop, and Mandy lost her footing. She sprawled onto the floor between the rows of seats with a loud oof. Some others gasped, a few tittered, but most just ignored the whole thing.

Abby stayed seated, as did everyone else. Mandy pushed herself off the floor and stood beside Abby, glaring down at her. The bus door opened, bringing the lights on and illuminating the inside.

Lieutenant Bowers strode through the open door and stood beside the bus driver, facing them. She immediately noticed Mandy. She barked, "You! Sit down!"

Mandy's color drained from her face and she sat down quickly, muttering, "Sorry, ma'am."

"What's your name?"

Mandy gulped audibly. She leaned forward and squeaked, "M—Mandy Flan . . ."

"Stand up when you address me!" Bowers interrupted.

Mandy sprang to her feet and stiffened to attention. Her knee slammed into Abby's seat back. Abby could hear the pain in her voice. "Yes, ma'am. Mandy Flannigan reporting for duty, ma'am."

"You wanna get kicked out before you even start, Flannigan?"

"N—no, ma'am!"

"That'd be a hell of a way to begin—kicked out before even getting off the bus. A world record. You wanna be that person, Flannigan?"

"No, ma'am!"

"Then sit down and follow directions. You think you can do that for me?"

"No—I mean, yes, ma'am."

"We'll see about that. Now everyone stand up and get off this bus!" she yelled the last part, making everyone jump out of their seats.

Abby stood and scooted to the aisle, acutely aware of Mandy standing close behind her. She thought she'd jab her in the back, or whisper some vile threat, but she didn't do or say a word. They had effectively cowed her for the moment.

They exited and stood in the cold, early morning darkness for a few minutes while the lines sorted out. The busses pulled away, leaving a trail of dust and exhaust to cover them. A few trainees hacked and coughed.

The training cadre referred to the buildings she'd seen as Bays. They explained that each building had two bays, with six cots in each. Bay assignments were decided by each trainee calling out a number from one to eight.

They went up and down the line, shouting numbers. When it was her turn, Abby said, "Seven." The rest of the women called out numbers. She heard seven again behind her and hoped to God it wasn't Mandy, but thought it might be. After the bus incident, who knew what revenge she'd take out on her?

"Get settled in your assigned Bays. No swapping!" Bowers pointed toward another building glowing in the darkness. Smoke and steam rose from pipes coming from the top and sides. "That's the chow hall. Meet there in your coveralls in one hour."

They hadn't received coveralls, so Abby assumed they'd be in their bays. She found Bay 7 and entered. Sure enough, the six cots held bedding and neatly folded coveralls.

Abby went to the nearest cot, but before she placed her bag on the cot, Mandy stepped in front and said, "This one's taken."

Abby shook her head in exasperation but held her tongue. All the other cots had already been claimed, so she took the one right beside Mandy's. She flung her bag on the cot and held up the coverall. It looked huge.

The other trainees held theirs up. They all looked far too big. Margie Wills, a tall blonde woman Abby knew from the WFTD, looked at the inside tag. "It's a men's small."

Abby looked inside hers. "Mine's a large."

Margie brought hers over and handed it to Abby. "The large will be too big for me, but it'll fit me better than it'll fit you."

"Thanks," Abby said, and took the smaller version. It would still drape over her, but at least she wouldn't trip over it. They made more exchanges and the women disrobed and put the coveralls on. They cinched the centers with belts, attempting to keep them from simply falling off. By the time they'd finished dressing, they gawked at one another.

"We look like hobos," Eberdeen Huss said in her silky southern accent.

The laughter started slowly at first but soon rose as they couldn't contain themselves any longer. Even Mandy reared her head back and laughed while holding her belly.

Alice Cathart strode past them, giggling all the way. She went to the middle of the room and pulled open the door, most likely leading to the bathroom. She stuck her head in, then went inside. A moment later, she emerged and she wasn't laughing. The others noticed and Margie asked, "What's wrong?"

"Uh, there's only two bathrooms and two showers."

Abby wiped the laughing tears from the corners of her eyes and said, "Well, that's enough for six of us, I guess."

"We have to share with Bay 8. I just checked. There are no other bathrooms or showers for them. We're sharing.

Eberdeen Huss said, "Twelve women sharing two toilets and two showers? Oh, my lord have mercy."

Abby suddenly had the urge to pee. They all hesitated for a moment, then rushed all at once. Mandy and Alice got there first. Mandy glared at Abby in triumph as she sidled up to the stall-less commode and struggled to unzip her stiff new coverall. "This damned zoot suit," she muttered.

Alice sat down beside her in full view. "Zoot suit. I like it. Guess the army doesn't care much about privacy, do they? Doing the morning business is gonna be something."

Abby suppressed her urge to pee and went back to unpacking. She carefully hung her clothes in the closet, making sure the buttons of her clothes faced the correct direction. She assumed they'd have bay inspections and she intended to keep her demerits down to zero.

While Mandy was still in the bathroom, Margie, whose closet was beside hers, asked, "So what's going on between you and Flanny?"

"I don't know. She's never liked me. I thought after WFTD, she'd relax, but I was wrong. It's nothing to worry about, though."

"I hope not. Sure would be nice if everyone got along, but I guess we're not living in a fairy tale, are we?"

Abby guffawed. "No, we sure aren't." Her thoughts drifted to Clyde and she glanced at where she'd already placed his picture beside her cot first thing.

"Is that your husband?"

"Yes, Clyde. He's fighting in the Pacific somewhere."

"He's a marine then?"

"No, army airborne."

"Airborne? Wow, you must be so proud of him. I hear the airborne are some of our best soldiers."

Abby's chest swelled with pride. "I am, but I'm also worried. I'd prefer he wasn't on the front lines."

"He must be proud of you, too."

"This all happened so fast. I sent him a telegram, and he gave me his blessing. But since then, our letters are taking weeks or even months, if they get there at all. He said not to expect much from him in his last letter, which can only mean one thing . . ."

"You poor dear. You think he's in combat?"

Abby nodded. "Did you see the newsreel about the parachutists in New Guinea?"

"That was him?"

"His unit, yes."

Margie put her finger on her chin. "As I recall, that was a very successful mission with few casualties."

"I would've heard from the army by now if something had happened to him, but it's so hard not knowing if he's safe. For all I know, he could be fighting for his life this very instant."

"You can't think like that, Abby. It'll make you crazy."

"I know. That's partly why I'm here; to keep my mind occupied. Well, that, and I love flying more than anything I've ever done before."

Margie beamed her bright smile. "Isn't it grand? Not only are we doing something we love, we're also helping our boys win the war."

"You have someone over there?"

Margie's eyes went distant. "Not a sweetie, but my two older brothers are somewhere in Africa, I think."

Abby touched her shoulder tenderly. Everyone had stakes in this damned war. "Do they write to you?"

"Yes, but they have families, so not too much. One's a gunner on a bomber and the others in the infantry. God, I miss them."

"Our men will beat this evil. I'm sure of it."

"I guess that's why we're both here, isn't it? To help in whatever way we can."

Abby stepped back and spread her arms, showcasing her baggy zoot suit. "Well, it's certainly not for the fashion."

15

DECEMBER 1943

Avenger Field
Sweetwater, Texas

Abby Cooper loved the feel of the stick in the BT-9 trainer. She occupied the backseat while the instructor, Frances Bledster, sat in front. The aircraft was a big step up from the Stearman. Instead of a biplane, the BT-9 had a single low wing, much like the pursuits and bombers they'd eventually be flying.

The weeks had flown by quickly. The days were hectic and long, but she loved every minute. Her favorite time, like everyone else's, was the four hours of flight time they received every day, weather permitting.

For the past two hours, they'd been practicing land navigation, mixed in with power stall recovery. None of this was new to her, but the BT-9 had its own set of idiosyncrasies to explore. Each aircraft had a certain feel all its own, and she loved the forgiving nature of the trainer.

Just for fun, the instructor would cut the engine occasionally and Abby would go through the emergency checklist while having to choose a suitable emergency landing spot, all while keeping tabs on her speed and angle to avoid a stall.

They approached Avenger Field, to practice touch-and-gos and whatever else the instructor had up her sleeve. She could see other aircraft circling the airfield. Some BT-9s, but mostly the double-winged Stearman filled the pattern.

Radios had recently been installed in the BT-9s, so she called into the tower and heard the harried voice of Larry Stockton. He talked fast and had a nasal tone that could be hard to understand. The first time she'd heard him, Abby did not know what he'd said and asked him to repeat himself. She'd gotten an earful from him before he finally repeated himself. She'd gotten used to his voice by now, but she still had to concentrate.

Mr. Stockton told her to make a turn away from the airfield to give him time to make room for her in the crowded pattern. She complied and made a lazy turn to the west. The instructor's head bobbed in front of her and Abby wondered if she'd fallen asleep. She had heard nothing from her in a long time now. That wasn't necessarily a bad thing, but she wondered.

"You awake up there?" she asked over the internal radio set.

Mrs. Bledster jolted in the seat, then looked back at her and gave her a thumbs-up. "Just going over some maneuvers we still need to perform." She held up her flight notebook as proof, but Abby thought she'd caught her catching a catnap.

Abby completed the turn and called the tower for further instructions. As she looked down on the tower, she noticed an aircraft moving in the opposite direction to the flow on the other side of the airfield. She took in a sharp breath. She'd become used to how things should look, and seeing such an obvious anomaly sent a shiver of fear up her spine.

"Do you see that, Mrs. Bledster?"

Bledster looked back at her, and Abby pointed. "Someone's going against the flow down there."

Bledster saw it and cursed. She immediately went to the radio and frantically called in the clear, urging the pilots to check positions. But it was too late. Abby watched in stunned, horrified fascination as the offending aircraft and the nearest aircraft flying in the pattern correctly seemed to draw together as if by magnetism. They met midfield and stopped in midair with a sickening crunch of metal. Both aircraft spun and twisted. Chunks flew off in every direction. Abby saw what could only be a body falling. A parachute strung out and partially opened before the pilot slammed into the ground.

Abby took in a sharp breath and watched as big and small chunks of aircraft rained down around the partially deployed parachute. Metal and fabric, mixed with blood and bone, plummeted to the ground and rolled into an unrecognizable mass, shrouded in dust and smoke.

"Oh my God," Abby said. "Oh, no." She didn't know who it was, but it didn't matter. All the WASP candidates were precious to her. Losing someone to demerits was bad enough, but losing someone this way, probably two, felt as though a cold spike had been thrust into her guts.

They didn't speak for a full minute as they took in the carnage. Finally, Mrs. Bledster said, "You need me to take over?"

Abby snapped out of her staring trance. She checked her flight attitude, then her gauges. "No, ma'am. I still have the aircraft."

Emergency vehicles raced to the smoldering wreckage. Water sprayed the largest chunks, while an ambulance pulled up beside the fluttering, partially deployed parachute. Abby doubted either pilot could have survived.

"Let's clear the airspace, Abigail."

"Yes, ma'am." She didn't want to leave, but knew it would be safer and give the controllers one less aircraft to worry about.

They made lazy turns over the barren flat ground for thirty long minutes, listening to the radio traffic. Neither of them said a word—both lost in their own thoughts.

Mrs. Bledster finally said, "Okay, let's turn back and land. Sounds like things have quieted down now."

Abby complied, turning the trainer back toward the airfield. She could see a thin string of smoke still rising. She wanted to cry. When she could see the tower, she radioed in again. "Avenger tower this is BT 134 Charlie, requesting permission to enter the pattern for landing. Over." It felt odd speaking as though nothing had happened.

Mr. Stockton's voice came to her, just as calm and cool. "BT 134 Charlie, this is Avenger tower. Cleared to land on 32. Wind negligible. Over."

"BT 134, Cleared to land on 32. Over." Her own voice matched the professional austereness of Mr. Stockton's. It broke her heart to think the world could carry on as if nothing had happened. She spoke to Mrs. Bledster. "It's surreal—as if nothing's happened."

It took a moment before she responded, but she finally did. "In the air isn't the right time for grieving. First things first, young lady. Concentrate on getting us down in one piece, then you can grieve."

Abby felt bitter, but knew she was correct. *I wonder if Clyde has had to deal with this?* She hoped he hadn't, but figured he must have. She remembered him telling her they'd lost men in training. Surely it must feel the same way she felt right now—like someone had ripped her guts out.

They took the rest of the day off from training that day. The entire class met in the chow hall. No one planned the meet. It was just where everyone ended up once they learned they had the rest of the day off.

By now, everyone knew the two women's names: Francine Buckleton and Tina Crossak. Tina was the one who entered the pattern incorrectly. Both had died—Tina on impact and Francine in the Sweetwater hospital an hour after she'd bailed out. Abby knew both of them, of course, but neither resided in Bay 7.

Margie Wills wiped a tear and said, "Francine has a husband and a two children."

"Oh my God, that's awful," Abby said as fresh tears wetted her cheeks.

"Her husband's 4-F, ineligible for service—bad back, I think. He's a plumber. The kids are four and five, if I recall. Two sweet girls. I met them at a picnic last spring."

Abby shook her head, not wanting to know more gut-wrenching details, but unable to tune it all out. "So sad. What will they do?"

Mandy Flannigan answered bitterly. "Well, they can't count on the government helping them out. As far as they're concerned, we're not in the actual military."

"What? They won't? But they died in service to the country. They'll have to honor *that*. Surely they'll have to make an exception."

"Nope. Not even a flag at the funeral."

Abby put her hand to her mouth to keep from sobbing. How could anyone be so cruel? "They won't even pay for the funeral?"

Some of the sadness turned to anger. The women shook their heads and murmured to themselves and each other—so unfair.

Eberdeen Huss, said in her southern accent, "We should pool our money. Send it along to their next of kin. It's the least we can do." There was a smattering of agreement.

Mandy said, "Tina caused it. Do we help her next of kin, too?"

Surprise and shock and stunned silence followed. A few nodded their agreement, but most just looked aghast at singling out the blame.

Margie Wills said, "Tina was my friend, too. Of course she deserves our help, Mandy. She made a mistake. Don't let that define her entire life. She was a good person. So eager and full of life . . ." her voice trailed away as she fought back a heavy sob.

Eberdeen added softly. "They were our sisters. They'll always be our sisters."

Mandy crossed her arms, but finally nodded. "You're right. I was wrong to say it. They both deserve our help." She flicked a tear away with obvious annoyance and stared at her feet.

Abby, sitting nearby, reached out and placed her hand on her shoulder. She'd never seen Mandy show any emotion other than vindictiveness and spite, but she couldn't help trying to console her.

Mandy flinched away at first, then met Abby's gaze. Her hard gaze softened and she put her hand on top of Abby's. She let the tears flow. It was as though a dam had broken. Abby wondered if Mandy knew Tina better than she'd let on.

The rest of the women went to her and soon formed a circle several layers deep. Everyone had a hand on someone else and they cried together for long minutes.

The next day, training resumed in earnest. The busy days didn't diminish the pain of losing Tina and Francine, but it helped keep their minds occupied.

The days at Avenger Field began early. They woke at 0500 in the chilly darkness of early morning. To avoid the morning rush of twelve women sharing two bathrooms and two showers, Abby learned it was much better to wait.

Some women were definitely *not* morning types. They'd fume and push and generally act unpleasantly. Abby had never minded early mornings. She rather enjoyed being up before the sun, but her jovial moods didn't make the non–morning people any brighter. In fact, some resented her good moods.

So, to avoid any conflict, she'd slip her zoot suit over her pajamas and wander toward the chow hall. There was a community toilet nearby and the line that early was usually short or nonexistent. She'd get to breakfast early and by the time most of the others came in, she'd be nearly done. Then she'd go back to the mostly deserted Bay 7 and do what she needed to do in the toilets and showers.

After breakfast, they'd form up outside and march to the large outbuildings, where they'd spend four hours at ground school. It not only covered the basics of flight, but they also learned how to take care of aircraft engines. Nothing too in depth, but enough to help them if they ended up stranded without a mechanic nearby.

Right before lunch, they'd exercise, following along as a military man standing on a platform performed calisthenics. They stayed as synchronized as possible. The instructor constantly berated and corrected anyone not performing well or in sync. A few even earned dreaded demerits. Abby enjoyed it, but felt bad for some of the women who just weren't coordinated. Failing out of the program just because you couldn't perform a proper jumping jack didn't seem fair to her.

After lunch, they'd head to the flight line. As long as the weather allowed, which it normally did, they'd fly. This was still everyone's favorite part of the day. Abby felt she could fly with the best of them now, even Mandy.

After flying, they'd do marching drills for an hour. Then they'd finally eat dinner. After dinner, their time was their own, but by then it was nearly ten o'clock at night, and lights out happened at ten thirty. If you missed it even by a few seconds, the instructors would descend upon the bays, ready to hand out demerits.

A week had passed since the accident, but it still weighed heavily on the group. The daily routine helped, but there was still an air of sadness. Consolidating donations and sending them to the next of kin helped ease the pain, but also reminded them that despite their commitment to helping in the war effort, the government didn't reciprocate or even acknowledge their commitment.

Abby had finally received a few letters from Clyde. Without coming right out and saying it, he'd implied that his unit had jumped into New Guinea. She could hardly contain her worry. He didn't get into specifics—he made it sound almost boring—but she wondered if he was giving her lip service to keep her from worrying. She adored his letters and raced to Bay 7 to read the latest one, which had arrived that morning.

It was shorter than the last few, and it sent a cold shiver up her spine. He didn't sound the same. She imagined it wasn't easy even finding a place to write in the jungle, but the scrawling, hard to read handwriting didn't seem like his words. The warmth she normally felt wasn't there. She read it a few more times, trying to figure out what it meant, but each time she came away worrying more. He sounded so different, almost hopeless. What had happened?

Alice Cathart, whose bed sat across the aisle from her, asked, "Is something wrong, Abby? Is that from Clyde?"

Living in such close proximity to one another made privacy a rare luxury and they couldn't help getting to know one another quite well. The accident had only brought them closer.

Abby looked up at her and gave her a tight smile. "Yes. It just came this morning. I've been dying to read it all day. I didn't think we'd ever get done marching."

"You're usually bouncing off the walls when you hear from him. What's wrong?"

Abby sighed. She folded the letter and put it back into the flimsy envelope. She noticed her hands shook. "He doesn't sound like himself. It's short and . . . I don't know . . . It feels cold. There's no warmth to it."

"Has—has he lost friends? Maybe he's just trying to deal with that."

"He wouldn't tell me if he had—well, unless it was his close friend Gil. I think he would tell me that. They're like brothers. No, this is something different. It's like it was written by someone else entirely."

A few other women filtered into Bay 7 and flopped onto their cots.

Alice assured her. "I'm sure he's just tired." Her eyes lit up. "You should write him a sexy letter. Men love that sort of thing."

Abby blushed. "I'm—I'm not sure how I'd go about that? I mean, I've never done anything like that before."

"Just tell him about a sexual fantasy. Make it spicy, something you wouldn't show to your mother."

A few other women became interested, including Mandy Flannigan. "What are you two talking about?" she asked.

Alice filled them in. "I'm telling Abby she should write her husband a sexy letter. He'll love it."

"You should," Mandy said quickly.

Abby didn't know whether or not she was being teased, so she didn't respond.

"I'll write it for you, if you'll let me," Mandy said matter-of-factly.

Abby blushed deeper. "What? No. Of course not. No one's writing dirty letters to my husband, except me."

"Oh, come on." She looked around the room of suddenly eager women and spread her arms out. "We won't send them, we'll just write them and you can pick and choose the parts you want to use for yourself. It'll be fun."

Abby looked from one to another. They all stared back at her with laughing eyes. "You're serious?"

Eberdeen Huss laughed and threw her mass of dark hair back. "I think it sounds amazing. But I'm warning you, I have quite an imagination." She sang the last word.

Mandy stepped forward. "We'll make it a competition."

"What's the prize?," Alice asked.

"Abby will choose the best one and whoever wins . . ." she tapped her lips with her index finger, thinking. She finally snapped her fingers. "Whoever wins gets first dibs on the shower in the morning for an entire week."

Everyone's eyes lit up. The prize was almost too much to fathom. They all turned to Abby. These women, even Mandy, had become her best friends. She didn't know she could be this close to anyone. She loved each and every one of them like sisters. Even though Mandy still sometimes made her feel small, she'd warmed to her, realizing it was just a part of her personality. A few women had been dropped from the program, but none from Bay 7 so far. She hoped that would never happen. It would be like losing a member of her own family.

"Well . . . okay." A roar of approval filled the bay.

One woman from Bay 8 poked her head in. Around a mouthful of toothpaste, she asked, "What's the big idea?"

They told her and she quickly spit out her toothpaste and told them Bay 8 would join the contest, too. After all, they shared the same showers, so it was only fair.

Abby laughed as the women flung themselves on their beds and started writing furiously. "This is going to be so embarrassing," she said. "Nothing too raunchy, okay?"

Boos and hisses erupted and a mass of pillows were flung at her. She reared back and laughed until her belly hurt.

The next night, she had a stack of dirty letters to read through. None of them had signed the letters, just handed her folded pieces of paper. They'd eaten dinner as quickly as possible and hustled back to Bay 7 so Abby would have plenty of time to read them over carefully.

Abby blushed mightily at the first letter. Embarrassment turned her face beet-red, and the women giggled at her discomfort. She placed the first one down and shook her head. "This is no good. I can't read these all to myself. They need to be read out loud."

Hoots and hollers filled Bay 7. The women from Bay 8 had crammed in as well.

Abby said, "Let's make it a game. I'll pass them around so everyone that wrote one has to read one out loud."

Mandy chimed in. "After each one, we guess who wrote it. If we get it right, we get an extra day with the shower."

For the next forty minutes, they each read someone else's letter out loud. By the end, everyone had laughed themselves to tears. Some letters were heartfelt attempts at sexiness, while others were clearly over the top. No one guessed the original writer correctly, but that didn't matter—only the laughter mattered.

By the time they had read them all, they only had minutes before lights out. Abby's stomach hurt from laughing so hard. The tension and pain from losing Tina and Francine had been washed away.

She'd always remember them, but she felt like she could move on now. The laughter and camaraderie seemed to have pulled them from a funk that the rigorous daily routine hadn't quite been able to achieve. For the first time since the accident, Abby felt good.

Two more weeks of constant, intense training passed. The accident never left Abby's consciousness, but it faded. Her flying abilities skyrocketed. She felt she could perform any maneuver the instructors thrust upon her.

She knew all the airframes inside and out and passed the tough ground school tests with high marks. She even found herself called upon to help those who were struggling, particularly with ground school. The unofficial tutoring brought her even closer to the other trainees and made her feel she was making a difference.

Then one beautiful day after lunch, she went to the flight line and mounted what she thought of as *her personal* BT-9. It was just like any other normal day, but when she entered the back seat, her instructor that day, Mrs. Valerie Leeds, hopped on the wing and gave her a wry wink.

"You know what today is, dearie?"

"Uh, Thursday, ma'am?"

"Yes, but it's also your instrument check-ride day."

Abby nearly lost her lunch. She gulped and responded. "Yes, ma'am."

She strapped in and took one last look at the outside world before they closed the blacked-out canopy. She couldn't see anything outside. The only light came from the soft glow of the instruments. She reached to where she hoped the flashlight still sat snugly strapped. She felt it and thanked her lucky stars that she'd remembered to check the batteries during her last flight. Undoubtedly, Leeds would turn off the instrument's glow at some point, mimicking a power outage, and she'd only have the flashlight to work with.

After the instructor got them airborne, she radioed. "Okay, Cooper. Are you ready to take control of the airplane?"

Abby gripped the flight controls, took a deep breath to calm her nerves and replied, "Yes, ma'am. I have the airplane."

For the next three hours, she followed the instructor's instructions. She turned to proper headings, adjusted her airspeed and altitude as requested, and even recovered from odd and unstable flight attitudes, which the instructor put her into.

Finally, the instructor called out a heading back to Avenger Field. She said, "I'm going to act as the tower. I'm going to give you directions, as though the airfield is obscured in heavy fog. Do exactly as I say, no matter if you feel it's wrong or not. Remember, don't trust what your body tells you, but what your instruments tell you."

She followed the directions to the letter. Many times her body insisted the airframe tilted right or left, but she ignored the urge for correction and concentrated on the level flight bubble, which told her the actual attitude.

The instructor finally told her to pull the tab holding the shroud in place and have a look around. Bright sunlight streamed in and nearly blinded her, but she saw she was on the final approach to the airfield.

"Now land, and we'll call it a day."

Abby landed soft as a butterfly and navigated off the active runway. She parked and shut down the engine. She felt she'd done well, but couldn't tell based on the silence from the front seat. Mrs. Leeds unbuckled and stood on the wing beside her. She finally broke into a smile and extended a hand. "Congratulations. You passed your instrument qualifications."

She beamed. The qualification was a stumbling block and had been the last flight for many trainees. They practiced exhaustively beforehand, but once the shroud went into place, at an arbitrary time of the instructor's choosing, you had one chance to pass. She'd done so, and with high marks, too.

With that out of the way, she only had to pass the final two check rides, one by the instructors and one by the military. Then she'd have the coveted WASP wings. She had many more flight hours to get through first, but she felt much better that she might actually reach that fateful day now that she'd cleared what some thought of as the toughest hurdle.

Her good mood shattered when she saw her dear friend Beatrice Malinsky racing across the tarmac with her packed bag slung over her shoulder. She wore civilian clothes instead of her zoot suit. Since Beatrice was an instructor and Abby a student, they'd barely said two words to one another over the past few weeks, but she still considered her one of her dearest friends.

Abby trotted toward her, waved, and called out. "Bea. Beatrice." When she didn't respond, she ran to her side and matched her stride. "Beatrice, whatever's the matter? Why are you dressed like that?"

Beatrice's eyes shone with tears. Her eyelids were swollen red, as though she'd been crying for a long time.

Beatrice scowled. "Because I'm done. They found out."

"Found out what?"

She touched her stomach. "That I'm pregnant." She stopped walking and placed her hand over her mouth in a vain attempt to stop her sobs.

Abby couldn't hide her own shock. "What? Pregnant? How?" Beatrice looked at her sideways and Abby put her hand to her mouth. "Oh my God . . . Stan? Stan's the father?"

"Yes, of course."

"And—and you knew?" She felt shame asking and wished she could take it back.

"Of course I knew," she replied with acid in her voice.

"I'm sorry, Bea. It's just a shock to find out. I—I didn't mean anything by it. I wish I'd known. I had no idea. How'd they find out?"

She cupped the bulge that looked obvious now that she wasn't wearing her zoot suit. "I couldn't hide it anymore. I think someone noticed me in the shower—I don't know—maybe they saw me throwing up too many times behind the shed."

Abby didn't know how to feel. A baby's a blessing, but not if you weren't ready. "But you couldn't hide it forever, Bea. I mean, it was only a matter of time until they noticed."

Beatrice stood to her full height and stroked her belly. "I know. I wanted to have it both ways." She looked off into the distance at a BT-9 in flight. "I love flying. I'm gonna miss it *so* much." She sighed and wiped the tears from her cheeks. "I don't know what I'm going to do now. I'm an unwed mother to be. Society doesn't look kindly upon our kind, even in wartime." Her eyes hardened and she said, "I thought about ending it, somehow.

Maybe put her up for adoption . . ." She continued stroking her belly, and her eyes softened as she looked down at the bulge lovingly. "But I want to keep it now. He or she will always remind me of Stan, and that'll never be a bad thing."

"Oh, Bea, I don't know how to feel. I'm happy and sad all at the same time. You're having a baby! But poor Stan. He would've loved her or him so much."

She hugged Abby, then pushed away. "Don't worry about me, Abby. I'll —we'll be fine. Get through the training and become a WASP. Do it for us."

An idea made Abby burst out. "Don't go, Bea. Stay in Sweetwater. Have your baby at the local hospital. We'll all be her mothers." She swept her hand to encompass Avenger Field and the WASP trainees. "We'll help you with the rent so you won't have to worry about getting a job. I know the others will help. Little Bea will be like the WASP mascot. Like the Fifinella gremlin patch they'll give us at graduation only a thousand times cuter."

Beatrice stared, unable to speak. "I—I was going to go to my parents, but the thought sickens me . . ."

"Then it's settled. Find a place to live in Sweetwater and we'll take it from there."

"Are you sure the others will help? You might have spoken out of turn."

"Nonsense. I hear the others talk about how much they like you as an instructor all the time. They respect you and think you're great. They'll chip in whatever they can."

Beatrice closed her eyes, and fresh tears seeped from the corners. She pulled Abby in for a tight hug and said into her neck. "Oh Abby, thank you. You're a dear friend."

16

OCTOBER 1943

Finschhafen, Papua New Guinea

The night attack in the jungle stayed with Clyde long after the gunshots had ceased. The enemy didn't try again that night, but he couldn't sleep. Whenever he closed his eyes, he saw his barrel against the Japanese soldier's head, the slight sideways glance from the stunned soldier, then his head snapping as he fired two rounds through his brain.

Morning light finally broke over the jungle and the sights of smoldering holes scattered through with enemy bodies. Some missing limbs gave him pause. He couldn't tear his eyes away from the carnage. Some of those bodies out there were men he'd killed.

Shouted orders and men moved out of their holes cautiously. Clyde didn't want to move. He wanted to curl into the bottom of his hole and drift away. His mind went to Abby. How could he tell her about this? He gritted his teeth and realized he never could. She wouldn't understand. No one who hadn't experienced it could understand the level of destruction and depravity. It was inhuman.

He tried thinking of them eating together in the small apartment over the dingy wet streets of Seattle, but the image wouldn't come to him. He couldn't remember her face and he felt his breath coming in quick gasps as panic rose in his chest.

He frantically dug into his pack and finally found what he was looking for: a pad of paper and a nub of a pencil. He knew he had a responsibility to the men, but he had to get some words down.

His hand shook, but he scrawled the words onto the page. With each word, her image manifested in his mind, as though piecing her together in a scrapbook. He had no intention of sending the words to her. In fact, he barely knew what he wrote and much of it was illegible, but it helped calm him and helped connect him to her.

He'd received letters from her since she'd left Seattle and moved to Texas. Her words had been full of power and joy as she described flying to him. He knew she truly loved it and it made him glad to know that she, at least, was thriving. But without him.

While she thrived and grew, he shriveled. His body ached and his mind reeled with images of death. How would he ever live a normal life? How would the hands that so callously took life ever be able to hold her face as he kissed her lips? She would feel his diseased brain and repel. By merely touching her, he'd ruin her.

He stopped writing. His hand shook, but not as much as before. Writing always helped calm him. He wrote more and more frequently in his journal. He stared up at the sky from the depths of his foxhole and decided he wouldn't survive the war. It wasn't his choice, but it would be for the best. Abby would remember him fondly as he used to be, not how he was now. He could never be who he'd been. He could never return to her. The jungle would be where he would die. He was certain.

A shape filled the space and Sergeant Huss's voice interrupted him. "You alive, Cooper?" He squinted and leaned toward the lip of the hole. "What the fuck are you doing? I asked for an ammo count and you're down there writing letters?"

Clyde sighed deeply and stuffed the notebook and pencil back into his pack. "I—I needed a second, sergeant."

"Well, don't let the U.S. Army or the Jap Eighteenth Division get in your way! Take your time by all means. I'll let Captain Stallsworthy know you needed some alone time."

Clyde pushed his way to a standing position. The bright sunlight lit up his face and he had to squint. Huss pulled back in shock. Clyde said, "I'm alright. It's not my blood."

"Well, clean it off then. You look like a walking corpse, corporal." He handed him his canteen.

Clyde's hand still shook, but he unscrewed the lid and poured the contents over his head, rubbing his face. The tepid water felt good. He felt his energy returning as he scrubbed. He turned his face up to Huss. "Did I get it all?"

"No, but it'll do. Now get out of that hole and get an ammo count. We're moving out."

Clyde felt dread. "Where—where to?"

"Back to Finschhafen. Command thinks we messed with the Nips enough for a while. Now that we found 'em, the flyboys and cannon cockers are gonna pound the hell outta them."

"We're not pursuing them?"

"Your ears full of blood, too?" He raised his voice. "We're heading back to the coast. Now hup-to, corporal! We've got a squad to run."

Clyde pulled himself from the hole and felt better for a moment, but the smell of rotting jungle mixed with torn flesh and sulfur nearly made him gag. Would he ever get used to it? *I hope not.*

A few hours later, they moved out of their fighting position. Men from Third Platoon had been tasked with sorting the dead Japanese soldiers. He was glad it wasn't Second Platoon. He didn't know if he could've done it. Besides the obvious, the duty was also dangerous. The Japanese sometimes played possum until a hapless soldier got too close. Then they'd roll over and explode a grenade, taking themselves and whoever was nearby with them. He hadn't seen it personally, but he'd heard countless stories and figured they had to be based on at least a few real incidents. The officers and NCOs made sure they stayed vigilant.

He walked with Third Squad back the way they'd come. The men still stared at him as though he weren't Clyde Cooper, but someone they didn't know. He hated it.

Gil Hicks veered his way and walked beside him. Clyde ignored him.

Gil finally said, "You okay, Paisano?" Clyde just grunted and kept walking, keeping his eyes on the treetops. "What you did last night . . ."

"What about it?"

"It was the bravest thing I've ever seen. I saw that Jap jump into Ollie's hole. I saw it plain as day, but I couldn't make myself move. You didn't hesitate for an instant. You did something. You might've saved Ollie's life."

Clyde saw the whole thing play out again in his head. He hadn't thought—just reacted. He wasn't proud of killing the enemy soldier, and Gil giving him accolades didn't feel right. "It was a stupid thing to do. I exposed myself. Our own guys could have shot me."

"Makes it even more brave."

Clyde looked around at the other men. A few turned away, as though they'd been secretly watching and been caught.

"Then why is everyone still looking at me like that?"

Gil answered. "They're in awe. I'm in awe."

"Looks more like fear and disgust."

They walked a few more yards. Their central position in the company made them feel somewhat safe.

Gil said, "It was brutal. Cold-blooded. The way you waited there until you had your chance . . ." he shook his head. "Then pow. I've never seen anything like it. None of us has."

"I don't know what came over me. It was like I was out of my body. I can't stop seeing the moment I pulled the trigger. The blood . . ." He touched his face as though he might still have blood on it. "I'm not proud of it."

"Well, don't sweat it. You saved Ollie's ass and everyone out here knows it. I'm happy you're our assistant squad leader, Clyde."

"That all?" Gil nodded and Clyde said, "Then get back in formation."

Gil smiled and veered away, but added, "You done good, Coop."

Clyde wanted to give him a wisecrack back, but nothing came to mind. He couldn't make light of the situation—not yet. It worried him. He'd always been able to put humor into situations. It helped defuse things, but now he struggled. There was nothing funny about what he'd done. For some reason, it felt more like murder.

Kill or be killed—he understood that, but it was a flimsy justification for killing a man and didn't make him feel any better.

After a long, uneventful march, they arrived back at the outskirts of Finschhafen. After being in the jungle with all its hidden dangers, it felt good to see streets and buildings again. The locals acted as though the Japanese hadn't occupied the area for the past few years. They whistled while they swept porches, and neighbors talked and shared food and drink. Bomb craters and a few destroyed buildings reminded them of their recent misery, and Australian soldiers strutted around with their hats skewed jauntily, but it seemed like business as usual. It reminded Clyde of home.

They went straight to the newly captured airfield. Carcasses of burned out Japanese aircraft littered the edges of the grass. Countless holes filled their metal frames and the slight wind made them whistle forlornly.

He learned the Australians had overrun the area just a week before they'd arrived, and that most of the damage to the airfield had come from a relentless air assault by the Fifth Air Force in the weeks before the attack. By the time the Aussies got there, the airfield had been unusable—holed and filled with destroyed aircraft. They'd gotten to work immediately, and now they'd pushed the wreckages to the sides and filled in the holes in the airfield, mostly.

Able Company spread out and men dropped their packs and took seats in whatever shade they could find. Second Platoon followed their lead. Clyde sat down with Third Squad and wiped the sweat from his brow.

"Listen up," Lieutenant Milkins ordered. "We're setting up here beside the airfield for the night. Our rides will come in tomorrow morning." A smattering of low hoots greeted the news.

Someone yelled out, "Where we headed, lieutenant?"

He raised his hands for quiet, but he smiled broadly. "We're headed back to Port Moresby."

The hoots turned to bitter groans. No one much liked the dingy port city. Too much filth and the place stank to high heaven.

Milkins raised his voice. "Listen up! We're officially off duty until 0500 hundred hours tomorrow. Take a load off and relax. You've earned it. I hear there are a few bars in town."

The groans turned to howls of delight. A cold beer sounded good to Clyde, but he had to write Abby first. She'd be worried sick and he owed it to her to ease her mind. He didn't have a good idea what he should write, but hopefully once he sat down with pencil and paper in hand, the words would come.

Soon, the edge of the airfield transformed into a tent city. Clyde strolled through the temporary camp until he found what he was looking for, an out of the way place to write a letter.

Gil ran up behind him. "Hey, Clyde, you wanna join us? We're going to find those bars Milkins mentioned."

Clyde held up his pencil and pad of paper. "I'll find you guys later, after I've written Abby."

Gil thumped him hard on the back. "Let her know I say hello. How you gonna find us?"

"I'll listen for the screams of terror from the Finschhafians."

"Ha, more like the Aussies. We're gonna show them how airborne troopers drink."

"Good luck. Those fellas know how to put 'em back. I'll see you later." Gil ran off to join a raucous group of paratroopers heading into town. Clyde watched them go, wondering if he'd ever feel like celebrating again. Drinking? Yes, but not celebrating. "I've gotta get outta this funk," he muttered to himself. "Acting like a damned sad sack."

He sat down and stared at the blank paper. He'd never had trouble writing to Abby before, but this one felt like an assignment from his high school English teacher. The words wouldn't flow. He tried to picture her laughing, but every time he closed his eyes, he saw the Japanese soldier's head snapping sideways, spouting a fountain of blood, and the way his squad mates looked at him afterward.

It took twice as long as normal to write, but he finally signed off. He didn't bother reading it. If he did, he knew he'd try to rewrite it. He wanted to be done with it. For the first time he could ever recall, he didn't want to think about or interact with Abby. He wanted to drink.

Sergeant Huss had warned him about socializing with the lower ranks, but he didn't want to drink with the other NCOs. He wanted to drink with his friends—particularly Gil. He set his mind to the task, but he needed to eat first.

He went to the temporary chow hall and ate dinner. Having a hot meal rejuvenated him. Even though the fare was mediocre, he went back for thirds. His guts would undoubtedly punish him in the morning, but at least he'd be able to relieve himself in a real latrine, not squatted over a log while keeping an eye out for poisonous insects and snakes.

By the time he left the tent city, it felt abandoned. Besides a few unfortunate squads left to guard their gear, the entire company had gone into town.

He walked at a leisurely pace as the colors of the sunset turned the sky into different shades of yellow, red, and purple. Sunsets in the tropics never failed to capture his attention. How many more would he see? He wished Abby were here to see it, but no—the last thing in the world he wanted was to have Abby in New Guinea. He pushed the thought from his mind and strolled toward the sounds of a party.

He found the first bar easily enough. The raucous hoots and howls led him right to it. He stopped to watch from across the street. Australians and Americans filled the place and spilled out onto the street. The smell of spilled beer and sweat overwhelmed him even standing fifty feet away. Clyde wondered if Third Squad was inside somewhere. He didn't relish finding out—too damned crowded. He'd need wings or brute force to even make it to the bar for a beer. He hadn't seen any military police presence. He wondered if Finschhafen had a police force. If so, they'd be busy tonight.

After a few minutes of watching the show, he kept walking deeper into town. He hoped there'd be at least one more bar. The noise faded behind him as he wound through the streets. It didn't take long to find the next one. The scene wasn't nearly as robust, but he still heard yelling, almost hysterical laughter, and the clinking of glasses.

He stepped through a flimsy gate, which seemed to be the edge of the property. A few soldiers milled around outside, drinking mugs of beer. He noticed a horseshoe pit and wondered if the Aussies played or if the Americans had set it up in the short span they'd been there.

He stepped inside the bar and the smell of stale beer mixed with cigarettes wafted over him like a physical force. He stood there for a moment, letting his eyes adjust to the low light. He bobbed and weaved through the crowd, then sidled up to the bar. The harried barkeep barely acknowledged him when he raised his hand, hoping for service.

He cupped his hand and yelled, "Gimme a beer!"

The barkeep glanced his way and nodded. Clyde turned away from the bar and looked around the place. He didn't see Gil or anyone else from the squad. He knew most of the faces and the ones he didn't were probably Aussies. Compared to the first bar, this scene bordered on sedate. He preferred sedate at this point.

The barkeep thrust the beer into his back. It overflowed and wetted the bar. Clyde flipped him some change, clutched the beer and drank it down by half. He held it up and looked at the color. It tasted good, but didn't resemble the beers from back home. Chunks of some unidentifiable substance floated in amber. He didn't complain, though. It went down smoothly and wasn't Halazone-laced water.

He drained it quickly, sent the empty glass back down the bar and held up two fingers when the barkeep glared.

"Cooper, is that you?"

Clyde spun around and saw Sergeant Huss. He couldn't hide his disappointment.

"It *is* you. Don't look so happy to see me. Chrissakes, you look like someone shit in your Christmas stocking."

"Hello Sergeant Huss."

"*Hello Sergeant Huss,*" Huss mocked in a feigned child's voice. "Don't give me that shit. We're off duty. Come join us in the corner." He pointed and Clyde saw an entire table of NCOs. "But don't come unless you've got beers. I gotta take a piss." Clyde noticed a slight slur.

"Got two on the way," he called to his back.

This time, he turned in time to catch the beers before they sloshed into his backside. He paid and took the beers to the NCO table. He recognized all of them, but he stood there like an idiot, gaping. A few were obviously drunk, swaying and giggling in their seats, while others simply looked buzzed and happy.

One of them finally noticed him. He squinted up at him. "Corporal Cooper!" Sergeant Plumly, the platoon sergeant, exulted.

Cooper didn't know what to say. His instinct was to brace and stare straight ahead, but no, they were off duty, so he set one beer in front of Plumly, then raised his own mug and said, "In the flesh," and drank deeply.

Plumly looked at the beer, then back at him as though he'd delivered him the holy grail itself. "Well, shit, Cooper, you think of everything. Have a seat."

The place didn't have a spare square inch to sit. Plumly stuck his paratrooper boot on the butt of Sergeant Gibbs from Fourth Platoon and kicked him off his stool. Gibbs sprawled. Cooper expected a fight, but Gibbs laughed uncontrollably—finding his new position on the floor the funniest thing that had ever happened to him.

Clyde sat in the newly vacant seat and took another swig of beer. He exchanged nods and grins with a few men he knew better than the others, both sergeants and corporals alike. He noticed that most of the corporals stood and the sergeants sat on chairs.

Plumly watched him closely. It made Clyde uncomfortable, so he drank more beer.

"Huss tells me you did a hell of a job with Third Squad," Plumly barked over the din of nearby conversations.

Clyde didn't want to talk shop, but couldn't very well tell his platoon sergeant that, so he nodded and said, "He's a good squad leader."

"Told me about that Jap in the foxhole."

The beer suddenly tasted like ash in his mouth. He swallowed it and stared into Plumly's hard but slightly glassy eyes.

"Can we talk about something else?"

The rest of the NCOs quieted and listened to the exchange. Clyde supposed they had talked about his actions ad nauseam. Gossip traveled through a combat unit even faster than a woman's Bridge Club. He wondered if the story had any resemblance to the truth at this point.

Huss came up behind them. "You about to tell us about the Jap in the foxhole?" He sounded like an excitable kid, wondering if the Easter egg hunt had started yet.

"I'd rather talk about *anything* else," Clyde groaned.

"Alright then, tell us about that pretty wife of yours," Huss said with a slight leer in his voice.

Clyde came off the chair with his fists balled. He faced Huss, ready to knock his teeth in.

Plumly hooked his thumb in one of Clyde's belt loops and pulled him back onto the chair. "Sit down, Cooper. You're wound tighter a snare drum."

Clyde sat, but he kept his glare on Huss. Plumly's voice hardened. "Tell us what happened that night, Cooper. We all wanna know how it went."

Clyde felt cornered. The last thing he wanted to do was relive the whole damned thing. Couldn't they just let him drink in private?

"You gotta get it out, son." Plumly pushed Clyde's beer up to his mouth. "Drink the rest of that, then down another." He raised his voice. "Bring him a whisky, too."

A whisky appeared in a dirty shot glass as if by magic. Clyde drank the beers quickly, then slammed the whisky in one gulp. It burned all the way and warmed his belly. His head swam and a feeling of calm euphoria hugged him like a warm blanket. He sipped another beer, which appeared in front of him.

Plumly said, "Alright, now that you're properly greased, tell us the story."

Clyde stared at the top of the beer. Where to start? "Well, I guess . . ."

Plumly interrupted him angrily. "No! Don't tell it like a simpering piece of shit leg. Tell it to us like a goddamned warrior. An airborne warrior, by God!"

A raucous roar of approval from the entire bar erupted. Men raised glasses and gathered around, eager to hear the story they'd only heard snippets of since it happened.

Clyde started again, but this time he told it as though recounting an action-packed Hollywood movie. The men loved it, cat-calling and slapping his back throughout. By the time he finished, he was covered in spilled beer as men hoisted and sloshed, but he didn't care.

He felt good and it wasn't just from the alcohol. He had flipped the script on the whole incident. Instead of feeling awful, he felt invigorated, like after his first jump. It was an ugly incident, one he wasn't proud of, but by God, he'd done his duty. These men—his paratrooper brothers—wouldn't judge him poorly for doing his duty. They'd see him through whatever came their way because they were all in the same damned boat. They'd get through it together, or die trying.

Plumly grinned like the cat that ate the canary. He raised his nearly empty glass and bellowed, "Now that's how you tell a story! Geronimo!"

The bar erupted in the chant, "Geronimo! Geronimo! Geronimo!"

Clyde woke in darkness. His head throbbed and his stomach ached from throwing up, but despite his physical ailments, he felt better than he had in days. Plumly had been right—telling the story to cheers and toasts had a cathartic effect. He felt as though a weight had fallen off his shoulders.

He heard groans as men rolled out of cots. As far as he could tell, the entire company had drunk too much last night. He wondered about Gil. He didn't remember seeing him. Hopefully, he wasn't cooling his heels in the brig—if there was a brig.

He didn't know the time, but his internal alarm clock told him it was time to get up. He felt his way along the corridor and pushed his way past the tent flap and outside. Still a little drunk, he swayed. The transports would come soon. He hoped it wouldn't be a bumpy ride. He didn't relish sitting among sick paratroopers as they rose above the Owen Stanley mountains and down into Port Moresby. It was never a smooth ride.

Steam rose from the temporary chow hall. He wove his way in that direction in search of coffee. The smell of eggs and toast nearly made him gag as he entered the tent. Low lights lit the space and he saw haggard paratroopers dotting the tables. A few looked up at him, then turned back to their coffee. None had food.

The server behind the table handed him a steaming cup of black coffee without being asked. Clyde took it gratefully. He stuck his nose in and let the steam warm his face. He sipped it and it scalded his lips and tongue, but he didn't care. It might be the best tasting coffee he'd ever experienced.

He sat among a small group of corporals. A few grunts and nods of recognition passed between them, but no one was ready to talk just yet. He sipped the coffee and tried to keep his mind off his throbbing head.

Finally, a corporal from First Platoon said, "You guys hear where we're going?"

"Moresby," another answered.

"No, I mean after that."

"There's an after that? Spill it."

Clyde peered at him over the lip of his steaming coffee. He didn't look nearly as torched as the others. He looked tired, but not as though he'd been drinking all night.

"I was posted outside the command tent last night—lucky me," he lamented. "Anyway, I heard 'em talking." He glanced around, then leaned in closer. "It's another airborne operation. I guess the brass was so impressed with the Nadzab jump, they want us to do it again."

"Another airfield?"

"I don't know about that. All I know is they're getting us ready for another operation."

Clyde said, "We were here less than a month. Seems awful quick to be starting into another one."

"Well, you know how that goes . . . hurry up and wait awhile."

"God, I hope not. All that time in Australia nearly drove me nuts. I'd rather get this whole thing over with."

"What's your hurry?"

Clyde concentrated on spinning his coffee cup slowly before he finally answered. "I've got a brother somewhere up in the Philippines, last I heard. He was stationed there when this whole shitty war kicked off. I think he's a POW, now. Heard it from the Red Cross, but that was over a year ago. Heard nothing since."

"Jesus. Might be better off dead than being at the mercy of the Japs."

Clyde couldn't disagree, but he knew his brother wouldn't quit. He'd never quit anything in his entire life. "Maybe. But if there's a way to survive, he'll find it, but only if we end this war in time. Every day that passes is another day in hell for those guys. There are thousands of POWs from the Philippines. *Thousands.* Sure, I wanna make the Japs pay for Pearl and all, but I really just wanna do my part and bring this war to an end and get my big brother back."

The distant sound of engines grew steadily, and they all listened intently. Clyde sipped his coffee. It resembled battery acid now. He wondered how long it had been since Frank had a strong cup of army coffee. He slugged the rest down in one thankful gulp.

17

NOVEMBER 1943

East China Sea

Frank Cooper didn't know how long it had been since he'd last seen sunlight. After boarding the ship in Manila Bay, they'd quickly shoved and pushed them down multiple flights of metal stairs. A fall would've surely killed them, but they'd all miraculously kept their footing and made it to the bottom.

Japanese soldiers and sailors cursed and shoved them toward the back, then shackled them to the beams running the length of the ship's hull. They seemed more brutal than normal, probably because of the recent airstrike. No daylight streamed through, but tiny sprays of seawater did, for they were far below the waterline. The ship remained at anchor for a full day. The hisses and bangs as sailors readied the vessel sounded loud and ominous in the darkness.

They had provided buckets to relieve themselves into, but rarely were they in place before their bowels exploded into the bilge. The stink should've gagged the rats that slunk over their bruised legs, but instead it seemed to invigorate them. Many prisoners screamed in the darkness as rats bit them viciously.

Finally, the ship's screws turned and the ship got underway. After a few hours at sea, their captors unshackled them, allowing them to move freely. Sailors wearing masks emptied the filthy buckets. Many gagged and vomited from the vile stench.

Now that they were underway, the Japanese set up a large trough that emptied into a massive container. Many prisoners made a point of staying close to it at all times. The filth and stink dissipated somewhat and the rats became less bold. Lights flickered to life overhead, spreading a yellow hue across the fetid space.

Twice a day, morning and evening, their captors delivered food and water. Surprisingly, the food was much better and more plentiful than what they were used to in Camp Bilibib, but it did little to quell their bowels and sometimes created more of a problem. Their systems weren't used to the increased calories, but Frank ate as much as he could get his hands on and he felt better.

"What happens if the ship goes down?" someone asked that first day.

It was a question they'd all thought about, but hadn't wanted to voice for fear it might come true. Someone had finally responded. "It would be a mercy."

After two days, Frank and Grinning Bear figured out the best place to spend their time was close to the hatchway the sailors used to deliver food and water. The hatch didn't open directly into the open air, but it provided a bit of freshness and they'd breathe it in deeply.

A Japanese soldier always entered before the sailors. He carried a rifle and aimed it at them while barking commands. Once they'd moved back a step or two from the hatch, the sailors would come in and deliver the food and water.

They worked quickly, not wanting to spend any more time in the diseased space than necessary. Despite their haste, they were careful not to spill. The hatchway remained open during the delivery. Even the short time it was open helped to freshen the air and lift their spirits.

After their evening meal, Frank sat on the step closest to the hatch. He could still smell the lingering fresher air, but it faded quickly. Grinning Bear sat on the step below him. He had his eyes shut, but Frank knew he wasn't sleeping.

"How long you think we'll be on this tub?"

Without opening his eyes, Grinning Bear answered. "Japan's a long boat ride from Manila. A week?"

"That's what I figure, too. The longer we're on here, the farther from our lines we get."

"It's not a direct route. We may be closer at the moment."

"You worry about our own guys sinking us?"

"I worry about the next minute, then the next hour, then the next day. There's no use worrying about something we can't help."

"With this door shut, we'll die down here. Doubt they'd open it for us. Rather have us die than escape."

"Hatch."

"What?"

"We're on a ship. It's not a door—it's a hatch."

"Right, hatch then. I forget you marines are just glorified sailors."

He opened one eye at that. "Watch your mouth, soldier boy."

They both settled in and shut their eyes. The stairs weren't comfortable, not by a long shot, but it beat sleeping deeper in the hold and closer to the filthy bilge water.

Aboard USS Dogfish
East China Sea

Captain Bodi Stanislaus swept his high-powered binoculars across the horizon. The sun would be up soon and he'd have to submerge the USS *Dogfish* to avoid being spotted by Japanese aircraft.

His mission was already a success. They'd engaged and sunk a Japanese Maru Class freighter two hundred nautical miles south of their current position. The enemy escorts had searched and even launched aircraft, but the Dogfish had slipped away easily enough.

Now they patrolled north of the Philippines, far from their base near Bougainville Island. The seas grew rougher the further north they sailed, but the air remained warm, although the mornings had more bite.

Ensign Wally Vilander stood beside him, scanning with his own set of binoculars. "Nothing but empty sea, captain."

Stanislaus looked at the fading stars overhead. "It's gonna be a clear day. We'll have to submerge soon. Jap aircraft frequent this area far too much for my liking."

A dark strip of land hung low on the horizon to the west. "Bring us to one six zero at ten knots."

Vilander let his binoculars hang from his neck and grasped the radio handset. He blew in it, then keyed the side and relayed the orders to the con. Below, Charlie Henshaw read the orders back and soon the Dogfish slewed to port and increased speed.

Stanislaus said, "We'll use the island for cover from anything coming from the west. I'd like to stay on the surface as long as possible. We'll see if any targets happen past."

An hour later, the Dogfish stopped a mile off the coast of the small deserted island. With the island as a backdrop, they'd be invisible to anything from the sea in either direction. The only way an enemy aircraft would spot them would be if they flew directly overhead, which would be bad luck.

"We'll stay here for the day. I don't have any interest in staying on the surface and giving some Jap flyer a wake to follow. We don't have enough battery power to stay submerged until dark."

Ensign Vilander didn't complain. He'd served under Stanislaus for six months and although he wasn't the most aggressive sub commander, he kept his men alive and still stung the enemy plenty.

"Aye, captain. We'll keep a watch topside."

"Keep men on the deck guns in case some Jap pilot gets lucky and flies over us." Vilander nodded and Stanislaus yawned then said, "I'm gonna rack out for a few hours. Let me know if you spot anything."

"Aye. Have a good rest, sir."

Stanislaus retired to his tiny room. He washed his face, shaved, and was about to strip and get into bed when the intercom hissed. Vilander's tinny voice said, "Sorry to disturb you, captain."

"What is it?"

"We have a plume of smoke to the east. Looks like another Maru, sir."

"Any escorts?"

"I don't see any. Estimate her speed at eight to ten knots. She's heading due north, near as I can tell."

"Sound general quarters. Let's get into the war."

He gave a longing look toward his bed, then stepped out into the corridor. A sailor almost bowled him over as he raced to his battle station. When the sailor saw it was the captain, he braced and saluted. "Sorry, sir."

"Move it, sailor."

"Aye, sir."

He squeezed past him and Stanislaus continued toward the control room, moving through the tight confines like a man who knew his ship better than his own mother.

The Dogfish's screws turned and she shuddered as she moved away from the island. Before Stanislaus ascended the conning tower to join Vilander outside, he ordered, "Load tubes one and two. Set torpedo running depths for ten feet."

He sprang up the ladder like a teenager, all thoughts of his bed long gone. He joined Vilander, who saluted, then pointed. The plume of black smoke was obvious. Stanislaus found the ship in his powerful binoculars. He brought it into focus. It was two miles away, he figured. He made a few quick mental calculations as he studied it, then said, "We'll be able to catch her easily."

"Yes, sir. A sitting duck."

Stanislaus scanned the sea around the hapless freighter. "I guess they feel pretty safe this far north. I don't see any escorts, either." He scanned the skies overhead. "They could have air cover, but I don't see any." He scanned for a few more seconds, then nodded, satisfied that the ship was truly alone. "Get the men below. When we're in deeper water, we'll dive." He didn't wait for Vilander to reply, but slid down the ladder quickly and went to the chart table.

Soon the Dogfish slipped beneath the waves. Red light diffused the inside, making the sweating sailors, some bare chested, look sinister. The smell of sweat mixed with oil and made Stanislaus feel right at home.

"Take us to ninety feet and give me ten knots, bearing 120 degrees."

They plotted the enemy position, an estimation, but a good one. Stanislaus estimated they'd be close enough for another look-see in eight minutes. Time ticked by slowly. He forced himself not to check his watch, but to count in his head instead. A calm, cool, and collected captain gave the men more confidence. *Submarine captain 101*, he thought.

"Bring us to periscope depth and slow to eight knots."

"Periscope depth at eight knots, Aye."

The Dogfish angled upward to sixty feet and slowed. When it leveled off, Stanislaus went to the periscope. "Up periscope." It rose from the deck and he knelt and extended the handles as soon as it was high enough. He immediately saw the enemy vessel, but scanned 360 degrees to make sure they were truly alone. He didn't see another ship anywhere and what he could see of the sky was empty and blue.

He held the periscope on the ship and said, "Mark target. Estimate speed six knots."

"Marked."

"Ready torpedoes one and two, and open doors."

The calculations went into the Torpedo Data Computer, but it was hardly needed. The Maru was truly a sitting duck. A few minutes later the TDC had a firing solution.

"Torpedoes one and two ready to fire."

"Fire one!" A whoosh of air and a shudder that he felt through the soles of his boots. The calm seas allowed him to watch the bubble track from the torpedo through the periscope. It ran straight and true. "Fire two!"

Another whoosh and he settled in to watch the show. He scanned the horizon again, not able to believe the ship could be out here all alone, but he saw nothing but open ocean.

"Ready torpedo three and four." He doubted he'd need it, but the Mark 14 torpedoes weren't as reliable as he would've liked. More than once, he'd watched in frustration as torpedoes struck targets but didn't detonate. He'd lost friends because of the damned things. That was also the reason he had them set to run at only ten feet. They settled deeper than their settings and often missed by passing below the keel. The magnets inside were supposed to detonate the torpedoes when they sensed the metal hull of a ship, but he'd never seen that happen. In short, he didn't trust the damned things.

Ray Callahan held a stopwatch. "Time to impact twenty seconds." At ten seconds, he started counting down.

Stanislaus watched, hoping the new camera was working. This would be a textbook attack. It might even make the newsreels back home.

"Three, two, one, impact!"

Nothing. Stanislaus gripped the handles until his knuckles turned white. "Another dud, dammit."

Callahan said, "Fifteen seconds to second impact."

"Fire torpedo three."

A whoosh as the third Mark 14 left the tube.

Callahan counted the second torpedo down. This time, when he called impact, Stanislaus saw an explosion. It looked small, but the hapless ship seemed to plunge downward, then rise quickly along with a towering spout of gray water.

"That's a hit!"

The crew erupted in cheers and backslaps.

"She's slowing. I see fire and smoke. Time to impact?"

"Two minutes," Callahan said excitedly.

"If it's not another dud, that'll put the final nail in the coffin."

It wasn't a dud and the Maru listed heavily and sank within minutes.

"Well done, men. Let's get the hell outta here before all that smoke brings the whole Nip air force down on our heads."

Frank knew they would serve breakfast soon, so he ascended the stairs, or ladder, as Grinning Bear insisted, and sat near the hatch. A few other POWs huddled there, anticipating the fresher air. It had become a prime spot to linger.

The seas had been rough overnight, although Grinning Bear assured him it probably wasn't as bad as it felt. Being this far down accentuated the pitch and roll. The creaking and groaning sounds of metal and wood didn't help either. But now the seas were blessedly calm. The ship barely moved up and down at all.

"Must be a lake out there this morning," Grinning Bear said. "Probably make good time today."

That didn't make Frank feel good. Every mile they traveled brought them farther from the front lines and farther from potential rescue. He hadn't given up on it yet, but he had resigned himself to long years of slave labor in Japan.

The hatch lug spun and Frank stepped away, knowing the big ornery soldier would come through with his rifle and shitty attitude.

The hatch swung open and the hinges squealed. It was only the third day at sea, but he equated that sound with food, water, and fresh air.

He and the others hustled down the ladder and hung around nearby. The slight breeze the open hatch brought had them all facing it and breathing deeply.

The soldier came down the ladder, eyeing them suspiciously. The four sailors behind him held vats between them as they carefully shuffled their way down the stairs to the eagerly waiting POWs. A fifth sailor held a large skein of water. He'd follow the feeders, squirting lifesaving water into their cups.

The soldier stepped to the other side of the ladder and faced Frank and Grinning Bear, his rifle barrel pointed directly at Grinning Bear's chest. It was like a ritual for them.

Frank glanced up at the wide open hatch. He didn't have thoughts of escape. He knew they'd shoot him if he made any move at all, but he wondered if he might glimpse a sun's ray bouncing off the deck. Would they ever allow them topside? He longed just for a glimpse of open sky. How long would they keep them down here? Weeks? Months?

The sailors put the vats of food down, prisoners lined up, holding their bowls and cups. Standing at the foot of the ladder meant Frank and Grinning Bear would be last in line. They didn't worry about missing out, their captors had plenty of food. He wondered if the better treatment would continue when they reached Japan. He doubted it.

An incredibly loud clang reverberated through the hull. Frank instinctively ducked and covered his ears. It reminded him of a Chinese gong being struck. He eyed the soldier, thinking he'd fired a shot, but he looked as confused as everyone else and his rifle barrel didn't smoke.

A hush as the prisoners and Japanese alike exchanged worried glances.

But the ship kept chugging along as though nothing had happened. If they were under attack, *something* would have changed.

The sailors barked orders, and the prisoners slowly rose, and the line continued. The Japanese soldier stayed hunkered, never taking his eyes off Grinning Bear, as though he might have had something to do with the loud bang.

Frank rose and shuffled a few steps toward the food. Suddenly, another bang followed immediately with an explosion sent him sprawling onto the foot of the metal ladder. Wrenching, overwhelming sound filled the space. He felt himself pressed into the deck hard, then it dropped away from him and he had the strange sensation of floating, then falling. The deck came up and met him and pain shot through his body. His hearing went black and so did his vision, but he wasn't unconscious.

Water washed over his body and he sputtered and saw hazy light. The ship settled and his hearing cleared enough to hear awful screams and moans. The ship's hold was unrecognizable from only moments ago. Where the vats of food had been now held only black water with floating chunks of debris, interspersed with struggling men.

Something hard smashed into his back. He spun off it and saw the handrail of the ladder. He'd floated nearly halfway up them. Instead of the overhead being thirty feet up, it was only fifteen feet. The water sloshed back and forth like bathtub water.

The filthy seawater suddenly receded, leaving him clutching the handrail as the current tried to rip him away. He saw a man floating face-down only feet away. Frank reached out and clutched the only thing he could reach—his hair. As the water rushed away, he held fast until the body slumped onto the metal steps and the water drained around him.

Frank glimpsed the hatch. It was still open. He leaned into the body and yelled, "Wake up!" But there was no response. He flipped him over and recognized Blake Greer. His eyes were wide and staring. He had a massive gouge in his forehead, as though a sledgehammer had hit him and crushed his skull without breaking the skin.

He let the body go, letting him flop back onto his stomach. The mass of floating humanity in the bilge splashed and panicked as they fought one another to get to the ladder.

His throat felt as though he'd swallowed shattered glass, but he yelled at them. "Come on! Come on, the door's open. It's the only way out!" He searched for Grinning Bear, but in the darkness and chaos, he couldn't tell one man from another. Many bodies were floating among the swimmers. He wondered where the damned Japanese soldier ended up. He'd surely gun them down if he thought they might escape.

A few men made it to the ladder and stumbled their way up to him. He pushed them forward, still searching for the big marine. A shot rang out and the man in front of him sprawled onto his face. Another shot and another bullet went through the prisoner.

Frank sat in stunned confusion. Where had it come from? It sounded close—right next to him. Beneath the ladder, he heard a guttural growl of anger and rage. He looked through the metal slats and saw the Japanese soldier holding a pistol. A prisoner tackled him and the guard pounded the back of his head with the butt of the pistol. They went beneath the water and didn't come up.

"Larry!" He recognized Grinning Bear's hulking mass and black hair just before they'd gone under. He tried going down the ladder, but panicked survivors filled them, pushing and shoving to get the hell out of there. With no other choice, he leaped over the rail and landed in waist-deep water. His ass hit the metal floor, sending shooting spikes of pain up his spine. He grimaced and waded toward where he'd seen Grinning Bear struggling with the guard.

The water erupted suddenly only a few feet in front of him and both Grinning Bear and the soldier came up, spouting oily water. The enemy soldier had lost his pistol, but held the marine from behind and squeezed his neck in the crook of his elbow. Grinning Bear beat on his arms and tried elbowing his guts, but the soldier was too strong and Grinning Bear had been in a POW camp for over a year.

The soldier met Frank's eyes and grinned. Rage welled in Frank's gut and he lunged forward. He led with his thumbs, jamming them into the soldier's eye sockets. He felt his right thumb sink deep and he hooked it into his skull and held on. The quickness and viciousness of the attack made the soldier release his grip on Grinning Bear, who fell into the water and submerged.

The enemy soldier screamed and thrashed, trying to free himself from the crazed banshee attached firmly to his front. Frank held on and pushed deeper. His eye popped out and swayed side to side grotesquely. The soldier spun and finally flung him off. The soldier staggered back, clutching at his bloody eye sockets.

Grinning Bear rose from the water. He shook his head, saw the struggling soldier, and sprang on him. He punched him in the stomach, then flung his head beneath the water and held on as legs and arms thrashed.

"We have to go! The ship's going down! We gotta get out of here!" Frank urged. He clutched at Grinning Bear, but he didn't release the soldier until he finally stopped struggling.

A few prisoners still struggled to swim their way to the stairs, but they were too weak or wounded to make it. The strong ones were already streaming through the hatch. The seawater near the back was deeper, nearing the overhead.

"It's pitching up. We gotta get off now!"

They fought their way to the ladder and made it to through the hatch and into a short gangway. There was sunlight streaming through. Men scrambled toward it, being pushed against the bulkheads as the ship lurched and pitched.

Another massive explosion ripped through the ship. An unimaginable force smacked into Frank's back and propelled him like a gunshot through a barrel. He felt searing pain, saw piercing light, then blackness.

18

Frank opened his eyes and did not know what had happened. He saw endless blue and finally realized he stared at the sky. He lay on his back, staring straight up. He suddenly remembered the awful explosions and the sinking ship. What the hell happened to the ship?

He lurched upright and his body revolted as his guts and back wrenched painfully. He gripped something hard and realized it must be wood. Was he still on the ship? He thought it would surely sink, but here he lay.

He heard a raspy voice. "Welcome back, soldier boy."

He recognized Grinning Bear's voice. He turned and saw his old friend lying beside him, propped on his bony elbow, grinning at him.

"What—what the hell happened?"

"Ship sank with us on it. Must've been a submarine. Hit us with torpedoes, I'm guessing."

Frank eased himself up into a sitting position. A few other prisoners stared back at him with sullen, sunken eyes. Frank recognized all of them: Neil Winstad, Gale Verona, Micah Winchuck and Glenn Madison. They'd all been through hell together at Bilibib. Their depredations never seemed to end. But where was everyone else? "This all of us?"

Grinning Bear shrugged. "Might be more, but who knows?"

Frank noticed they weren't on a boat, but half a boat. The bow tilted forward, but the middle had been sheared off. Shredded wood stuck up in sharp, jagged pieces, and water lapped in through the damaged slats.

"Jesus, are we sinking?"

"Easy does it, Frank. We're afloat, but only just so." He glared at the others. "They didn't want to pull you aboard. Thought one more would sink us." He tapped the butt of a pistol sticking out from his tattered pants. "But I convinced them otherwise."

"Where'd you get that?"

"I took it off that Jap guard in the bilge. Held onto it somehow through the blast. Guess all those bastards telling us to never let go of our weapons during training paid off." He looked around at the other men. "Glad I did, too. We'd both be in the drink."

Frank looked at the other men. They looked scared and hopeless. "How long was I out?" Frank asked.

"Ship went down three hours ago, I guess."

He looked around and saw bits of floating debris, but not as much as he would've thought. "Where are the Japs? There must've been more survivors."

"There were, but not much left for them to hold on to. I didn't see any other emergency boats, just floating chunks, hardly big enough to get up on. We lucked out finding this." He tapped his pistol again. "I dissuaded any of 'em from making a play on us, though. Now the current seems to have a hold of us." He pointed to a distant outline of land. "Taking us closer to that island. We've been trying to paddle there, but we have little to work with."

Frank squinted through the bright glare of midday. "Thank God. I don't think this thing'll float much longer. Seen any signs of life?"

"A few birds here and there, but nothing on two legs so far."

"What if the Japs are on there? What then? I don't wanna be captured again."

Grinning Bear said, "Me neither."

Another hour passed. The current brought them closer and closer to the island. They could see breakers and even a strip of beach beyond. Soon the half boat lurched against a band of coral reef. The grinding of wood put

Frank on edge. Glenn carefully stepped off the boat and pushed them off the reef, dragging them toward the island. He hopped back in and the half boat sank a little and water came over the sides, but stabilized.

"Figure we're about a half mile from the beach. Should we swim for it?" Frank asked.

"Let's stay with the boat as long as possible. The reefs will tear our feet to shreds," Glenn said.

Grinning Bear glared at him. Frank knew something bad had happened while he'd been unconscious. Best to air out any grievances now, he thought. "Look. I don't know what happened back there, but we've gotta work together or we'll all die."

Grinning Bear turned on him, and Frank repelled at the brief but violent glare. "I'll tell you what happened. They tried to keep me, then you, out of the boat, Frank. If I didn't have the pistol, we'd both be fish food by now. *That's* what happened."

Glenn and the other three men all looked crestfallen and ashamed.

Glenn held up his hands and said, "He's right, Frank. I'm ashamed of myself." He gestured to the others. "We're all ashamed, right, fellas?"

They all nodded emphatically, and Glenn continued. "Look, it was in the heat of the moment. We thought the extra weight would sink us. I know it's not an excuse, but—well—I was scared. We all were. It was a mistake and we know it was wrong. I hope you can forgive us someday, Larry." The silence stretched for a long moment and when Grinning Bear didn't respond, Glenn added, "But in the meantime, Frank's right. If we are going to survive, we need to work together. We won't cause any trouble. We fucked up and we know it. You can count on us whatever the hell happens now."

The others nodded their agreement, looking truly sorrowful. Frank raised an eyebrow at Grinning Bear. Grinning Bear finally gave a slight nod. It wasn't much, but Frank knew he'd work with them, even if he'd never quite trust them again. Frank doubted he ever would, either.

The half boat nudged up against an impassable span of coral reef and stopped. Frank and Grinning Bear carefully stepped out, not wanting to cut their feet. The sun blazed overhead, making them yearn for the shade of the thick jungle just one hundred yards away.

Glenn stepped out to stabilize the boat while the other three stepped onto the coral as gingerly as possible. There wasn't anything to gather from the boat. They'd escaped the sinking ship with whatever they had on their backs, which was mostly rags.

Grinning Bear made sure the pistol stayed secure in the waist of his pants. He only had eight bullets, but those bullets would certainly come in handy, especially if they ran into trouble on the island.

Frank had no illusions, though. If the Japanese had any kind of presence, they'd be outmatched and certainly outgunned.

They carefully eased themselves over the coral. When they came to deep spots, they swam. The water felt wonderful, but once on shore, the dried salt would mix with the sand and grate on their skin.

Frank said, "First priority is finding water."

Grinning Bear nodded and kept pulling himself along. "Water, shelter, and food."

Glenn added, "Water. Oh God, I hope there's water."

Frank saw the desperation in his eyes. They'd all been through countless days of misery. Thirst and hunger were just a part of the equation of being a POW. He'd trained his mind not to think about the deprivation. Once you started down that path, it usually led to more misery. His thirst threatened to consume him now, though. He fought to suppress it the best he could.

"When we get to shore, stick together until we know if we're alone or not. There might be natives, too," Frank said.

"Let's hope they're friendly," Grinning Bear stated flatly.

"No reason they wouldn't be. More likely, they're oblivious to the whole war . . . unless the Nips are here."

"They might be headhunters," Grinning Bear said, and Frank didn't have the energy to ask if he was joking. He hoped so.

They finally weaved their way through the coral and made it to the soft black and white sand beach. They gazed at the jungle for a moment. The island showed no signs of human activity. Thousands of tiny crab tracks crisscrossed the otherwise pristine sand, but no human tracks.

Grinning Bear drew the pistol and they walked up the beach toward the shade of the palm trees. They stopped in the first shade they came to and sat down heavily.

Frank wanted to shut his eyes and sleep. His body ached and he felt as tired as he'd ever felt. He had countless cuts and bruises, but by some miracle, he hadn't sustained any more serious damage, despite being launched from the doomed ship and flung a hundred feet into the open ocean.

None of the others had suffered any serious damage either, although Glenn's right arm had been burned from the shoulder down to the elbow. The skin had peeled and ugly, puss-filled blisters formed and popped occasionally. The pain must be excruciating, but he seemed more concerned about his thirst. Perhaps he was in shock.

Frank wanted to go in search of water, but his mind shut down and he couldn't keep his eyes from drooping and finally closing.

He woke what only seemed like a few seconds later, but he could tell by the angle of the sun that he'd slept at least an hour, probably more.

He sat up and felt every muscle scream in protest. He winced and couldn't stifle a whimper. His head swam as though he'd been on a fast merry-go-round.

Grinning Bear noticed him awake. "Welcome back."

Frank tried to speak, but felt as though his mouth was stuffed with dry cotton. His tongue felt immense, and didn't seem to fit in his mouth properly. He couldn't form words. Although uncomfortable, it wasn't a new feeling. He simply nodded back at the marine. Grinning Bear, of course, understood.

"We need to find water." Grinning Bear's voice sounded raspy and tired.

Frank saw the others were still asleep. Glenn's burnt arm glistened with wetness and had taken on a pinkish hue. Tiny pustules of puss dotted the burn site. Frank raised a questioning eyebrow.

Grinning Bear shook his head. "Let 'em sleep. We'll come back for them."

Frank nodded and tried to get to his feet. Despite his best efforts, the coral had cut his feet. There was no avoiding it. He hoped they wouldn't become infected, but thought they most likely would.

They walked gingerly along the edge of the jungle and the beach.

Hopefully, they'd come to a creek emptying into the sea. They had to scramble over sections of rock and, at one point, they swam through a beautiful tidal pool. Fish darted and flashed as they swam, and crustaceans dove into rocky hiding places.

"At least there's plenty to eat," Grinning Bear uttered.

Frank had finally generated enough saliva to respond. "Won't be too easy to catch."

"Whittle a piece of bamboo to a sharp point and skewer whatever we need."

Frank wanted to crack a joke about him being a Native American, but he couldn't muster the extra energy. He just grunted and kept following along.

They'd traveled a half mile or so when they saw a distinct change in the landscape. Instead of a sandy beach, the ground turned to wet pebbles and rocks. Their feet sank into them and water lapped over their feet. This high up the bank, it had to be fresh water.

Frank reached down and scooped some to his mouth. He slurped and said, "It's fresh water."

He bent to scoop more, but Grinning Bear clutched his hand and pointed. "Let's go upstream. There's bound to be a pool."

It was all frank could manage not to slurp more of the muddy water. They struggled through the pebbles and rocks. When they reached the edge of the jungle, the ground turned solid. There was no sign of the creek, but they could hear moving water somewhere close. They pushed through a copse of massive leaves and came to the edge of a pool.

Frank slipped and half his body submerged. He sucked in great mouthfuls of water. He closed his eyes and savored the taste as though drinking the finest beverage. Hands grabbed his ankles and pulled him out and onto the grassy edge. He took a deep breath of fresh air. He wanted to dive his head back in and continue drinking, but he saw Grinning Bear's stunned face.

Standing only a few yards from them, stood ten native women half submerged, staring at them, all completely naked. Their beauty struck Frank like a slap. A few were older, but most were young and their breasts were full and their bellies tight. Despite his thirst and battered body, he couldn't help staring.

Grinning Bear slumped to his knees and swayed. He leaned down and stuck his head into the water and drank deeply. Frank tore his eyes from the women and joined him. He thought once he'd hydrated enough, the vision of the women would fade away. Surely they couldn't be real. It must be a hallucination. He'd heard of such things happening and even experienced it for himself occasionally.

But when he rose with his whole face dripping precious water and looked again, they were still there, just like before, staring at them with wide eyes and bare breasts.

Grinning Bear came up. He had his eyes closed. He said, "I saw the most wonderful vision before."

Frank said, "Open your eyes. It's not a vision, they're real."

Grinning Bear slowly opened his eyes. He shook his head and murmured, "Did we die? Are we in the happy hunting grounds?"

"Would they let my kind in? No, we're not dead. Just damned lucky."

Frank and Grinning Bear slipped into the luxurious water, slurping it as they swam steadily toward the women, who simply watched them come.

When they could touch bottom, they stood and trudged their way to the nearest of them. They didn't retreat, but watched them as though having their own vision. They stood in front of them and looked them over, still not convinced they were real.

Grinning Bear reached out and touched the nearest woman's arm. She took a quick step back and babbled to the others. They all backed away, not showing them their backs. Frank found himself mesmerized by their swaying breasts—completely enamored by them. He tried to avert his gaze but couldn't. He felt as though he'd entered some alternate universe, something from ancient times involving goddesses. He hoped there wouldn't be serpents.

His thirst finally got the better of him, and he leaned forward and drank more water. The women covered their mouths and laughed as though he'd done something funny.

Frank glanced at Grinning Bear, who continued to stare at them as though in a trance. "Why are they laughing?" Frank asked.

Grinning Bear finally snapped out of it and answered, "They probably bathe here. We're drinking their bath water."

"I don't care." He stuck his hand in and scooped more into his mouth. "They could've peed in it and I wouldn't care. It's the best tasting water I've ever tasted."

The women continued laughing and talking among themselves. One of the older ones stepped forward. She spoke softly, but they couldn't understand her. She reached out both hands to them. They looked at one another, then walked to her and they each grasped a hand. She smiled and pulled them along like children.

The others walked beside them, and Frank couldn't take his eyes off their womanly parts. The older woman led them to a well-used trail. She broke her grasp, spoke, and pointed at the path. The women filtered into a line in front of them and Frank and Grinning Bear kept their eyes on their strong, sinewy butts.

"What about the others?" Frank finally remembered the men they'd left on the beach.

Grinning Bear mumbled something Frank couldn't quite decipher, but he got the gist—forget those assholes. Frank didn't disagree.

Time passed as though they were in a fog, but they finally entered a wide area that gave way to a village. More shapely women watched them with keen interest. Strong men holding spears and small bows also watched from the edges. Some glared, but most were simply curious. They must seem like apparitions, white, emaciated, ghosts. Had they ever seen white men before?

The women led them to the center of the village and stepped away from them as though presenting them as new found treasure, or perhaps parasites. The older woman spoke to an older man in low tones.

The man lifted his chin and strode to them, looking them up and down. He circled them as though inspecting cattle. They both fought the urge not to turn with him. They knew instinctively that they shouldn't.

The Shaman, for that was how he seemed, stopped in front of them. He was shorter than both of them, but seemed taller. He had scars all over his body, making him look as though he had some bizarre skin condition. They stood stock still, as though being inspected by a visiting general.

The man finally spoke directly to them. He had a high voice that didn't quite match his swarthy look. The language sounded singsong. They'd heard nothing like it before, and didn't understand a word. When they didn't respond, the Shaman looked back at the woman and he seemed to switch languages, although it may just have sped up. He looked back at them and raised his eyebrows.

Frank cleared his throat, then said, "We don't understand. We are friends. Friends," he repeated hopefully, while clutching his hands to his scrawny chest. Then he put his hands together as though in prayer. "Thank you for not killing us. We mean no harm. Friends."

The women covered their mouths again and tittered and laughed. The men also smiled, but fell short of outright laughter.

"Did I say something funny?" Frank said while leaning toward Grinning Bear.

"I think our language must sound funny to them."

"Well then, we've got that in common. Theirs sounds like a damned cricket chirping."

A well-built young man, also with scars, but not nearly as many, approached the elder. He leaned in close to his ear and spoke. The elder nodded and the young man circled behind them, just like the old man, but instead of coming to their front and facing them, he came up behind Grinning Bear and snatched the pistol from his waistband.

Grinning Bear couldn't help reacting. He spun quickly, but the deed had already been done. The young man held the pistol by the barrel. He grinned and said something, then threw it up in the air and caught it again as though testing the weight and balance.

"Careful, young fella. It might go off and blow your face off," Grinning Bear said with a broad smile across his face.

The young man studied the pistol, then grasped the pistol grip and aimed it at Grinning Bear while squinting down the sights. Grinning Bear kept smiling, but he lifted his hands as though surrendering. "Easy does it, pal. Easy does it."

The young man made a popping sound with his mouth while pretending to shoot.

Grinning Bear nodded and said to Frank, "They've definitely seen guns before. Not sure if that's good or bad. This kid's gonna plug me if he's not careful."

The man suddenly spun in a circle as though dancing, exposing more scars on his back. He danced his way to the elder's side, then stopped and held the pistol out to him as though presenting a precious gift. The elder took it and inspected it as though he'd seen plenty. He then stepped forward and handed it back to Grinning Bear.

He spoke in that high singsong voice and Grinning Bear smiled and said, "Thank you." He tucked it back into the back of his tattered pants.

The next few hours Frank and Grinning Bear spent in relative ease. The islanders fed them as though they were long-lost brothers. The bare-breasted women brought them food, mostly fish and various types of crabs. They ate more than their bodies could hold and both men excused them-selves hurriedly and puked into the jungle, but they soon returned and resumed eating, only slower this time.

They waved the women off and rubbed their bellies, hoping the women understood the basic gist of "we can't eat any more." They smiled sweetly, took the food away, and left them alone. It didn't take long before they both fell asleep on the surprisingly comfortable thatch bedding.

Frank woke with a start. He looked around the dark hut in a momentary panic, before he remembered where he'd ended up. He felt to his right, expecting to feel Grinning Bear still sleeping beside him, but he wasn't there.

Frank's belly hurt, but he wasn't complaining. He'd eaten too much, too fast, but he wouldn't have it any other way. He stood and tested his legs. He felt good. Marvelous what food and water could do for a man. He felt his way forward, letting the flickering light seeping into the building guide him.

He felt a pang of guilt as he thought of the men they'd left on the beach so many hours ago. They might've died of exposure by now, for all he knew. Time to bring them in.

He found the door and pushed it open. He stood in the doorway and took in the village. Grinning Bear sat with the four other men from the beach. They looked dazed as they greedily ate and drank their fill. Grinning Bear sat next to them, staring into the fire.

Frank stumbled his way out of the hut and walked toward them. A few women noticed, and one of the younger ones darted to his side and put her arms around him for support. Her soft skin against his made him reel. A dizzy spell passed quickly, but she steadied him. He regaled in her womanly scent. Perhaps she'd rubbed flowers on her body. He wanted nothing more than to take her into his arms and lie with her on the comfortable thatch bed he'd just left, but he resisted the urge and let her help him toward the fire ring.

The young woman guided him to a carved-out stump across from the others. He didn't want her to let go, and when she finally did, he felt an emptiness. She smiled demurely and he shook his head in wonderment. "That look. It may as well've come from someone back in my hometown. The world's the same all over, I guess."

Glenn, Neil, Gale, and Micah kept eating while they stared at him across the flames. Finally, Glenn said around a piece of some kind of meat, "Glad you guys found this place."

"It's like heaven on earth, isn't it?"

They all nodded and continued tearing into the food. "You might wanna slow down a bit. Larry and I both threw up from eating too much, too fast."

Neil nodded emphatically, swept his filthy hand across his mouth, and said, "We already did that." Then he went back to eating.

Frank put his hands out to the fire's warmth. The night wasn't cold, but it was an automatic response.

Micah wiped his mouth and directed a question at Grinning Bear. "He know about the Japs?"

Frank's eyes widened and his body tensed. "What did you say? Japs? What Japs?" he looked around frantically, ready to bolt into the jungle.

"Easy does it, Frank." Grinning Bear lifted his chin toward his right and Frank's left. "Over there, just outside the light."

Frank strained to see, but the fire's glare was too much, so he stood and took a few cautious steps. It took a moment for his eyes to adjust, but he saw three huddled Japanese men eating quietly shoulder to shoulder.

Frank felt a coldness in his guts. "Who? What? What the hell are they doing here?" he finally asked.

"The natives found them somewhere. I'm sure they must be survivors from the ship. The currents that brought us here did the same for them."

"Are—are they armed? Are we prisoners again?"

"Course not. They didn't have any weapons. They're as haggard and tired as we are."

Frank chafed. "I doubt that very much! They weren't POWs, for chrissakes."

"True, but they also weren't our captors. They're navy boys, far as I can tell. I don't think any have much rank either. The one in the middle might be a corporal or something, but I can't tell. I don't think they'll be a problem."

"What if there's more? What if there's more that are armed?" He looked around frantically. "They could sneak on us as we speak. I won't let them take me prisoner again. I'd rather die, Larry."

"Relax. The natives won't let 'em get close. I checked. They're watching the whole area."

"But they've only got spears and bows. The Japs could have rifles or even submachine guns. We gotta get outta here."

"I led them to our guys here, Frank. They're skilled. They move like ghosts. Any Japs that turn up, they'll see 'em long before they get seen."

"But do they know how dangerous they are? Do they know about them?"

"I watched 'em with the Nips. They don't treat them the same way they treat us. The women won't go near them, in fact—they make a point of keeping far away. They must've had some run-ins with them before."

"Then why don't they just kill the sorry little bastards?" He regretted his tone as soon as he'd said it, but the prospect of being captured again caught him off guard. It made him angry. He couldn't imagine having to go through the entire ordeal all over again. He'd kill whoever needed killing to avoid capture, or die trying.

"I don't know. I can see they don't like or trust them, but they never threatened them. They just keep a close watch." He pointed and Frank saw three strong young men crouched, holding spears nearby. They focused on the Japanese sailors as though on guard.

"I won't be able to sleep with them nearby. What if the natives get sloppy? What if the Nips try to cut our throats?"

Grinning Bear pulled the pistol from the back of his pants and hefted it up and down. "I'm armed, remember? If they come at us, I'll shoot 'em." He tucked it back into place. "I've already made a point of showing it off to them. We don't speak the same language but they understood alright."

"I don't like it. What if their navy comes looking for them? The ship must've gotten an emergency radio call out. If they come looking for survivors, the first place they'll look is right here."

"Hadn't thought about that."

"That's because you're just a stupid fucking marine." He meant it in jest, but it came out harshly.

Grinning Bear bristled. "Watch your mouth, soldier boy. Nothing we can do about it now, anyway. If it makes you feel better, we can put together a watch schedule tonight."

The thought of trying to stay awake on watch seemed laughable. He wanted to eat, then sleep for the rest of his life—maybe have some fun with the pretty young native gal first. A watch schedule? Nah.

He was about to say so, but Glenn beat him to the punch.

"Is that necessary? Doubt I'd be able to stay awake for long. I can barely keep my eyes open as it is." The other men nodded their agreement and kept shoving food into their mouths.

Grinning Bear stood up abruptly. "I don't remember asking for your permission." He paced back and forth, then stopped and said, "We'll get our beauty sleep tonight, but in the morning, we need to figure all this out. I'm with Frank. They will not take me prisoner again. I'll die first."

Everyone nodded their agreement as they stared into the flames.

19

NOVEMBER 1943

Camp Knothead, Burma

Shawn Cooper and the rest of Operational Group Bellevue finally arrived back at Camp Knothead after the Myitkyina operation. The long trek drained their supplies, so they'd scrounged and foraged for food the last few days. They'd all learned to live off the land, but they didn't relish eating lizards, snakes, snails, and whatever else they came across. Each man dreamed of eating Chef Watson's meals again and kept their gnawing hunger away by talking about it constantly.

They didn't stay long at Camp Knothead. After only a few days of rest, orders came, sending them northeast toward the Hukawng Valley, where the largest concentration of Kachin tribesmen trained to fight under the tutelage of other operational groups in the area.

Shawn considered that mission the best he could hope for. Traipsing around, ambushing and sabotaging Japanese soldiers was fine, and he was imminently qualified, but he'd seen enough combat for a lifetime. The prospect of training the indigenous mountain people appealed to him. He looked forward to staying in one spot for a while.

It would take a week to travel on foot from Camp Knothead to the upper reaches of the Chindwin River, where the legendary Kachin chief,

Zhang Htaw Naw lived. Shawn had heard stories about the man ever since he set foot in Nasira. He had a reputation as a fierce fighter and a stalwart leader. Even Didi spoke of him in hushed tones of deep respect.

By now, traveling overland for miles upon long miles felt normal. Despite being far behind enemy lines, they had little to fear from Japanese patrols in the vastness of Burma. By now, they knew how to avoid their strongholds, and if they came across Japanese patrols, they were easy to avoid.

They still moved cautiously, and if they came across signs of enemy soldiers, they marked the area, then skirted around. When they came across Kachin villages, they described the Japanese locations. The Kachin invariably already knew, but they'd smile, wave, and nod their thanks.

They finally dropped from the mountains and descended into the wide open plains of the mid-Hukawng Valley. The Chindwin River meandered through the lush valley, growing ever larger the farther it moved down the valley. From the mountains above, the river and its many tributaries looked like an arterial tree Shawn remembered from his high school human anatomy class.

They crossed the valley cautiously, although they saw few signs of the enemy. They traveled upstream, often dipping their canteens and feet into the river. Tigers loomed along the edges, making easy meals of unsuspecting animals of all sorts. The OSS men avoided them even more diligently than the Japanese.

Soon the grassy plains gave way to steep, jungle-filled mountains. The Chindwin River's banks closed in and the placid waters turned rough in spots where steep drops and rocks formed roaring rapids.

After they passed one of these deep canyons, high above the river, Kachin men wearing brand new U.S. Army uniforms met them. They carried M1 Garands, carbines, and Thompson submachine guns. When Shawn first saw them, he thought they were regular U.S. Army soldiers, but as he closed on them, they looked more like children playing dress up. The uniforms fit well, even though the Kachin were generally smaller in stature than American boys. For once, the U.S. Army sent them appropriately small sizes.

Their strong presence in the valley made Shawn feel at ease, but he wondered why the Japanese hadn't assaulted the area. Surely, they must know about the sudden threat in the middle of their territory, or perhaps not.

They finally arrived in a sprawling village on the top of a flat-topped mountain.

"This is the chief's village," Boyd said as he walked beside Shawn.

Shawn looked around excitedly. He had an image of the man in his mind's eye as a towering, chiseled warrior. He doubted his image matched reality, but it was a pleasant thought. He didn't see anyone that looked like a warrior chief, however.

The resident OSS operational group members met them. Shawn hadn't seen many of them since they'd trained together near Shangri-La in Maryland. It felt like a homecoming. He shook hands, slapped backs, and caught up on their lives. Most of their stories were like his own, although few had seen actual combat yet.

They all looked vastly different than they had back in the states. Shawn passed the news that Fenton and Mackie had both been KIA and Hutch wounded. They'd already heard the news, but hearing absolute confirmation from the men who'd been there had a sobering effect.

"How about you guys? You lose anyone?" Shawn asked Grant Hollins, a friend from the early days of airborne school.

"Not yet," Hollins answered. "Lost a few to malaria and shit like that, but they all recovered and came right back. You Knothead guys have seen more combat than we have, though. We've been mostly training the Kachin."

"That's why we're here, too. I hear they're really ramping things up, getting ready for Stillwell to come sweeping down from China."

"You got that right. We're getting plane loads of supplies nearly every day. When we're not training, we're busting our humps bringing in scattered gear. Those flyboys have improved markedly, but when they first started, they had a lot of mis-drops." He spread his hands to the vast skyline. "There're hundreds of thousands of dollars' worth of gear out there if you can find it. Most likely be there for eternity."

"Hopefully, the monkeys don't figure out how to use the stuff." Shawn elbowed Veatch, who looked chagrined. "Veatch here nearly got us killed by the sons of guns. He fancied some monkey meat, so he shot one of 'em. It really set the others off. If they'd been armed . . ." he ran his finger across his neck. "They were mad as hell."

Hollins laughed. "Armed monkeys. Maybe we could train them to kill the Nips, too. They wouldn't do even half as well as these Kachin fellas, though."

"We've been fighting alongside a few of them ourselves." Shawn thought of Didi and the dead Burmese porters. "They're brutal but effective."

"You got that right. That's exactly what we need out here. The Japs are just as brutal, but the Kachin can outfight them any day of the week. The Nips really messed up when they ticked them off."

"So they're taking to the training alright?"

"Hell yes. It's as if they have an innate understanding of our weapons. They master them quickly, and I'm not just talking about rifles and carbines, but heavy machine guns, mortars, even ack-ack guns. Hell, the head honcho wants us to teach 'em how to use the howitzers."

"You have howitzers here?"

"They dropped a few in pieces just last week. Ammo is supposed to come soon, too. Also, a few fifty pounders."

"By head honcho, you mean the Zang Ding Tang fella?"

Hollins shook his head and lowered his voice. "Don't make fun of him where the Kachin can hear ya. You might wake up dead. It's pronounced, Zhang Htaw Naw."

Shawn repeated it until he got it right. Hollins said, "You got it now. To answer your question, yes, that's the Kachin head honcho. He's the real deal."

"He's in charge of *all* the Kachin?" Shawn asked. Hollins nodded and Shawn continued, "Even the ones to the east and south of here?"

"Yep. All of 'em. He's charismatic as hell—a natural leader. They love him and would willingly die for him. He's sharp, too. Speaks English well enough to understand him and he just started learning it a few months ago. You shoulda seen General Donovan and him jawing like old friends. He hates the Japs more'n we do."

"Donovan met him?"

"Yeah, crazy son of a bitch came all the way here from Nasira."

General Donovan was known for pulling such stunts. He never sent his men where he wouldn't also venture.

Shawn asked, "When you think they'll be ready to take the Japs on? I mean, as a regular fighting force."

His eyebrows raised in surprise. "They already are. Haven't you heard? They've been hitting Jap outposts for almost a month now."

"We were out at Myitkyina for a few weeks. Been out of the scene around here. They're having success?"

"Oh yeah. You've seen the way they move through the jungle—they're like ghosts. They get in close, then assault with brutal efficiency. They hit hard, then retreat. The Japs barely know what's hit 'em before they're gone again. Nips have learned not to pursue 'em, too. The Kachin are patient and deadly ambushers. Best damned troops I've ever seen. The brass has labeled their battalions American-Kachin Rangers."

Shawn squinted at him. "Rangers? Come on, they can't be that good. As good as us?"

"Let's just say I'm glad they're on our side. They haven't lost a single man, and they've killed over three hundred."

"Three hundred? They must be exaggerating. That's common enough."

"I've seen their handiwork. They wiped out an entire company-sized unit last week. Believe me, when Stillwell gets 'em all armed and ready to go, the Nips won't have a chance."

"Well, I'll be damned. I'm looking forward to diving into the training, but it sounds like we might be a day late and a dollar short."

"From what I've heard, Bellevue will accompany them on the raids. You fellas have seen more combat than the rest of us, so they want you to fine tune anything that needs tuning."

"Really? Doesn't seem too fair. You guys have been here the whole time. You know 'em a hell of a lot better'n we do."

Hollins shrugged and spit out the weed he'd been chewing. "Oh, we'll get our share, too. That's the problem. Now that the Kachin have weapons and they know how to use 'em, they're champing at the bit to go after every Jap outpost within a thousand miles. The brass wants to reign 'em in to keep 'em ready for the main event. Get the rest of them armed and trained up first. A couple of hit-and-runs are okay, but they don't want the Japs to know just what kind of force we've got here. As good as they are, if the Japs can pinpoint 'em, their air force will pulverize them. The Kachin have never been under a sustained artillery barrage or heavy bombing runs. They don't dig holes and hide—it's just not who they are. They're stalkers and attackers. We've gotta use 'em wisely at the right time or they'll be wasted and the offensive will fail."

"I see," Shawn said, somewhat overwhelmed. "Well, I'm just glad to be a part of it all. Sounds important as hell."

"It is. By attacking Burma, the Japs will have no choice but to pull troops from the Chineses front. It's something the brass has been promising good old Chiang Kai-shek for years. It's why he allows us to have bases in China in the first place."

"I feel like a damned pawn in a massive chess game."

"Ha, you're not far off, only I don't think us OSS men are pawns, more like bishops." Shawn raised an eyebrow. Hollins added. "Bishops can slice deep behind enemy lines." He punched his chest proudly. "That's us."

"Okay, bishops then." He made a mental note not to play chess with Grant Hollins.

Shawn and the rest of OG Bellevue spent the next week getting familiar with the Kachin they'd be going out on patrols with soon.

They watched as the other OSS men guided them through more training scenarios. It became immediately apparent that Grant Hollins hadn't been exaggerating—the Kachin were born infantrymen. They understood tactics as though they'd grown up studying them.

They also inherently understood the weapons systems and needed very little instruction to figure them out. They learned quickly how to dismantle and put them together again, too. Some of their timed sessions rivaled long-standing records set back at Fort Benning. Shawn wondered if their small hands helped them.

Their movements through the mock exercises the OSS men set up for them, bordered on genius. They moved stealthily and knew instinctively how their brethren Kachin would move, making the whole operation smooth and efficient.

Now the time came to put their training to the test. The next day, OG Bellevue would accompany a new fifty-man strong platoon of Kachin Rangers in search of the enemy. They'd head southeast where there'd been a surge of Japanese movement reported.

Shawn sat around a low campfire watching a mess of what looked like potatoes wrapped in leaves, cooking slowly deep in the coals. The Kachin huddled around other fires dotting the camp. Laughter, sometimes raucous and loud, permeated the camp. The whole place had a buzz of nervous excitement.

Shawn looked over his shoulder at a nearby group of laughing Kachin. "Looks like they're happy to be going out tomorrow." He turned back and leveled his gaze at Umberland sitting across the fire from him. "You have any idea what we'll be facing?"

"Yeah, actually I do. The Nips have built up an area about twenty miles southeast of us. It's an ammo dump with a platoon's worth of soldiers guarding it."

"An entire platoon? How are you so sure?"

"The other great thing about the Kachin besides them being gifted fighters is their capacity to gather intelligence. Everyone knows everyone else. They have a natural network of ready-made informers everywhere. The information passes quickly even without radios, but now that we've got those, we get up to the hour intelligence reports. From all accounts, it's astoundingly accurate."

JoJo chimed in. "You're not worried about the numbers being evenly matched? What about overwhelming odds and all that?"

"It's a concern, but command told me not to sweat it. They said one Kachin Ranger is equal to ten Japs."

Shawn said, "You've seen 'em training all week. You think that's accurate?"

Umberland nodded. "Yeah, I do. Don't you? You've seen 'em, too."

"Maybe veteran units, but you know how it is with green troops. Anything can go wrong and usually does. We don't know how they'll react under real stress."

"That's what we're there for. Once we get eyes on the ammo dump, the Kachin will give us their plan of attack and we'll say yes or no—give them suggestions if need be."

Boyd asked, "If it doesn't go as planned, we'll be on our own out there with a cadre of green troops."

O'Keefe guffawed. "So, what else is new?"

Umberland stood and stretched his back. "We'll leave at 0300 and arrive sometime tomorrow evening. We'll have the evening to look the place over and come up with a workable plan, then we'll hit 'em the next night. Get some rest. We've got a long trek tomorrow."

The Kachin Rangers kept a steady pace all day, stopping only a few times to drink water and gnaw on strips of meat. The mules they brought along seemed to be as durable as them.

They moved with little fear of enemy patrols. The network of informers would've warned them of any enemy movements along their path. But even with that information, Shawn was happy to see the Kachin still moved with stealth and wariness.

They understood that the intelligence network could work both ways. The Japanese had their own informers. Although the Kachin wouldn't shy away from a fight, they'd rather get to the destination unobserved. They seemed eager to prove to the Americans just how effective they could be.

As they neared where the ammo dump should be, two Kachin men met them. They appeared from the bush as though they'd been a part of it. They greeted the other Kachin warmly and led them the rest of the way. They pointed out the copse of trees hiding the sight, then faded back to wherever they'd come from.

They'd traveled the twenty miles in just five hours. Shawn and the other Bellevue men didn't carry more than they usually did. The Kachin carried their own packs but used mules to carry the mortars, mortar shells, and the four .30-caliber machine guns, along with extra ammo. Shawn wondered what would happen if they lost the mules. Would they be able to haul the gear back out or abandon it in the field?

They set their base camp in a thick stand of trees less than a quarter mile from the ammo dump, which sat in a copse of trees across a wide stretch of waist-high kunai grass. The mules grazed lazily, not caring one whit about the war.

Once they'd dropped supplies and set out security, they scouted a route to get across the field and get into the grove of trees shielding the ammo dump. They could use the cuts and natural defilades in the ground to move without being detected, even in daylight.

They made it across the grassy plain easily, and Shawn crawled forward until he could barely see the edge of the ammo dump. The Japanese had thinned the area, but kept the overhead foliage to shield the place from any passing Allied aircraft. They'd used the cut logs to build revetments around the ammo dump itself.

One road led into it, but didn't come out the far side. As he lay there watching, a truck trundled in and he watched as shirtless Japanese soldiers loaded a few large boxes into the back. The driver lit a cigarette and leaned on the side of the truck, watching the other men work. When they finished, the driver turned the truck around and drove back the same way he'd come.

From his low position, he couldn't see the entire ammo dump, just the leading edge. Despite that, he saw quite a few enemy troops. They didn't seem overly concerned about their safety. A roving patrol passed by, but barely glanced their way. They walked along a well-trodden path. They passed only fifteen yards from him and the others. He watched their faces and decided they weren't too serious about their job. They seemed bored. *That'll change*, he thought grimly.

After a good look around, they retreated along with the Kachin Rangers. They moved back across the field to their rendezvous point. Shawn was glad to see their own Kachin Rangers taking their guard duties seriously. He barely saw them before they showed themselves and let them pass. The grazing mules barely lifted their heads as they passed.

The Kachin officers retired into a secluded area to form a battle plan. It only took half an hour before they emerged wanting to discuss things with Bellevue.

Shawn and the others stood around a scraped out area. The Kachin had made a rough sketch of the ammo dump in the dirt. A pile of sticks formed a pyramid representing the actual ammo. Smaller sticks and rocks represented the enemy positions they'd observed on their scout.

From what Shawn had seen, it looked accurate. The far side of the ammo dump also had detailed depictions of defensive layouts, but he'd just have to trust them, since he hadn't ventured to that side.

In stilted English, the ranking officer, a man the Americans nicknamed Honcho, laid out the plan. Shawn was happy to see they'd kept it pretty simple. Simple plans with less moving parts worked better once the bullets flew.

Forty Kachin Rangers would form a semicircle around the western edge, where the road entered. Six men would hang back and stop any trucks that might come for resupply or try to bring reinforcements. They would set two machine guns up on either flanks facing the ammo dump, one would be in the center and the fourth would cover the road from a raised promontory far back near home base. It would provide more insurance against reinforcements and could also cover their withdrawal back to the rendezvous.

The rest of the Kachin would simply assault the dump. They'd take the enemy by complete surprise, set charges in the ammo dump itself, then escape. The machine guns would then go to work, pinning the enemy, not allowing any survivors to defuse the C-4 plastic explosives.

Umberland pursed his lips and nodded. He glanced at the OSS men. No one raised any red flags. The plan seemed sound and effective.

Umberland clapped Honcho on the shoulder and said, "It's a good plan." He held his thumb up. "Guess you didn't need to haul those mortars all this way," he said as an afterthought. "The tree canopy will keep them from being effective."

Honcho smiled a toothy grin. "Mortars there." He pointed, and at the edge of the tree line, the three mortar tubes along with the stacked mortar shells sat ready. Two grinning Kachin stood beside each tube.

Umberland scowled. "They won't do any good with the tree cover."

Honcho smiled again and said, "White hot."

Umberland squinted, unsure what he meant.

"White phosphorus?" Shawn offered.

Honcho nodded emphatically. "If no boom. White hot make boom." He mimicked the white phosphorus settling through the treetops and onto the stacks of ammunition represented by the pyramid of sticks.

"Well, I guess you've thought of everything."

The moon shone through a thin layer of clouds and lit up the grassy plain leading to the grove where the attack would occur. Shawn felt odd being out of the action. He stood with the fourth machine gun crew on the promontory overlooking the road. If the Japanese had a reaction force nearby, which the Kachin intelligence network had somehow missed, the .30-caliber would have a perfect position on them as they came up the road.

The main Kachin force left home base at midnight. They planned to attack at 0230, so they had plenty of time to get into position without tipping their hand. Despite knowing the Kachin were out there on the grassy plain, Shawn barely saw them. He briefly saw slow-moving shapes that eventually disappeared into the trees.

The minutes passed slowly. The clouds skittered overhead and the moon peeked out occasionally to light up the landscape in silvery shafts. He checked his watch. Only fifteen more minutes before showtime. He figured they must be in place by now.

A part of him wished he sat ready to fight beside the rangers, but his rational mind rebelled against the thought. He'd seen his share of combat. He didn't mind sitting this one out.

He wouldn't be able to see much of the action from here, but he'd certainly hear it. He crouched beside the .30-caliber crew, who looked impossibly young. He guessed neither of them could be older than fourteen or fifteen—maybe younger.

Despite their age, they manned the machine gun as though about to go into action, even though they might never get the chance. They clearly hoped the Japanese would pursue the Kachin as they retreated, but Shawn doubted that would happen. They'd most likely be too stunned to react.

He checked his watch again. They'd synchronized with Honcho's just before they'd pushed off. Shawn remembered how Honcho had stared at the brand new, American supplied, watch. He coveted it as though it were made of precious emeralds.

The time clicked to 0230 hours, and Shawn held his breath, but nothing happened. The onslaught of sound and slaughter he expected simply didn't occur. He squinted at his watch, thinking he'd read it wrong—but no.

Finally, at 0234 hours, he finally heard a shot, followed immediately by more shots in quick succession. The distinct staccato of Thompson submachine guns joined in and mixed with blasts of grenades. He saw flashes in the trees.

From here, it didn't seem too intense, but he knew the Japanese would see it much differently.

The fire intensified suddenly, then almost dropped to nothing. A few more grenade blasts, then only the sounds of far off yelling sifted through the trees. Was it already over?

The ripping sounds of the three .30-caliber machine guns firing in short bursts filled the air. Even through the trees, he could see the tracers ripping through the night. A few ricocheted wildly into the treetops with bizarre twang sounds.

He checked his watch again. If everything had gone to plan, the C-4 fuses would ignite at 0300 hours. He expected that to be quite a light show. Based on what he'd seen, the ammo dump held thousands of pounds of high explosive ammunition. It would light up the sky for miles around.

The clouds parted, and moonlight shone down. He touched the gunner's shoulder when he saw the first of the Kachin Rangers sprinting away from the grove of trees and into the grassy plain. No fire from the enemy position followed them and soon the field filled with dark shapes moving back to home base in an orderly manner. The lead men stopped to cover others just emerging, just the way they'd trained. His respect for these fighting men grew deeper.

The young machine gunner kept his barrel pointed at the road and he gave Shawn a toothy smile. On the other side of the machine gun crew, JoJo sat watching the spectacle. He held his carbine loosely. He gave a low whistle, then said, "Smooth as silk, so far."

The machine guns in the grove abruptly stopped. The silence made Shawn's ears pop, as though missing the sounds of combat. More Kachin Rangers filtered out from the grove of trees and stopped, facing back the way they'd come. Soon he saw men trotting along, holding tripods and boxes of ammunition. Next, he saw the men carrying the .30-caliber weapons themselves. He could see the orange glow from their still-hot barrels.

He wondered if they'd burned through any. It wasn't uncommon, particularly for men new to the adrenaline of combat. There was nothing like the feeling of power that came with firing a belt fed machine gun, and even the most stalwart veterans could burn barrels out in the heat of the moment. But he doubted the Kachin had suffered from the same affliction. He had heard no bursts longer than ten rounds. They'd learned well.

The Kachin Rangers sifted back through the grass, leapfrogging from one position to the next, always covering one another. Finally, a few rifle shots rang out from the ammo dump. Shawn expected a storm of return fire from the Kachin, but they kept their disciplined withdrawal.

The Kachin machine gunner shifted his barrel from the road to the grove of trees. Shawn could feel his eagerness to join the fight. The attack force had nearly made it across the grassy plain and into the cover of the rendezvous point, leaving the field free for engaging any enemy forces stupid enough to pursue them.

Shawn checked his watch. "The C-4 should blow that place sky high any second now."

0300 hours came and went, but no explosion. More and more rifle shots rang out from the grove of trees. Flickers from the enemy muzzles lit up the edges of the grove. Shawn sensed the gunner's eagerness to get into the fight. Shawn touched the Kachin gunner's shoulder. "Give 'em the business. Open fire!"

Shawn doubted he understood his exact words, but he caught the gist. He settled into the sights, then pressed the trigger. The sudden roar made Shawn jump, even though he knew it was coming. He watched the initial burst of pure tracer fire lance into the tree line a little high. The gunner adjusted, then fired a longer burst, sweeping the barrel across where they'd seen the muzzle flashes.

Shawn pushed to his belly, expecting return fire. The gunner kept his bursts short, but relentless. Still no explosion from the ammo dump. Either the Japanese had found and defused them, or the Kachin hadn't set the timers correctly. The acid activated fuses could be temperamental sometimes.

The familiar sound of outgoing mortar shells made him look up. He thought he could see the shells arcing into the moonlit night gracefully. He watched the treetops. The sudden brilliance as the white phosphorous shells burst in them took the rest of his night vision.

More shells landed, and each time they burst lower in the trees as they burned their way through. He couldn't tell for sure if they were on target, but it looked about right from his vantage point.

He had a love hate relationship with white phosphorous mortar shells. The white hot phosphorous burned at over 1,400 degrees Fahrenheit. It burned through anything it touched. It was great for burning down structures and trees, but it had horrifying effects on human flesh.

He didn't have time to ponder what it was doing to the Japanese soldiers still alive at the ammo dump, because the ammo dump suddenly and violently exploded. It was too late for him to close his eyes. He only saw spots behind his closed eyelids. He instinctively pressed his face into the dirt as the shock wave swept over their position. His floppy hat flew off his head. His ears rang, despite having the forethought to cover them with his hands.

The roar reverberated through the valley. He wondered if they'd hear it all the way up in China. He remembered General Stillwell famously telling the 101 Detachment brass that he wanted to hear booms in the jungle. Well, this would certainly qualify. He hoped the son of a bitch was listening.

When Shawn lifted his head and looked back at the grove, it looked nothing like it had only moments before. Fire consumed trees and a cloud of black and white smoke rose steadily, finally blocking out the moon. Nothing could have survived that blast. He stood and brushed the dirt off his backside.

JoJo stood beside him. He gave him his hat back. "Found this for you."

"Holy shit! That was impressive." His ringing ears made him talk too loudly. He replaced his hat and looked down at the machine gun crew. The gunner still peered over the barrel, searching for new targets. The barrel hissed and smoked.

Shawn said to him, "I don't think there's anyone left to shoot down there."

JoJo raised his voice. "You think the C-4 finally cooked off or did the Willy Peter get to it?"

"Hell if I know. Smart of them to bring the mortars, though."

JoJo shook his head at the growing conflagration. "I'd say these Rangers are ready to be released into the wild—wouldn't you?"

"We couldn't have pulled it off any better ourselves. We better get the hell outta here before the whole Jap Eighteenth Army comes up the road."

"I'll bet these guys would welcome the challenge."

"You're right—they might even whoop their asses."

20

Operational Group Bellevue, along with the Kachin Rangers, packed up and left their temporary attack HQ soon after hitting the ammo dump. The destruction left by the incredible explosion from thousands of pounds of ammunition igniting simultaneously had filled Shawn with awe, and he still remembered the tremors that had shaken his body.

They didn't venture back into the area, but he doubted anyone could've survived. Intelligence said an entire platoon of Japanese soldiers had guarded the ammo dump—all gone in a flash of violent carnage.

Spirits were high as they used the remaining darkness to move as far away from the area as possible. Soon the place would crawl with Japanese searching for revenge.

They didn't hide their tracks, but walked along a well-used dirt road. Their prints looked the same as countless hundreds of others. The further up the Chindwin River valley they traveled, the more secure they felt. Shawn could sense the Kachin Rangers becoming complacent with the passing of each mile. It made him nervous. They were still far behind Japanese lines, and dawn approached quickly.

The sky had just lightened in the east when he strode up to Lieutenant Umberland and voiced his concern. "Are we gonna find cover soon? Sun's about to come up."

Umberland pursed his lips. "I suggested it, but Honcho wants to keep pushing. There's a village another two miles up—he knows them and wants to stop there for the day."

"It'll be full daylight by then."

"Yep. He feels pretty safe this far up the valley."

"Nips are gonna be looking for payback."

Umberland nodded his agreement. "We discussed it already. He wants to keep going."

"You could overrule him."

Umberland glared at him with growing annoyance. "For chrissakes, I know that, Cooper."

Shawn understood that the conversation was over. Being an OSS man allowed him some levity with the officers—they respected *and* expected every other operator's opinions, but Shawn knew when to stop pushing. Umberland was as competent as they came and he'd follow him anywhere. He just wished they'd get the hell out of the open.

The sun rose and the air itself seemed to turn a reddish-yellow as it shone through the low clouds on the horizon. *What was the old saying? Red sky in the morning, sailor takes warning.* He didn't think the same thing applied on this side of the equator, and it didn't help his outlook.

The ancient road wound up the valley, mostly in a straight line. He crested a low rise and, from his position near the back, he could see the front of the column of men and mules.

They'd bunched up, as though they weren't deep behind enemy lines, and the Japanese Air Force didn't own the skies. He felt profoundly uncomfortable. He could sense the other OSS men felt the same way. They'd poked the hornet's nest just a few miles back and a few hours before, and the Rangers acted as though they'd single-handedly won the war.

He finally saw the village in the distance. The sun had burned through the low clouds and it shone down on them in full force. Sweat formed on his brow and dripped off his nose. He searched the skies—clear and sunny, and thankfully devoid of enemy aircraft. He yearned for low clouds and rain.

A group from the village hustled down the road and met the lead men of the column, slowing their progress. Even from his position near the back, he could hear the excitement in the Kachin Ranger's voices, as they no doubt regaled the villagers with their war stories. He wondered if they resembled the truth.

Then he heard what he'd feared—the droning engines of aircraft. The column of men and beasts halted at the same instant and listened. The engine sounds reverberated across the valley, making direction hard to pinpoint. Odds were it would be an enemy aircraft. It could be a C-47 on a supply drop, but he doubted it.

Umberland yelled, "Get off the road! Take cover!" Even though the airplane wasn't in sight yet, Umberland wasn't willing to wait around and find out if it was a friendly or not.

Shawn agreed with his assessment. He sprinted off the road and flung himself into a ditch about forty yards off the road. He considered running to the nearest clump of trees, but doubted he'd make it before whatever was coming arrived.

The engine noise increased steadily and he pinpointed the direction. It came along the same route they'd come from—following the road. He chambered a round into his carbine—for all the good it would do. He saw a flash of movement near a far off ridge and his heart sank. Two Zeros rose over the ridgeline, obviously following the heavily used road, hoping to get lucky.

The Japanese pilots couldn't help but see them. The Kachin Ranger's luck had just run out. He hunched low. The grass would help conceal him, but not from above. Had the others found concealment in time? He peered over the grass and saw men sprawled out near the road. The mules still stood stoically in the road, grazing on nearby grasses as the whine of the engines rose. Mortar tubes stuck out of their loads conspicuously. Would the Japanese notice them as they flew past at over two hundred miles per hour? He doubted they'd need the evidence to attack. After the ammo dump, everything on the road would be fair game.

The Zeros came steadily. They spread out and climbed, obviously getting a better view. He guessed they swooped over his position under five hundred feet. He caught the glint of glass and the lead enemy pilot's head peering down. The mules stopped their grazing momentarily to glance up, then resumed. Shawn willed them to run away, but they were oblivious to his wishes.

The Zeros sped past, then pulled nearly vertical. They'd definitely seen them. They only had moments to find real cover. Shawn didn't need coaxing. He sprang to his feet and ran as fast as his legs would take him toward the relative safety of the trees.

He heard the whine of engines, then the hammering blows from the Zero's powerful 20mm cannons on the wings and the 7.7mm machine guns on top of the engine cowling. He dove and rolled behind a downed tree, and made himself as small as he could manage. The ground shook with bullet impacts.

When the Zeros screeched past, he raised his head and saw they had riddled the road. Geysers of mud and dirt obscured it, mostly. He strained to see the mules, but couldn't see through the cloud.

The Zeros arced into the sky gracefully. They'd make passes until they ran out of ammunition or were driven off. Perhaps they'd already radioed their position to other hunters. They had to get the hell out of there.

The pair of Zeros lined up again, parallel with the road. Shawn couldn't help himself. He propped his carbine on the log and fired the contents of his thirty-round magazine. He tried for a leading deflection shot, but nothing happened. The first Zero's deadly machine guns opened fire again, and this time they strafed further off the main road.

Shawn reloaded and readied himself for the next aircraft. He heard the distinct sound of one of the Browning .30-caliber machine guns open fire. Tracers lanced up at the Zero, and the gunner used them to guide his shots, but they passed harmlessly behind. It was enough to throw the enemy pilot's aim off, however. His strafing run was brief and off target.

As Zeros screamed past, this was their chance to get out of the open and into the trees. He heard yelling and the Kachin were on their feet and sprinting. The Zeros arced up again, then gracefully leveled off and dove toward them once more. Shawn suspected this might be their final strafing run. He couldn't remember the ammunition capacity of the A6M Zero, but they must be close to bingo.

The pilots adjusted as they saw the fleeing troops in the open. The .30-

caliber machine gunner opened fire again and this time his tracers surrounded the lead Zero. Shawn wondered if it was the same crew he'd stood beside during the ammo dump raid. He hoped not, but suspected they'd be the ones fearless enough to try it. If they survived, he'd congratulate them on a job well done.

Chunks fell off the lead Zero and the wings wavered side to side as the pilot used the rudder pedals to yaw the aircraft and slide it out of the way of the machine gunner's sights. The front of the aircraft winked as another round of strafing resumed. Despite the brutal attack by the Zero, the accurate fire from the Browning continued to slam the airframe.

The Zero pulled up and Shawn heard the engine catch and grind. He rolled onto his back and fired straight up, as it seemed to pass only yards over his head. He saw smoke billowing out the bottom and sides of the engine cowling. The fuselage was filled with smoke and he wondered how the pilot could continue flying without being able to see.

The Zero gained altitude quickly and disappeared over the ridge. He turned in time to see the second Zero unleashing a deadly stream of bullets. The geysers of dirt and debris walked toward the machine gunners. The bullets swept over the position and he saw a piece of a soldier fly into the air. He thought it looked like an arm, but he couldn't be sure.

The Zero finished his deadly work and followed his leader over the far ridges. Shawn got to his feet and squinted toward the machine gun position. He couldn't see anything but black churned up ground. He felt sick to his stomach. The gunner had undoubtedly saved men's lives with his heroics, but he'd likely paid with his life. He hoped it wasn't the ridiculously young soldiers, but had a bad feeling.

He stepped into the dust cloud still hanging over the road and walked along the carnage. He saw the remains of the mules. They'd likely died on the first pass. At least they'd died quickly. As suspected, the machine gunner was dead. His body was riddled with gaping holes, and he was missing an arm and a leg, but his face looked pristine. It was the boy. He wished he knew his name. *So damned young.*

Umberland yelled, directing the Kachin to gather what they could and get into cover. At first, they walked aimlessly about—stunned—but the calls for help and the pained groans from wounded men pushed them into action.

They were under the cover of the jungle with what remained of their supplies, along with their wounded and dead within half an hour.

"We should tell the villagers to vacate. The Japs won't spare them," Shawn said as he helped place a wounded man onto the ground beneath a thick banyan tree trunk.

Umberland replied. "Already done. We didn't even have to tell them."

Two hours later, the droning of more aircraft filled the valley. Twin engine Betty bombers flew in low. The first wave strafed the hapless village. From their position overlooking the area, they could see structures splinter and walls fall down. The next wave dropped what looked like five hundred pound bombs from their gaping bomb bay doors. They reduced the town, which had stood for generations to rubble in just a few minutes. He hoped they had evacuated everyone.

The Kachin watched the destruction with mounting anger, but also regret. If they'd left the road before daylight and taken cover beneath the jungle canopy, this tragedy wouldn't have happened. Foot soldiers may have searched the town, possibly even killed or arrested some people, but the town would still be standing. It was a hard lesson, but one Shawn knew the rangers would take to heart.

Shawn reclined on a warm rock face, allowing his feet to dangle over the Chindwin River far below. Beside him, JoJo and O'Keefe threw rocks. The rocks arced high, then descended inexorably to the placid waters, creating perfectly round ripples. It reminded him of home. How many times had he done this exact thing with his cousins on camping trips?

He hadn't thought about his cousins for a long time. They were more than cousins to him—more like brothers. Frank was a prisoner in the Philippines. He'd heard it from Clyde in a letter that had somehow found its way to Nazira and forwarded to him at Camp Knothead a few months before. He thought how hard that had to be for his aunt and uncle, not knowing if Frank was dead or alive. Frank was one of the toughest men he'd ever known. If anyone could survive, it would be him.

Clyde also informed him he had followed in his footsteps and joined the airborne. Shawn didn't know specifics, but assumed he must be in the war by now. He'd have to send a letter to his aunt and uncle and find out his address. He didn't know when that would happen, though. Getting a letter out from here would be nearly impossible. Perhaps he and Team Bellevue would get some time back in Nasira soon. Then he could catch up on his correspondence.

He had to remind himself that Burma wasn't the only show in town. In fact, in the whole grand scheme of the war, it played a minuscule part. He doubted the folks back home could even find it on a map, let alone knew the ins-and-outs of the war that raged here.

"You guys hear any news lately—I mean, about the war in general?"

JoJo shook his head. "Nothing more than scuttlebutt."

O'Keefe added. "I heard things are turning around for us on this front, despite most of the focus being on Europe. You know the marines took back Guadalcanal, I suppose." Shawn nodded he had. It was old news. O'Keefe held up a finger as though remembering something important. "I heard the Italians quit."

"Quit what?" JoJo asked.

"The war, dummy."

"You mean they surrendered?" Clyde asked.

"I guess so. I heard Burbank and Gunnison talking about it."

"I'll bet my cousin Clyde's over there somewhere."

"He the one who's airborne, too?"

"Yeah. I wonder if he was one of the guys that jumped into North Africa. I know they got torn up pretty badly. They were fighting both the Germans and the Italians, I think. You think they'd tell me if he bought it?"

JoJo answered. "A cousin? Naw, I doubt it. Next of kin, sure, but not a cousin."

"I feel so isolated out here in the middle of nowhere."

"Well, if he's dead, there's nothing you can do about it, anyway. Best not to know."

"Yeah, I guess so, but if he's dead, I'd rather not send his parents a letter asking for his address and upset them more."

"You got any plans for the new year?" JoJo asked.

It was an old joke, but still made Shawn laugh. It also made him a little sad, reminding him that his life wasn't his own. Until the war ended or he was killed or wounded, he would be here fighting the Japanese for the foreseeable future. He couldn't make plans until the job finished. He couldn't help feeling trapped.

If given the option, he wouldn't choose to be anywhere else, but not having the choice in the first place made it hard to swallow sometimes.

"Maybe 1944 will be the year the war ends," he said hopefully.

JoJo threw another rock and it sailed out into space, then sliced into the water far below with barely a splash or a sound.

Overhead, the hum of high bombers made them all glance skyward. Since the attack on the road, any airplane sounds made them jumpy. The planes were too high to see, though, and they relaxed. Friend or foe, they couldn't be sure. The Japanese had been bombing targets in northern Burma and even into India for the past week. He doubted it had anything to do with their ammo dump raid, but it was worrisome. Did they know General Stillwell was preparing to attack or was it just routine daily destruction?

O'Keefe spit over the edge. "Wanna make it a wager? Hundred bucks says it doesn't end in '44."

Shawn wanted to be hopeful, but he doubted it, too. The war wasn't winding down, but ramping up. At this rate, it may never end.

"Naw, I'm not taking that bet."

JoJo agreed. "That's a sucker's bet. Double or nothing for 1946," he offered instead.

"'46?! For chrissakes, I hope not," Shawn guffawed, but thought even that might be optimistic.

21

DECEMBER 1943

Avenger Field
Sweetwater, Texas

Abby loved flying more than anything. The next few weeks at Avenger Field, the WASP trainees transitioned to flying the T-6 Texan trainer, and she immediately fell in love with the aircraft. The powerful Pratt and Whitney Wasp-style engines more closely resembled the fast pursuit aircraft they'd be flying once they received their wings.

The trainer had two seats, but they flew alone most days. They performed long cross-country routes with only a map strapped to their thighs, a compass, and their sharp eyesight to guide them. Despite the vastness and relatively featureless landscape, she'd become proficient at navigation.

She rarely flew from point A to point B, however. Thunderstorms and rain squalls often forced her to adjust her route. Keeping intricate track of the map compared with the ground features took extreme concentration and skill. Getting lost was the easiest thing in the world and also the most gut-wrenching.

She loved it, though. It was like solving a massive puzzle. Watching the ground pass beneath her wings and having it match her map was so satisfying. Finding the designated waypoints, then flying the indicated heading to the next one successfully, made her almost giddy.

They flew long routes all over Texas. Sometimes she'd land at designated airfields, fill up with gas and head out again. Sometimes she'd get a hamburger or a Coke from the stunned airfield crews, most of whom had never met a female pilot.

Abby loved every minute. Flying had become a natural part of her psyche. She couldn't imagine *not* flying. She wondered if someday Clyde would allow her to take him up for a joy ride. That would be a wonderful day. She imagined him in the back of the T-6 with the canopy wide open, his hair blowing in the breeze as she dodged between puffy clouds and they both laughed.

His letters kept coming and thankfully, they weren't as hopeless and scary as the one she'd received the month before. He told her he'd met the enemy and came out on top. He didn't sound proud, just relieved that he'd been able to do his duty when called upon. He didn't get into specifics, but he didn't need to. She knew him well enough to know that he'd seen and possibly done terrible things.

He mostly told her about the other soldiers and the funny anecdotes that inevitably sprang up when a large group of young men lived together in tight confines. It sounded like a glorified summer camp, but she knew it was anything but that. He also asked her to write more sexy letters. She told her fellow trainees that, and they laughed and laughed—but got straight into writing more.

She wrote him telling him that her mother had somehow gotten her address and written a few letters. She told him she sounded like a different person.

She'd noticed a change in her before she'd moved, but figured it was because of her affair. The thought made her cringe once again, but according the Meredith's letter, she'd called it off and was trying to make her marriage work.

The letters were more personal than she would've liked. It made her stomach queasy to even think about, but at least she'd opened up to her. But she still didn't sound happy. She wondered if she'd ever find happiness married to her father.

Abby told Clyde that she didn't want to acknowledge the letters at first, but finally ended up writing her mother a long letter. She couldn't go into specifics about the WASP program, but told her it was the most exciting thing she'd ever done in her life—besides marrying Clyde, of course. She told her she was happy and hoped she could be, too.

Thank God, mother hasn't mentioned visiting. She wouldn't be able to stomach that. Besides, she only had about an hour a day to herself and she spent that time writing letters to Clyde or studying. If her mother did visit, she'd barely be able to see her. They didn't allow any outsiders, family or not, onto the base. Perhaps she should tell her mother that to forestall any unannounced visits.

She'd just landed back at Avenger Field. She hopped out of the cockpit and stood on the wing, and watched the sun dip beneath the horizon. The clouds turned from white to pink and orange in an instant that nearly took her breath away.

Her flight mechanic, Estelle Winker, came out from the hangar, wiping her dirty hands on a filthy towel. Her powerful forearms flexed, reminding Abby of a man's arms. Despite her manly arms, Estelle had a beautiful, womanly face.

"Any problems, ma'am?"

Abby slid off the wing and landed beside her. "Nah. She's purring like a kitten. I put a lot of miles on her, though."

"I'll give her a once over. You have a big day tomorrow."

"I do?"

"You don't know?"

"Know what?"

"The board has you and a couple other gals taking your final check rides tomorrow."

Abby didn't let on, but the news didn't make her fill her with excitement, but worry. Was she ready? She didn't feel ready. Surely they couldn't expect her to pass already—but then she remembered that her training was quickly coming to an end. *Of course I'm ready*, she chided herself.

Training group 43-6 had lost many young ladies to various failures and even two to death. But she and the rest of her group had weathered it all. If she wasn't ready now, she never would be, but it still terrified her. What if she forgot everything? What if she failed on the very last test?

She hustled to the message board outside the mess hall. Sure enough, she read her name there, along with five other trainees. The first check ride would be with Mrs. Leeds, the same pilot who'd checked her off on her instruments. She was tough but fair. Abby couldn't ask for much more than that. A U.S. Army Air Corps pilot would give the second check ride. The name said Captain Ralph Snyder. She didn't know a thing about him, but wondered why a captain would give check rides to WASP trainees.

She filled in her flight hour logbook and recorded her flight notes in the official register. She'd flown over three hundred total hours now. Many in the low wing T-6 Texan. The same aircraft she'd be flying for her final check ride. She hustled off to the mess hall. Since the first few hours of the check ride were spent on the ground going over ground school questions, she wanted to study as much as she could before lights out that night.

She filled her tray without really noticing the contents. She barely made eye contact with the servers, keeping her head down and steadily moving down the line. She took her loaded tray to the nearest table, but stopped when she heard her friends from Bay 7 calling for her to join them. She veered to their table and sat down heavily.

"How was your flight?" Margie Wills asked.

"Fine. No problems."

"Did you fly to Beagle?" Mandy asked her. Abby nodded absently and stirred her food with her fork. Mandy added. "Did you see dreamy Mark the mechanic while you were there?"

Abby nodded. "Yeah, he was there."

"Was he wearing that cut off shirt and all sweaty?"

Abby shrugged and tried to eat a string bean. She chewed it, but the taste nearly made her gag. It wasn't the bean's fault. She was too nervous to eat.

"What's the matter with you?"

She looked up abruptly at Mandy's harsh tone. "I'm on the list for the check ride tomorrow."

Mandy said, "So what? So am I. That's good news. It means we're one step away from earning our little Fifinella gremlin wings."

Abby smiled, thinking about the small caricature that Walt Disney himself designed for the WASPs. It was a cute little gremlin dressed up in flight gear, complete with a leather helmet and goggles. They made it into a patch that they'd wear with almost as much pride as their wings.

"What? Are you nervous?"

"Well, yes. Aren't you?"

"Not really. What could they possibly throw at us we haven't already seen a hundred times already? I've never felt more prepared for anything in my life. I just wanna get it over with so we can start working. You've got nothing to worry about."

Abby glanced around at the others. Many of them would join her tomorrow and the rest would likely follow only days apart. By this time next week, class 43-6 would be history. Members of Class 43-7 were most likely already on their way here from across the country.

"I guess you're right. Of course I'm ready. We all are." She looked at her bland food choices. "But I can't eat this stuff right now." She pushed the tray away and left the mess hall. She wanted to study until lights out.

The next morning she awoke at 0500 and pulled her zoot suit over her pajamas just like any other morning at Avenger Field. But there was a distinct difference. By this time tomorrow, she'd either be a fully qualified WASP pilot or packing her bags.

She forced herself to eat breakfast, knowing she'd need the fuel if she hoped to perform even marginally well. The reconstituted scrambled eggs and greasy sausage sat in the pit of her stomach like a lead ball. Much to her chagrin, despite ample cups of cut coffee, she didn't have an urge to visit the toilet. She tried to will it to happen, even sitting down on the toilet just in case, but had no luck. *Oh God. What happens if I have to go up there during the check ride?*

The time came and she checked into hangar number four. She found Mrs. Leeds and they dove into the verbal ground school portion. Once she got going, she felt much better. She flew through the questions easily. It only took an hour. She went to the bathroom one last time to pee. The weather was perfect. There was no reason to call off the first flight.

She breezed through the flight tests. She was used to Mrs. Leeds and vice versa. She didn't take it easy on her, but Abby knew there was nothing she could throw her way that she couldn't deal with. They performed several touch-and-gos and also simulated takeoffs in different conditions, such as muddy field takeoffs and short fields. She breezed through it all easily. By the end of it, she was having fun.

She finally landed and while the T-6 was being refueled, Mrs. Leeds told her she'd passed the first check ride. She shook her hand with both of hers. "Just one more hurdle, but I don't see why you'd have any trouble passing. You're a wonderfully talented pilot."

She glanced over Mrs. Leed's shoulder and saw a tall U.S. Army Air Corps captain striding toward the fueling station. "Is this Captain Snyder?"

Mrs. Leeds turned, smiled, and waved at him. He waved back. "Hello Valerie," he said, as though he'd known her his whole life. He had an easy smile and Abby guessed him to be in his thirties. She wondered why he wasn't overseas. Perhaps he had been and was simply on rotation back in the states. She knew the army used veterans to train up-and-coming combat pilots, but she didn't think WASP trainees qualified.

Mrs. Leeds introduced them and added, "I think you'll find Mrs. Cooper a good stick, captain."

He gave Abby a tight smile and shook her hand. "We'll see about that." He searched the sky and it seemed to her it was more than just a weather check. She wondered if he was looking for Luftwaffe aircraft or Japanese Zeros. "If you're all ready, I am, too," he stated.

Abby made sure the fuelers had topped off the tanks to full, then did a walk around, making sure nothing seemed out of place. She went to the wing and he offered to help her up. She reached past his hand and helped herself up. She glanced back and caught him staring at her butt. She ignored it and dropped into the front seat.

She strapped in and waited for him to do the same. She checked in with the tower, then taxied to the end of the runway and went through the run-up sequence. She'd already done this during her initial flight, but did it again anyway, just in case the captain expected it. He didn't say a word until they were climbing away from Avenger Field airspace.

"Okay, Mrs. Cooper. I know you've already shown Valerie the basics, but I'll need to see them, too."

He told her what he wanted her to do and she complied with skill and confidence. After an hour of jumping through the required hoops, she felt great. She'd done every maneuver perfectly so far.

As they floated at twelve thousand feet, he said, "It's a shame they don't let you gals practice aerobatics."

She answered. "Well, since we won't be going into combat, they don't see any need for that sort of thing."

"So you're telling me you've never done a barrel roll or a loop while you're all alone on some long cross-country?"

The question bothered her. Of course, they'd all done that very thing, but she didn't know Captain Snyder from a hole in the wall. Was he trying to trick her into answering him truthfully? If she told the truth, would he immediately fail her?

She took the safe road. "No, sir." She said with finality. "It's against the rules."

"Oh, come on, really?"

She turned in her seat to gauge him. He smiled back at her and she nearly told him, but she'd worked too hard to take such a chance on a whim.

He finally said, "I can take you through some maneuvers. Would you like that?"

She thought she could probably do them better than he could, but didn't let on. "It's against the rules, captain. I'm the pilot in command of this aircraft, so the answer is no."

"What if you find yourself in a combat situation someday? You won't survive if you can't maneuver."

"We're not training for combat, sir. We're simply flying from point A to point B. Besides, we're not going overseas where the fighting is."

His voice took on a somber tone. "Not yet, but who knows? We're losing a lot of pilots over there. I've heard the Russians use female pilots in combat roles. They're good, too. Deadly in fact. The Germans fear them. Would you like to do that?"

She looked back at him. The smile had vanished from his handsome face and even through his goggles, she could see that his eyes looked pained.

"No, I wouldn't. Who would want to do such a thing?"

"There's nothing like it. But it's not like everyone thinks. I mean, I've flown hundreds of combat missions and it's mostly just flying in circles, looking for the enemy. When you actually see them, which is rare, the fight lasts for seconds, a minute at the most."

"Where'd you fly? Europe?"

"Yeah. Flying against Germans mostly, sometimes Italians, but mostly 109s and 110s. The 109s are a good aircraft, can climb with the best of 'em, but they don't dive too well. The trick is to stay way above 'em and dive straight past after giving them a dose of fifty-caliber. Even if you don't hit 'em, it's usually enough to break up their formation." His voice trailed off as though remembering. "They're damned good at altitude, too."

She wondered if he suffered from shell-shock. She'd heard of men having to deal with mental issues after being in combat—mostly infantry-men, but she supposed air combat would be just as stressful, if not more so. Perhaps she should let him take her through a few barrel rolls. Perhaps it would help his brooding—but no. *Stay focused on the task at hand.*

"What would you like me to do next, sir? Perhaps it's time to head back to the airfield?" she suggested.

"Not yet. How about you climb to fifteen thousand feet and put her into a spin?"

Abby gulped. She loved the T-6 Texan, but the one idiosyncrasy it had was in the spin. Its stable platform made it very difficult to put into a spin in the first place, but likewise, once in a spin, it was even harder to recover from. They'd been instructed to avoid the situation.

She wondered if Captain Snyder knew the T-6 even half as well as she did. She was the pilot in command. Was she being tested? Did he expect her to explain the aircraft to him and why a spin wasn't a good idea?

She climbed to fifteen thousand feet and leveled off, tossing the question about in her head. She couldn't help herself, she had to ask. "You do know the T-6 is a notoriously bad . . ."

He interrupted her, "Spin it!"

He startled her, but she closed her mouth, added full power and lifted the nose straight up. She felt the rudder pedals beneath her boots. She'd need to work them like a fine instrument to pull this off. She watched the floating ball and worked the pedals to keep it centered.

The aircraft slowed quickly and the stick felt mushy in her hands. The nose seemed to hang on the propeller for an eternity.

It finally lost its battle with gravity and swung violently sideways and backward at the same time. The world spun crazily, but Abby released the back pressure on the stick and cut the throttle way back. She worked the rudder pedals and subtly nudged the ailerons, trying to pull the aircraft out of the increasingly fast spin.

It felt like they might start rolling at any moment. Abby knew that wouldn't happen, but it still felt awful. The altimeter unwound as they headed straight down, spinning crazily. She kept working the aircraft, slowly getting bits of control back, but also getting dangerously low.

She heard Captain Snyder over the intercom. "Have you got it? Have you got it?" She ignored him and kept working the controls. "Uh, I'm taking the aircraft."

"No, you are not!" she screamed. "I have the aircraft!" If he even touched the controls, it would be an automatic fail and her worst fear would come true. She'd get them out of this.

The flight surfaces finally flew again. With only two thousand feet of altitude left, perhaps one more full spin, she pulled out and leveled off. Sweat poured off her brow.

She glanced back at him. He stared back at her, but she thought he'd lost some of his bravado. "Like I was saying before, the T-6 doesn't like to spin and likes recovering even less."

"Noted. Take us back to Avenger Field, Mrs. Cooper. Congratulations, you passed."

Abby couldn't wipe the smile off her face. The flat, desolate landscape beneath her had never looked so beautiful. Everything felt good. The air inside the cockpit, her zoot suit against her sweaty skin, even her partially steamed goggles, felt good. She'd never felt so alive.

As they entered the pattern and lined up to land, Captain Snyder asked, "Would've you let me take the controls, or would you have taken us into the ground?"

"Like I said, I had the aircraft. I don't have a death wish, captain."

"Well, I'd put you up against any male pilot any day of the week. That was some good flying."

"Thank you," she said, and her smile almost hurt.

She landed and taxied to parking. She saw the other women who'd already finished their tests, standing around holding their leather flight helmets with broad smiles on their faces. From the smiling faces, she figured they'd all passed as well.

She shut down the engine, going through the process automatically. The other women flocked to her aircraft and stood beside the wing, waiting to hear the news.

Captain Snyder hefted himself out of the back and smiled down at them. "Hello, ladies," he said.

They smiled coyly back, but kept their eyes squarely planted on Abby. She pulled herself out of the cockpit, doing her best to keep from looking their way. She wanted to keep them in suspense for as long as possible.

Finally, Margie called out, "Well?"

Abby finally spun around and couldn't help screaming and dancing on the wing.

Captain Snyder laughed, and the girls joined in the merriment. Abby slid off the wing and the women clumped together and bounced, screamed, and hugged in delight.

Snyder jumped off the wing and stood watching. Abby broke away from her friends and turned to him. She extended her hand and he shook it. She said, "Say, were you baiting me up there?"

"I don't know what you mean."

"I mean, if I'd of taken you up on your offer for aerobatics, would you have failed me? Was it some kind of test?"

He smiled. The women had quieted and stared at him in accusation.

He held out his hands. "Well, I'll never tell." He put one hand on her shoulder. "You passed. That's all that counts."

He walked away, and Abby watched him go.

Alice asked, "What was that all about?"

Abby told them about their conversation. Everyone agreed he'd been trying to trick her into breaking the rules, but Abby still didn't know.

They interlaced their arms and walked toward the hangars. They'd all passed their check rides and would be successfully graduating. It was a dream come true.

Mrs. Winker approached them. She held up her hands as though cheering for a football team. "Hurray! You're the last one today. You obviously passed."

"Yes, ma'am."

"How'd it go?"

"He had me put it into a spin, ma'am."

She and the others gasped in unison. Mrs. Winker said, "Oh my. That must've been frightening."

"It was. He tried to take over, but I wouldn't let him. I finally got control back at just two thousand feet. It was close."

"I'll have a word with him. He must not know the intricacies of the aircraft."

"I think he does now."

The group broke up and Abby and a few others retired to Bay 7. When they entered, banners and balloons fell from the ceiling. Beatrice blew on a party horn and sang, "Congratulations!" Her other hand held her now distended belly.

Abby went to her and hugged her tightly. She felt the large pregnant bulge. She dropped to her knees and kissed it through Beatrice's dress. "How are you doing in there, little one?"

"Never mind that. Y'all are WASP pilots. You did it. I'm so proud of y'all."

Abby laughed and threw her head back. They pulled in for a group hug. She didn't think she could be any happier.

The rest of the week felt surreal. No longer did Class 43-6 need to wake up at 0500—but they still did. The days, which had seemed too short to fit everything inside, now felt too long.

She wrote Clyde a long letter, telling him she'd qualified. She told him how proud of him she was and that she hoped her own efforts flying as a

WASP might somehow bring the war to a close quicker and, as a result, bring him home to her sooner.

As she wrote it, she thought it might not be completely true. Yes, she wanted the war to end so they could get on with their lives, but she also knew that the WASP program would likely wither away once that happened. Things would go back to normal and her flying days would end. She wanted to fly as much as possible before that happened.

She felt guilty for having such thoughts. She tried to put it out of her mind. The war was in full swing and appeared it might go on forever. But things seemed to have turned in the Allies' favor slightly.

During training, she had little time to read the papers. War news came in snippets after big events occurred—usually bad news. But now that she had time to read more, there were more stories of battles being won than lost.

She sealed the letter to Clyde and put it in the to be sent pile of other posts from Bay 7. She would leave Bay 7 tomorrow to make room for the next class. She'd still be in close contact with most of her friends, at least for another day or two, but once they received their assignments, they might be sent to the far corners of the country.

The day before, they'd chosen which of the three types of missions they wanted to fly. They could tow targets for the navy while the new gunnery recruits blasted away, learning how to lead a target and so forth, or they could fly at night in mock attack runs to let the men train how to find them with their massive light systems. Or they could choose to be ferry pilots. Everyone wanted to be a ferry pilot, including Abby.

Basically, it entailed flying an aircraft from point A to point B, but it usually meant long cross-country flights with just their wits and their aircraft to keep them safe. Ferry pilots could be away from their home bases for weeks. Often after delivering one aircraft, they'd be assigned to fly another aircraft somewhere else. Sometimes even flying from coast to coast and flying many different aircraft.

Abby thought it sounded amazing. It reminded her of stories she'd read as a child about the Pony Express riders of the old west. It sounded glamorous and exciting, but she didn't sign up for that.

"What do you mean?" Beatrice asked with an edge to her voice. "Why not? You want to tow targets? I don't understand."

"Towing targets sounds fun, too. It's not permanent. I can switch anytime if I don't like it or get bored."

Beatrice rubbed her distended belly. "But, ferrying's what I used to do. You'd love it. I thought it's what you always wanted to do."

"Yes, it was. But not now." She glanced down at Beatrice's belly.

Beatrice's face changed. "You're doing this for me—for us, aren't you?"

"I want to be here for you when the baby comes. If I'm ferrying, I'm almost guaranteed to miss it. I don't want you to have to go through that alone, Bea."

"No! I refuse to let you do this, Abby. I'm a big girl. I can take care of myself."

"Really? Who will take you to the hospital when the time comes? Everyone's being sent to the far corners of the country. If I'm not here, no one else will be around to help you."

"I'll go to my parents. I probably should have from the start."

"You're due in a month. After the baby comes, I'll switch to ferrying. If I'm towing targets, I'll be around. I won't be somewhere in New York or California. I'll be with you, and the little one."

"They don't have tow targets here. You'll be in Norfolk and I doubt they'll let you commute in one of their airplanes."

"You're right, but we can do that together. We'll drive your truck to Norfolk."

"You really want a bunch of wet-behind-the ears kids to fire live rounds at you?"

"It's just a job. All I care about is flying, and that's flying. Probably less dangerous than ferry piloting."

"I doubt that. Ferry pilots aren't dodging live ammunition."

Abby could see Beatrice warming to the idea, though. She reached out and touched Beatrice's belly. She felt something move, probably a foot or a hand. She giggled. "It's important to me. I really want to help you through this."

A tear sparkled in the corner of Beatrice's eye. "You're a good friend, Abby. We don't deserve you."

22

DECEMBER 1943

Seattle, Washington

Sal sat on the edge of the bed in the run-down hotel room in Seattle. He'd paid for three days, but it had stretched to nearly three weeks. He hoped it wouldn't take long to find himself an apartment to live in and it wouldn't have if he'd had the motivation to look. But he couldn't bring himself to hit the pavement and start looking. He'd never been so bored in his life, or so angry with himself. Before he could get on with his life, he had to talk with Meredith.

He went to the lobby and asked the concierge if he could use the phone to place a local call. After some handwringing, the concierge finally agreed, but he told him to keep it short. He shut the door behind him as he entered the booth, as though hiding him from his boss.

Sal called the Brooks estate, knowing he'd most likely speak with Mr. Hanniger. He didn't relish him knowing his purpose, but he couldn't avoid it. Mr. Hanniger sounded genuinely pleased to hear from him, but he didn't ask questions when Sal asked to speak with Mrs. Brooks.

A few awkward minutes later, he heard Meredith's voice on the line. "Sal? Is everything alright?"

"Yes, yes, of course. I didn't mean to alarm you, but I was wondering if you'd be able to meet me somewhere for a coffee or lunch, perhaps? Today, if possible."

"Are you sure you're alright? This is so unlike you."

"Please Meredith. I need to talk with you in person, and the sooner the better."

They worked out the details, and Sal hung up the phone. He stepped from the booth and thanked the concierge by palming him a quarter.

He hailed a cab, and it only took a few minutes before he found the small diner she'd suggested. A bored waitress seated him and brought him a menu. The diner was mostly empty. He'd never heard of the place and he wondered if Meredith used it for her secret meet-ups with her ex-lover. He didn't remember ever dropping her off here before.

He glanced at the street, wondering if she'd take a cab or be driven in the Rolls by Mr. Hanniger. It would be odd seeing Mr. Hanniger in the Rolls. He hoped she took a cab.

The bell over the diner rang as a Meredith entered. He stood and waved. He didn't see the Rolls or a cab leaving. She gave him a reserved smile and went to the table, looking around the place suspiciously.

She gave him her hand and he grasped it lightly. "Thank you for meeting me. Please, sit down."

She sat in the booth across from him. He didn't think he'd ever seen her in such a normal setting. She normally ate at fine restaurants or the posh country club. She looked comfortable but out of place at the same time.

"Of course, Sal. It sounded quite urgent."

"Well, I'd say more pressing than urgent."

"I had Mr. Hanniger park around the corner. He assured me he'd be fine."

Sal wondered if he'd made a mistake. Perhaps he should press her about anything besides what he actually wanted to talk about. He could ask more questions about Miss Watson—but no—he had to get this off his chest once and for all. He wouldn't be able to move on with his life until he knew.

"This won't take long, Meredith."

The waitress came over and asked if they'd like to hear the specials. Sal didn't have an appetite. "Can we just have some tea, please?"

Meredith gave him a wan smile, then nodded at the waitress. "Yes, just some tea would be nice."

The waitress rolled her eyes and left quickly.

Meredith stared at him. She reached across the table and clutched his big hands. "What in the world is the matter? You look like you've eaten a rotten egg."

Her hands on his sent a shiver up his spine. He blew out a sigh and looked into her beautiful eyes. "Meredith . . . I have to know."

She squeezed his hands when he hesitated. "Know what?"

He didn't see any hint in her eyes at what he wanted to know—no recognition at all. Had he imagined it all? No. "The night we spent together . . ." He couldn't finish. It didn't feel right.

She released his hands as though they'd suddenly burst into flames. She looked around the place as though someone might've heard.

"Oh my, Sal. Is that what this is about?"

He stared at her and he felt as vulnerable as he'd ever felt. He hated it. He couldn't bring himself to speak.

She leaned back and collected herself, then leaned forward again and placed her hands gently on his. She searched his eyes and he had trouble not looking away. He felt like a damned fool.

She said, "We both decided that night was a mistake, Sal."

He'd already gone this far. He may as well finish hurling himself off the cliff. "I know, but for me it meant—well, it meant a lot to me. It meant the world to me."

Her eyes changed and he saw what he'd dreaded seeing: pity.

"Oh, Sal. It was so long ago. It—well, it's a happy memory for me, but . . ." She removed her hands and set them daintily on the edge of the table. "I don't want to hurt you, Sal."

He fought to maintain a stoic, hard face. He hoped he succeeded. But at that moment, he would've preferred to relive his year in the trenches of France than be sitting in this booth across from the woman he'd spent half his life pining over.

He straightened his back and lifted his chin. "It's all right. I shouldn't have brought it up, but I wanted to clear the air since I won't be around much anymore." He sounded lame even to his own ears.

"My God, Sal. I had no idea you still think about that night. We were children."

He leveled his gaze and raised an eyebrow at her like a question. "Speaking of children."

Meredith shook her head slowly. "No, no, I don't think so."

"The timing would've been right."

Meredith looked around again. The waitress came over, holding two steaming cups of water and packets of tea. She placed them down carefully as Sal and Meredith stared across the table, never wavering. She didn't stick around long.

When she'd gone out of earshot, Meredith leaned forward and shook her head emphatically. "No, she's not yours. She looks nothing like you."

Sal leaned back and crossed his arms. He saw more of him in Abby than Victor, but he'd kept it to himself all these years. How could Meredith not see it? Perhaps it would be too much for her to bear.

"If you say so."

"Don't be an ass. Don't . . ."

He interrupted her. "Do you have her address? I'd like to visit her."

She couldn't speak for a moment. Her mouth moved, but she couldn't form words.

He put her mind at ease. "Not about that. I'd *never* bring that up, believe me. I love her too much. I simply want to set things right with her. We didn't part on the best of terms, and I want to know why."

Meredith caught up with her breathing after taking a few long breaths. "Yes, I have it. Do you have a pencil?"

He pulled out a scrap of paper and the nub of a pencil. He pushed it across the table. She wrote the address and pushed it back to him. He read it, "Sweetwater, Texas."

"She's still in training, I think, but she could finish any day now. She lives at an airfield, I think. You might not have access. It's very hush-hush."

He folded the paper and stuffed it into his shirt pocket. "I'm sorry, Meredith. I didn't mean to upset you."

She clutched his hands again and her eyes softened but they weren't the eyes of a lover but of a friend. He hated it, but understood.

She said, "I'm sorry you've been feeling that way all this time. You should've come to me much earlier."

Sal just shook his head, not wanting to talk about it for one more second. "I've changed my mind about getting an apartment." He tapped his shirt pocket and smiled. "I'm going to visit our girl."

Meredith shrunk slightly, but smiled back at him. "Will you give her my love, Sal? Will you tell her how much she means to me?"

"Of course I will."

She scooted out and stood abruptly. He stood as well. She wiped a tear off her cheek and strode with purpose toward the door. Sal watched her go. He felt an ache deep down, an ache that might never go away. The little doorbell rang as she left. She didn't look back.

Sal sat on the train staring, but not actually seeing the flat landscape of Texas flash past.

After his meeting with Meredith, he'd boarded a train the very next day and now he trundled his way across half the country. Abby had taken this same route months before. It made him feel good to know he was seeing the same things she'd seen. He hadn't been back to Texas since he'd trained there in 1917. This time, he wasn't preparing for war—or was he?

The train lurched to a halt and the conductor called out, "Sweetwater Texas."

He gathered his things and stepped out into the aisle. Many eager young women stood waiting to step off. He'd noticed them before, and learned they were heading to Sweetwater to join a brand new WASP class. He'd engaged them a little, gleaning some information, but his heart wasn't in it. He'd told himself he could wallow in pity over Meredith's denial for the duration of the train ride, but no longer. Now it was time to put it out of his mind and move on.

He'd heard a few of the women wondering if talking with the big man with the scar across his cheek was safe. They giggled and whispered he might be a spy sent by Hitler to sabotage the program. They kept their hands over their mouths as though that would be enough to hide their voices from his keen ears.

He didn't let on that he'd heard them, but thought about the irony. He'd killed the Hun in countless bloody encounters during the war to end all wars. Spying for them now would be quite the turn of events.

The side doors opened and even before he stepped off the train, he smelled manure. He hadn't been to this part of Texas before, but he remembered that smell. He decided it must just be the way Texas smelled. Did it start right at the border? The thought made him grin.

He stepped off the train and stood on the small platform. A sign read "WASP trainees" and an arrow. He figured he could tail the trainees all the way to Abby, but thought better of it. The women might really believe he *was* a spy then.

It might be better to keep a low profile. Even though he'd read about it WASPs in the papers—maybe it *was* a top secret program. The last thing he wanted was to be detained by some local yokel sheriff's department while they checked his story.

Since these women seemed to be a new batch of students, he figured Abby must already be done with her training. He wanted to find her before they sent her off to some far-flung part of the country.

The only accommodations nearby was a little hotel called The Blue Bonnet, but the WASP trainees filled it and the owners had the no vacancy sign up.

With few options, he walked down Main Street. He couldn't help but like the place. Besides being ridiculously small, it was also well-kept and friendly. People smiled and waved at him as though they'd known him all their lives. He wondered if the WASP program had acclimated them to strangers or if they were always this friendly.

Before the war, everyone must've known everyone else. He pictured a packed Sunday sermon followed by a community breakfast and games for the kids. He didn't see many young men, but that made sense. Little places like this always sent their boys off to fight first, it seemed. Did the young men have more of a sense of patriotism, or just a need to get the hell out of a small, suffocating town, and if it took a war to do so—so be it. He wondered how many would be lucky enough to return—and how changed they'd be.

He found a small diner and went inside. A little bell rang and he thought he'd stepped back in time. A few folks with cowboy hats on sat at a table and gawked at him. They didn't seem quite as friendly, but he didn't get a sense of danger, either. He understood how he might confuse them. He wasn't a local, he wasn't a trainee, he wasn't wearing a uniform, and he was middle-aged. He had them perplexed. Perhaps they'd talk about him for generations to come: the mysterious scarred man who came to town back in the winter of '43. They made legends with far less.

The haggard-looking youngish woman behind the little bar put down her copy of the newspaper and motioned him to sit wherever he liked. He sat at the bar facing her and set his suitcase down beside him.

She gave him a tired smile. "Hi, honey. You want a menu? We ain't got much, but you can take a gander if y'all want to."

He never got used to locals saying "y'all" even if addressing only one person. Even though he'd never been to Sweetwater, it seemed like any other small Texas town he'd ever passed through almost thirty years before. But this diner smelled different.

"Coffee would be fine."

"We got chicory coffee."

"That'll work."

She poured it, set it in front of him, and he realized it was the reason for the odd smell. He'd tasted the vile stuff before, but this place seemed to have absorbed the smell into the walls. How long before the smell of regular coffee replaced it? Or would there always be a hint of it here, like an odd chapter of a book that didn't quite fit, but forever changed the story.

He sipped it, and the waitress watched him as though wondering if it might finally kill someone. When it didn't, she picked up the newspaper and offered it to him. "I've already read everything. You want it?"

"Nah. I read it on the train."

She shrugged and stuffed it behind the bar. He noticed recruiting posters along the wall behind her. Every branch of the armed services was represented. There was even a picture of a semi-goofy, semi-evil looking buck-toothed Japanese soldier with a long knife stalking a beautiful brunette woman. The caption said, "Know your enemy."

He doubted the Japanese looked anything like the depiction and wondered what message the makers were trying to send?

The bell rang as someone entered. He didn't turn but saw the waitresses manner change from amicably bored to hostile in an instant. She crossed her arms and said, "What do you want?"

A woman's voice answered. "Don't get your panties in a wad, Tessa. I'm here to pick up the milk delivery."

Sal turned on his stool. A beautiful tall woman, very far along in her pregnancy, stood there with her hands on her distended belly. He thought she might pop at any moment. He immediately felt the need to help her.

The waitress, Tessa, reached under the bar and hefted a gallon of milk. Condensation dripped down the sides and made Sal's mouth water.

Tessa's biting voice said, "If I'd a known it was for y'all, I wouldn't have agreed to it."

The woman waddled her way forward and stood beside Sal. He stood quickly and grasped the milk jug before she did. He handed it to her and she smiled sweetly at him. His heart skipped a beat. She demurred, "Why thank you, sir. Chivalry isn't dead after all." She'd raised her voice so the men in the corner could hear.

To Sal's utter surprise, a cowboy he guessed to be a little older than himself answered her. "Not for shameless hussies like yourself."

"Get the hell outta here!" another one of them said, his voice dripping with scorn and hatred.

Sal couldn't believe how they treated this beautiful pregnant woman. His shock turned to anger and he turned his impressive frame to face the table of cowboys. Her husband wasn't there to defend her, but he'd be damned if he let these yahoos speak to her that way.

"I'll ask you to apologize to the lady. Now."

The men exchanged glances with each other then stood, pushing their chairs out of the way.

Sal evaluated them quickly from a professional's point of view. They were tough, most likely strong from a life of hard work, but had zero training. Perhaps they'd served, probably in peacetime. He likely wouldn't take them all down, but he might not have to, just their leader—the one who'd spoken first. The one leading them to where he stood.

"We ain't apologizing to no whore."

Sal didn't have to look back for her reaction. He knew she couldn't be a whore. If she was, she'd be wasting her talents horribly in a small, backward town like this. Besides, she held herself with poise and confidence. He didn't know who she was, but she wasn't a call girl. He'd bet his life on that. And even if she was, these bozos were way out of line.

"Then I'm going to bloody you. No one talks to a lady like that and gets away with it. If her husband were here, he'd do the same."

"Mister, I don't need much of a reason to fight, but I'm gonna explain it to you, so you know who you're defending." He pointed at her with an accusing finger. "She's pregnant, but she ain't married. Around here we call that sort of thing a whore."

Sal turned and saw the woman raise her chin in defiance. Her beautiful brown eyes sparkled and he felt something move in his soul. She didn't cower, but rose to the challenge. His respect and admiration for this woman went up tenfold. "I don't care if she's gonna have Satan himself's baby—I won't stand for it. Now, who wants a broken nose first?"

The men stood shoulder to shoulder. They removed their cowboy hats and set them down carefully. The leader spit in his hands and rubbed them together. "We like nothing more than teaching city boys how to behave in our town. Particularly whore-loving city boys." The others nodded their agreement.

While they nodded and readied themselves, Sal was already moving. He gripped the nearest chair and hurled it at them. They cowered and put their arms up to block it. The chair smashed into the leader and the loud smack and cursing told Sal he'd hurt him.

As the chair was still falling to the ground, he lunged and landed a quick jab into the leader's nose. It flattened and spattered blood as though he'd burst a hose. The leader clutched his face and dropped to his knees. Sal kicked him in the chest and sent him sprawling into a table. He hit his head hard on an edge and lay on the ground, rolling side to side in agony.

Sal ducked beneath a right hook from the fighter on his right, then jabbed his elbow into the man's kidney. He curled and dropped, clutching his side, desperately trying to breathe and get out of the way.

Sal sensed the third man charging directly behind him. He curled his back and felt the hammer blow of a fist, but he hit nothing vital. Sal swept his leg and took the man off his feet with a crash that shook the small diner.

He leaped and plunged his elbow into the man's nose. It also broke with a sickening crunch of cartilage, broken teeth, and spraying blood.

He spun off him and crouched, waiting for the fourth man's attack, but it never came. The cowboy stood looking over the sudden and violent carnage and had second thoughts. He held out his hands and stumbled backward. Sal lunged, making him yelp as he tried to turn and run away. Sal grabbed him from behind, clutched his arm and pulled it up his back, making him cringe and gasp in pain. "Please, please. Don't break it, I—I gotta work the farm."

Sal hissed in his ear. "Then say you're sorry to the nice, pretty pregnant lady." When he didn't say it right away, Sal barked into his ear. "Now!"

"S—sorry for calling you a whore, Miss Malinsky. I—I didn't mean nothing by it."

Both Tess and Miss Malinsky stared with their mouths wide open. The pregnant woman recovered quicker than Tessa. She shook her head slowly and looked Sal up and down. He couldn't help feeling self-conscious. He hoped he didn't have too much blood on his face. He had the ridiculous notion that he wanted her to find him handsome. He felt like a damned high school student wanting to ask the prettiest girl in school to the big dance.

She smiled, and her eyes sparkled. Sal thought it the prettiest smile he'd ever seen and thought he'd like to lose himself in the deep depths of her brown eyes.

All she said was, "My, oh my."

The door burst open and in walked the last person Sal figured he'd see. "Abby!" he blurted.

Abby's mouth dropped even lower than Tessa's.

"Sal? Is that—is that Sal?"

He pushed the fourth man and he tripped over the group leader, just getting to his feet. They both sprawled onto the floor again. Sal went to Abby with his arms spread. He saw a flash of anger for an instant, and thought she might hit him, then she rushed to him and they hugged.

. . .

Sal stood inside a tiny house on the outskirts of Sweetwater proper. They'd left the little diner in a hurry when Tessa threatened to call the sheriff. He paid her for the damages and she'd calmed down a little, but still wanted them gone. The cowboys cussed and threatened, but they'd been beaten and they knew it.

In their hurry to leave, he hadn't had a moment to talk to Abby. Now that they were safely inside the house, she turned on him and pointed a finger at his chest. "What the hell are you doing here, Sal Sarducci?"

He'd just helped Miss Malinsky into a chair. "I wanted to see you. Is that a crime?"

"How'd you get this address?"

"From your mother."

She shook her head and he could see the fear and anger in her eyes, but also something else. She carried herself differently than he remembered—with more confidence and poise. She had a shorter haircut and she looked healthy and strong.

She paced as though processing what she should do. He watched her, seeing himself in her with each step. He looked back at Miss Malinsky and said, "Beatrice, right?"

She beamed at him and adjusted herself and her baby before answering. "Yessir. I remember you. You drove and picked up Abby from the airport back in Seattle."

"That was a long time ago." He suddenly realized the age gap between them. She could easily be his daughter, but he couldn't help the attraction he felt and unless he was grossly mistaken, it was mutual.

He pushed it out of his mind and turned back to Abby—the reason he was here. "I didn't mean to bust into your life like this." He held up his hand, which had a few minor cuts on the knuckles. "The address just had Avenger Field. No house address. I went into the diner for a bite to eat and —well, I think you know the rest."

"You can't be here, Sal," Abby lamented.

He looked at his feet. The words hurt him more than Meredith's. Did all the Brooks women want to hurt him instinctively?

Abby continued. "I just graduated from WASP training. I'm about to do something real for the first time in my life and *you* show up?"

He glanced back at Beatrice, but she was no help. She looked at her fingernails as though they were suddenly the most interesting things in the world.

He turned back to Abby. "Congratulations. I don't really know what that means, but it's impressive."

Beatrice hefted herself to her feet and waddled to Abby's side. She slung her arm around Abby's shoulder and said, "It means she's a pilot. She's earned her WASP wings, which only a few hundred other women have done before her. She's on her way to greatness, Mr. Sarducci."

He hated the way his name sounded in her mouth. He felt like an old pervert stalking a young woman, but he focused his attention back on Abby. "That's fantastic!" he exulted. "I'm so proud of you. Your mother will be, too."

Abby couldn't keep from smiling. She kissed Beatrice's arm. "I couldn't have done it without Bea's help. She got me into the program in the first place."

"Maybe, but *you* did the rest."

They talked as though he wasn't there any longer. He felt like a third wheel. He wondered if he'd made yet another mistake by coming here.

"Well, look. I'd stay at the Blue Bonnet, but it's full of new trainees. I'll just stay tonight. I can sleep on the floor. I—I'll leave on the next train."

"Doesn't come until next week," Beatrice said with a gleam in her eye.

"Then I'll take a bus or whatever the hell they have here. I won't intrude."

Beatrice stepped away from Abby and gave her a hard look. Sal pretended not to see. He checked his wristwatch. "I suppose I might find a bus tonight."

Abby crossed her arms and said, "Why are you here, Sal? Why aren't you home with Daddy?"

"I retired." He let that settle in and before Abby could say anything, he added, "I wanted to see you one last time. I'm not sure I'm staying in the Seattle area. I—well, I got the feeling you're angry at me. The last time I saw you . . ." he shrugged. "I need to know why. I can't move on with my life knowing I've hurt you somehow. I want to know how to fix it. You're like a daughter to me."

Abby suddenly looked extremely uncomfortable. She glanced at Beatrice, who only looked confused. Sal was convinced that something had definitely happened back in Seattle and it was bad enough that she hadn't even discussed it with her best friend.

Abby finally said, "You can stay, but only until the next train leaves. I have a new life with the WASPs here. You're a part of my old life, a life I'm trying to leave behind."

He didn't get the answer he sought, but she wasn't kicking him out, so he had a week to set things right. He glanced at Beatrice, who gave him a sly little grin. That might also be worth exploring.

He could tell they needed a few minutes alone, so he excused himself with the excuse of using the bathroom. He took a wrong turn and instead of the bathroom, he entered a bedroom. He saw a picture of Clyde and realized his mistake.

He quickly retreated, then stopped in his tracks. Sitting on a small table in the corner among a stack of textbooks with titles pertaining to flight, he saw a small leather-bound notebook. Among the textbooks, it stood out. It seemed out of place and he thought he may have seen it before.

He checked to see if anyone was watching. Beatrice and Abby still talked things over in low voices. He strode across the floor and stared down at the odd little book. He picked it up and opened the cover, instantly confirming his suspicions.

Abby hadn't destroyed Miles Burr's journal after all. He suddenly realized why she was so mad at him. She knew what he'd done. She knew about the arson and the role he'd played. He placed it back down. Now what?

23

DECEMBER 1943

Unnamed Island
East China Sea

Frank Cooper felt better than he had in a long time. The natives seemed to have endless supplies of food and fresh water. They'd been on the small island for only four days, but it felt much longer.

Four more Japanese sailors had turned up on shore, but the natives found them quickly and brought them in under a close watch. They'd placed them with the other sailors. They brought them food, water, and provided shelter, but kept watch over them day and night. Frank noticed one of the new ones seemed to hold some authority over the others. He wasn't an officer, but possibly a sergeant or their navy's equivalent. They stayed together mostly. None of the newcomers had weapons either.

Frank realized their numbers were more evenly matched now: six to seven in favor of the Japanese. If it came to blows, Grinning Bear still had his pistol with eight rounds, but the natives seemed to understand the importance of keeping watch over the Japanese, so they didn't worry too much.

Frank wished he could communicate better with the natives, but their complicated language eluded him. He could actually speak better with the

Japanese sailors if he'd been so inclined. Being in a Japanese POW camp for the past few years, a man couldn't help but learn the language. He hadn't deigned to speak with them, but sometimes he sat close and tried to hear their murmured conversations.

Now that his health was slowly improving, he'd join the natives on short hunting and fishing expeditions. He marveled at their skills in both the water and the jungle. They didn't mind him tagging along, although he thought he must annoy them with his bumbling. He couldn't help noticing that each man had scars across his body seemingly randomly, but mostly on their legs. The older men had more scars than the younger men. He wondered if it was some kind of rite of passage they had to go through continually. The women's skin was spotless, as far as he could tell.

It was another pleasant evening. He followed a group of boys to the beach and sat on a rock whittling the end of a piece of bamboo into a sharp point, while they spear fished in the tidal pools. He used a sharpened stone. It was difficult and slow going, but he had nothing but time. He longed for a knife, but never complained. He was free and wouldn't have cared if he had to gnaw the bamboo with his teeth.

Something caught his eye on the horizon. He looked past the three perfectly brown children lunging with their spears and more often than not coming up with writhing fish or thick crabs and grinning ear to ear.

There was smoke on the horizon. He dropped the bamboo and stood. He shielded his eyes and squinted into the sparkling distance. Had he imagined it? No, it was definitely there. The smoke seemed to get more visible every second, and soon he could see the faint outline of a ship.

He didn't know the exact position of the island, but he doubted an allied ship would be on this side of the Philippines. It had to be an enemy ship. He wondered hopefully if it could be the submarine that sank them, but discounted the idea. Submarines didn't trail smoke.

A boy saw him looking. He turned and looked too, then yelled to the others. They swam like fish to the edge, then darted into the jungle toward the village.

Frank ran after them. He'd regained some strength, but it would take months, possibly years, to become truly strong again. He lumbered after them and was soon out of breath, but he kept trotting along until he came to the village. His legs burned and it felt as though his lungs would burst. He hunched over with his hands on his knobby knees, trying to catch his breath.

The boys had already alerted the adults. The shaman emerged from his hut, along with a few men with spears and bows and arrows. More joined them when they heard the commotion and soon half the village sprinted toward the beach.

The shaman saw Frank huffing and puffing and he said something to him that he couldn't understand, but pointed and he figured he meant he should join his comrades. He saw the Japanese sailors eyeing him from across the compound. He glared at them and wondered if he should watch them while the natives were distracted.

In the four days since landing on the island, they'd barely interacted. The Japanese sailors obviously saw that they were treated differently than the Americans, but they didn't seem perturbed. They just seemed happy to be alive. He figured he could leave them untended for a few minutes.

He found the others lazing around near one of the fresh-water pools, watching bare chested women laundering skimpy garments of clothing. He'd spent many hours doing the exact same thing and understood their fascination.

"Hey, there's a ship on the horizon!" he called out.

They all tore their eyes from the women. The women also looked his way. One of the younger ones smiled broadly and waved at him, her breasts swaying enticingly. He waved back, feeling immediately foolish. He wanted nothing more than to lie with her, but he didn't know if the natives would frown upon it, so he abstained. Truthfully, he doubted he had enough stamina to actually perform the deed. He was still too weak, but he would've liked to have the opportunity to try.

"Where?" Grinning Bear asked.

Frank pointed. "It's still too far away to tell if it's friend or foe, but probably a Jap ship."

"Way out here, you're probably right."

"What the hell are we gonna do about it?" Glenn asked. They'd talked about this possibility, but still didn't have a solution. They were still getting used to their freedom.

They'd discussed using the natives' long canoes made from sturdy palms to find a bigger island, but as far as they could tell, they only used them for fishing, or traveling around the island, seemingly just for fun. No other islands dotted the horizon in any direction and they couldn't simply ask them if such a thing existed. Besides, the canoes didn't look seaworthy enough to cross large swaths of open ocean.

The island itself had little to offer in the way of hiding spots, either. The highest peak was more like a hill, and they hadn't come across any caves or anything they could use to hide in their limited exploration.

Grinning Bear pulled the pistol from his waistband. He carried it around everywhere in case the Japanese sailors tried anything. He'd cleaned it as best he could, but without gun oil, it didn't look too good. Ugly streaks of rust dotted and streaked the barrel. He was confident it would still fire, though, but wasn't willing to waste ammo to find out. Besides, just the mere threat the gun posed might be enough.

"What are you gonna do with that thing? If the Japs come ashore, you'll be outmatched a thousand times over."

"I'll kill the Jap sailors, then hide. If we leave 'em alive, those bastards'll tell their buddies all about us and they won't leave until they find us and put us back in chains."

Glenn said, "We shoulda done it a long time ago. We ain't got time to bury them now."

Neil, had grown up on a small farm in Nebraska and, despite endless deprivations doled out by his captors, he still clung to a young boy's naïveté. He said, "We can't just kill 'em—can we?"

Grinning Bear said, "Why the hell not? It's them or us. They're not taking me prisoner again, no way." He waved the pistol. "I'll use the last bullet for myself if it comes down to that."

Frank felt the same way, but he couldn't wrap his head around shooting unarmed men in cold blood. "You can't do it, Larry."

Grinning Bear glared at him and Frank said, "You think they'll just sit there quietly while you put a bullet in each of their heads? Would you? Besides, Glenn's right; we don't have time to bury them. And what'll the Japs do when they find the bodies? They'll kill every man, woman, and child on this rock, that's what. And we'd be responsible."

"They might do that anyway," Gale suggested. "They're not known for their compassion."

"What do you suggest, then?" Grinning Bear directed the question at Frank.

"We take 'em with us at gunpoint and we all hide."

"Too risky. With just one pistol and eight rounds, it's not enough of a deterrent. If they make a break for it, most of 'em would make it. I might knock one down if I'm lucky. Besides, there's no good hiding places. They'd find us for sure."

"Maybe they aren't coming here at all," Frank said.

With nothing decided, they trotted toward the beach. Frank noticed the Japanese sailors walking cautiously toward the beach, too. It was the first time he hadn't seen them guarded and they took advantage.

Grinning Bear noticed, too. He glanced back at Frank, then veered their way, the pistol clearly visible. "Hey!" he barked.

The sailors jumped in surprise and huddled closer together. The new man with rank said something low and earnest and the sailors kept walking, trying to ignore Grinning Bear.

Grinning Bear stepped in their path and aimed the pistol at the leader's forehead. "Stop right there, Tojo."

The rest of the Americans surrounded the sailors. Frank wished he had his Thompson submachine gun, or at least the sharpened bamboo stick. Despite being shipwrecked, the Japanese were much healthier and stronger.

The lead Japanese sailor stopped and faced Grinning Bear defiantly. He spoke in low guttural tones, and Frank caught a few words here and there.

"I think he's saying something about rescue."

"I don't like his tone," Grinning Bear hissed dangerously. He looked him up and down and the sailor glared back at him with dripping hatred. "I think I recognize this guy, Frank. I think he was on Corregidor. Yeah, I remember him killing Manny and maybe even Newsome."

Frank tore his eyes from the sailors and stared at Grinning Bear as though he'd lost his mind. He saw pure hatred and murder there.

The sailor's face hardened and he said something, but he never finished the thought. The pistol barked, and blood misted out the back of his head.

He swayed for a moment, then tilted forward like a felled pine tree. Grinning Bear stepped out of the way and he hit the ground with a soft thud. Blood and grayish bits of brain seeped out of the small hole in the back of his head.

The other sailors turned pale. They backed away slowly, their arms stiff at their sides, terrified.

"Jesus, Larry—what you do that for?"

"I didn't like the way he looked at me."

The natives rushed from the beach and, seeing the dead sailor, formed a circle around all of them. The shaman stared at the dead man, then at the smoking gun barrel, still firmly in Grinning Bear's hand.

The shaman stepped forward, his face a grim, deeply lined mask. He spoke and suddenly the spear-toting men raised their points at all of them and forced them into a tight circle.

They pushed the Japanese and Americans into a tightly packed group. The sailors shied away from Grinning Bear as though to touch him would burn their skin. Frank's skin crawled as he pressed up against the Japanese, but there was nothing he could do. The Japanese seemed equally disgusted, if not more so.

He could see anger mounting in Grinning Bear's face, so he said, "Don't do anything stupid, Larry."

"Maybe I should just finish the rest of 'em off and be done with it."

Micah spoke through clenched teeth, "Haven't you done enough? You'll get us all killed."

"I've got just enough to finish 'em. They're packed nice and tight. I might even have some left over if I get a two for one."

"Cut the crap!" Frank barked. "You shoot and they'll skewer us."

"The ships on the way. May as well go down fighting," Grinning Bear reasoned.

The shaman raised his hands and spoke in his sing-song language. It was beautiful in its own way, and Frank wondered if it would be the last thing he heard. It wouldn't be too bad.

His mind drifted and he wondered what his little brother Clyde was up to. He hadn't thought about him or his parents in quite some time. He wondered if the Red Cross had delivered his letter. There was no way for them to respond. He chuckled to himself, thinking about the address they'd have to use to make that possible: "to Frank Cooper—POW somewhere in the Philippines."

He figured Clyde was probably neck deep in the war by now. Hell, he might already be dead. He hoped he wasn't fighting in this region of the world. Perhaps he was fighting the Germans somewhere far to the north. Maybe he'd been smart and gotten himself some rear-echelon job passing out candy bars and sandwiches to high-ranking officers, but he doubted that. Even though he didn't think of Clyde as a hothead, he'd want revenge for his older brother. He wished he could talk him out of it, but figured he wouldn't listen anyhow. He could be stubborn.

He broke from his thoughts of home and family and focused on the here and now. They were being corralled toward the center of the village. The points of the spears were only inches from their faces and exposed bellies. The natives who'd seemed so friendly and accommodating now seemed angry and harsh.

He glimpsed the horizon and thought he saw a plume of smoke against the grandeur of the setting sun. Was the ship passing on by? Was it all a false alarm?

He put his hand on Grinning Bear's shoulder and pointed. "You see the smoke? You see it? It's passing. They're not coming after all."

Grinning Bear nodded. "Well, I'll be damned."

Glenn's voice dripped with contempt. "We coulda gone on living in paradise, but you had to go and shoot that sorry son of a bitch."

"Stow it, or you might be next."

They stopped them in the center of the village. Thatch huts surrounded them. The women stood in clumps watching the spectacle. Frank saw the one who always smiled at him, but now she had her arms crossed and wore an angry scowl.

The shaman said something and the men stepped back a few paces, but kept their spears ready and aimed. Bowmen had nocked arrows behind them.

The shaman stepped forward, heading straight for Grinning Bear. He stood stock still in front of him. He extended his withered hand. Grinning Bear was supposed to give up his pistol.

When he hesitated, Frank hissed, "For chrissakes, give it to him."

"I don't wanna."

"What are you gonna do, shoot your way outta here? Give it up."

Finally, Grinning Bear unloaded the bullets and handed the pistol over. The shaman shook his head slightly and held his other hand out for the bullets.

Grinning Bear looked at the snubbed rounds in his hand, then hurled them in an arc, spreading them far and wide.

"Jesus, Larry." Frank expected to be skewered any second. The spearmen poised, the bowmen had their strings tight and their arrows aimed. The irony of fighting in a modern war and being killed by tools from the Wild West made him chuckle.

The shaman shifted his gaze from Grinning Bear to Frank. He said something he couldn't understand, but it sounded like a question, so he answered what he thought it might be.

"I'm laughing 'cause this son of a bitch is a full-blooded American Indian and he's about to be skewered with tools his ancestors used to kill us white men with on the high plains about a century ago. Just damned ironic." He couldn't keep from laughing and the other Americans joined in nervously at first, then raucously. The Japanese looked at them as though they'd completely lost their minds.

The shaman watched with a deep scowl, then he finally joined in. He spoke, and the warriors lowered their spears and bows. They smiled too, then laughed when the shaman laughed. Frank wondered if they had even a remote clue what he'd said. He was sure they didn't. They wouldn't know too much about American history out here, even if they understood English. But it broke the tension and he didn't think they'd kill them just yet.

That night, all of them, including the Japanese sailors, were unceremoniously forced into a hut together. Men with spears surrounded the hut and never wavered in their watchfulness. In the distance, the sounds of construction kept them on edge and awake.

"What d'you think they're building?" Micah asked.

"I'm guessing a cage," Neil answered.

The thought of losing his freedom made Frank want to die. Even though he doubted it would be even half as bad as his previous experience, he didn't want to be behind bars again. They'd experienced freedom if only for a few days, but the thought of losing it again kept him from sleeping.

He stared into the darkness, listening to Grinning Bear's soft snores. He wanted to throttle him. It was his fault they'd lost their freedom this time. They'd been through hell together—helped each other survive—but in that moment, he truly wanted to kill him. How could he sleep soundly knowing he'd doomed them to imprisonment?

He finally drifted off to sleep. The sounds of construction filled his dreams. He dreamed he was being held underwater until nearly drowned, allowed one gulp of precious air before hands pushed him down again. It happened repeatedly.

He woke to the sounds of urgent native voices. Frank sat up from the thatch mat and wondered if this would be his last day. Perhaps the natives would simply do away with the problem.

Grinning Bear rubbed his face and struggled to his feet. Frank glared at him. "This is all your fault."

Grinning Bear ignored him and stepped to the door where the natives stood beckoning them forward. Frank slowly stood. The Japanese sailors watched them warily, but they seemed to have lost some of their earlier swagger now that they'd lost their leader. Perhaps the killing had been a good thing after all.

Frank stepped through the door and into bright sunshine. In days past, he'd felt happy here, but today he felt only dread. Once they were all together in a tight group, they corralled them along a little-used path. Frank's stomach growled. He hoped they wouldn't starve them to death. He'd rather be shot full of arrows.

The path wound through the jungle and finally expanded onto a field. He saw what they'd been building throughout the night. It wasn't a cage as he'd thought, but some kind of playing field. Stacked in the center were thick bamboo poles. Most were freshly cut, but two had obviously seen a lot of use and looked different. They were longer and had large bulbous coconuts attached to each end.

The field had long strands of bamboo laid end to end surrounding it, and it looked like a perfect square. In each corner sat boxy structures, again made of bamboo. A shallow line was dug through the center of the square to separate the two sides. In the line, three balls, a little smaller than basketballs but bigger than softballs, sat equidistant from each other.

"What the hell is this?" Grinning Bear said under his breath.

"If I'm not mistaken, it's some kind of sports field. I mean, it has to be. The bamboo is the out-of-bounds line. The things in the corners are goals and there are even balls and sticks."

The entire village emerged from the trail and spread out around the field. They oozed excitement, as though in anticipation of a show. They stood watching them and pointing. Frank saw the young woman wave at him. Her broad smile had thankfully returned. He smiled and waved back, thinking that perhaps they wouldn't kill them outright. But what the hell was going on?

"Looks like the whole village has showed up to watch. Is that a good sign or a bad sign?" Gale wondered.

The crowd of spectators buzzed as they pointed at them and smiled and giggled.

"Are we expected to play?" Grinning Bear asked.

The shaman held up his hands for quiet. It took a moment, but soon the low buzz of excited voices quieted and he had their attention. He spoke in his sing song language for a full five minutes. The crowd smiled at some points and frowned at others. Frank wished he knew what the hell he was saying.

The shaman raised his voice and lifted his arms. When he finished, the crowd erupted in cheers and dancing. Twelve young native men took the field. They went to the center and picked out bamboo sticks. Two heavier men took the two with the coconuts on the end and retreated to opposite ends to what Frank could only assume were goals.

The others separated, so six men were on each side of the center line. The young men's eyes sparkled with excitement. Each of them looked eager to play. A few smacked their bamboo sticks on the ground and they snapped with a whip-crack sound. Frank realized they had split the ends. He wondered for what purpose.

The shaman signaled and they pushed the prisoners forward until they faced him. He spoke as though they could suddenly understand him, but they stared blankly. Finally, he pointed to his eye, then to the playing field. He wanted them to watch.

They stood on the sidelines. The Japanese sailors spoke in low murmurs, just as confused as the Americans. One woman sauntered out from the other side. She went to the ball closest to the center. She picked it up and kissed it, then yelled something. The men stood ready with their sticks, their muscles flexing in anticipation.

The young woman threw the ball in the air and rushed back to the sideline. The men stepped forward to the mid-line and lashed out viciously at one another with their poles while others leaped for the ball and smacked it back. It reminded him of a jump ball at the start of a basketball game.

The ball rolled awkwardly, as though on the heavy side. A player smacked the end of his pole down hard over the top of the ball and the split bamboo tips spread over it. He lifted, and the ball stayed at the end of the bamboo, secure in its grip. He darted across the midline and sprinted toward the nearest corner goal. The players all whooped and hollered. The defenders attacked him, viciously hitting him with their poles, but he kept running as though he didn't feel pain.

His teammates pushed forward with him, trying to clear a path. They smacked the other players, sending a few sprawling in the grass, but they sprang up quickly and re-entered the fray.

The player guarding the opposite goal sprinted to the unguarded goal. He stood in front of it with his thick double coconut ended bludgeon. A player from the offensive team got too close and the goalie hit him in the side with the coconut end. The player went flying with a yelp of pain. The crowd on the sidelines erupted in cheers, groans, and laughter. They smacked one another on their backs and jumped around, urging the players on.

The player with the ball reared back and flung the stick forward, sending the ball zinging toward the goalie. He expertly swung the bludgeon and smacked the ball with a loud crack. It flew into the air and the players converged on it, all the while smacking one another with the sticks and shrugging into each other with lowered shoulders.

The ball hit the ground and a player used his stick to roll it toward the other goals. It rolled awkwardly because it wasn't completely round, but more oblong. The players spread out and another player smacked his stick onto the ball and the bamboo spread and gripped it tightly. He lifted, but instead of running headlong into the melee, he stepped back, then flung the ball across the field to a waiting player. It bounced at his feet and he let it hit his leg and bounce up. He redirected its path with a smack from his stick and it rolled toward the open goal. The goalie yelled and charged, but he wouldn't get there in time.

The player helped it along the ground, finagled it around another player, and nudged it into the goal with his foot. He raised his stick in triumph, and the crowd cheered heartily. Frank couldn't help noticing all the women's breasts bouncing up and down as they jumped and clapped.

The players reset. The men had a sheen of sweat and a few had bloody gashes, but they were all smiles. They left the ball in the goal and once again a different woman went out and threw a new ball in the air to start the next point.

Frank said, "Now we know where all their scars came from."

Grinning Bear asked, "What d'you think the balls are made of? It's dark like leather, but it's not quite right."

"I dunno. Maybe animal hide around woven thatch?" he guessed.

They watched the rest of the brutal game. They surmised that the goal with the ball still inside was now off limits, making it harder to score since only one goal needed to be guarded for the down team.

The game tied. Now that each team only had one open goal, the brutality increased tenfold. The young men became fatigued as the game wore on, and they used more strategy, passing the ball around expertly. Some even caught the ball at the end of the stick, but that happened rarely and when it did, the crowd cheered wildly.

Finally, the last ball found its way past the goalie, and the game ended. The players hugged and caressed sore muscles and split skin. They drank water and dumped it over their heads to wash off the sweat and blood. No one had deep wounds, but all had small cuts and gashes. Even the goalies had taken a few thrashings. The women trotted out to rub their wounds with animal skins and cooed into their ears.

. . .

The shaman clapped his hands and the merriment dropped off quickly. He raised his voice and the men guarding them separated the Japanese sailors from the Americans.

He murmured to Grinning Bear, "There's six of them and six of us. They want us to play, I'll bet."

Sure enough, the women brought out the balls and placed them on the center line. The guards pushed them onto the field and separated the Japanese and Americans onto the separate sides.

The men who'd just played handed them their bamboo sticks. Frank hefted his. They were heavy and he didn't relish the possibility of being struck by one. They weren't as heavily made as the hated bamboo sticks back at Bilibib, but it wouldn't be pleasant. The double-ended goalie stick they handed to Grinning Bear. He hefted it and swung in, testing how it felt.

The Japanese received their sticks. They murmured and nodded among themselves, feeling the weight and taking a few practice swings themselves.

Frank swung his through a wide arc. The split end created a slight whistling sound. A native rolled one of the balls his way. They did the same for the Japanese. They clearly wanted them to practice before playing an actual game.

Frank leaned down and lifted the ball to get a better look. He held it up and gazed at it carefully. Then he flung it away and wiped his hands on what was left of his tattered pants. "It's a fucking human head!" he exclaimed in disgust.

Grinning Bear picked it up and scrutinized it. "They've knotted off the neck." He knocked on the outside. "It's soft, like they broke the skull and stuffed it with something to keep its shape."

He tossed it back to Frank, who dodged it and let it fall at his feet. "I don't wanna inspect it, dammit." He took a step back, then smacked the pole over the top, as the natives had. The end wrapped around the head and gripped it snugly. He lifted it. It was heavier than it looked and he strained to lift it, but once it was over his head, it was easier to control. He trotted around with it, getting the feel.

Gale waved his pole. "Throw it here."

Frank reared back and threw it overhand. It sailed out with force and plopped at Gale's feet and rolled a few feet. Gale trotted beside it, helping it along with the stick as though playing hockey. He whacked it and the bamboo gripped it. He lifted it and ran a few paces.

"That works surprisingly well," he chuckled. He flung it at Neil, who shied away, but then put it through the paces. After a few more minutes, they enjoyed themselves. Frank even managed to catch the ball in the air once, gaining a few nods of respect from the native men.

The Japanese also picked up the concept quickly and easily. Soon they flung the ball around as though they'd been playing for years. Just like the Americans, they enjoyed themselves.

The shaman let them practice for about half an hour. Then he raised his hands and his voice. He spoke slowly and the spectators listened intently. Frank had no idea what he was saying, but he could tell by the worried look on the young woman's face that it wasn't good.

When he finished, silence hung over the field. The edges of the playing field were now lined with scarred native men holding sharpened spears at the ready. Bowmen with notched arrows stood a few paces behind them.

"What the hell's going on?" Frank wondered aloud.

"If I'm not mistaken, I think this next match is gonna be for all the marbles," Grinning Bear stated. "I guess the guards are there to keep us from trying to run away."

"What? You think they want us to play to the death?" he asked incredulously.

Grinning Bear shook his head while watching the shaman closely. "No, I think whoever wins lives."

They pulled closer together, a feeling of dread sweeping over them. The Japanese were in far better shape overall. They hadn't spent the past few years deprived of food and water and been worked to the bone. But they might not be as tough and resilient. The six Americans had survived, despite the odds stacked against them all the way. What harsh experiences did the Japanese have? There was no way of knowing, but Frank doubted they'd suffered even half as much. But their strength and reactions would be far better.

The women gathered the three balls and laid them along the center line, then stepped away. Instead of smiling, they looked truly saddened and even anxious.

Grinning Bear pulled the team in close. "Look, if we're gonna beat these guys, we have to even the odds." His eyes hardened and his voice slipped into a low growl, similar to the way it was just before he'd shot the sailor in cold blood. "Let the Japs get the ball first. Stay out of their way, but if you get the chance, swing for their heads." He hefted his bludgeon. "I'm supposed to guard the goal, but when they come across, Micah will fade back to defend it while I use this to crack some heads."

"Jesus, Larry. You sure?"

"They're in far better shape than us. The only way we'll score is if we outnumber them. I'll take as many out as I can. If one goes down, give him an extra whack to make sure." He held up a finger as though coaching a little league team of fifth graders. "Don't spear 'em though. I don't think it's allowed."

"And bludgeoning them to death is?" Glenn asked.

Grinning Bear shrugged. "Guess we'll find out."

They were called up to the line by the shaman's sharp yell and emphatic hand gestures.

Frank stepped to the line. He'd played high school basketball and once again he thought this part was eerily similar to the tip off. The young woman walked out from the sideline. She picked up the ball, which had once been some unfortunate human's head. She stared at him and gave him a furtive smile, as though she didn't expect to see him alive again. Then she kissed the head where the lips might've been in life. She threw it far into the sky and ran back to the sideline.

The Japanese thrust forward, swinging viciously at them, but the Americans faded back, allowing the Japanese to gain control of the ball. Micah faded back to the nearest goal, replacing Grinning Bear, who stepped forward menacingly.

The Japanese holding the ball ran straight for the undefended goal. Frank swiped at his legs as he ran past, and his stick scraped a long groove across his shin, drawing blood. A nearby sailor rushed at Frank headlong, the stick over his head like a samurai sword. Frank ran in the opposite direction and the player veered toward the goal with his comrade.

Brutal thwacks reverberated as poles found flesh, but most of the blows found only air as the Americans tried to stay out of the way. The sailor with the ball gave a war cry as he approached the open goal. He leaped and flung the ball. It bounced just in front of the goal, then slammed into the back net.

He lifted his hands and yelled in jubilation, but it cut short suddenly when Grinning Bear's coconut end slammed into the side of his head with crushing force. The side of his head collapsed and blood spewed out his nose and both ears. He dropped like a sack of rice and his body writhed and twitched on the grass.

A stunned silence fell over the field and the crowd, who'd just begun to cheer for the score, held their hands over their mouths. Two Japanese sailors dropped their sticks and ran to the downed man. They fell to their knees and draped themselves over him, but it was clear there was nothing to be done. His body finally stopped twitching.

The Japanese collected themselves and glared at Grinning Bear who still held the dripping bludgeon. One of them yelled and the others rose and ran at him, but the shaman raised his voice and the native men immediately stepped forward and filled the gap between the charging Japanese and the Americans, stopping the attack.

They pushed the sailors back to their own lines, but the Japanese yelled and screamed in frustration and hatred at the Americans. Frank couldn't take his eyes off the dead man. He felt sick to his stomach. Yes, he was the enemy and he hated them for starting this war, but this just seemed wrong.

The others also looked sick to their stomachs, all except Grinning Bear, who glared at the remaining Japanese with renewed hatred. "One down, five to go," he uttered.

The shaman conferred with his men. They spoke in a tight circle. Frank guessed they discussed whether or not they'd broken a rule. Surely men were injured during this game, but had any died? The act had definitely been on purpose and right after a goal, too. Would that matter? A feeling of dread overtook him as he wondered if they would kill one of them to keep the teams even.

The natives finally broke their circle. Two men hauled the body off the field and flung it unceremoniously into the weeds.

The shaman raised his voice and spoke to the rapt crowd. His words brought low murmurs of discussion. He raised his hands the way he'd done to start a new point in the first game.

The Japanese conferred with one another and the goalie stick passed to another man. He hefted it and stared at Grinning Bear with raw hatred.

Grinning Bear pulled them close again. Frank could barely look at him. He saw the coconut still dripped blood.

Grinning Bear's rough voice sounded devoid of emotion, but Frank thought it must chew him up inside.

"Okay listen. They're gonna want payback. They're coming at us to kill. Buddy up. Don't get ganged up on and try to score as quickly as possible."

"Score?" Neil said incredulously. "How 'bout just survive?"

Grinning Bear's voice dropped and he went nose to nose with him. "If you wanna survive, we have to win this game. I just made that possibility easier, but we still have to score to win." He pulled back. "It's dirty work, but the more we injure them, the better." He hefted the bludgeon stick. "This thing's got a lot of hitting power, but I doubt they allow it to cross the center line of this batshit crazy game. Anyone that tries to come across, I'll try to kill. I think they'll try to sucker us like we just did to them, though. So watch each other's backs. If possible, go after their goalie, but keep out of the way of his stick."

The shaman yelled and the natives made them come forward and forced them to the line where the young woman held the next ball, ready to heave it into play. The groups broke up and moved to the line. Frank could feel the hatred from the sailor's stares. Fear gripped him, but he turned it to anger. He marveled at how easily he achieved it. He glared back at the man across from him.

Glenn stood in the center, ready for the tipoff. The young woman threw the ball into the sky and darted away. While all eyes went up, Frank sprinted toward the center. He rushed at the Japanese sailor across from Glenn.

Glenn watched the ball, but the sailor charged and lunged his stick at his guts. Frank noticed he'd peeled a few of the broken ends off of the tip, leaving a sharp end.

Glenn leaped up, trying for the ball. The sailor's stick pierced him at the belly button, but before he could sink it all the way through, Frank slammed into the pole, tearing it from his hands.

Glenn screamed in pain and dropped, bleeding from the gash in his belly. Frank swung his stick as hard as he could and felt it crash into the sailor's ribs. He hoped he'd broken a few and, by the sailor's loud expulsion of air, he thought he had.

The ball landed between them. Frank smacked his stick over the top and lifted it over his head. The other sailors retreated, ready to bludgeon to death anyone that attempted to come onto their side, leaving the sailor he'd hit writhing on the ground.

Frank reacted without thinking. He flung the stick and ball down as hard as he could onto the sailor's back. The noise and the feel of the crushing blow would stick with Frank for the rest of his life. The sailor's back arched and his mouth opened, but he had no breath to yell or scream with.

The ball stayed in the stick and he lifted it over his head again, but before he could land another blow, a Japanese sailor ran at him, aiming to jab his stick straight through him like a bayonet.

Frank backpedaled and tripped over Glenn, who still writhed and held his bleeding belly. The stick barely missed Frank's head and he saw in crystal clear clarity that the Japanese sailor's stick had also been modified for skewering.

The sailor tripped over them and fell onto their side of the playing field. Grinning Bear was on him immediately. He swung the bludgeon like an axeman chopping wood. He brought the coconut end down on the back of his skull, crushing his face into the soft grass with a sickening crunch of bone and brain.

Again, the world seemed to stand still. The only sound came from their heavy breathing and Glenn's panicked whimpers as he tried to keep his intestines from spilling out.

The shaman yelled in utter frustration. There was nothing melodic or sing song about his voice now. The native men flooded onto the field and gripped their spears, ready for the order to kill them all. They smacked the player's sticks from their hands and women ran to pick them up. They ran them to the shaman and placed the Americans in a pile and the Japanese's in a different pile.

Frank, Gale, and Micah ran to Glenn's side. He looked at them in stark terror, his face as white as the clouds drifting lazily overhead, oblivious to humanity's foibles. Neil stood frozen at the goal box, staring at the bloody scene. Grinning Bear still stood over the body of his most recent victim, his chest heaving as he breathed in deep gulps of air.

The shaman inspected the American's sticks. He threw them down, then did the same with the Japanese sticks. All the Japanese sticks had been modified into sharp points. They clearly planned to skewer the Americans and end the game.

The shaman held the sticks up as proof for the crowd to see. He bellowed and raged, and soon the rest of the natives yelled right along with him. They threw fruit and coconuts at the Japanese, who cowered and packed into a tight group.

The Japanese collected the man Frank had attacked. He couldn't stand straight and he spit blood. He had broken ribs and possibly a ruptured kidney. The man leaned on his friends to stay upright.

The shaman raised his voice and the crowd slowly grew quiet again. His voice leveled and Frank thought he heard a deadliness instead of beauty. A moment later, the bowmen stepped forward. Frank thought they'd kill them all, but their arrows flew straight and true and into the huddled Japanese. They screamed and writhed as they seemed to suddenly sprout arrows from their backs and necks. They took a long time to die. So did Private Glenn Madison.

24

DECEMBER 1943

Port Moresby, Papua New Guinea

Clyde Cooper read Abby's letter with both pride and concern. She'd done it! She'd completed the WASP training and was now officially a WASP pilot. He still didn't know exactly what that meant. He'd read a few newspaper snippets his mother had sent to him about the program. Apparently, they needed civilian pilots because they had sent all the regular male pilots off to war. That made sense to him, but he didn't understand the secrecy surrounding the program. Even her letters hadn't shared too many specifics. She told him she'd graduated but didn't tell him what she'd be doing exactly.

When he'd arrived back at Port Moresby, a stack of her letters awaited him. He read them all in one sitting. The one telling him of her WASP achievement had been written less than two weeks before. A new record. A few of them had been extremely spicy.

She explained how her girlfriends had urged her to write him sexy letters and they'd even helped her write them. At first, it made him extremely uncomfortable, thinking Abby shared their most intimate moments with people who were strangers to him, but he soon realized it was all in fun, and he had to admit he liked the letters a lot. Some of those girls had some serious imaginations.

Her last letter told him she had to leave Sweetwater, where she'd trained, and move to Norfolk, Virginia, so she could start her new career. She didn't have an address yet, but she told him her pregnant friend Beatrice would forward any letters she received, so he should keep sending them to the Sweetwater address until further notice.

He was stunned and confused to hear that Sal, the Brooks family driver and security man, was also there in Sweetwater. She explained that he'd quit working for his father-in-law and planned on helping Beatrice with her new baby. Abby spent half the letter explaining how wonderful her friend had done during the birth. And how she'd been able to leave her duties in Norfolk to be there at Beatrice's side. It was all overwhelming.

Norfolk held a large naval base, and he wondered what in the world she'd be doing for the navy. He hated not knowing. He wrote to her, asking for specifics. Perhaps she couldn't give them, but if not, she should tell him that, so he didn't wonder.

He heard heavy footsteps in the hallway. They had given the NCOs of Able Company a plush row of barracks, and they each had a room all to themselves, which included a door. For once, he was glad to be a corporal.

Sergeant Huss burst into his room without knocking, causing him to jump. Clyde cussed him. "Dammit, sergeant, what's the big idea?"

"There you are. You hear about Kinsler?"

"You mean our esteemed CO *Colonel* Kinsler? No, what about him? He got another harebrained scheme up his sleeve for more training?"

"He's dead."

Clyde turned from the letter he'd just sat down to write and looked at Huss, stunned. "Dead? Dead how?"

"Shot himself. At least, that's the word right now. They're still investigating."

He ran his hands through his hair and leaned back. "Shot himself? But why? I mean, I didn't like the guy, but I didn't want him dead." He narrowed his gaze. "You sure someone else didn't shoot him? You remember that fella that wanted to shoot him after he got those guys killed crossing the river? Maybe he still holds a grudge."

"Nah, they're pretty sure he shot himself. He was holding his own pistol when they found him."

Clyde tried to feel some remorse, but that sort of thing had become harder to come by since he'd seen men die in combat. Death wasn't as surprising or tragic anymore—it was just something that happened to people—to everyone, eventually.

"Does this change our plans for Cape Glouster?"

"Nope. Colonel Jones is taking over command. He's senior to Tolson and Lawrie."

Clyde knew little about Jones. To him, he was just another highly polished piece of brass. The brass didn't ask corporals for their input.

He reflected on Kinsler. "You know, Kinsler took a lot of heat for those training casualties. I remember being mad as hell—thought he was an incompetent asshole. Hell, I wanted to shoot him, too. But I gotta hand it to him, he pulled us together. We were a fragmented mess when we arrived in Cairns, but by the time we jumped into the Markham Valley, we were firing on all cylinders."

"I remember those days. I thought he was bonkers, too, but his results speak for themselves."

"Wonder why he did it? Did he leave a note?"

"A note? You've read too many bad novels. No, he didn't leave a note."

Clyde fiddled with his pencil. "That all you wanted to tell me?"

"That and they've given us a date for Cape Glouster." Clyde looked at him expectantly. Huss said, "Day after Christmas."

"That's a hell of a way to spend Christmas night . . . getting ready to kill Japs. Do they celebrate Christmas?" He'd never thought about that before.

"Hell if I know. If they do, we're gonna give them some kind of great present. Maybe we'll shove candy canes up their asses," he laughed as he left and shut the door behind him. Clyde could hear him whistling jingle bells.

For the next few weeks, they trained for the Cape Glouster jump. The brass thought it would be a tougher nut to crack than the Markham Valley. Like that operation, they planned to jump onto an occupied airfield, but whereas Nadzab airfield had been in disuse, Cape Glouster was a known hive of enemy activity—so they trained hard.

As Christmas approached, so did the drop day. Clyde tried to keep his letters to Abby upbeat. He tried to talk about Christmas positively, knowing how much Abby loved the holiday. Who didn't? But this year, 1943, he dreaded the day for he'd be boarding a C-47 and dropping onto a heavily defended airfield. It may very well be his last Christmas.

Abby might start the new year as a fresh widow. He wasn't afraid for himself as much as he was for her. It would break her heart to lose him in the first place, but the day after Christmas? It would forever ruin the holiday for her. The rest of her life, she'd equate it with the day she lost her husband. But she'd move on. She'd find someone else and move on easily —perhaps she'd forget about him altogether.

He kicked himself for thinking like this. Sometimes he couldn't help slipping into his old ways—his self-defeating miasma of self-pity. *I'm an airborne warrior, by God!*

He remembered fondly how Sergeant Plumly had labeled him that night in Finschhafen as he told his story about killing the Japanese soldier at point-blank range.

Thinking about Abby didn't make him feel that way now, though. He felt lonely. Being away from her was hard enough, but being away from here at Christmas was even harder. This damnable war had torn apart how many millions of men and women? He shuddered at the thought.

Christmas Eve finally arrived. Port Moresby did its best for the holiday, but Japanese airstrikes were still a possibility, even though it hadn't happened in months. They still couldn't string lights outside. They'd cut down and decorated a "Christmas tree." It was the first time Clyde had seen lights strung around a palm tree. Presents decorated the base, mostly homemade, lewd gifts to make each other laugh. The highlight was a talent show. The most popular act featured a voluptuously dressed Tojo and Hitler dancing together. A disgruntled and jealous Mussolini sat in the corner dressed like a baby sucking on a pacifier.

They tried—but the merriment felt forced—the laughter almost hysterical rather than joyful. The jump loomed too close and their fates hung in the balance.

The First Marine Division had already landed on Cape Glouster and the reports of the fighting were intense, but the real enemy was the incessant rains and deep mud. The rains wouldn't keep the C-47s grounded, however, for the cloud ceiling and visibility were within safe jump parameters.

They spent the wee hours of the day after Christmas standing by at Port Moresby's airfield, some three miles out of town. The strip was lined with freshly painted C-47s. They'd been arriving all week and there'd been many jokes about them being Santa's little helpers, much to the pilot's annoyance.

Clyde wrote his last letters to his parents and Abby and dropped them off with the quartermaster on Christmas morning. He didn't mention that it might be his last letter. He kept it light, knowing the recipients would be celebrating Christmas *or they would be tomorrow*. He remembered the time difference. His letters wouldn't arrive for weeks, possibly months or not at all, but he couldn't make himself write a glum letter on Christmas morning, despite his own grim circumstances.

His breakfast sat heavily in his gut. The cooks had outdone themselves as they always did on the morning of a combat jump, and the old familiar jokes about the last supper zipped around the ranks.

He'd checked his own gear and that of the squad countless times. The men were ready for whatever was coming. Now, he just wanted to get the whole thing over with. He remembered feeling the exact same way as they waited for the Markham Valley jump. Unlike that time, General MacArthur didn't show up to inspect them. He figured he'd be celebrating Christmas for real somewhere.

He heard yelling coming from down the line of seemingly endless paratrooper sticks. The din grew as word passed. He heard groans mostly, but also a few barks of laughter. He stood and stretched his aching back. His butt had gone to sleep while he was sitting on the side of the airfield. He wiggled his legs to bring back blood flow.

Lieutenant Milkins strode down the line, addressing different sticks of paratroopers from Second Platoon. Clyde saw various reactions, but the main one was frustration. *Must be another delay*, he thought bitterly.

Milkins finally stood in front of Clyde's stick. "Men, they've called the whole thing off."

Clyde stood in stunned silence. He didn't think he'd heard him correctly. Called it off? They were supposed to board any minute. They'd been training intensively since November 2nd. How could they call it off? Was it bad weather?

"The marines overran the airfield we were going to jump onto. We no longer have a mission."

With no mission, Clyde suddenly felt hollow. He'd been training hard for a perilous mission, and now he had nothing to fear or look forward to. Instead of feeling grateful for not having to face a life-and-death situation, he felt cheated somehow. They all did.

Gil spit on the floor of the recreation center and kicked at the rat scrabbling in the room's corner for scraps. "How long we gonna sit here on our hands?"

Over the past few days, they'd asked Clyde the same question at least a dozen times. "Until they tell us otherwise, I suppose." Gil looked annoyed, as though he should know more than he did, so Clyde added, "They don't keep corporals in the loop, for chrissakes."

"Well shit," he picked up a bottle cap and flicked it from between his fingers with a snap. It caromed off the wall just above the rat's head, but instead of scampering away, it hissed at him, then went about its business. "Jesus, even the rats are rebelling."

"It's weird, isn't it?"

"What is?"

"We'd be four days into the operation by now. Who knows—if the marines hadn't overrun the airfield, we might be dead by now. Corpses rotting in the jungle."

"Yeah, well, I guess that *is* weird to think about. But thinking that way will drive you nuts. That's not what happened, so knock it off."

"Yeah, I know. The really weird part is that I'd rather have jumped than be sitting here right now twiddling my damned thumbs."

Gil stared at his hands. "You know—I feel the same way. Despite how crazy that sounds, I wish we'd gone through with it, too."

"If we had and we'd survived till now, we'd probably be talking about how we wish we were back here cooling our heels."

Gil snorted a sharp laugh. "Human nature, Paisano. We're never satisfied. I guess that's why wars happen in the first place, huh?"

Clyde looked sideways at him. "Didn't figure you for the philosopher type."

Gil raised his middle finger at him and flicked another bottle cap at the rat, which had stepped closer to him. "In some ways, this rat has a better life."

Clyde stared at the rat. It had mottled fur with scars across its nose and one of its legs looked as though it had been broken at some point and healed incorrectly. It had seen better days, yet still survived, fighting for every scrap of food. He wondered how many scuffles it had endured? How many times had it fought over carrion or garbage?

"That son of a bitch has led a hard life. How d'you figure he's better off than us?"

Gil shrugged. "He knows exactly what he needs to do to survive. Every day there's no question what has to happen. It doesn't care about being satisfied or happy. If it's alive, that's enough."

"Guess you're right. But that sorry bastard doesn't have many days left, I'm thinking."

"Yeah, but even that doesn't concern him. If he has to die, he's fine with that, too."

"You need a hobby, Hicks, you really do." He sauntered to the open window and peered out over the grounds. He pulled a crinkled cigarette from his front pocket and put it into his mouth without lighting it. "Looks like something's happening."

Gil shot to his feet and joined him at the window. "Yeah? What's going on?"

Unlike the past week of paratroopers mostly walking with their heads down, now they darted around with sudden renewed purpose.

They left the recreation center and strode across the courtyard. The muddy ground reeked like a cesspool, despite their best efforts to keep it clean.

Sergeant Huss walked toward him with purpose. He had a half-chewed cigar sticking from his crusty mouth. He shoved it to the side and stood with his hands on his hips. "Well, we're finally getting the hell out of this shit-hole."

"Another mission?" Clyde asked.

"Not exactly. We're heading back to Cairns . . . back to Gordonvale where this whole thing started."

"But we only just got here."

"Don't you worry, corporal, they won't let deadly killers like us sit around too long—trust me—there's plenty more for us to do in this damn war."

The Last Test of Courage
A Time to Serve Series, Book 4

Clyde Cooper and his fellow paratroopers have returned to Australia after a highly successful operation in New Guinea. But the respite is brief as a new mission looms on the horizon. Jumping onto Nooemfor Island will push the veterans to their limits, and plunge them into deadly combat against an enemy that refuses to admit defeat.

Clyde's brother, Frank, has escaped the iron grip of the brutal Japanese POW camp and landed in a tropical paradise. But he's not content to let the war roll on by. With help from his native hosts, Frank braves the seas, determined to rejoin the fight. But when he finally re-enters the fray, he may regret his decision.

Cousin Shawn remains deep inside Burma battling side by side with the Kachin Rangers as an OSS operative—taking the fight to the enemy in their own backyard. But the Japanese are far from defeated, meeting the offensive with unexpectedly stiff resistance. Unfamiliar with the Burmese jungles, Shawn's OSS cadre and the Kachin Rangers struggle to gain the advantage. But they must retain a foothold in Burma at all costs...or risk losing one of the most important Allied supply routes in the region.

Meanwhile, back in the US, Abby Cooper is embracing her new role flying for the WASPs. But she quickly realizes her profession entails dangers beyond what she ever imagined. Now, Abby is questioning everything she's worked so hard to achieve.

There is no end in sight to this worldwide calamity. Tragedy and sacrifice surround the Cooper family on all fronts. And the only way forward is through their strength, resolve, and faith in one another.

Get your copy today at
severnriverbooks.com/series/a-time-to-serve

ABOUT THE AUTHOR

Chris Glatte graduated from the University of Oregon with a BA in English Literature and worked as a river guide/kayak instructor for a decade before training as an Echocardiographer. He worked in the medical field for over 20 years, and now writes full time. Chris is the author of multiple historical fiction thriller series, including A Time to Serve and Tark's Ticks, a set of popular WWII novels. He lives in Southern Oregon with his wife, two boys, and ever-present Labrador, Hoover. When he's not writing or reading, Chris can be found playing in the outdoors—usually on a river or mountain.

From Chris:

I respond to all email correspondence.
Drop me a line, I'd love to hear from you!
chrisglatte@severnriverbooks.com

Sign up for Chris Glatte's reader list at
severnriverbooks.com/authors/chris-glatte

Printed in the United States
by Baker & Taylor Publisher Services